THE GREEN CATHEDRAL

KERRY McDONALD

WITH LEE TIDBALL

This book is printed on acid-free paper.

Published by:
Level 4 Press, Inc.
13518 Jamul Drive
Jamul, CA 91935
www.level4press.com

Library of Congress Control Number: 2019944544

ISBN: 978-1-933769-92-9

Printed in the USA

Dedication

To Cynthia, my Rimi

PROLOGUE

———

Central Pacific Coast—Republic of Costa Rica
Circa 1905

Juanito, a boy of ten, ran out of the little house that he and his mother, father, and sister lived in just back from the pristine beach that formed at the mouth of the Rio Palma. It was sunrise and time for his favorite chore of the day. He carried a bucket filled with rats that he'd trapped around the house and in the storehouse where freshly picked bananas were kept until they could be picked up each day by the wagon that took them on their long journey to San José. Sure enough, there at the mouth of the river, the old, toothless crocodile lounged, just like he'd done for nearly all Juanito's life.

His father had found the fifteen-foot behemoth there one morning and could see that a fight with something, perhaps a shark, or even something man-made like the propeller of one of the boats that occasionally steamed down the coast toward the new canal project going on in Panama, had stripped the thing of most of its teeth. Knowing that being without teeth would eventually cause the croc to starve, Juanito's dad, an American named James, had taken to feeding the beast. And now, that was just another chore that either he or Juanito did every day. Juanito's mother, Juana, a native Costa Rican, told them they were both *loco*, and his sister, Julisa, was too small to care, but still, Juanito and James faithfully fed the croc.

Perhaps this was because James, though strict with Juanito, was also an unusually kind man. Juana had told Juanito that that is why she had married him. James had been a convicted criminal who had chosen to go to Costa Rica and help build the railroad from San José to Puerto Limon on the other side of the country, rather than rot in an American prison. It was hard work, and James had survived many trials, including a knee injury that had hobbled him and a bout with malaria. Many other workers had died outright.

But after finishing with the railroad, James had gotten what he'd worked for—freedom and a small tract of land near a village where everyone worked for an American company that grew bananas and sent them back to the United States. James had been so grateful, Juana had said. And when he'd seen Juana's first husband, a foreman on the banana farm, whipping her for not pleasing him, James had beaten the man up and reported him to the boss man. The foreman was fired and sent away, and Juana refused to go with him. Instead, she married James and enjoyed a kindness she'd never felt before. So she didn't mind when others looked at her strangely as she went to market with her white American husband. Her man was kind to her and their children. That was all she cared about.

But being kind to a toothless crocodile was ridiculous!

Juanito laughed as he tossed rats into the croc's open mouth. He thought having a toothless crocodile was the most perfect pet for their family in the whole world.

Juanito now dropped his bucket and picked up his fishing pole. He ran to where one of their family's dugout canoes was lying and pushed it skillfully into the gentle waves of the Pacific Ocean. The beach stretching down the coast from the mouth of the Rio Palma was sheltered by a small but not insignificant island a little over a mile out to sea. This island broke the waves enough so that they were calm and gentle, unlike the waves farther down, where the surf pounded onto the beach directly from the ocean.

Juanito loved to fish and to be out on the water, so he spent an hour or so every morning around sunrise out in one of the canoes, hoping for fish to bite while he enjoyed the sun rising behind him and gradually turning the water from opaque to a crystal blue.

But today, as he sat in his canoe with his fishing line in the water, something was disturbingly different.

The sun was definitely rising behind him, but before him, coming in from the ocean, there was another bright sun approaching, lighting up the sky nearly as much as at midday. It became brighter and brighter. Juanito, confused and terrified, wanted to paddle for the shore and find his father, but he couldn't take his eyes off the approaching light. It was mysterious and terrible, captivating and fascinating.

There was an enormous booming sound that swept across the waves, and then the light separated into two—a giant fireball diverting up the coast, and a much smaller one approaching as if it were aimed right at him!

"Juanito! Get outta there!" his father's voice called frantically to him, but Juanito was frozen in a dreadful fascination. He looked at the light that streaked up the coast. It moved with unimaginable speed, then suddenly disappeared and collided with the land somewhere far away. Juanito could hear a muffled roar, and then seconds later, a mighty wind swept over him like a tidal wave. The water rocked violently, and Juanito tumbled out of his canoe. Skillfully, he grabbed onto it and waited for several seconds as the wind finally blew out and the water calmed.

He turned to see the small light. It, too, was racing toward the Earth at an unfathomable speed. Juanito was sure that it would strike the water right where he was and he'd be tossed around like a toy boat in a bathtub. Suddenly, though, the light faded some, and the object seemed to slow. It dipped lower and lower and then disappeared behind the island. A shudder went through the water. A brief roar of wind came but stopped almost as soon as it started.

And then, all was calm.

Juanito's father rowed up beside him in the big family canoe. "Come on, buddy! Let's go check it out!"

That was another thing about James. He was insatiably curious, and once he got an idea in his head, he was unstoppable. Juanito pulled himself up into his father's canoe, tethered his own to the stern, grabbed a paddle, and stroked for the island with his father. Juanito was excited. He'd never been to the island before. He didn't even think his father had been there. It was hard work paddling so far for so long.

Finally, they pulled their boats up onto a large beach and looked back at the village and their home, both of which appeared very small.

"Sweet Jesus," marveled James, and then he signaled Juanito to follow him.

They crossed the beach and ran into the jungle, which was more like a forest, with tall, arching trees covering smaller trees and scrubby undergrowth. Everything was dazzlingly green, and the trees reminded Juanito of the tall arch over the door to their church, which was couched under a tall bell tower. He wondered if such magnificent arches were what the cathedrals in big cities like San José looked like.

They ran farther in, watching their steps because both were barefoot and had no shirts on, only pants that came halfway down their legs. James led the way, an amazingly agile man considering his past injuries, and as Juanito followed, he thought he saw through the forest an area where many trees had fallen. Just as he noticed that, his father called out, "Stop, son!"

Juanito did, and then saw the reason why. A huge brown cat, a puma, was lolling in a tree above them. It gave a threatening growl, then stood menacingly on the limb it was on, as if daring the two humans to go farther. Juanito went to James and held on to his waist, terrified, as James studied the big cat.

"Let's move a bit to the right, son," James said without taking his eyes off the puma, and he and Juanito took a few steps.

But the cat growled loudly and leaped to another tree limb directly in front of them. Both father and son jumped with surprise and fear.

"I don't guess we're going any farther into this forest today, son. Let's back up toward that beach. Keep your eyes on the cat."

The two slowly backed away several paces, then turned and dashed back the way they'd come, not stopping until they got to the beach. Both shaken, they took one more look into the forest, noting that the big cat had followed them, but at a safe distance. They hastily pushed their canoes into the water and were off.

What they didn't see, though, was that above the puma, walking along a tree limb as if she'd done it hundreds of times, was a small girl, perhaps seven or eight years old, with brown skin and uncommonly large green eyes. She watched them go as well.

CARTAGENA

1

—

f one had seen the three men standing together on the ramparts of
the massive walls of the Castillo de San Felipe de Barajas, one might
have thought they were typical modern tourists. That's because they
were staring at portable electronic devices rather than taking in one
of the Western Hemisphere's most beautiful and historic cities. To
the left was the Laguna de San Lazaro, and farther beyond, the Bahia
de Cartagena and the skyscrapers of the hotels along the Bocagrande
peninsula. To the right were the Laguna del Cabrero and the green
parklands along its shores. And straight on in the center was the crown
jewel of Cartagena: its storied Walled City. It was filled with cobble-
stone streets, colorful colonial adobe homes and hotels, ornate cathedrals, historic government buildings, and restaurants of every description. All these were surrounded by four kilometers of venerable stone
and mined coral walls, which had shielded the city for centuries from
countless attacks by invaders and pirates.

But these three men couldn't have cared less.

Two were dressed in business suits, one a smallish man with a classic Spanish look, complete with the pointy goatee. A much larger man

stood beside him. He looked as though his suit was stuffed with boulders beneath a much smaller head.

The other man, though, was swarthier, dressed in khaki cargo pants and a button-down thrown over a black T-shirt. He was taller than the Spaniard but not as large as the other man beside him. His Caucasian skin was deeply tanned, and his arms rippled with muscle. Though lithe in build, one would not question that his clothes most likely hid a similarly impressive physique. His name was Abel Nowinski, former US Navy SEAL and current special agent with the American Drug Enforcement Administration, the DEA. A smile cracked his somewhat craggy face as he watched the balance of his secure Internet bank account suddenly grow by $200,000. The transfer had gone through without a hitch. He almost looked like the thirty-seven-year-old that he was rather than the older man his overly weathered face usually indicated.

Next to him, the shorter Spaniard, who went by the outsized title of Don Vicente Galvan, frowned and twisted his goatee as he pocketed his cell phone.

"There. I hope you're happy. I feel like I've just been robbed."

Abel smiled. "I imagine it does hurt a bit. Kind of like I used to feel when I was a kid and had to pay a day's worth of lunch money to my big bruiser friend on the playground so I wouldn't get my ass kicked. I used to pity the fools who couldn't pay up. They didn't get it all the time, but, boy, when they did . . . I'd never seen so many bruises on one nine-year-old body. Kind of like your competitors down in Urabá are feeling right now after their hundred-million-dollar shipment was seized last night by my DEA friends in Miami."

Don Vicente winced ever so slightly as Abel pocketed his cell phone.

"But you, my friend," continued Abel, "have just purchased an insurance policy guaranteed to keep you safe from pain like that." At this, Abel gave Don Vicente's gargantuan enforcer a wink. "I'll make a call later this week. The next day, you'll be depositing a hundred million."

"And if I'm not," spoke Don Vicente sharply, "I'll be depositing you in my pond filled with crocodiles. Do not trifle with me, Mr. DEA Agent Abel Nowinski."

Abel gave him a grim smile. "No 'ifs,' no trifling. I'll take that backpack now." He indicated a daypack that Don Vicente's giant had slung over his shoulder. "I've got an appointment to keep."

He grabbed the bag as soon as the giant let it slide down his sleeve and unzipped its main compartment. Five packets of American one-hundred-dollar bills, just as ordered. He zipped it back up and slung it onto his back.

"Aren't you going to count it?" asked Don Vicente dryly.

"Just did," replied Abel. "Gotta run. Besides, we trust each other, right?" He gave Don Vicente a condescending pat on the cheek, then walked swiftly away.

Scuttling down some old stone stairs, Abel found his electric rental bike among others in the rack near the fortress's entrance. He hopped on it, donned a simple helmet, and whisked himself away onto the busy avenue that would take him into the Walled City. The bike's electric motor barely made a whir as he sped along.

Back on the fortress wall, Don Vicente looked to his monster protector. "He's being followed, eh?" The big man nodded silently. "And his apartment?"

"An older building near the Hyatt Regency," said his man, sounding almost as robotic as he acted. "Our team is in place."

"*Bueno,*" said Don Vicente. "Kill him at the first sign of trouble."

E-bikes were a new thing in the Walled City. Like other larger cities, the Walled City struggled with too many cars on the same roads as hordes of pedestrian tourists, and e-bikes were an excellent alternative to cabs and Uber drivers. For just a few thousand Colombian pesos, which wasn't even a dollar, they were the perfect mode of transportation. Tourists could get from place to place without having to walk endlessly in the hot, sticky afternoon heat. Someone could get to places quickly and cheaply without being assaulted by the city's herds of prying street vendors.

And, for Abel, they also served a more clandestine purpose. They assured him that he would be tough to follow, something that Abel was sure one of Don Vicente's minions was doing now. Because e-bikes had a top speed of only about twenty-five miles per hour, cars could not discreetly follow them. A car would have to go too slow to blend in with the traffic flow, and thus become highly conspicuous. He could also quickly lose a tail once in the Walled City, with its narrow streets and broad plazas, by zipping through places where cars could not go.

And so, barely ten minutes after leaving the Castillo de San Felipe, Abel had identified and deftly lost Don Vicente's tail and was zipping through one of the tunnels of Cartagena's famous Torre del Reloj gate. From there, he crossed the Plaza de los Coches, with its famous yellow colonial clock tower. Abel didn't even give it a glance as he sharply turned left, then right up to Calle 33. He zipped past a pleasant park known as the Plaza de Bolivar and then passed the Palacio de la Inquisición. Abel had always thought he'd enjoy a tour of its museum of post-medieval torture devices.

Not long after, he approached one of the most popular and well-preserved areas of the city wall, just a matter of meters from the Caribbean itself. He parked his electric bike, locked it, checked once again to make sure his tail was nowhere in sight, and then looked for a stairway to ascend the steep rampart.

For the entire time he'd been riding, Abel's mind had been whirring along with the sound of the bike's tires. His boss, Victor Garza, a veteran DEA special agent with fifteen years' experience in foreign service, had asked Abel to meet him this evening at the Café de Vista Sol, an unusually quiet international eatery located on the city wall literal steps from the shore of the Caribbean. It was a place famous for its multiple food selections, serene atmosphere, and incomparable views of the sunset over the sea. Being one of the most sought-after dinner spots in the Walled City, Abel knew that Victor must have planned well ahead to secure such a dinner date. Then again, he might also have a connection with the owner, or be a regular. Victor had led the DEA post in Cartagena for years, and anyone who was anyone seemed to know him.

But it was why Victor had called him there, on that night of all nights, that had Abel's nerves uncharacteristically tingling. Victor knew Abel's past well, since he had been the one to hire him out of the Navy almost as soon as Abel had resigned his commission. He knew that Abel had served on a Navy SEAL team for a body-crunching, mind-numbing ten years after graduating from the University of Iowa. He knew how Abel had been a three-sport walk-on athlete there, excelling in all three, then joined the Navy with his eyes set on SEAL training. He knew that Abel had breezed through his two and a half years of SEAL training and had served his country with honor in nearly every corner of the globe. And he knew that a single .30 caliber machine-gun round fired by an ISIS soldier had shattered both his right knee and right elbow. Both joints had been repaired and replaced, but despite his best efforts to continue on, Abel had had to call active duty quits. Victor knew how Abel had been crushed, his heart rent by having to leave his team, and also how he'd never considered a desk job. Abel had resigned instead and signed up with the DEA, where the physical requirements weren't quite as rigorous, but his SEAL skills and toughness were prized. And he knew that Abel was an action junkie, a man who lived for the high brought on by heart-pounding adventure and life-or-death struggle. For such a man, though, living in between such episodes was challenging, to say the least. And because of that, he knew that Abel feared the future more than anything because his body could never keep up with his need for speed.

Victor had tried to help Abel with these things occasionally during their two years together in Cartagena. Victor knew that Abel was a good man who wanted to do good things. But he also knew Abel's intense needs could drive him to the dark side if he weren't careful. But Abel had shrugged it all off. To do anything else would be to lower his standards or change his course, each of which, to Abel, meant giving in to weakness. Abel could never accept the idea that he was not still the robust and invincible being that he had always been.

But as the time went by and Abel discovered that the dull routine of investigation consumed much more time than action in the field, Abel knew that Victor had noted his increasing restlessness. He knew that Victor had been disappointed when Abel's focus wandered at work, the result of late nights spent overindulging. Victor had even had to discipline Abel twice for reporting to work unfit for duty.

Now, Abel's intuition told him that tonight could be a night of reckoning. Perhaps Victor would finally fire him, something Abel had thought could have happened on several occasions. Maybe Victor would have him reassigned, sent back to the US. He could get his act together there without tearing down years of hard work infiltrating and destroying the drug cartels that, like cockroaches, seemed never to die.

Abel wondered if Victor might know about the deal he'd just done. Victor knew that Abel had finally given in to his urges, his need for action and adrenaline, his impulse to live dangerously in a dangerous world. Could Victor have found out about the $200,000 that had been transferred into his secret offshore account by the very drug lord that Victor was trying to bring down? Or the $50,000 cash that was in the backpack Abel now carried into the Café de Vista Sol? Might he realize that the deal he'd made with Don Vicente Galvan was to make sure all of Galvan's drug shipments to the US were protected from DEA and US Customs inspectors from now on? Abel couldn't imagine how he would. Abel knew the system well, and he'd taken all the right precautions and covered all his tracks.

. . . But still, what if Victor knew?

Abel smiled as he bounded up the steps to the top of the wall and spotted the café just fifty meters away. He could already feel his heart pounding harder as adrenaline rushed through his veins. For better or worse, at least he now had his fix.

2

"Well, there he is, my favorite sniper," quipped Victor, a tall black man whose voice and physique seemed to Abel to be the perfect combination of two legendary movie stars: Samuel L. Jackson and James Earl Jones. Abel slid into the dining booth on the opposite side of the table. The Café de Vista Sol had a colonial interior design with most of its tables either in the large main dining room or out on its expansive outdoor veranda. There was no shortage of booths, though, where people who enjoyed privacy and conversation as much as good eating could feel comfortable. Despite his uneasiness, Abel was glad that Victor had chosen a booth. If things suddenly turned sour, it would happen in private rather than in the open for all to see.

"What are you drinking tonight?" asked Victor as he waved a waiter over.

"Beer," replied Abel. His tastes had never been fancy or strong, at least not until lately.

"On tap or bottled?" inquired the waiter.

"Tap, whatever your house brew is."

"Ah, as I suspected, a back-to-basics, red-blooded American soldier," said Victor.

"Hu-ah!"

"I'll have a flute of your house white," said Victor, and the waiter departed. "It took a long time for me to start enjoying the finer things in life, Nowinski, and to be honest, they're rarely as good as they're cracked up to be, but white wine in the evening, well, that's become something special. You should try it sometime."

"Maybe I will," said Abel. The waiter brought them each of their drinks. Abel lifted his ice-cold mug. "But not tonight."

Victor laughed, and the two clinked their glasses and drank up.

Then Victor sat back in the cushioned booth and gazed out the window at the sinking sun, its redness reflecting on the water and making it look as if it were on fire. "I'm not one with a lot of social graces, Nowinski, but I've got to tell you, this place has one hell of a view. Check that out. Where the hell else in the world can you see a sunset like that while you're eating dinner?"

"I've watched plenty of sunsets while I was eating dinner," replied Abel, "all over the world. They all get rolled into one for me. I can't keep them straight anymore, so I don't try."

"Yeah." Victor chuckled. "But what meals you were eating?"

Abel smiled. "MREs mostly." They both laughed.

"You see," said Victor, "that's what makes this special." He shifted his fit, yet somewhat bulky frame around to sit up straighter and looked over the menu. "Tonight, along with your sunset, you have real food. Now, how many times have you experienced that?"

"Touché." Abel smiled.

Victor said, "I'm having my usual, the filet mignon done medium rare with a baked potato on the side. They're both to die for, and the bread and fresh mango that come with them are amazing. You'll find everything from burgers to stuff written in French and Italian that I don't even care to look at, even Asian stuff like Thai chicken and chow mein. I personally recommend the vegetarian lasagna, but that's probably not your thing, so the real kind with the meat and the red sauce is just as good. Find yourself a real meal to enjoy with the sunset, Nowinski, and then I've got some things to talk about with you."

So far, Abel had felt at ease, but Victor's last comment put him on edge. He pretended to study the menu. Abel started to wonder if, perhaps, Victor *did* know what he was up to. Having never been in a purely social setting with his boss, it caught him off guard that the man could be casually enjoying a sunset in an expensive restaurant one minute, and doing a 180 and talking as if he were back in his office the next. Abel thought he'd have to be careful not to telegraph any signals that might clue Victor in to his uneasiness.

The waiter returned. Victor gave the man his order, then the waiter turned to Abel.

"I'll have the lasagna, the meaty kind, with extra cheese and red sauce," said Abel.

"Gracias, señor," replied the waiter, then primly strutted away.

"So where are we at with the Vicente shipment?" asked Victor as he and Abel sipped their drinks and gazed out at the sun. The entire Caribbean was now so red it looked like its waters had been transported across space and time from when Moses turned the Nile River to blood so many centuries before.

Abel didn't miss a beat. "It's all good, sir. I just came from a meeting with my contact. It'll be arriving in Miami in a week or so, and they've already been notified. We'll nail this one for sure."

"Great. These new young bucks like Don Vicente think they're going to be the millennial version of Pablo Escobar or the Cali Cartel. We're not going to let it happen. We get so much more cooperation from the Colombians these days. Places like here in Cartagena have become tourist meccas, UNESCO sites, ports for every cruise line in the world. The economy's booming, everyone's employed, and no one wants some Papa Pablo wannabe screwing it up. You're right, Nowinski. We'll nail them, nail them for sure. How much is that shipment again?"

"About a ton," replied Abel. "Over a hundred million, street value."

"That's great. Second one in as many months. Good work, Agent."

Abel took a swig of beer to hide the gulp he had just taken and to assuage the ensuing heartburn. Victor was one of the good guys, and he obviously thought Abel was still one, too. Abel felt a sharp twinge of shame, but he quickly dismissed it. No more Boy Scout routine for him anymore. He had his own problems, and he would fix them in his own way, regardless of how Victor might feel about that. Being back in action felt good, and skimming a small portion off the top of the millions that these cartel crooks dealt in was nothing to them, and could go a long way toward securing Abel's future and giving him the means to enjoy his one, short life. As their food came and the two began using their mouths for eating rather than talking, Abel felt satisfied that everything tonight would end up just fine.

But Victor wasn't done yet. "Abel," he said between devouring mouthfuls of steak, "there's something I've meant to ask you since I hired you, and haven't had the chance. I'd done lots of research into SEAL training and the like, and I always wanted to ask you about your trigger. Abel, what was your trigger?"

Abel barely caught himself in time to continue putting a forkful of lasagna into his mouth rather than stop mid-bite with his jaw hanging open.

"I'm not sure that's any of your goddamn beeswax, sir," he growled as he chewed his meat and noodles, red sauce seeping from the corners of his mouth.

"Really?" continued Victor, not missing a beat as he sliced off some more mignon. "You don't think it's important for a DEA station chief to know what motivates his agents, what causes them to want to put their life on the line each day?"

"I told you that in my interview," said Abel. "I want to serve my country and be a part of the action, not standing on the sidelines, but I couldn't continue doing that with my SEAL team. All due respect, sir, but maybe you just forgot?"

"I'll tell you for sure that I didn't forget, but you didn't let me finish. I'm sure you're aware, as I am, that your outward motivation doesn't have anything to do with your SEAL trigger."

Abel ate silently, his head down.

"Your SEAL trigger is the one person, thing, or ideal that keeps you going when everyone else has quit, what causes you to attempt the impossible, to hang on when you can't hang on anymore, to tap into an inner reservoir of strength that no one else even knows exists because you must continue living for the sake of that—"

Abel banged his fork on his plate. "I know what a goddamn trigger is!" he said sharply, glaring at Victor, "and it's none of your goddamn business!"

Now Victor was angry. "What do you know about my business?" he shot back. "I'm the agent in charge of this DEA post, and I'll decide what is and is not my business. I've watched a number of agents come into this country with all the high-and-mighty motivations you talk about—serving the country, being where the action is—all that kind of shit, and before they've even made it through a year, they're sullen, they're frustrated, itching to do something when there's nothing to do, griping, complaining, showing up late, twisting in the moral wind. Does this sound like anyone familiar to you, Agent Nowinski?"

"That's a helluva low blow, sir."

"I don't give a damn!" continued Victor. "We're talking about your life, the lives of other agents around you, and the mission of the DEA, and whether you can be trusted with those things. With stakes like that, I don't care if the blow was so low it ruptured both your balls."

"You saying you don't trust me, sir?" Abel sneered, his own anger boiling up even more.

"I've trusted you with my life and the mission of this post and everyone in it for going on two years now, Agent Nowinski, so I think I deserve a bit more respect than that last comment, but to be totally honest, over the past few months, I don't know what to think. That's why I'm asking you about your SEAL trigger."

"You don't have a trigger if you're not a SEAL."

"Bullshit! Everyone needs a reason to live—a reason they have to pull through and survive—especially in this business. You know what happened to those other agents that lost their focus like you're doing now? They got corrupted—all of them. Some don dangled more money in front of their faces than you'd make in a whole career as a Navy SEAL, or they'd make in ten lifetimes as a DEA agent, and they went for it, because they didn't have anyone or anything—any trigger—that would bring them back from whatever precipice they were teetering on and give them the moral strength to resist the temptation and do the right thing!"

"What happened to them?" asked Abel blankly. "I mean, this isn't all hypothetical bullshit, is it?"

"The lucky ones are dead," said Victor. He picked up his knife and sliced up a bit more filet, stuck his fork in a piece, and chewed it for a long moment. He took a drink, swallowed, and eyed Abel, now with a more somber look. "There were six by my count over the years. What got them killed was they all, later on, got remorseful and tried to get out, but that's not how it works in the cartels. Once you're in, you're either in or you're dead. They knew that, but no one ever really believes it when they're in the middle of all that shit."

"What about the unlucky ones?" asked Abel.

"They got caught. Because the cartels they collaborated with also engaged in the murder and torture of DEA agents, they were charged as being complicit. Both pleaded guilty and are serving multiple life sentences in the ADX Florence in Colorado."

Abel couldn't help but shudder, though he hoped not too obviously. The ADX Florence in Colorado was more commonly known as Supermax, the one prison in the entire federal system specially designed for prisoners considered so dangerous to themselves, to others, to the nation, or to the whole freaking world that even a prison's maximum-security facility was not deemed secure enough for their incarceration.

Victor continued. "They're hanging out now with people like the Unabomber, the Shoe Bomber, the Underwear Bomber, the Oklahoma City Bomber, the Boston Marathon Bomber, the 1993 World Trade Center Bomber, one of the 9/11 World Trade Center bombers, and a few dozen other assorted bombers, murderers, crime bosses, cartel dons, and traitors. Hell, you put the sentences of all those guys together, you'd probably have five or ten thousand years' worth of prison time. Twenty-three-hour-a-day solitary confinement, all meals in your cell, no entertainment, no visitors. See what I mean about unlucky?"

"All right, you made your point," grumbled Abel, who was not feeling nearly as good about the $50,000 in his backpack as he had an hour ago. The deal was done, though. A cartel hit man would probably be tailing him or spying on the place where he was staying now for God knows how long. He had to make the best of things. "My SEAL triggers all died a long time ago, or may as well have."

"And now?" asked Victor.

Abel just shrugged. The two each finished their dinners in silence. Victor watched the sunset over the Caribbean while Abel started in on his second beer. Finally, Victor broke the silence.

"I didn't bring you in here tonight just to have some kind of heart-to-heart," he said. Abel looked up. "I've got an assignment that I need someone for, but it's not around here."

"I'm listening," said Abel.

"We've got a contact up in Costa Rica, a small-time don who we allow to stay in business because he gives us inside shit about the big boys down here. Every now and then, we send someone up there to 'raid' his facility, make a few 'arrests' and such so that the dons down here don't get suspicious and think he's a collaborator. It's beautiful country up there, lots of sand and surf, jungle, wildlife, great weather, nice little hotels and beach houses, and the friendliest people you've ever met. Hell, it's almost like a working vacation. I usually leave it open on a first-come-first-served basis with the team, but I thought I'd give you a little early heads-up?" He gave Abel a questioning look.

Abel finished his beer. "Sounds boring," he said. He put his napkin on the table. Victor polished off his wine, left a wad of cash with the waiter, and the two stepped outside onto the wall. The sun had almost entirely set by now. Darkness was closing in.

Victor headed toward a small footbridge that crossed the street below and some stairs that led to a small dock that protruded out into the Caribbean, the café's seaside entrance. A small fishing trawler was waiting. Abel knew that it was actually a well-armed DEA boat filled with weapons and sophisticated electronics.

"What's up?" he asked.

"Nothing much," Victor replied. "Doing a little fishing tonight with a couple of others. I suppose you could come if you're not busy."

Abel smirked. "Fishing" was the post's term for taking a boatload of contraband drugs out into international waters after it was no longer needed as evidence, setting it afire, and eventually blowing the boat up, sending millions of dollars of coke down to Davy Jones and friends.

"Thanks, but I'll pass," Abel replied. "You all enjoy. I'm sure you'll have a blast."

Victor laughed as the two shook hands, then he took to the stairs and boarded the trawler. He waved goodbye to Abel, who returned the gesture. The boat pulled away, its bright light cutting through the growing gloom.

Abel watched it for a while, inwardly heaving a sigh of relief. Though the evening had had its uncomfortable moments, it didn't look like Victor knew of his duplicity. Yet, try as he might, he couldn't put all the things that Victor had mentioned out of his mind. Words like "once you're in, you're either in or you're dead" and "the lucky ones are dead" and "serving multiple life sentences in the ADX Florence" clung to his mind despite his attempts to dismiss them. As the boat finally faded from view, Abel grabbed his backpack, scuttled down the other side of the wall, found his e-bike, and left.

3

—

Once Victor's trawler had reached a point where they could no longer see the lights of Cartagena, he checked with his radar and navigation men to make sure that they had the larger boat on radar. They did. Then he had his crew kill all the lights as they approached it. Victor had, of course, lied to Abel about the kind of "fishing" he and his other agents would be doing that night because he knew Abel wouldn't want to go. Had Abel come, it would have put him in a highly tricky situation with the DEA that would undoubtedly have landed him in prison. On land, he'd at least be safe from that, though he'd face a whole different set of dangers there. Victor shook his head. Abel was on his own now, set free, even though Victor knew he was most likely as treacherous as Benedict Arnold, and probably could have proved it by merely opening the guy's backpack. But Victor hadn't done that. He knew that, behind Abel's roguish bluster, the former Navy SEAL was really just a lost, lonely man looking for some direction, and Victor had decided that, because of that, the guy deserved another chance. Perhaps someday he'd get his act together, find the "trigger" he so desperately needed to keep himself out of trouble, and make a new start.

One could only hope. But there was no time to contemplate that now. The real "fishing" was just about to begin.

The big trawler had all its lights killed as well, but Victor knew it was tricked out to be an oceangoing fishing boat, the kind often used by drug smugglers to cross the Caribbean or go up the Pacific coast before unloading their tons of cargo onto smaller boats out in international waters to take the haul to shore.

The opposite was true as well. These modern mega-cartel wannabes didn't have the money or sophistication yet to develop a vast fleet of oceangoing semisubmersible vessels or "narco submarines" like the cartels of the '80s had. They still had to rely on the older "go-fast" boats—boats similar to speedboats, but beefed up with bullet-resistant hulls and other enhancements—to get their kilos of cocaine from tiny shore outposts to their larger oceangoing vessels out in international waters without attracting the attention of land-based police or Coast Guard units.

Only, the oceangoing trawler that Victor's boat was now approaching was not manned by drug smugglers of Don Vicente Galvan's Clan de Cartagena like the incoming go-fast boat crews were expecting. It had been quietly overtaken by Victor's DEA agents who had infiltrated the crew before the ship's departure from port. Just a few of the original crew members were still with the ship; the rest of the individuals on the boat were now DEA agents. The ship's decks were filled with three rigid-hulled inflatable boats (RHIBs) that were quietly being assembled, armed with M240 pedestal-mounted machine guns, and lowered into the water.

Victor's boat pulled up next to the bigger trawler, and he was hoisted on board. Two more DEA agents, one bearing a helmet and body armor for Victor, met him. Victor listened as he was brought up to speed.

"Welcome aboard, sir. Everything's ready. The RHIBs are assembled, launched, crewed, and in position on the other side of the ship. All the spotlights are in place and manned."

"Good, Agent Dolan, very good," replied Victor as he donned his body armor. "How about the fish?"

"Everyone's left their dock according to our ground reports. Should be in the area in five minutes or so."

"And the Colombian police?"

"They'll be coming right behind them."

Victor nodded, then walked over to the ship's bridge, where three cartel crewmen sat stoic and expressionless. "You've got one job—light the bridge and the fantail running lights on my command, then one of you waves to the first boat that approaches and lights you up. You got it?"

"Sí, señor." They all nodded.

Victor continued. "Once the shooting starts, go belowdecks and stay there. When things are all over, you'll be driven by DEA agents in unmarked vehicles to your homes, where you'll have fifteen minutes to pack. Then you and your family will be taken to a secure airport where you'll be put on a private DEA jet and flown to the country of your choice in the Western Hemisphere. Papers will be made for you in flight. Once you land, you're on your own, unless you choose the US, where you'll be met and processed immediately as asylum seekers. That's the best we can do for you. The governments of the United States and of Colombia thank you for your service."

As Victor was about to leave, one of the cartel crewmen spoke in heavily accented English. "Señor, they will still kill us, no matter where we are."

"Maybe, but at least they won't do it tonight."

The sound of high-powered motors whined in the distance.

"Sir, it's time," said Agent Dolan.

Victor grabbed an assault rifle racked on the bridge. "Have these men taken to their positions, and flip on the bridge and fantail lights. Let's you and I find a place near the spotlight on the bridge, and get me the ship's mic."

"Yes, sir," said Dolan. As the two found the bridge spotlight and settled in, Dolan asked, "Sir, where's Agent Nowinski?" The area now was live with the whining buzz of several go-fast boats approaching. The bridge and fantail running lights were lit. Suddenly, a bright spotlight seemed to emanate from nowhere and splash the trawler amidships. The cartel crewman waved and motioned the boats to come in.

"I sent him on another assignment," grunted Victor. With that, he called into his headset mic, "Let's light 'em up, boys!"

Spotlights instantly blazed from three different locations on the trawler. At least six go-fast boats were instantly illuminated, with others just on the edge of the light. Victor used the ship's mic and called out in Spanish, "Halt. You're all under arrest! Kill your engines, throw your weapons in the sea, and you won't be harmed!"

A few boats' crewmen did, but others pulled out, and one charged, firing at the spotlights. Dolan and Victor dove for cover. The RHIBs roared out from behind the ship. Machine-gun fire blew up the offending boat, while all four occupants of another were riddled with bullets as they tried to fire back with assault rifles. A couple escaped, but gunfire and lights could be seen not far away across the water.

The Colombians, right on time.

"Yeah!" shouted Agent Dolan. "We got them, sir!"

Upon hearing no reply, he looked around, then gasped. Victor lay dead beside him, a bullet through his head.

4

—

A bel lived in a small brick apartment building just a block or so from the luxurious Hyatt Regency Hotel Cartagena. The apartments had probably been pretty swanky decades ago when there was still very little development on the long Bocagrande peninsula that stretched for several kilometers to the southeast of the Walled City, forming the seaside of the placid Bahia de Cartagena. Now, though, that strip of sand was lined with thirty- and forty-story modern hotels and condominium buildings, giving it a look not unlike Miami Beach, and Abel's apartment building looked like a little three-story orphan in comparison.

Abel didn't mind. It certainly wasn't some filthy flophouse. But still, he didn't actually spend much time there. Being a loner didn't mean that he necessarily thrived on solitude. Abel's restless energy frequently took him to places where lots of people gathered just so he could be around them and feel their vibe. So this night, after returning from his dinner with Victor Garza, he'd returned briefly to his apartment to open the windows, then headed out to one of his favorite people places: the ritzy bar at the Hyatt Regency. It was expensive, but also classy, and a mecca for the English-speaking foreign tourists, businessmen, and local expats who were usually a fun and intriguing lot to hang out around. *Tonight, though, will be extra fun*, he thought as he carried his backpack with its secret load of cash in and plopped down at the bar in front of one of the English-speaking TV screens that featured twenty-four-hour news. He splurged by ordering an appetizer of hot wings and mozzarella sticks along with the house beer. The crowd tonight was not large or overly loud, so he even considered buying a round for the lot of them, but then, glancing at the TV, he did a double take, and his mouth fell open, a half-chewed hot wing plopping onto his plate.

"Some breaking news just coming in now," said a news commentator. "Agents of the American Drug Enforcement Agency, in cooperation with the Colombian National Police, have just seized yet another large shipment of Colombian cartel cocaine, this time as it was apparently being loaded onto an oceangoing fishing trawler allegedly bound for the port of Miami in the United States. The seizure took place in international waters off the coast of Cartagena, though government officials are assuring the public that the Colombian National Police forces did not actually operate outside of Colombian waters but caught several so-called go-fast boats as they were trying to escape back to the mainland. With the total amount of drugs seized put at well over one hundred million US dollars, this marks the second time in as many months that the US DEA, in cooperation with the Colombian National Police, has seized a sizable shipment of northern Colombian cartel cocaine before it could hit the streets." A jubilant CNP spokesperson thanked the Americans for their help in "killing off these nits before they can turn into lice," referring to new cocaine cartels that have sprung up over the past few years, including the Clan de San Juan de Urabá and the Clan de Cartagena, and the so-called dons that run them. The spokesperson also said that Cartagena city police were now beefing up their visible presence and bracing for cartel reprisals that may follow. The report mentions, "there were casualties on both sides in this operation," but no specifics were given.

"Holy shit!" Abel yelled at the TV. He was so loud that others in the bar turned in alarm. "Holy fucking shit!" he yelled again, and he suddenly tore out of the bar, nearly bowling over a cocktail waitress serving a table near the door.

Abel's mind was racing a mile a second as he charged out of the Hyatt and dashed down the street for his apartment.

Shit! Shit-shit-shit! he thought. *That was my shipment! My fucking shipment! The one I was supposed to protect—when it got to Miami!*

At the same time, another thought leaped into his mind as he pounded toward the old brick building, which was now in sight. *Victor knew!* He knew even as he was sitting there chatting with Abel casually eating his dinner. He knew when he invited Abel to go "fishing" with him, for Christ's sake! The whole damn dinner date with him had just been one big charade! Abel knew that cartel hitmen had followed him into the Walled City. It was a good bet that, at some point, they'd gotten back on his tail after he'd left. Maybe they'd even checked out where he lived and what kind of car he drove before they'd met him. *The building might be staked out!* The sooner he got out of the city—out of the goddamn country—the better.

Breathlessly arriving at the apartment building, Abel crashed through the doors, now focused on just what was important enough for him to spend one minute grabbing before he'd head for his car when suddenly, he stopped. *My backpack! The money! I left it at the bar!*

Abel dashed through the doorway and charged back down the street. He was less than half a block away when an ear-splitting explosion caused him to leap with surprise, and then the explosion's blast wave swept over him, knocking him off his feet. Abel turned around just in time to see his entire apartment building collapse as if someone had chopped the poor old structure's legs out from under it. A choking wave of dust and tiny debris fragments swept over him. Abel coughed and spewed sandy spit but quickly recovered his feet as he dashed back to the Hyatt.

More thoughts flooded his mind as he ran. *Was that blast meant for me? Are Don Vicente's hitmen that close? Where will I go now?* His car was parked down the street. *Will it be safe?*

He dashed back into the Hyatt, pushing through crowds pouring from the bar and the lobby to see what the explosion down the street was about. He charged through the bar and found his backpack right where he'd left it, then took off again. By this time, he'd decided that if the cartel dons were willing to blow up the entire building that he lived in just to retaliate, it was a good bet that his car was probably rigged to blow as well. Charging through the main entryway to the hotel, he skidded to a stop and headed for the kiosk where bellhops and valets kept the keys to the vehicles of people checking in. He snatched a key fob from a small rack and began clicking it, listening for chirps or car horns. Upon seeing one car's lights flash, he ran for a boxy little Kia Soul that was just on the other side of the entry area, threw open the driver's side door, tossed his backpack inside, and screeched out toward the street.

At the same time, he noticed several men in suits who had been scanning the crowd. They suddenly turned, pulled handguns, and opened fire on him. The other people ducked, covered, and ran in all directions, helping Abel escape the volley as he burned rubber out onto the wide Carrera 1, one of the main drags along the Bocagrande, heading back toward the Walled City. He gave the little car the gas, and it surged forward—excellent for a small car, but not near what he might need if he was being followed. Two sedans and a Jeep weaving in and out of traffic behind him in his rearview confirmed that. Increasing his speed, he came to the dizzying intersection with Carrera 2, also known as the Avenida San Martin, where the left turn he had to make around the traffic circle nearly caused him to roll the Kia. Those following him zipped around it with ease and were now closer still.

The vast, looping maze where the Avenida San Martin intersected with the Avenida Blas de Lezo that diverted inland just south of the Walled City came rushing at Abel and his stolen Kia. In the dark, it looked doubly confusing. He zipped off to the right as if to swing around the Walled City on the Blas, then screeched his vehicle left again and jumped onto a loop that took him back to Carrera 1 and 2, which were now called the Avenida Santander. He smiled as he saw one of the pursuing sedans not make the turn in time and fishtail around on the Blas, then get T-boned by another car as it tried, too late, to make the turn. He still had two vehicles behind him, and now they were racing along the Santander with the city wall off to the right and the Caribbean close up on the left. The margin of error was slim, especially since it was dark and they were all weaving in and out of traffic, going at times over a 100 kph on what was essentially a wide, multilane city street.

Abel saw the Café de Vista Sol and the triangular fortress that it was a part of coming up rapidly on the right, high on the wall at the city's farthest protrusion into the Caribbean. It was the one place where the wall actually came within a few feet of the roadway as it curved to the right around the point. Abel's quick mind snatched at an idea. He weaved to the outside lane and slowed slightly. The pursuing Jeep took the bait, quickly speeding up to come alongside the Kia. Abel saw two men with assault rifles lean out the windows and take aim. But they were now right where Abel wanted them. He suddenly swerved the Kia to the right, causing the driver of the Jeep to do the same to avoid a collision. It skittered off the shoulder, and the men with guns opened fire, but the firing stopped an instant later as the Jeep plowed head-on into the solid stone of the city wall. Abel winced as he heard the impact, and seconds later, he saw a fiery explosion in his rearview. The pursuing sedan barely escaped the fireball and flying debris. The chase continued.

As he sped along, keeping the sedan at a safe distance by both going insanely fast and weaving in and out of traffic, Abel contemplated his next move. He knew that he could ride the Avenida Santander almost all the way to Cartagena's Rafael Núñez International Airport, where it would once again go through a mazelike intersection where the coexisting Carrera 1 would branch off, then head into a jumble of streets filled with shopping centers, fast-food joints, hotels, private residences, and even the Carrera 3, which actually went to the airport terminal. Abel felt that if he could get to this area unscathed, he could once again lose the hitmen, then park somewhere and enter the airport, a place where it would also be easy to get himself lost while he caught a flight out to just about anywhere that wasn't in Colombia. The heightened security in the city might also help him, with airport police being on alert for known cartel operatives. But the cartels could have men there as well, figuring that Abel would be looking for the fastest way out of the country.

Fuck it, thought Abel. Whatever was going to happen, it would all be over in less than fifteen minutes. The airport was that close, and they were going that fast.

And he was right. Before he knew it, there was the big, messy intersection, all lit up with streetlights that, along with car headlights, made everything look glaring and garish. Abel feinted that he was going to continue on straight, then, at the last minute, swerved right and back onto Carrera 1. The car behind him flew off into some landscaping but quickly swerved back onto the road behind him.

The sedan's momentary off-road escapade had caught the eye of a Cartagena police cruiser. It now joined the chase, and before long, two other cruisers as well.

The first one must have at least run the sedan's license number and reported something suspicious, thought Abel. That was good. Maybe the cops would get rid of his tail for him.

No sooner had he thought it, though, than he found that another police car, this one unmarked, had turned on its lights and siren between him and his pursuers.

Well, I am driving a stolen vehicle in flagrant excess of the posted speed limit.

He spotted the big, sweeping left turn where Carrera 1, now called Calle 70, curved into the airport environs. He sped up suddenly and flew around it, catching the cop car off guard. He came almost immediately to a street where well-lit signs directed returning rental cars to turn right. Abel turned left instead, and then right almost instantly, went down the street for a block, then parked near a small park, squashed in with many other cars. After sitting with the engine off for well over a minute, Abel decided he must have lost the police car. He had no idea what might have happened to the cartel hitmen.

Abel got out of the Kia, patted it affectionately on the hood, grabbed his backpack, and locked the doors before tossing the keys on the back seat and slamming the back door shut. He walked calmly toward the airport drop-off area, a mere block away. He figured he was pretty safe for now. The police didn't know who he was or what he looked like, and the cartel hitmen had hopefully been waylaid long enough by the Cartagena police that they would no longer be a factor.

As he crossed the street through a menagerie of cars, taxis, small trucks, and shuttle buses, though, he discovered that a couple of men in jackets and jeans were walking toward him almost immediately.

Damn, they're everywhere, he thought, *and they do know what I look like!*

He saw a policeman patrolling nearby and walked swiftly toward him.

"Por favor!" he called. The policeman came toward him, and the other two backed off, but not far. "Can you please take me to the ticket counter? I don't know where to go."

The policeman pointed toward a couple of sets of automatic doors. "In there," he said.

Abel became agitated. "I know 'in there,' but which one will take me to Haiti?" he retorted. "I don't know if any of the airlines go to Haiti, and I have important business there tomorrow."

The policeman sighed, then signaled for Abel to follow him inside, which he did, as did the jeans-and-jackets guys.

Abel was becoming increasingly frustrated. It wasn't like he couldn't handle the guys, but doing so in the middle of an airport's ticketing area without being seen would be tricky at best. And who knew if others were around? The policeman left him at the counter for the SALSA d'Haïti airline, and the jeans-and-jackets guys stood on the other side of the ticket area, leering at him.

"Fuck it," said Abel to himself. He ditched his place in line and headed for a public restroom close to a nearby security clearance complex. A furtive glance back confirmed that the jeans guys were following, along with one other man who was in between them and Abel.

Abel entered the restroom, and as soon as the other man came in, Abel grabbed him, hauled him to a bathroom stall, and shoved him in.

"Lock the door and don't come out," he ordered.

The terrified man complied. Abel turned now to see the boot of one of the jeans guys just pushing open the door. Abel rushed at the door, smashed the guy's foot with it, then flung it open, threw the howling man inside, and slammed the door in the face of the second guy. In seconds, Abel extracted the knife that the smashed-foot guy was now trying to brandish, despite barely being able to stand, and used it to slit the guy's throat. Then he turned to face the second man, who furiously charged him through the main door, also with a knife. Abel dodged the blade and slammed his fist into the guy's larynx, creating a sickening crunching sound. As the guy unsuccessfully gasped for breath, Abel dragged him into another bathroom stall, threw him on the toilet seat, and left him to die. He did the same with first man, who was rapidly bleeding out and nearly unconscious. He closed both stall doors, then banged on the first man's stall as he left.

"You can come out now," he said, then disappeared out the bathroom door.

Back in the expansive ticketing lobby, Abel quickly slipped out a different door than he'd come in. To his surprise, what he was looking for came in a familiar form. The car with the unmistakable Uber sticker on its front windshield was a Kia Soul, this one a delicious-looking chocolate brown. He hopped in.

"Where do you need to go, señor?" asked the driver, a young man probably in his twenties.

"South, on Route Ninety until we're well out of the city," said Abel. He tossed a hundred onto the front seat. It was the equivalent of three hundred thousand Colombian pesos. "I trust this will be sufficient for a good thirty or forty kilometers."

"Sí, señor!" replied the driver enthusiastically.

"Bueno," said Abel.

As the driver pulled away, Abel watched tensely for a while, still not sure if other cartel hitmen might have been posted at the airport and seen him leave. After ten or fifteen minutes of checking the car's rearview and turning around to actually see the traffic behind, it was apparent that no one was following them. It looked like it was a clean getaway.

Abel pulled out his secure smartphone and saw he had a text message from Dolan, Victor Garza's second-in-command at the post. Abel's jaw dropped at what he read:

Garza killed in seizure operation. Assuming command until replaced. Apprise of mission status when able. Avoid airport. Use scenic routes.

Abel was stunned. Victor was dead. But even more shockingly, before he died, he apparently had told Dolan that he had assigned Abel to the Costa Rica mission. Victor had not told Dolan about Abel's treachery! Dolan now was advising Abel about the best way to get out of the country and avoid cartel reprisals rather than ordering him in to face justice for collaborating with Don Vicente's cartel. The implication of it all nearly took Abel's breath away as he stared at his phone. Eventually, even as the full impact had not yet sunk in, Abel texted back.

Mission status en route via scenic routes. Able to avoid cartel reprisal attempts. Sorry about Garza. You'll be a fine acting post commander, Dolan.

Abel stowed his phone, then closed his eyes and put his head back as his driver took him out of Cartagena. Twenty minutes later, Abel told the young man to stop at the tiny bus depot in a town called Aroja.

The two got out, and Abel made the young man an offer he couldn't refuse. He'd buy the Kia for $10,000 in cash and be on his way while the driver took the bus back to Cartagena. Either that or he'd be forced to steal the Kia and kill the driver to cover his tracks. The guy was smart. He took the money. Abel grabbed some water, fruit, and snacks from a nearby convenience store that was open late, then continued his journey south.

SAN JERONIMO

5

—

Abel was now in one of his favorite situations—on the road, by himself, heading out on a mission. It had been his preferred modus operandi ever since he'd failed to make it back on to his SEAL team two years before. Since being with the DEA in Cartagena, Abel had, of course, been civil and professional with the other agents at the post, but he'd never quite clicked with anyone on a personal level. Indeed, his conversation with Victor Garza earlier that night was as private as he'd ever gotten with anyone in Cartagena, DEA agent or no. Victor had been right—nearly dead right—about him. He was drifting, floating aimlessly around in the moral cesspool that DEA agents dove into every day, easy pickings for the crocodiles that swam around in it. And were it not for Victor, he'd have been devoured already, either by the cartel, whom he'd failed, or by the agency itself, whom he had betrayed. Victor had single-handedly spared him from it all—in one night, no less.

Abel shook his head at the thought. Why in the hell would a guy do something like that for him? He'd screwed up, after all—screwed up royally. Abel had learned in the SEALs that if you screwed up, you were fucked, and not just you, but everyone else who depended on you. The world was dangerous and unforgiving, and people who didn't get that, or refused to understand that, always ended up fucked in the end. Why had this one man decided to mess with the natural order of things? And he'd gotten himself killed in the process! There was a side of Abel that wished he could thank Victor when he thought of that, but he dismissed it quickly. It made him feel uncomfortable. He didn't understand it, and there were more important things to be thinking about at the moment.

And so Abel drove on through the Colombian night, down highways that were narrow and traveled on by few. He passed through a couple of bona fide cities on his way south, the brightness of their lights nearly blinding him, and countless little villages that he had almost traveled entirely through before he even realized they were there. He had practically no idea what the country looked like. It was pitch dark everywhere that his headlights didn't pierce, and so it was hard to tell whether he was going through forests or open plains, farmland or rancheros where cattle might be grazing. It certainly wasn't a jungle, but that was about all he knew.

As time passed, he thought of other things, more immediate matters, like his present situation, and what he'd have to do to acquire those things that he didn't have, and when. As to the current situation, it wasn't that bad, but far, far from ideal. He had the clothes on his back, a pair of good tennies on his feet, his usual weapons that he never went anywhere without—meaning his Glock 19 compact 9mm handgun and two spare magazines, his SOG SEAL Team Elite all-purpose knife, and his Walther PK super-small handgun on his leg in honor of one of his movie heroes, James Bond—and a serviceable vehicle. But other than that, things looked bleak. Food, water, and heavier-duty clothes and footwear would be essential. Some raingear and a more durable backpack to haul everything would be nice.

His ace-in-the-hole asset was his money, the now $40,000 in cash stashed in his backpack, as well as the additional $200,000 in his secret offshore bank account. The cash alone was the kind of money that could get him everything he needed and more, as well as get him to his final destination in one piece if he was careful. Or it could disappear in a heartbeat if he got careless with it and made himself a magnet for thieves, who would be hiding in the shadows virtually everyplace he'd be going from now on. He reminded himself to stash rolls of it in various different places on his person, just in case the worst happened.

Another resource, mostly unknown to Abel but reputed to be reliable, was a small network of DEA assets stationed in strategic places on the way between Victor Garza's post in Cartagena and the various DEA posts in Central America. Abel was heading for one of those assets now, a pilot based at the tiny airport in Vista Bonita, a small town on the Colombian coast of the Gulf of Darién, a backwater of the Caribbean that must be crossed to get from Colombia into Panama. That would allow Abel to board transportation at a place well away from the typical hubs where cartel assassins may be lurking, and also to get over the gulf and into Panama in a fraction of the time it would take if going by sea, as most people did.

The reason why Abel didn't simply drive into Panama was that there literally was no possible way to do it. The border between Colombia and Panama, for nearly fifty kilometers on either side, was covered with a trackless morass of swamps and jungle known as the Darién Gap. It was called the Darién Gap because it was the one place in the entire length of the great Pan-American Highway, which stretched all the way from Fairbanks, Alaska, to the southern tip of Argentina, where there was actually a gap in the roadway. The pavement stopped at the terminus of a long, shaky footbridge across the wide Chucunaque River in the heart of the tiny town of San Jeronimo in Panama, then started again on the Colombian side in another town called Turbo, the central hub for people making water crossings of the Gulf of Darién. Both would likely be patrolled by cartel hitmen looking for him.

The Gap itself had no roads at all, not even Jeep trails. The only transportation across it was either on foot (and be sure to bring your

sharpened machete) or hollowed-out, flat-bottom wooden river canoes, the main form of transportation for the various indigenous tribes
in the area and others who'd built fledgling plantain and banana farms
there. Danger lurked everywhere for the uninitiated in this trackless
jungle. Poisonous frogs and scorpions hopped and scurried alongside
fer-de-lance snakes and fire ants. Animals from wild pigs to pumas
prowled the thick undergrowth and lofty tree branches. Even the trees
themselves could be dangerous, the ubiquitous black palm's bark bris-
tling with sharp barbs that were coated in disease-carrying bacteria.
The national park within the Darién was a UNESCO World Heritage
site for its pristine, pre-Colombian jungle terrain and preservation of
the culture of its indigenous people, but like many natural wonders, it
was intensely wild, with no regard for the tastes of civilized humans.

Despite these, the biggest reason for someone like Abel to avoid
the Gap was that it had for decades been the domain of the cartels,
where smugglers from Colombia could move their product along into
Panama and points north without fear of official interference. In recent years, though, the elite Panamanian police force known as the
PNP had begun to crack down on this illicit activity, at times turning
the Gap into a guerrilla war zone. One's mere presence without the
specific permission of the PNP would land you in jail, or perhaps
even in a grave, and likewise, a chance encounter with cartel guerrillas
could bring with it an even more gruesome fate. Agent Dolan apprised
Abel of this in a voicemail that Abel listened to over his car's speakers
as he drove.

So the plan was, according to the voicemail and subsequent texts
from Dolan, to board a plane in Vista Bonita, clear the gulf, and fly
as far as the pilot was able to take him. Dolan estimated that he could
make it as far as the Costa Rican border, perhaps even farther, depending on the plane. This would get him well clear of Colombia and, most
likely, any cartel thugs. It sounded terrific to Abel. After being on the
run all night, after a harrowing evening the night before, he could use
a little snooze time on an airplane.

But Abel's heart sank as soon as he parked the Kia. The lone plane on the runway near Vista Bonita was a tiny single-engine Cessna Skyhawk, a four-seater usually only used as a pilot-training aircraft. The man whom Abel presumed to be the pilot came running out of a small adobe building alongside the runway.

"*Hola!* Hurry, *ándele!* We must go immediately!"

Abel swung himself out of the Kia and grabbed his backpack. "What's the rush?"

"Get in. Get in! There's no time to explain." The man, who was short and probably in his sixties, tossed Abel a heavy leather jacket with sheepskin lining similar to a World War II flight jacket. Abel looked at it as if it were an alien life-form, then grabbed the arm of the bustling little man and swung him around.

"Listen, whoever you are, I'm not setting foot inside that little toy airplane of yours until you tell me what the situation is here," he growled.

The man sighed. "My name is José, and the situation is that my petrol pump is not working, and the man who is coming to fix it is coming later today, but if I'm not here, he will not fix it, and I will go another week with no petrol pump, which means that I will once again only have one tank of fuel to make it through the week. This is terrible. I have crops to dust, mail runs to make, people like you to fly across the gulf. I cannot afford to run out of petrol again."

"Wait a minute," said Abel, alarmed. "Are you saying that you're out of fuel?"

"No, *estúpido!*" he cried. "But I will be once we land in San Jeronimo. There, I'll refuel, and then I will come back, and if I miss the man who is going to fix the pump, I will only have what's left in my tank to last the week."

"San Jeronimo!" Abel was furious. "You were supposed to take me all the way to Costa Rica."

"Ha!" José laughed. "That is, how you say, hilarious." He put his own leather jacket on and started to climb into the little pilot's seat.

"I can't go to San Jeronimo! It's dangerous," yelled Abel. The guy was strapped in. He was serious.

"Not if you don't cross the bridge into the Darién. The only other things that are there are little concrete and wooden houses and a few cantinas and shops and *fondés* where you can eat really cheap. There's even a PNP post there next to where the old Spanish *fuerte* is. They issue permits to go into the Darién and send out patrols to watch for cockroaches trying to enter the country from the jungle. How could you be safer?" He turned the ignition, but the plane failed to start.

How about landing somewhere on the other side of the border with Costa Rica? Abel thought.

This was turning into another nightmare, and he'd barely gotten over the one the night before. José tried the ignition again, but the engine refused to turn over.

"Aiee! Sometimes this happens, especially when low on fuel. You go, give the propeller a pull."

"A what?" asked Abel incredulously.

"A pull! You know . . ." He mimicked someone pulling down on the propeller.

"You gotta be fucking kidding me," Abel grumbled to himself as he set his backpack down and moved to the propeller.

"Not on that side, the other side," yelled José. "You want to get your arm sliced off?"

Abel did as he was told. José turned the ignition and Abel pulled, but it was hard, and the propeller wouldn't budge. The plane's engine sputtered.

"Again!" cried José.

This time, when José turned the ignition, Abel gave the propeller a mighty yank with both arms, then jumped to the side as the engine revved and the propeller became a whirling blur.

Abel walked back around the plane, retrieved his backpack, and grabbed the leather jacket.

"How high are we going?" he yelled to José. Abel had jumped from

planes as high as thirty thousand feet back in his SEAL days, but what
he was looking at wasn't exactly standard-issue Navy SEAL gear.

"Ten thousand feet!" called José. "We must cross the mountains on
the coast. Much better for you. You can catch the highway and drive
from San Jeronimo, or even rent a plane if you want. See! I am good
Colombian—help DEA get rid of the cockroaches!"

Great, thought Abel. *Just high enough to freeze my ass off, and all so
I can land in a potential hornet's nest of cartel thugs.*

At that moment, he knew that if Dolan had been there, he'd have
slugged him smack in the nose. He hoisted himself into the cramped
rear seat and strapped in. A SEAL was taught to adapt to changing situations, but the events of the last eighteen hours had been taxing. José
worked the controls in front of him, and they bounced down the old
runway, taking off into the dawning sky.

6

—

Colonel Rafael Ochoa, commander of the Darién Brigade of the PNP, grimaced as he read the paper just handed to him. A US DEA agent bound for Costa Rica is flying in within the hour, it said. Don Vicente Galvan of the Clan de Cartagena had put a price on his head. The don's operatives in the Gap were already aware of the reward. The bounty was posted on the dark web. The request was being made by the DEA post in Cartagena to protect him and see him on his way. It had been sent to General Javier Vizcarra, the national commander of the PNP, and he had contacted *el presidente* himself to get his official go-ahead.

Colonel Ochoa shook his head. Panama's economy lived and died according to its relationship with the US. Panama rebuilt its economy after the days of dictator Manuel Noriega on foreign tourism and expatriate resettlement. Panama's program for *pensionados* offered the most comprehensive benefits of any country in the world to foreign nationals who moved to Panama to spend their retirement years. All they had to do was be at least fifty years old and provide evidence that they received a pension from some source in their home country. This had brought tens of thousands to Panama, many of whom stayed, some even obtaining dual citizenship. By far, the most significant number of foreign retirees came from the US. That meant that their relatives came to visit them as well. Though Panamanians officially controlled the Panama Canal now, the US still maintained a significant presence there to help protect the most vital waterway in the world from attack. Billions of US dollars were spent by the shiploads of tourists that came through the canal on cruise liners, many based in the US. If a US DEA agent needed protecting now, not only would it be done, but it would become the top priority of those in charge.

Within the hour, thought Colonel Ochoa. *Not much time.*

Perhaps this explained why his patrolmen had already detained more than a half dozen men this morning. Some came out of the Gap without the proper papers. Others had crossed the river into San Jeronimo at places other than the footbridge or simply were strangers who nobody knew and looked suspicious. Could there be others on the way? Colonel Ochoa's Darién brigade consisted of five hundred officers and patrolmen, but most were scattered along the border or on patrol in the Gap itself. There were probably only about fifty patrolmen currently stationed in San Jeronimo, along with the local constable and his volunteer deputies. Whatever the colonel did, it would have to be decisive, and it would have to be quick. Neither time nor resources could be wasted.

He figured that he probably had one advantage, and it was a big one. The cartel hitmen and the bounty hunters didn't know when this DEA agent was coming or in what way, or if he would even show up in San Jeronimo at all. In fact, most of them probably had only a name and a picture and were just guessing that he might show up here because most everyone coming out of the Gap did.

He decided to take a low-key approach. He turned to his communications officer.

"Send Code Jaguar," he ordered.

Code Jaguar indicated to his men and the local constable that there was a reason for a heightened number of strangers or illegal activity to be about. It was a call to be extra alert and to question or detain anyone who aroused suspicion. It also put his airport security force on high alert, though it did not call for them to obviously deploy themselves.

Then Colonel Ochoa made a couple of more overt moves. These would help facilitate his still-formulating plan to get this DEA agent on his way as inconspicuously and efficiently as possible. He ordered that his post helicopter get airborne and go out as if on a normal fly-over of the Gap. But also, while taking off, it would briefly fly out over the jungle surrounding the airport and make a sweep to detect if any assassins were perhaps staking out the airport. He ordered his personal turboprop to be prepped and readied for takeoff, and at least one armored Humvee to be put in place as well. Then he got into his private police SUV and headed for the airport.

The airport at San Jeronimo was not actually the San Jeronimo Airport. It was just a single strip of runway carved out of the jungle a few kilometers up Highway CA-1 (also known as the Pan-American Highway) and a cluster of service buildings and PNP offices. Its primary function was to be an aerial hub where supplies and men could be moved in and out quickly. Patrols within the Gap could be quickly resupplied or given cover in case of attack, and humanitarian aid could be efficiently dispatched. It did also serve the public as a landing point for private, non-jet aircraft, but no commercial flights of any kind were allowed there.

As he drove, Colonel Ochoa finished formulating his plan. He and his men would apprehend this DEA agent the moment he stepped out of his plane. Then they would put him on Ochoa's PNP turboprop and get him off the ground and away in less than five minutes. Simple, quick, and efficient, the way Colonel Ochoa always tried to operate. In the remote possibility that his helicopter flyovers detected assassins in the jungle with weapons that could shoot down planes, they'd make a run for it in the Humvee instead.

But there was something that bugged the colonel about the entire situation. Only in his best-case scenario would he actually get the man to safety and off the cartel's radar. If the agent could be apprehended, put on the turboprop, and flown out of San Jeronimo, the man would get away. The cartels would have no idea what his destination would be. The man would have months, maybe even years, to figure out how to disappear for good. In every other scenario, though, the people who were searching for this man would know at least which way he was going and would have maps to track where he might go next. Even if the colonel sent him into the Gap, which most considered a death sentence anyway, the cartel's men inside would quickly hunt him down. The fact was, wherever the man went, no matter how far away from Colombia it was, the cartel would continue to hunt him down until he was dead. That's how it was for people they wanted badly enough. Short of the DEA and the Colombian National Police destroying the cartel itself, the only thing that would stop them would be the man's dead body. And that incredibly sobering thought set Colonel Ochoa's mind to contemplating different, more ominous contingencies to his plans.

He headed out of town and eventually turned his SUV onto the dirt road that led to the airport. As he drove, he wondered just what this man had done that made Don Vicente Galvan so angry? The drug lord didn't seem to have vendettas out on the other DEA agents in Cartagena, or at least no more than usual. Perhaps he would ask this DEA agent about it when the man arrived if there was time.

Moments later, Colonel Ochoa pushed through the door of the airport office of his PNP command. He was just in time to hear the report coming in from his helicopter. It had just completed its first pass over the jungle around the airfield.

"I saw several people scurry for cover as I passed over," the man in the helicopter said over the radio. "It was impossible to tell how many, but certainly at least five or six, all armed with automatic weapons. We're coming around to check out the left side of the runway now."

"Acknowledged," said the radio operator.

This news was very troubling to Colonel Ochoa. The jungle was cleared for a quarter mile around the runway. The forest's edge was also walled off with a perimeter fence eight feet high and topped with razor wire. This ensured that the airport was safe from the vast majority of weapons preferred by the cartels: assault rifles and handguns, even bazookas. However, there were any number of heavier weapons such as high-caliber sniper rifles and late-model RPG launchers that could effectively reach the runway, or even the airport buildings. That is, if a bounty hunter or cartel hitman could somehow haul it in from the impassable Gap or over the surrounding mountains without being detected by his patrols. And there was always the question of whether an aircraft could get high enough once it took off to get itself out of range before crossing over the jungle. Overhead, he heard the chopper coming in for another high-level pass over the area.

"I'm looking through the binoculars now. I see more men running for cover under the trees, or back into the bush—one, two, three, some more—at least six, perhaps more." The observer was referring to men caught in a fifty-yard swath of jungle on the other side of the fence where the undergrowth around the trees was regularly cut back to aid in exposing potential intruders who might try breaching the fence.

"One had a very big, long gun. That is all I could make out for sure."

"Acknowledged. Gracias," droned the radio operator.

Colonel Ochoa sat back on a desktop to contemplate this new situation. What was developing was not due to the luck of some bounty hunters or a few cartel hitmen happening to be in the right place at the right time. This sounded like a planned effort, an attack that had been coordinated and prepared in advance. *How could that be? Only if—*

Suddenly, in the distance, he heard the whine of a small plane coming closer. *The plane carrying the agent is arriving already?* Colonel Ochoa sprang off the desktop.

"Operator, contact the tower. Tell them to wave off the incoming plane. It must not land here! It must go to El Real or some other place farther up the valley."

The operator did as he was told, but the sound of the plane was now even closer. The radio operator turned.

"Sir, the plane is out of petrol. It must land here, here and now. Otherwise, it will crash."

"No! It cannot!" cried Ochoa.

This could not be happening. The plane was flying into a gauntlet! Just then, he caught sight of it, a tiny single-engine Cessna by the look of it. Closer and closer, it came to the ground. Ochoa waited for the fusillade to begin, but nothing happened. The plane skipped along the runway, then rolled in toward the office building and stopped by the adjacent hangar. Ochoa was speechless. They had let the plane land.

There must be something more to this.

Suddenly, Ochoa sprang into action.

"Operator!" he commanded. "Send orders to Lieutenant Garcia at the *fuerte*. Order him to bring half the garrison to the airport, approach with stealth, join forces with airport security, and once he hears gunfire, his men are to sweep through the jungle on both sides of the runway and kill whoever they find."

"Yes, sir," replied the operator, and he immediately got to work.

Colonel Ochoa stepped from the building and told one of the guards at the door to follow him. He and the guard walked to the plane, which had now pulled up close to the airport's small refueling station and cut its engine. José and Abel climbed out.

"Hola!" called out the colonel in a friendly manner. "Welcome to San Jeronimo. I am Colonel Rafael Ochoa, the commander of the national police garrison here. If you can both come with me, we need to do some debriefing and have you sign a few things and the like before we let you go on your way." He gave Abel a slightly longer look, and he hoped the warning was understood.

"Yes, sir," said Abel sharply.

José, on the other hand, balked. "Respectfully, señor, I must refuel and get back into the air immediately. I have an appointment to keep back in Vista Bonita that is very important."

"I'm sorry, señor, but it is required. They are just routine things, checking papers, signing some things." At Ochoa's nod, the guard gave José a little nudge. "We'll have someone refuel your plane while you're inside."

They walked back toward the airport office building. Abel said, "He's running on fumes. He's got a guy coming out to fix his refueling pump back in Vista Bonita, and if he's not there, the guy won't come back again for another week. 'Mañana time,' I guess."

"I see," replied Ochoa tersely, clearly not appreciating the American's cynical reference to the slower pace of life in many Latin countries. "Don't worry about him." He nodded to one of the mechanics nearby, who went to the refueling pump and started it up.

After they came through the door, Ochoa ordered the guard and a secretary to take José to a room down the hall while he escorted Abel to his office. Once the door was closed and the blinds were drawn, Ochoa turned and gave Abel a hard look.

"You are Abel Nowinski, the DEA agent?"

"Yes, sir," replied Abel. "I guess the Cartagena guys got my message. Thanks for your help. I'll be looking forward to getting out of here and letting you get back to your business."

Colonel Ochoa's face relaxed for a moment. "Agent Nowinski, protecting people from the drug cartels and other unsavory characters is our business."

He sat down at his desk. An orderly knocked on the door. Ochoa admitted him, and the man tossed a piece of paper on the colonel's desk and left. Ochoa read what was on it, smiled grimly, and then asked, "How well do you know this pilot?"

"Just met him a little over an hour ago. He's a DEA asset they use to get people across the gulf. He was supposed to get me all the way to Costa Rica, but he had this fuel thing, and this is as far as he—"

"Agent Nowinski," said Ochoa, "I'm afraid that you and the DEA have been betrayed." He handed the visibly shocked agent the note he'd just been given.

"Over half a tank?" he mumbled. Then his face turned from shock to anger. "His plane had over half a tank of petrol in it?"

"There is also a small convention of cartel operatives and bounty hunters lurking in the jungle around this airport, apparently waiting for you to leave so they can obliterate you and whatever manner of transportation you're leaving in," explained Ochoa. "I can assure you that holding conventions of cartel operatives and armed mercenaries is not something we're in the habit of doing here in San Jeronimo. In fact, had they not been tipped off, I'm sure none of them would be here at this moment."

"That lying weasel!" yelled Abel. He sprang out of his chair. "I'll kill him myself—"

"No, you won't," interrupted the colonel, "and you will leave this airport in a few minutes. It just won't really be you." Ochoa gave Abel a meaningful look, and Abel sat back down. "You understand what will be happening here, then?" Abel nodded. "My orderly will escort you to the restroom and give you a PNP uniform. I'll require all your clothes, effects, and identification, as well as your backpack and all its contents."

Ochoa noted that Abel's face suddenly paled. "Actually, there are just a few things I'll need to get out of that, weapons, money, you know."

"I'm sorry, Agent Nowinski. I will require all of its contents. I'm sure you understand. There may be an explosion or fire, rendering a body unidentifiable. But if there are other things, things only you would have—"

Abel jumped up. "Oh, yeah? Well, some of those 'other things' I'm gonna be needing and can't do without, so—"

"Agent Nowinski!" Ochoa commanded. "Sit down!"

Abel refused. Ochoa pressed a button on his desk phone. A giant, well-muscled orderly arrived instantly, brandishing a policeman's club. "Orderly, take this man to the restroom and remove all his clothing and anything in his pockets. If he resists, handcuff him to the lavatory seat."

The orderly advanced on Abel, tapping his police club in the palm of his hand. Abel backed off. He put out his hands and sat down.

"Okay, okay. No need for violence," he said.

Colonel Ochoa glared daggers at Abel. "Agent Nowinski, I have been charged by *el presidente* of Panama with your safety, and I will fulfill his orders to me, which means that you will obey my orders. Is this clear to you now?"

Abel gave the colonel a disgruntled smirk. "Yeah, yeah, whatever. Let's get to it."

Colonel Ochoa looked to the orderly. "Get this man a uniform, everything, including weapons, ammo, gear, the works." The orderly dismissed himself. Ochoa turned to Abel. "You do have aliases with legends, correct?"

"Of course I do, but the papers are—"

"In the backpack?" asked Ochoa.

"No. They were in my apartment when the building blew up last night," groused Abel.

"My sympathies. I'll contact your acting commander in Cartagena immediately. What was his name, Dunham?"

"Dolan," corrected Abel.

"Ah, sí," said Ochoa. "Such a shame about former Commander Garza. He was a very good man, an old friend of mine."

Abel was silent.

Ochoa continued. "You'll have the new papers by tomorrow morning. It won't be safe for you to travel before then anyway. We'll discuss the details later. Right now, we should be about the business at hand."

Colonel Ochoa led Abel, now dressed as an ordinary PNP patrolman, José, now dressed in Abel's garb, complete with a backpack slung over his shoulder, and a couple of orderlies out to José's plane, where Ochoa opened the cockpit door to let José climb in. The man was shaking like a leaf but still tried to continue with the charade.

"Why is this that I have to wear that man's clothes?" he asked. "No one would tell me."

Ochoa actually appreciated how well José was carrying through with his innocent DEA asset sham. It was saving the colonel the hassle of having to gag the man and actually force him into the plane and allowed him to show in plain sight to the many eyes out in the jungle that a man looking just like Abel Nowinski was now boarding the Cessna. His secretary had done an excellent job on the man, even using some of her makeup to make José's face look more Caucasian.

"You are helping Agent Nowinski to be safer," remarked Ochoa. "This way, if anyone is watching, they will report that the agent has gone back to Colombia, and in the meantime, he will escape San Jeronimo and continue on his mission without harassment."

"That sounds dangerous to me," whimpered José, sweat now beading on his face.

"Of course it's dangerous," replied Ochoa, "but you are a fine, patriotic asset of the DEA and the Colombian National Police, no? You help them clean out the cockroaches, right? I'm sure your bravery will be noted and rewarded. In fact, let me reward you myself for being so cooperative with the PNP. Here are ten thousand American dollars."

He handed José a pack of money that Abel recognized had come from his backpack.

So Ochoa wanted everything to be in the backpack, huh? Everything to be just the same as if José was really Abel.

Abel could only wonder what Ochoa had done with the other $30,000. Probably stashed it in some safe back in that office somewhere. The guy was as corrupt as anyone in this putrid part of the world.

Ochoa continued. "I suggest that you get away immediately. The airport is safe, but there could be cartel spies about or perhaps a bounty hunter. You know the clan in Cartagena has put a price on this agent's head. When you're seen, you don't want to be around long enough for anyone to do anything about it. Then, once you're home, you may ditch the clothes and go on with your life as if nothing happened. You should be fine!"

José did not look fine. In fact, he looked sick. Ochoa closed the cockpit door, and Abel passed by it as the colonel and his orderlies headed inside. He looked in at José.

"Thanks for everything, *amigo*," he said wryly.

Abel watched with Ochoa and his office staff as the little Cessna rolled to the near end of the runway, then leaped to life as José began a very aggressive trip down the runway and took off well ahead of where such a plane would typically become airborne.

"He's making a run for it," remarked Ochoa. "If he can get high enough quick enough, he just might make it."

As the plane rose, the jungle all around the runway suddenly erupted with automatic rifle fire, making it sound like the area was a giant popcorn machine. Mixed in were lower, more ominous booms from what were probably .50 caliber sniper rifles that had been propped up by their gunners to operate more like anti-aircraft guns. Tracer bullets gleamed faintly in the morning sunlight and crisscrossed near the plane. Suddenly, the plane's landing gear was shredded off. Then a single RPG round streaked out of the jungle, wobbled around a bit, and dropped short of the aircraft before exploding. Two more such rounds followed within seconds as it looked as if the plane, even minus its landing gear, was about to make it. Seconds later, though, one of the RPGs found its mark. The plane disintegrated in the thunderous explosion, and its parts rained down onto the jungle perhaps a half mile from the end of the runway.

"Good," said Ochoa grimly. "This is good."

The popping of weapons had not ceased with the explosion, though. In fact, it sounded to Abel like it was increasing. "What's that all about?" he inquired.

"Oh, it is just my patrolmen. They are going in now to exterminate the cockroaches, or at least sweep them out the door. It should give us some peace around here for quite a while. Operator," he called to the radioman. "Contact Lieutenant Garcia and tell him to break off in fifteen minutes if he hasn't chased them all away by then. Any dead should be laid out in the hangar here for identification. Any wounded or those who surrender should be taken to the processing center in town as usual."

"Sí, señor!" replied the radioman.

"The rest of you carry on with your duties. You are dismissed." The office staff got back to work.

Ochoa now turned to Abel. "Agent Nowinski, I have received word from your acting commander that your two aliases, complete with passports, credit cards, bank account information, etcetera, will arrive by tomorrow morning along with some cash. The secretary will show you to a room upstairs that we often use for guests. It has an air conditioner and a bed, and the restroom is at the end of the hallway. You may use the office break room for snacks and drinks, and when you want a meal, just ask the secretary, and she'll send an orderly to get whatever food you'd like in town. Please limit your time outside. We don't want some suspicious sniper who still might be around to discover that the fox hasn't left the chicken coop yet, as you Americans say. I'd also like to have dinner with you at my headquarters in town at seven o'clock. An orderly will drive you there."

"Is all that an order, sir?" Abel smirked. He was still more than a little peeved about the fate of the contents of his backpack.

Ochoa softened slightly. "For the most part, no, just suggestions and information. The dinner at my headquarters, though, that is an order. Not only because I'd like to treat you to a nice dinner, but I have much information to pass on to you about the situation with the cartels here in Central America. Things are changing fast, and not for the better. Enjoy your stay in San Jeronimo, Agent Nowinski."

The next morning, not long after sunrise, Abel found himself in a cushy swivel recliner in Colonel Ochoa's personal turboprop, with its customized-for-comfort interior, lifting off from the same runway as José had the day before, sans the flying bullets and RPG rounds. Apparently, the ruse had worked. The airport and San Jeronimo itself were clear of cartel assassins and other mercenaries. Tourists were crossing the footbridge and climbing into river canoes for guided tours, and hikers were geared up and catching ferries to the far side of the Chucunaque just as always.

Abel wore a new pair of quick-dry khaki cargo pants and one of several Coolmax tees. He'd also been given a utility vest, a standard PNP bulletproof vest, another Glock 19 with extra ammo and magazines, and another Navy SOG SEAL knife. He also had a new backpack stocked with standard rain and survival gear, and $20,000 in cash to buy food, more clothes, and a serviceable vehicle once he touched down in Costa Rica. Colonel Ochoa had made a point to take Abel to the safe in his headquarters the night before, open it, and hand him the two packs of $10,000 from it. It was all contraband recovered from captured or killed cartel dons, bounty hunters, or other criminals, he'd said, and he was allowed to use it for government business subject to strict accounting and auditing.

"We are not thieves here, Agent Nowinski," he'd said, "nor do we assume that we deserve some kickback from all the money that we confiscate. Corruption is insidious. In the PNP, it is not allowed to take root. If and when it does, the perpetrators are executed by firing squad the minute guilt is established."

Ochoa had seen Abel's smirk and said that if Abel was wondering about the money in his old backpack, most had been consumed in the explosion of José's plane, though some $5,000 had been recovered after the criminals had been driven away from the airport and the plane's wreckage had been found. Ochoa had pointed out several packets of partially burned bills in the safe.

Abel called to the pilot about how long it would be before they reached their destination. The pilot had replied that it would be over an hour, maybe two, and that they'd be passing over much beautiful country, including several volcanoes and lakes. Abel thanked the pilot, then pulled out his new Apple smartphone and began to set it up using the plane's secure Wi-Fi network.

At the same time, Colonel Ochoa had watched the plane take off and then followed it with his eyes all the way until it disappeared. As he returned to his SUV and headed to his headquarters, he contemplated the decision he'd made. The routine search he'd made of Abel's backpack had told Ochoa all he needed to know about why the cartel was following Agent Nowinski and hiring assassins and posting bounties. This man had made a deal with the cartel devils, and something had gone wrong. Now, they would never let him go. Even despite the ruse that they'd successfully executed, which could buy him considerable time, eventually, they'd find out. They always did, and perhaps even sooner than later in this case. If Agent Nowinski was going to where he said he was going in Costa Rica, things could become complicated very quickly. The small-time don he was to "inspect" for the DEA was a man much more clever and slippery than one would believe, and he'd also become much more ambitious. He may have even made contact with the clan in Cartagena already. If so, Agent Nowinski would once again become a dead man walking.

Ochoa had briefly considered arresting Nowinski, but his evidence, other than the blood money, was nonexistent. Also, his old friend Victor Garza must undoubtedly have known of his agent's corruption. The man could smell it, like an ugly stench, as Ochoa remembered. For some reason, in the case of Agent Nowinski, Garza had chosen not only to ignore it but also to send his corrupt agent on an assignment to Costa Rica. Ochoa was sure that, in the older man's mind, there must have been a reason—a very compelling reason—to act in the way that he did, and he, Rafael Ochoa, would not stand in the way of whatever higher purpose his old friend had seen in this very flawed man.

PLAYA DE PALMA

7

—

Caleb Forrest signed his name on the papers, authorizing his use of the older-model Jeep Wrangler. He was checking it out of the DEA post garage in Jacó, Costa Rica. Abel was still having trouble getting used to signing that name naturally, without thinking twice or having to make a correction.

"You're getting better," said Commander Lopez, the agent in charge of the Jacó post, "but I still saw some hesitation. You really need to practice more, Agent Forrest. You're heading out into the field again, and if you're still thinking somewhere that you're Abel Nowinski, one day you'll be signing your death warrant doing what you just did."

"Yes, sir," replied Caleb as he caught the keys that Lopez tossed to him. What he really wanted to say was, "Yes, Mr. Lopez. I'll do exactly as you say, Mr. Lopez. And fuck you, too, Mr. Lopez." Abel had felt like a schoolboy ever since he'd arrived in Jacó a couple of weeks ago. Lopez had told him his new alias for this mission. Then Lopez had given him his new passport, credit cards, driver's license, and other identifying information as well as his legend. Lopez had instructed everyone on the post staff to call Abel by his new name, Caleb Forrest, and ask him questions about his new identity. So, Abel would pass through the office every morning, and the receptionist would ask him about where he grew up (California, not Iowa), what the name of the high school he graduated from was (Joseph Gregori rather than Mason), and what its mascot was (jaguar instead of Mohawk Indian). Others in the briefing room would ask him how long he'd been in the DEA, what had he done before (he still was a former Navy SEAL), and where his first posting had been (South Florida). And, yes, he had been there when a new recruit, Abel Nowinski, had been briefly assigned there before being sent to Colombia. He knew Nowinski had come from a Navy SEAL background also and seemed a bit smug about it. He was sure that once this Abel got to Colombia, it wouldn't be long before he'd either be dead or corrupted. He was repeatedly asked to write down his birthdate (February 26 rather than September 17) and to say his social security number or give them its last four digits (9899, one of the more natural things to keep in mind). Everyone, at virtually every moment, systematically uninstalled Abel Nowinski from Abel's inner hard drive and replaced it with the fictitious Caleb Forrest.

Of course, Abel knew that all this was a critical—potentially lifesaving—process, and he did his homework. The DEA had been very generous about helping Abel recover from the trials of his recent escape from Colombia and the ever-spreading tentacles of Don Vicente Galvan and the Clan de Cartagena. There was an expansive Marriott resort outside Jacó. Abel was given a suite there, complete with a kitchen and free run of the resort's many pleasures for two weeks. Abel had spent several days snorkeling and one day learning to surf, and taken several jungle tours. In these, he'd seen all sorts of wildlife and ridden zip lines underneath the rainforest canopy that reminded him of his old SEAL days. He'd even tried his hand at golf, but it proved to be so slow and frustrating that he'd quit after just nine holes. He'd been allowed to buy his own car, a 2014 Kia Soul he'd seen at a used car dealership and snapped up immediately. To do it, he had to use the lion's share of the cash Rafael Ochoa had sent with him to make the purchase quick and easy, but it was worth it. He took himself out to simple restaurants where he could get used to ordering basic American foods again. It was all so enjoyable that a side of Abel began to feel like a normal person again.

But there was another side that hadn't even approached becoming normalized. It made Abel chafe at this new situation almost as much as he had with the old one in Colombia. He knew that everything was temporary, that soon he'd be back out into some backwater excuse for a town doing a lot of mostly tedious DEA work. He knew that his money would run out and that his salary wouldn't be enough to pay for the expensive, action-packed lifestyle that he craved. With Abel Nowinski officially dead, he wasn't sure if he could even access the account that contained the money that Don Vicente had paid him, much less spend it.

And speaking of Don Vicente, he might actually be there as well at some point. In briefing Abel about his new assignment, Commander Lopez had mentioned that Abel's contact, a fat, lazy-looking don of surprising cleverness and ambition named Monti Ruiz, had talked recently of Colombians reaching out to Costa Rican dons.

"Knowing him, they've probably reached out to him, too," Lopez had quipped.

The Colombians needed waystations to refuel and resupply the ships, planes, and subs that now carried cocaine up the Pacific coast instead of crossing the Caribbean, where the Colombians were tired of losing money. Costa Rica's many offshore islands apparently were ideal locales for such depots. The eventual involvement of Don Vicente Galvan seemed inevitable.

All these things made Abel feel trapped and angry.

"Once you're in, you're either in or you're dead," Garza had said. That truth was now becoming all too real. Everything—the DEA, the drug lords, the financial instability, the security that he'd had so briefly, and that security being lost all in one night—it all clung to Abel's mind like a ball and chain.

Damn! he thought. *Damn the DEA and the whole fucking mess.* Garza and Dolan and the other Boy Scouts at the Cartagena post had ruined everything.

What he left out, of course, was that it was he who had gotten himself into this inescapable mess, he and his overarching restlessness, loneliness, and need for some kind of security, which expressed itself these days mostly through greed, envy, and bitterness. Feeling emotionally bereft and confused by the puzzle of himself, Abel chose to simply ignore it all.

And thus, he was, inside at least, one very angry man, whether it be Abel Nowinski or Caleb Forrest.

Abel drove the Jeep back to his suite at the Marriott and geared up for a short pre-mission that he'd planned. The village that this Monti Ruiz worked out of was called Playa de Palma, a tiny little speck of a town, like so many along the central Costa Rican coast. Each was mostly dedicated to the service and comfort of foreign adventurers, tourists, and surfers, who came in droves during high season to kick back, surf, or explore old jungle trails that locals would guide them through. Abel wanted to visit Playa de Palma clandestinely first so he could get a feel for the place before he returned a few days later as Caleb Forrest, DEA agent looking for weapons caches and stores of cocaine. He decided to go in a full camouflage outfit and face paint, but to carry only his sidearms and his compact range-finding monocular so he could look things over more precisely from afar. He didn't want to burden himself with anything else. Since the jungle virtually met the ocean along this part of the coast, he'd try to sneak his way in toward the village as far as he could and not be seen.

After about forty minutes of bumping down Costa Rica's Pacific coast "highway," he came to his destination. It was an intersection with a tiny dirt road marked by a small sign that said Playa de Palma was three kilometers off to the right. Abel pulled his Jeep onto the rutted road and quickly found a space to pull into the jungle and hide his vehicle. Cramming on a camouflaged cloth hat and securing the chin strap, he headed into the jungle, roughly paralleling the road on his left side and the Rio Palma, the river that gave the community its name, on his right. It was the kind of hike where he'd usually use a sharp machete to hack through the thick rainforest shrub layer, but that would make his stealthy approach impossible, so he soldiered on without one—and got soaked as he did from the moisture of the dense undergrowth.

It was not long, though, before he came upon something that looked like an outbuilding next to a small wooden structure, a cottage or maybe an office that someone lived in. A perimeter was cut into the jungle around the facility, but not so much as to expose it. Abel peered through the monocular and saw several men hanging out on the porch that surrounded the wooden cottage, which was built on stilts.

Abel suddenly heard the sound of a motor, and the three men got up and walked toward the outbuilding, a mostly corrugated-metal structure with a double door. An old US Army–style Jeep emerged from the jungle near the building, and Abel could see a barely visible track that it had apparently been following. The driver got out of the vehicle with a clipboard. A man from the house signed it, then was given a paper by the driver. The man stuffed the paper into a pocket, then both he and the driver joined the other two men, who were unloading heavy crates from the rear of the Jeep. The double door of the building was thrown open, and the men carried the crates into the dark mini-warehouse.

Abel recognized the crates. They held boxes of ammunition. Zooming in, he saw that it was the standard caliber used for American M16 or AR-15 assault rifles and various types of semiautomatic handguns. He also noted one crate that carried belt-style ammo designed to be used with a heavier-caliber weapon with full-automatic capability.

Looks like the DEA will definitely find a reason to check out that facility, thought Abel. He pocketed the monocular and continued along toward the town.

It didn't take long for Abel to note several other things as he crept through the jungle. There was no other road to the building complex he'd just passed. Its only vehicle accessibility was the Jeep track that the ammo vehicle had used that must have come from the main highway. There was, however, a well-used footpath winding through the area that looked like it probably led all the way down to the town itself. There was a small school building on the other side of the dirt road, and younger, elementary-age children played *fútbol* on a grass-and-mud playground. Others hung out in the shade or played on a brightly colored play structure. That meant that older kids were probably bussed out to Jacó or perhaps down the road to Parrita to attend high school. He noted a small cemetery alongside the road. The jungle had been cleared from around the headstones, and a fence was around the site to make sure it stayed that way. As he got closer to the town, he noted that the river curved toward the road, squeezing his space and putting him dangerously close to the walking path that led to the facility he'd just passed. The area soon broadened out, though, as the river curved away from the road again.

He then began to encounter townlike buildings, a small motel and adjacent restaurant tucked away in a carefully manicured jungle clearing, and a larger facility along the other side of the river with an iron footbridge that was twenty to thirty meters wide and brown in color. A car driving through the jungle toward the lodging facility told Abel that another road went that far into the forest from the coast.

Suddenly, Abel stopped himself in his tracks, barely managing to keep from falling. The trail to the storage facility had veered suddenly toward his line of walking. One more careless step and Abel would have left a distinct boot track in the trail mud, a sign that may have tipped off a vigilant guard that a stranger was about. Though Abel had seen no sign of guards or even found any evidence of surveillance equipment, he couldn't afford to get sloppy. A slipup would undoubtedly come at the same time Monti Ruiz and his men decided to tighten their security. Eyeballing the path in its new direction, Abel saw that it came out in another clearing around an American-style frame house at the back door of a building that looked like a garage. Taking more mental notes, Abel went on.

The jungle was thinning now, and the sky was becoming clearer and brighter through more significant gaps in the trees. Abel knew that his recon journey to Playa de Palma was just about over. There would be no more jungle to hide in. He heard the quiet rush of falling water from the river to his right and veered that way. Falling water could mean some higher place, an overlook of some kind, where he could survey the village from a superior point relatively unobstructed. Encouraged by the lightness ahead, but wary also, Abel finally came to the river's edge.

The Rio Palma did drop gradually down, and Abel's sharp eyes noted a zip line, probably for tourists, which began on a platform in the trees on the far side. There looked to be a steeper drop just a hundred meters or so farther down the stream that the zip line disappeared over. Cautiously, he hugged the riverbank as he proceeded toward the light. Finally, the jungle opened slightly, and the water dropped over a small escarpment. And there, laid out below him like a panoramic photograph, was the heart of the town of Playa de Palma, and immediately beyond, the turquoise blue of the Pacific Ocean.

The main road that he'd been paralleling was now several hundred yards to his left. It emerged from the jungle there, then turned, serving as a beachfront main street of sorts as it followed the Pacific, crossed the Rio Palma about two hundred meters from where Abel sat, and continued down the coast. Several beautiful beachfront motels and quaint little restaurants were clustered in the area, easily visible by the clearings in the jungle where they were set back from the ocean. One in particular, on the far side of the river crossing, looked almost elegant. Its main residence area surrounded a well-maintained swimming pool, an asphalt parking lot, and several beachfront guesthouses within easy walking distance to the main building. Across the bridge were substantial restaurants and another, quainter establishment.

That's where I'll be staying, thought Abel.

Farther back to his left, the beach made a little bay, and the roadway turned. Around that nook, a plethora of colorful adobe buildings was built along the sides of another dirt road and several small offshoot tracks that branched from it. The buildings on the beachside looked to be more small motels and eating establishments. Those on the other side were service establishments, such as a prominent food store, several shops that sold clothes and souvenirs, an ATM kiosk, surfing gear, paddleboat rental facilities, and more. There was a town square of sorts where there was a building that served as a bus depot. It was along a road that continued right down to the very edge of the Pacific where it turned into a pier along which several boats of various sizes were moored. There was also a well-tended park and even a soccer field with cut grass and some old aluminum bleachers along its touchlines. Farther back, Abel could see a gas station with a two-bay garage for making auto repairs. Next to it was something that looked like a visitor center or city hall building, and, of course, the most impressive building, the local Catholic church, complete with a spire topped with a bell tower.

The clean Pacific waters were alive with surfers and swimmers. On the inviting beaches, sunbathers enjoyed the brilliantly clear day from their beach towels, umbrellas, and even cabanas that seemed to be the property of seaside motels. Not crowded, to be sure, but definitely not deserted either.

Abel did note one area where there seemed to be more activity than other places. This was the head of the pier, where a large man in a Hawaiian shirt sat in a big lounger in the shade of a wide canopy held up by poles secured deep in the sand. On a table next to him, safely in the shade, were perhaps a dozen cups filled with big candy lollipops. Coming and going like bees from a hive were many children. They would take a cup of lollipops, then circulate among those on the beach, selling the delicious goodies. When they'd sold all the lollipops, they'd run back to the big man, give him a wad of money, and then take another cup full of confections and repeat the routine. The man would count the money and put it in a cashbox. Then he would return to talking to various adults who wandered over from time to time and sat in a beach chair next to him. He appeared very jovial with everyone, though it did seem as if the adults' behavior was overly obsequious upon coming and going, lots of exaggerated laughter, elongated handshakes, and stiff little bows.

Monti Ruiz holding court, thought Abel with a smirk, all while using children to make money for him. There wasn't a more perfect caricature of a small-time drug lord in all the world. It was hard for Abel to imagine that this man could be as shrewd and ambitious as Commander Lopez had warned. Perhaps Lopez was being overly cautious in his assessment, but Abel decided to remain wary. He may be just a greedy buffoon, but what a great way to disguise the devious, ambitious scoundrel that could be the man inside.

Having taken all this in, Abel was about to stand when he heard screaming behind him. He dove for cover, then peered out from behind a shrub to see two people on the previously noted zip line fly through the trees and past his hiding place on the other side of the river, flying on down to the fancy motel that he'd picked out for himself. Abel shook his head.

You know you've been out of the field too long when you're not paying attention to a freaking tourist zip line, he scolded himself.

His business now done, Abel was about to put his monocular back in its belt pack when something that he'd failed to take note of caught his eye.

There was an island in the ocean directly out from the beach. Abel pulled out his monocular again and zoomed in on it. How could he have missed this?

Must have been too laser-focused on the town and the beach, he decided. He estimated its range to be not more than a mile and a half out. It was flat and covered with jungle on one end, with prominent beaches that extended out into the ocean. But on the other end, there rose a significant peak, probably an old volcano, perhaps a few hundred feet high. It, too, was covered with jungle, except for the very top, which was barren, and where it abutted the sea, it ended in sheer cliffs that dropped all the way down to the water. There, the woefully thin beach was covered with boulders and black sand. It did not appear there was any sign of people on the island at all.

Abel put his monocular away, and as he carefully made his way back to his Jeep, he found himself almost salivating thinking about the island. Finally, a new and potentially exotic place to explore. Who knew what dangers or wonders there might be to discover? For the first time since his SEAL days, Abel felt genuinely alive again. It was like a breath of clean, fresh air was washing out all the angst and worry that had polluted his psyche for so long. This job would be more than just routine DEA muckraking, Abel decided. It would be exciting, engaging, and hopefully action-packed as well. He could hardly wait.

It was a good thing he had no idea how prophetic his thoughts were. Had he known, he probably would never have shown up at Playa de Palma ever again.

8

—

The next day, Abel was packed and ready before he even hit the Marriott's breakfast buffet. And why not? The number of things he had to pack was the sum total of the outfits and gear that he'd been given by his DEA commander and whatever else he'd bought for himself with the money from Colonel Ochoa back in Panama. Much of the cash had gone into his Kia Soul that was now stored at the DEA garage, and the rest into a small start on a new wardrobe that he'd made shopping at Jacó's various clothing shops in the absence of large department stores. It all fit very nicely in the carry-on size suitcase he'd also bought and the military-grade duffel bag that he'd been given by the DEA.

Everything else he'd owned was gone.

Most, of course, had been blown up with his apartment in Cartagena a little over two weeks ago now: his clothes, his guitar, his simple kitchen items and dishes, including his special ceramic Wheaties breakfast cereal bowl his mom had gotten for him when he was ten. She had always demanded he start his day with the "breakfast of champions." He still loved Wheaties, but it wasn't as satisfying to eat them in an ordinary bowl.

Likewise, his bedroom things were gone. Most of what he'd had was just stuff he'd bought at garage sales and thrift stores, but his 100-percent memory foam Tempur-Pedic queen-size adjustable bed was no more. It was one of the original, ultra-firm types that's no longer made. He'd spent $3,000 of college graduation money on it because his former box-spring mattress gave him backaches, and he wanted to have a bed that he truly loved to sleep in to come home to when he was in the military. It always felt like lying on a board at first, but within seconds, the memory foam would warm and wrap itself around every contour of his body. Going to bed had felt how coming home should feel—a sigh of relief, and a warm embrace—but not anymore.

All of his bathroom things were gone as well, but what he really, really missed were his photos. Framed photos were the sum total of the interior decorating that he ever did, and they were not only gone, but irreplaceable. These had either been given to him or taken on old film cameras or early digital cameras when one-megapixel seemed like a wonder. Having a sharp eye for both panoramic scenery as well as por-traits of people, the walls of his various living spaces had always been covered with a selection of his simply framed shots, whether it was some scenic marvel he'd been to in his SEAL team travels or on vaca-tions or intimate shots of his SEAL mates, his friends from college, or his now-deceased parents and estranged brother and sister. Sometimes, when home, he had just sat in his recliner, another piece of his life that he sorely missed, and gazed at his pictures, remembering moments and reliving times he never wanted to forget. The memories were still there, but the reminders were gone, and Abel was afraid that without the reminders, the memories would fade as well.

And then there was the one picture—a picture he'd taken of the only woman he'd ever been truly in love with, one that seemed to cap-ture all of her pure loveliness, both inside and out, in one inimitable expression. It was a perfect portrait of the closest thing he'd had to a lifelong companion. She was gone now, of course, hopefully more content with someone who could make her happier than he had, but he still loved looking at her photo, partly because it was such a damn good portrait and partly to remind him that he once had made a woman of such beauty very, very happy, and because of that, perhaps there was some shred of hope that he could do it again.

Abel had grieved for a couple of days, but, of course, he knew deep down that the absence of these things from his life had been his fault, the result of what had been a risky, foolish decision. He wasn't totally convinced that the decision had been entirely foolish, though. After all, had things gone as planned, he'd be rich, not someone with nothing to his name but what was packed in two bags. Then again, given the tenacity of those who were after him, maybe it was time just to come clean and, little by little, start to rebuild some semblance of what he'd lost. But if the right opportunity came along—

Ack! Enough of all this, he told himself.

Leaving his bags on the bed, he headed down to the breakfast buffet dressed in his new favorite outfit—khaki cargo pants, a breathable light-blue button-down that was nicely tucked in, and waterproof trail runners that made his feet feel invincible. Time to load up on calories, then load up the Jeep with all his worldly possessions—and a few DEA-issued weapons—so he could make life interesting for "Fat Monti" Ruiz over the next few days.

At that same time, in Playa de Palma Fat Monti Ruiz was making his morning rounds after breakfasting at home with his dutiful wife, Maria, and his little granddaughter Lucia, who was a very spry eight-year-old. She had made sure that her *papi* had finished his entire breakfast burrito and both his quesadillas before running off to school, a distance longer than eight hundred meters. Monti kissed Maria goodbye, then headed out from his house, an impressive wood-framed building with aluminum siding and a composite roof that looked stately compared to all the adobe buildings in town.

The first stop was always up the road at his son's place, also a stately wood-framed house with a big corrugated metal garage behind it, just a block or so away. Monti preferred to take care of the family business before anything else. Today, Monti had to talk with his son, Paco, about the recent ammunitions shipment that came in the day before. Paco was his quartermaster who kept an inventory of everything in the business and distributed it to whomever might need it, among other things. All seemed to be in order except for a couple of boxes of handgun ammo, forty-five-caliber bullets that obviously wouldn't work in the business's 9mm Glock and Beretta pieces. Along with the larger ammo, his Mexican supplier had shipped two new forty-five-caliber semiautomatic pistols for free.

Monti had scoffed. "He's trying to get rid of those old cannons he's had around forever. Doesn't he understand that no one walks around with a holster on his hip down here? Why doesn't he sell them to one of the cartels up there who have to fight with the Mexican Army or something?"

"Probably because he thinks we're small-time down here, and we don't know the difference between a big weapon and a useful weapon," answered Paco. Paco was far too skinny, Monti thought, and he continually urged his wife, Sonia, to fatten him up, but she'd just laugh and say that food went through Paco like water.

"Send them back," Monti had directed, "the ammo, the guns, everything."

"Just the forty-five stuff, right?"

"Sí, of course. And tell that jackal that just because we can run our business down here without fearing that the *Federales* will interrupt our breakfast doesn't mean we're *estúpido*."

"I'll tell him, Papa," answered Paco.

"How is our product flow?"

"All is well, Papa. Our sales on the *playas* are above normal for this time of year, and the hotel business is steady. I believe that as long as we continue to give our vendors the twenty percent commission that we started last year, we will continue to see sales figures remain stable," surmised Paco.

"And how about the lollipops?" Monti smiled.

"Ah." Paco chuckled. "Their sales are rising like a fleet of hot-air balloons. You're very clever, Papa. The amount of product we use is not enough to make someone an addict, but it is enough to give a nice little buzz. People don't know why, but they can't get enough of them." They both laughed.

"*Sí*, and the kids love to hustle them." Monti smiled. "Make sure that there is strict, separate accounting for all sales from them. The profit is to go entirely to the school. And if that stuffy schoolmaster gets suspicious, make sure he knows that part of those profits will go to raising his salary, as well as that of the *maestras*. This town will have the finest primary school on the *costa*. It is our obligation to your children and Lucia, as well as all the rest. We're not jackals like those cartel *muchachos* back in Michoacán."

"Speaking of cartels . . ." said Paco, more seriously.

Monti lowered his voice. "You've heard from the Colombians, no?"

"Ah, sí," replied Paco. "All of the dons you reached out to have responded. All expressed frustration with shipping across the Caribbean. The profits do not keep up with the losses. However, most didn't have the capital to move in a new direction—yet.

"There was one, though, who was very excited and wished to move quickly. He heads a cartel in Cartagena called the Clan de Cartagena. He would like to meet with you in person sometime soon. He says he has procured a narco sub recently that he'd like to move a large shipment of product with, but cannot afford another loss. He says he can get it to the Pacific side of his country, but it will need a discreet refueling stop somewhere along the Costa Rican coast. He says that assuming we do have a suitable island available as you said, he would like to invest in developing it with us so he doesn't have to pay the inflated fuel prices and tributes that other dons have to pay at more established waystations."

Monti squinted his eyes with skepticism. "And you believe this fairy tale?"

"It was contained in an email that came through our secure network," replied Paco.

"The one the DEA has hacked, or the one that they haven't hacked—yet?"

"The new one, Papa. As far as we know, it's not even on their radar yet."

Monti harrumphed and made like he was about to leave.

"Think about it, Papa. This could be our big break, a way to get the kind of money we'd need to put our plans in motion and lift our whole village out of poverty. Isn't that why you contacted the Colombians in the first place?"

Monti looked away and longed to walk out the door. Yes, this had been why he'd contacted the Colombians, but he had no idea that he'd be taken seriously or responded to so soon. He had no specific plan; he hadn't even started to figure out what the costs might be, and then there was the problem of the island itself.

"Gracias, Paco," he mumbled. "I shall be thinking about this while I'm out on my rounds today." He headed for the door.

"Don't think too long," admonished Paco. "If we really want to do this, it's not an offer that we can afford to refuse. He'll simply go somewhere else."

Frustrated, Monti whirled around. "If this man and his clan are not legitimate, or if they're treacherous jackals like those we left in Mexico, it is an offer we must refuse! If this man is so impatient that he must be communicated with now, give him the numbers for our offshore deposit account. Tell him that if he wishes to do business with us, he will gladly deposit one—no, two million US dollars into our account within twenty-four hours or he can take his submarine and find another bathtub to play in! Only then will we talk."

He then marched out the garage door as Paco called out something about the DEA to him. Monti didn't want to hear it. It was time to be out greeting his friends.

He first stopped at the comparatively majestic church, its brick and adobe walls inlaid with stained-glass windows and its towering belfry dwarfing any of the village's structures. He went in. A few devotees were kneeling in prayer as they always did in the morning. He saw the padre preparing the sacristy for the midday mass and tipped his old sombrero to the man. The priest gave him the sign of the cross in return. He saw that a bus was pulled up to the depot, and he greeted some of the visitors who got off, gave directions to some, smiled, and tried to be pleasant. Then he continued down the main beach road, stopping at the little hotels to give morning greetings to the managers and, more importantly, find out how many new guests had arrived overnight. He crossed the footbridge and checked in with Faviola, the manager at the Best Western Rio Palma Inn, the one real, *norteamericano*-style hotel that he'd attracted to his village—three stars in the American Automobile Association's motel ratings and a rating of four and a half out of five stars from three hundred reviewers on the Tripadvisor website. Yes, they were full, she said. It was that time of year. And then he crossed back over the bridge and walked down the other side of the road, doing the same for all the shops and restaurants that were open so early.

And all the while, the wheels were turning in the back of his mind. He wasn't thinking so much about this offer from some new Colombian cartel that he'd barely heard of. He'd find out soon enough if they were someone he wanted to deal with, and if so, he'd be the one dictating the terms, or he really would tell them to take their submarine and go play in someone else's bathtub. A deal like this could be a boon to him, his family, and the village—the means to make many mutual dreams come true. But one must be careful and precise with these cartel people, or all the nightmares that he'd fled with his family from Mexico would soon revisit them here.

No, what was really occupying his mind now, as he came to the boat dock and noted the early-bird surfers and paddleboard riders making preparations for the day, was what Paco had reminded him of as he was leaving Paco's garage. The DEA agent was due today. The single biggest reason why Monti and his family were able to operate their little cocaine-selling business was that the American DEA allowed them to. In exchange for being able to operate without harassment, he was expected to pass on useful, actionable intelligence about the more significant drug-smuggling operations that were going on along the coast. This arrangement had worked very well over time. When competitors had gotten too big, or someone new had tried to move in on his territory, Monti would merely inform the DEA, and his competition disappeared. But in order for it all to look legitimate and for him, Monti, to not be fingered as an informant by his partners in crime, the DEA had to periodically "raid" or "inspect" the village, "seize" product, "confiscate" weapons, "close down" a warehouse, sometimes even make arrests. He was always forewarned, of course, and he knew that no arrests were to be made this time, but he would be expected to allow weapons and small amounts of product to be seized, and, of course, to provide tips on whatever might be going on in the local drug world.

And he'd forgotten all about it.

Ah, the ravages of being over sixty, he lamented.

Gazing out at the boats along the dock and the beautiful island that held so much promise—and problems—for his future, he planted himself on a park-style bench that was one of several installed around the dock and caught his breath. Though he was still, at six feet two, a powerful man of considerable strength, much of his former muscle mass had unfortunately gone to his girth. It was the price of a safe and peaceful life, he always told himself with a wink.

He fished out his smartphone from the side pocket of his cargo shorts and punched a speed-dial number.

"Hola, Paco!" he said. "Sí, sí, I'd forgotten. *Muchas gracias*. Those handguns, we'll let the DEA man find them, and the ammo as well. Throw in some of the other ammo, too. Put aside five—no, ten kilos of product, and I think I'll let whoever it is confiscate a boat as well. Maybe we'll put all the stuff in the boat. Ha! I'm a genius, I know. *Gracias*, my son. *Buenos días.*"

9

—

Though Abel knew whom he needed to see and precisely where that person would be, he decided that he'd play tourist on his trip down the dirt road toward Playa de Palma, stopping at a few places along the way to the town center and the beach. He pulled his Jeep off at the elementary school and went into the airy office. A chubby woman sat behind a counter at a messy desk, typing away on a computer while talking on the phone in Spanish. It was early in the morning, probably just an hour or so after school had started, so no children were out playing. Abel stood patiently. His eyes, trained for situational awareness, noted things like well-constructed walls, good glass in the windows, a suitable and sturdy desk (despite the mess) for the woman, modern communications equipment, and another smaller desk surrounded by shelves and functional file cabinets.

A welcoming yet efficient office space, he surmised, like any elementary school he'd been to in Iowa, maybe even more modern than some. Not exactly what he expected to find in a small village cut out of the jungle along the Pacific coast of a country like Costa Rica. And that made him curious.

"Hola, señor," said the woman, who was now standing in front of him behind the counter. "I am Leticia, the administrative assistant here at Palma School. What is it that I can do for you?"

Abel smiled at the professionally dressed woman who was perhaps a bit older than he, but not too much.

"Oh, hello," he said cordially. "Actually, I'm here on business and was hoping you might be able to direct me. I was wondering—"

"Just follow the road, señor. Whatever your business is, you will get there if you just follow the road. It is the only way in, and the only way out," replied Leticia. "Once you get to the town square, you can park your vehicle across from the bus depot and walk to wherever you want."

"Well, that sounds simple enough," said Abel. "This is quite the place you've got here."

"Yes, it is, isn't it." Leticia smiled. "Were you expecting something else?"

"Ah, well, no, I guess," stammered Abel, "but I grew up in the US, and there were a lot of places that didn't—"

"Have schools as nice as this one?" Leticia smiled knowingly. "Señor, we are just a tiny town in a tiny country where just about everything is lovely, especially our children. They are our highest priority, and we actually mean it when we say it."

"Well, that's nice to hear. I appreciate your help." Abel gave the woman a crooked little smile, then left.

Wonder if they care about their kids as much in the next village down the road.

He smirked to himself as he drove away. *Nice to see that Ruiz at least did one thing good with his drug money.*

Continuing down the road, he noted the large frame house he'd seen with the metal garage out back where the footpath that started at the warehouse ended. He saw a tall, slim man in front of it, tending a flower bed. Abel stopped his Jeep and got out, and the man stopped his work. The two met by the side of the road.

"Hola," said Abel. "My name's Caleb Forrest, from Jacó. I've got an appointment this morning with an older fellow, Monti Ruiz, a bit taller than me, kind of heavyset. Do you know him?"

Paco chuckled quietly. "Señor, everyone in Playa de Palma knows Monti Ruiz."

"Oh, really?" said Abel sardonically. "Well, maybe you could tell me where I might find him. He told me to meet him here, but didn't give me an address or—"

"That's because there aren't really addresses here, señor, and Monti Ruiz is seldom in a building anyway, at least not during high season. You'll find him sitting under a pavilion near the pier, probably with a few boxes of lollipops on a table beside him."

"That sounds refreshing," said Abel. "Why bother with an office in a place like this, right?"

"Exactly, señor," replied Paco.

"Will we be able to talk in private somewhere? Our business is kind of confidential."

"I'm sure he can make an accommodation for you, señor." Paco smiled. "But I must also warn you, confidential things have a way of becoming, eh . . . how you say . . . un-confidential here in Playa de Palma."

"I guess that'll be his business then, not mine." Abel turned back to his Jeep. "Thanks for your help," he called, and then drove off.

A couple of minutes later, Abel found the parking lot just as Leticia had said (and he'd seen the day before) and found a spot that he hoped wouldn't get blocked in. The area was made of crumbling old asphalt, and parking lines were faded, if they'd ever been there in the first place. All manner of vehicles were parked there—old beaters and pickups that went back to the seventies, muddied SUVs, small economy cars with roof racks for surfboards on top, even stylish sedans and clean SUVs that were most likely tourists' rental cars. Abel locked the Jeep and headed out on foot toward the pier, which was not much more than a glorified dock. He was aware as he passed the bus depot and the "city hall" that there was another dirt road off to his left where shops and food stands were opening, and surfers were hitting the morning waves in earnest. Joggers and walkers of all ages could be seen, most certainly tourists out for their morning constitutionals. The smell of peppers and chilies was in the air along with the pungent smell of the ocean, whose crashing waves lent an irresistible sort of white noise to the whole scene—but Abel didn't take any of it in.

He was focused on the large man under the cloth pavilion who sat in an extra-large outdoor chair with several other beach chairs strewn around him at the head of the pier. His back was turned to Abel, and Abel figured that the man was probably messing around with a device, like everyone else these days. He was about to call out Monti's name when the man suddenly spun his chair around and faced Abel with a jolly smile that would make him look like Santa Claus if he had a white beard and wasn't wearing a flowery Hawaiian shirt. He even had a small child in his lap. The child held a book as if he'd been reading to the big man. Abel was so genuinely surprised that he just stood there in the sand.

"Caleb Forrest of the DEA," announced Monti in his big, jovial voice. "Welcome to Playa de Palma. Don't look so surprised. Your presence precedes you, especially when—"

"It wasn't that," said Abel as he sauntered forward. "I knew you'd know I was here when I first pulled up to the school and had that nice chat with Leticia, probably a relative, right?"

"Ah, sí. You're very perceptive," replied Monti.

"It was just a guess. I know news travels faster than the birds in a place like this. I was just surprised that you had a kid reading to you in your lap instead of some dinner-plate-sized smartphone that you were busy tweeting on."

"Ah, the children are our life here," said Monti.

"So I've heard," replied Abel as he moved to sit down and held out his hand. "Monti Ruiz, I presume?"

"You presume correctly. Please, have a seat." The two men shook hands as Abel sat down.

Abel took a glass of cold lemonade from the little boy who had been reading to Monti Ruiz. He had scampered off to a restaurant across the street and was now handing it to him. It looked freshly squeezed and tasted as good as anything Abel had had to drink since coming to Costa Rica.

"It is Melissa's own special recipe," informed Monti, speaking of the restaurant's proprietor as he, too, took a long drink. "She mixes the raw lemon juice with just a touch of mango juice, then adds sugar fresh from the cane that comes in from Jacó each week. There is nothing like it anywhere else."

"Is that so?" remarked Abel. It really was great stuff, but there was more important business to get to. "So, Señor Ruiz, I'm here for a few days because the DEA has intel that there might be illegal drugs cached here awaiting shipment to Mexico and then to the US. It's my job to confiscate any such contraband that I might find here, along with any illegal weapons or ammunition stores that would exceed the legal limits of the government of Costa Rica."

"I can assure you, my friend, that I have no idea where you may have heard these lies. We here are law-abiding citizens and would have nothing to do with such an unsavory business. You will have my full cooperation in your work, and if you do find such contraband, we will bring to justice anyone you can prove is participating in such lawlessness. Our entire community is open to you. I just ask that you are not rough with our citizens. As I said, we are peaceful people, and courtesy will get you further than strong-arming."

"I'll be as strong-armed as I need. If everything you say is true, that shouldn't be much, right?"

"Sí, not much. Not much at all," said Monti. Both men laughed as they played their little game. "Perhaps you'd like to check out the many motels that we have available and find a place you'd like to stay. Then I shall escort you to wherever you wish to go."

"I already know where I want to stay—that Best Western just across the bridge down the road."

"Oh, I'm so sorry, sir." Monti shook his head regretfully. "It is high season, and that motel is always sold out for months in advance. But I can recommend—"

"Well, it's not going to be sold out today," replied Abel casually. "In fact, I'm pretty sure I heard that one of those beach house guest rooms will be cleared out and clean by noon."

"I don't think that you heard that, señor," said Monti, in a noticeably more serious tone. "In fact, Faviola was quite clear this morning that the motel was sold out. Perhaps you are mistaken."

"No mistake," said Abel, almost as if he hadn't heard what Monti said. He got up to leave. "Maybe you'll need to remind Faviola. I want to spend a little time walking around town, get the lay of the land, you know. Then we can head up to that big frame house up the road. I need to check out that garage he's got up there. Let's hope I don't have to use too much strong-arming to find out what I need to know because after that, I'm really going to need to settle into one of those beach house guest rooms for the rest of the day. *Comprende?*"

"Sí, señor," answered Monti, his voice smooth as a dagger's blade. "*Comprendo* completely. Shall we meet back here in, say, one hour?"

"Sounds good to me," replied Abel. He started off toward the rows of motels and restaurants along the edge of the main surfing beach.

"*Señor!*" called Monti. Abel stopped. "Enjoy my town and my people. There is much beauty in both of them!"

"I'll keep that in mind," Abel called back, then went about his business.

Monti made a phone call as he watched Abel go.

"Paco, make sure all is ready in the garage," he said. "Sí, sí, in about an hour. This one acts like he's a tough little shit . . . I can't tell yet, but we'll need to be careful . . . I can't tell that yet either, but we'll both find out soon enough. Adios, *mijo*."

Abel walked along the smaller dirt road that ran behind Playa de

Palma's main recreational beach, the one on the left side of the pier. Midmorning had brought out many more surfers, sunbathers, and parents playing in the water with their children. Abel was surprised again at something he saw. Two lifeguard towers were on the beach, one near where he was walking and another farther down on the other end of the beach. They weren't just cheap little things that you might find at some school swimming pool either, but big Southern California-style towers with an enclosed supply house behind two high, swiveling seats with footrests, all under a canvas shade to keep the sun off. Abel noticed two young people, a boy and a girl, each probably high school age, getting out supplies and preparing their station for the day ahead.

Abel called up to them. "Hola!"

The young man, dressed in standard lifeguard-red board shorts, saw him and came closer. "Hola! ¿Cómo estás?"

"Fine, thanks, and my Spanish is shitty," answered Abel.

"No worries," said the boy. "My English is near-native. How can I help you?"

"I didn't know there were lifeguards on these beaches. Is it like this all the way down the coast?" asked Abel.

"Only here," replied the lifeguard.

"Playa de Palma has the only lifeguards on the central coast, from Jacó to Quepos," added the girl, likewise dressed in a standard, lifeguard-red swimsuit with white boardshorts pulled over it.

"How come?" asked Abel, genuinely intrigued.

The two young people shrugged. "I guess they don't have the money to pay for them," replied the girl. "This is the only town that advertises for lifeguards during high season besides Jacó and Quepos."

"Interesting," said Abel. So Monti Ruiz's money also makes the world safe for tourists. Abel was begrudgingly impressed. "How about school? Don't you guys go to school?"

"Not during high season," said the boy. "We go to school during the green season so we can get jobs and help the tourists during high season. Without tourists, Costa Rica is nothing but banana farms. We don't want to become banana farmers." The two laughed.

"That makes sense," said Abel. "So, where are you guys from, around here?"

"She is," said the boy, nodding to the girl. "I'm from Jacó. They've put me with a very nice family while I live here. Part of my pay goes to them to help pay for my food and stuff."

"So what do you guys know about that island out there?" Abel asked. When there wasn't a ready reply, Abel noted that the girl was coyly shaking her head no to the boy, who seemed puzzled by her expression. Finally, the boy spoke while the girl resumed her work.

"I don't know anything about it, but the people around here are really afraid of it. They call it Isla del Diablo, and no one ever goes there. I'm sorry I can't tell you more."

"Huh," said Abel.

"I'd better get back to work," said the boy. "Enjoy your stay here in Playa de Palma, señor."

Abel was now doubly interested in the island. All he was expecting to hear was that it might be covered with jungle, or maybe there was a beach there that kids went to and had parties, or perhaps Monti Ruiz, entrepreneur that he was, might have created an island tour, and they used the bigger boat at the pier to take tourists out there. But to hear now that it was a place shunned by the town, and referred to as a "devilish" place—well, that opened a whole new set of possibilities for what might be there.

Abel continued his slow walk down the beach, stopping at several fresh fruit stands, a couple of restaurants, and several surfboard/paddleboard rental outfits. Whenever he brought up anything about the island, some version of the same reaction happened. One woman said it was cursed. Another said that it was ruled by a ghost. No one could recall how long it had been since a boat had gone there. Many just didn't want to speak about it at all, dismissing him as soon as he brought it up and making the sign of the cross as he left.

Too soon, it was time to return for his meeting with Monti Ruiz. *Refocus*, Abel told himself. *You've got a job to do.*

Still, he could hardly wait to hear what Monti Ruiz might say if he should casually bring up the subject of the island.

"This is my son, Paco," said Monti Ruiz as he, Abel, and Paco stood in Paco's garage.

"We had the pleasure of meeting earlier this morning," said Abel. "I'm assuming that at least this conversation won't become 'un-confidential.'"

Paco smiled and winked at Monti. "Yes, well, of course," said Monti. "I want to assure you, Señor Forrest, that a sizable amount of contraband has been set aside for you in a very suspicious place, which will allow you to confiscate both product and weapons to put in the newspapers and the Internet and leave us more than enough plausible deniability to retain our reputations. And I'm confident that it will not be necessary to strong-arm anyone to get it.

"I've also secured your beach guesthouse at the Best Western. It should be ready by the time we finish here."

"I'll be sure to thank Faviola," replied Abel.

"I wouldn't try it," retorted Monti. "She'll probably slap you as soon as you open your mouth."

"Maybe I could include a couple thousand dollars," returned Abel.

"She'd still slap you, but maybe not quite so hard."

Abel chuckled. Monti didn't.

"I'd like to take a look at your warehouse up near the highway," said Abel, getting down to business.

Monti and Paco exchanged a glance.

Clearly, Abel thought, *they don't know how I know about it.*

"I'm afraid I cannot allow that," said Monti slowly. Abel raised his eyebrows. "You doing so would violate our arrangement with the DEA. Just as I don't confiscate all your things when you arrive, search through them, and maybe decide that you're a DEA agent who is trying to destroy my business, you do not pry around in places where we do not give you permission and decide that we are a drug cartel that needs to be eliminated."

Abel put his hands up plaintively. "Just curious," he said.

"Curiosity kills more than cats," replied Monti. "Now that we understand each other, I have some information for you."

"I'm all ears," replied Abel.

"There are several new Colombian cartels that are reaching out to us, asking for help moving their product up the coast on their way to destinations in Mexico. They have become frustrated with the cost of doing business across the Caribbean—they say their losses are beginning to outweigh their profits—and are looking for new ways to get product to buyers in Mexico and the US. They feel that using ships or subs and planes in the Pacific would ultimately be more profitable even though the route is more expensive because, in the Pacific, there is so much less chance that their shipments will be seized.

"What they need from us here in Central America are waystations where their boats and planes could refuel inconspicuously. Islands are highly preferred, and, of course, Costa Rica has a large number of coastal islands, many of which are not occupied by anyone at all."

"Including one that's just, what, a mile and a half or so off your own little part of the coast here," inserted Abel.

"That is another matter which I may discuss with you at some other time," Monti said dismissively. "Now, most of the cartel dons there in Colombia do not have enough money at this time to buy ships, subs, and planes. They're exploring possibilities, though, and working hard to get together the needed funds. But there is one who seems eager to get started. His name is Don Vicente Galvan, who is the head of the Clan de Cartagena."

The name caused a reflexive chill to go through Abel like someone had poured cold water down his spine. He hoped that it wasn't too noticeable.

"He lost a shipment off the coast of Cartagena just a few weeks ago. It was a really big deal for all the DEA posts in the region," commented Abel, hoping to cover his dismay. *Don't these cartel guys ever go away?* He'd just gotten back to some semblance of emotional normalcy, and now here he was again, Don Vicente fucking Galvan. No wonder everyone called the cartel guys cockroaches. "That's probably what's got his beehive all stirred up. What's his play here?" Abel asked.

"He's offering millions to help any of the local dons who are near suitable islands to develop them into all-inclusive waystations, complete with piers, docks, refueling equipment, even airstrips. Don Vicente tells them that, if they cooperate, they will be partners with him, and they will both share in the profits of running the waystation, which would be used by other cartels for huge fees."

"Sounds like quite a plan," observed Abel. "Any takers around here yet?"

"No, not so far," answered Monti. "There is not much stomach on the Costa Central for partnerships with the snakes from Colombia. We all value our tourist trade too much. If the DEA could pressure this Don Vicente and somehow force him out of business, we would all be grateful. It is only a matter of time before someone cracks and goes for the money, and then we'll all be in danger."

"I'll be sure to bring it up with Commander Lopez as soon as I contact him," said Abel. "They're having the same problems in Panama. We don't want it getting any farther north."

"Gracias, señor," replied Monti. "And now, *mi amigo*, I leave you to get yourself settled in your beach house and enjoy the many wonders of our little town. And should you wish to explore the coast in one of our boats, perhaps do some fishing, feel free to choose any on the pier for your pleasure. They all belong to me."

"Really?" Abel smiled. "Any one in particular that you'd recommend?" He suspected that this might be more than just an invitation to explore or go fishing.

"Actually, the bigger one at the end of the pier is mine only because it was parked there a few nights ago, and no one has come back to pick it up," said Monti with a grin. "The keys were still in it and I think you might especially enjoy this one. I have not had the chance to use it yet, but it looks like a fine launch. Perhaps you can let me know how it performs after you go for your little ride."

"Hmm." Abel chuckled. "I'll be sure and do that. Muchas gracias."

All three laughed as Abel left, Monti especially at how Abel massacred Spanish words with his very American accent. Once Abel left, though, and Paco watched until he was out of sight, Monti and Paco closed the door and spoke again between themselves.

Monti said, "Now, what's so urgent to talk about before I've even had my lunch?"

Paco took Monti over to the small office area that included his desk. He lifted the lid of his laptop computer. "I thought you'd want to know about this," he said, pointing to the screen. It was open to a website for their business account with a bank in the Cayman Islands. A new deposit had been made—two million dollars. The two looked each other in the eyes.

"After your lunch, you can sleep on this for your siesta," said Paco.

10

—

bel found his car in the now very crowded parking lot across from
the bus depot and squeezed it through the mostly unmarked lanes
of parking spaces and out onto the road that ended at the pier.
Making a right, he continued down the beachfront, an area a little less
crowded than the beach on the other side of the pier because this part
of the beach seemed to be reserved for the guests of the motels that
lined the road.

Then he skidded to a stop as he passed a restaurant with a sign that
screamed "All-American Food." He pulled in and ate his lunch at an
outside table: a really greasy cheeseburger with fresh lettuce, tomato,
and pickle on it; even greasier fries fresh out of the deep-fat fryer; and a
chocolate milkshake made thick and creamy with real ice cream behind
a classic soda-fountain counter. The whole meal cost about ten dollars,
but Abel doubled that with a tip for the expat who ran the joint. His
name was Ron. A retiree living on a modest schoolteacher's pension,
he'd still wanted to fulfill his lifelong dream of living on a beach, so
he'd come to Costa Rica where he could do that and even afford it.
He'd missed American food, though, and lots of tourists he'd met felt

the same, so he'd opened up the only totally American food restaurant in Playa de Palma. Soon, he met an American woman, Elaine, who'd run a diner in a small Midwestern town, and she'd really put pizzazz into the place. They'd gotten married and were both happy as clams. Abel took some pictures of the establishment with his phone, including one of himself and the owner underneath the "All-American" sign (which Elaine had taken), then told them he'd stop by some morning for scrambled eggs and hash browns.

Now stuffed, he went on over the Rio Palma bridge, parked in the Best Western's asphalt parking lot, and headed in. There in the airy, spotless lobby behind the registration desk stood a young male desk clerk. Abel introduced himself and told the young man, probably in his twenties, that he had a reservation for one of the beach guesthouses. The young man excused himself for a moment, made a very short phone call, then checked through his reservations on the front desk computer. As he did, a family with young children tumbled out of an elevator nearby. They all laughed and giggled as they sat in the lobby, apparently waiting for something.

"Is there some problem, Javier?" asked Abel, reading the clerk's name badge.

"Oh, no, sir, not at all. Will you excuse me for just one moment?" The clerk went into a room behind the front desk, and a brown-skinned, middle-aged woman in a business suit with the sternest face that Abel had ever seen on any woman appeared from the room and took the young man's place.

"So you are Caleb Forrest of the United States here on vacation," said the woman in an equally stern, almost too-loud voice. "And you have reserved one of the beach guesthouses." She clattered away on the keys of the front desk computer.

Faviola, Abel surmised. No doubt about it, and she was everything Monti had promised.

"Fine," said the woman. "I am Faviola, the house manager, by the way. I was told to give you our most special treatment and accommodations, so I have you in Guesthouse Number One for the week, just down the sidewalk out on the beach. If you could just initial where I've indicated and sign below, that will be fine. Also, enter your vehicle information and tear off the parking permit at the bottom, which you should display on your vehicle's dashboard each night you're here. Your accommodations are already paid for, so there will be no charge."

Abel took the paper and started to initial items, noting that the lobby seemed to have gotten very quiet even though the young family was still there. Then he did a double take at the paper, then a triple take. Something was weird about the items he was initialing. One said, "Asswiper." Another, "Son-of-a-bitch," and still another, "mother-farter." Under the line where he had to sign his name were the words "Caleb Forrest—Ugly Americano," and on the vehicle registration sheet, the kind of vehicle was already filled in. "Shit-mobile." He looked up, and Faviola gave him a look as cold as an Arctic iceberg. "Will a couple thousand dollars make things any better?" he said.

"Probably—for them." She indicated the family behind him. "This is the family that had reserved Guesthouse Number One for the week before I was told to give you our most special treatment and accommodations. I thought you might want to make some sort of accommodation for them since they graciously gave up the house they'd reserved more than three months ago. So go ahead, give it to them—now."

Abel pulled out his roll of cash, which was getting uncomfortably small for his taste. He peeled off ten one-hundred-dollar bills and handed them to the man who looked to be the father of the family. "Here. Thanks, muchas gracias."

"Do not take that!" ordered Faviola to the father. He stopped and looked at her. Faviola glared at Abel. "The gentleman mentioned to me *a couple* thousand dollars. I'm sure that he miscounted when he offered you his money since he was only giving you one thousand dollars. You should not take the money until he has recounted and made it the proper amount."

Abel grimaced. "Oh, right. Sorry for the mistake," he growled, eyeing Faviola, who stood like a proud peacock behind the front desk, and then seeing the stony faces of the father's family watching his every move. Abel counted out ten more one-hundred-dollar bills, added them to what he'd already counted, and handed it all to the father.

"There you go, señor. Two thousand American dollars," groused Abel, trying his best to smile.

"Gracias, señor," said the father, who accepted the money with a little bow and a "gotcha" sort of smile. "Muchas gracias." Then he and his family romped out of the lobby toward the beach as if nothing had happened.

"Yeah, 'muchas gracias' yourself," Abel grumbled. He moved to leave.

"Don't forget your copies of your registration and your vehicle permit," called Faviola. Abel swung back around and grabbed the papers off the counter.

"Breakfast is served every morning from six until ten o'clock in the room right around the corner. The pool is open daily from six a.m. until ten p.m., and you can get free coffee, bananas, and chocolate chip cookies here in the lobby twenty-four hours a day. Parking is in designated spaces only, and please use caution on the riverside of the property. There are American crocodiles that sometimes lurk along the banks, hunting."

"Which ones are worse, the ones along the river, or the one behind the front desk?" quipped Abel.

For the first time, Abel saw Faviola smile, though not very widely. "I will leave that to you to decide," she said.

Abel gave her a wry grin, then headed out, found his Jeep, and drove it down a narrow asphalt pathway that led through a tiny arm of the jungle and opened into a small parking area behind Guesthouse Number One. Abel grabbed his two bags of gear and entered through the back door. He found himself in a small utility room with a compact washer-dryer arrangement as well as a showerhead with a concrete drain under it, obviously a place to wash off salt and sand before entering the house. Impressed, he opened the door to the rest of the house and stepped into a place that even he, as callous as he was, thought was simply majestic.

He stood in a large, open kitchen with a breakfast bar directly in front of him. Beyond that was a casual living room complete with a forty-inch flat-screen TV, a couch, some comfortable chairs, and a couple of nice end tables topped with lamps. At the far end of that room were two giant open-air windows that looked out over a porch and then the beach and the Pacific itself, stretching as far as his eye could see. The open-air windows appeared to have both blinds and solid wood shutters that could be lowered over them for privacy and to mitigate sunlight, which would, in a few hours, come full bore into the house as the sun set over the ocean.

Noting a door off to the side of the kitchen, Abel entered and stepped into a master suite that was sort of a smaller version of the living room, except done up with a king-sized bed and an en suite bathroom that was simple yet elegant. Abel especially appreciated the large, glassed-in shower. A door on the backside of the master suite led to a second bedroom behind it with two double beds and its own bathroom, which also had a door opening out onto the parking area. Both bedrooms had private entrances from the beach.

Abel tossed his two bags onto the floor of the master suite, removed his shoes, and plopped down on the king-sized bed. Piling up some of its many pillows, he sat back and gazed out the huge window nearly the size of the wall that faced the ocean. A gentle breeze blew in, pungent with the smell of the sea, and Abel could hear the clatter of palm branches overhead that shaded the beach house. Nothing but sand, sun, sky, and the awesome ocean could be seen. It was like having his own private home on his own private beach. The beauty was breathtaking, even for him.

And then he noted the island he'd seen earlier in the day, looming across the water, seemingly within touching distance. He'd definitely take that boat Monti had mentioned for a spin, and he just might find a discreet way to get out to that island without being too conspicuous.

After all, he wouldn't want to set the whole town buzzing about the American who went out to the "Isla del Diablo." Someone might take him for an emissary of evil himself.

He got up and within five minutes had unpacked the entirety of his things and was ready for his boat ride. He snatched up the altered motel registration form and was about to ball it up and attempt a three-pointer into the nearest wastebasket when he stopped. He looked over the paper again and smiled. Where else would he get a unique memento of this particular journey? He decided then and there that it was time to start collecting memorabilia again. There was no getting back all that he'd lost in his Cartagena apartment, but he could start again, and he decided that this odd piece of gallows humor would be the first thing for his new collection. On the way to the boat, he'd stop by the general store and see if he could get a few photos that he'd taken printed and enlarged, and he'd buy some pushpins to stick them on the walls of his guesthouse bedroom. It was nice, for the first time since leaving Cartagena, to feel like things were finally safe enough to make a small attempt at starting over with his life.

11

—

Abel waved at Monti, who was planted in his chair at the head of the pier, doing his lollipop-selling thing. Abel vaguely wondered what the whole deal with the lollipops was, but for the moment, it didn't concern him. He'd walked from his motel this time rather than driven and stopped into the general store to see about getting his pictures enlarged. Sure enough, they had a self-service kiosk where he could upload images directly from his phone, pay for the size of the prints that he wanted, and come back a few hours later to pick them up. He found the pushpins he'd seen before and set aside a box with the store's owner, a tiny woman with a winning smile, and told her he'd be back after his boat ride to pick them up. She'd smiled at him like she thought he was a movie star, and said she'd be there when he came back.

Then, with his backpack slung over his shoulder, he continued down to the road and walked to the pier. Anticipating lots of sun, he wore light pants and a short-sleeved button-down with half the buttons undone. He brought a few snacks and water, his monocular, and a warmer shirt to throw on if it got colder, and he wore the same trail runners he liked so much, but he also had some sandals with him in case he just wanted to hang out on the deck. To top it all off, he wore one of his camouflage-style SEAL cloth hats with a broad-enough brim to keep the sun off his face and neck. And, of course, scuttled away into one of the backpack pockets was his Glock 19 with two extra clips of ammo.

Tipping his hat to Monti as he passed by, he walked out on the pier to the last boat, as Monti had instructed. It was a very bland sort of boat of moderate size, with a wooden hull, a wood deck with guard-rails that went entirely around it, a small cabin of which most was below the deck line, a raised bridge where the helm was with a deck that was roofed over and had cheap glass on three sides, and a stairway that went down to the deck level and also through the main hatch into the rear cabin, which Abel assumed led not just to the cabin but the hold as well.

Like any Navy officer would, Abel inspected the entire ship, stem to stern, and down in the cabin area, as expected, he found the con-traband that he was supposed to find, ten kilos of product along with a couple of old forty-five semiautomatics and some ammo. The pistols looked serviceable, but seriously, they were probably left over from the Vietnam War. They did have holsters with them, but then again, who carried holsters these days besides beat cops? Abel left all the stuff where he'd found it, figuring that he'd call in his find sometime later, and someone from the Jacó post would come down and pick it up.

But he wouldn't do it right away. Whoever came would probably want to impound the boat as well, and Abel wanted to use that boat for at least a couple more days. Today was just a day to get a look at the island, maybe find a suitable mooring place so he could go ashore for a few minutes. But he'd most likely want to do some serious ex-ploring at some time, so he'd continue using it to search out more contraband for now.

Seeing that his fuel tank was full, Abel headed away from the beach areas and pointed the boat toward the mouth of the Rio Palma and his beach house. Once there, he took a few pictures of the place from out at sea, then continued down the coast for another half mile before heading out farther into the ocean. With a keen eye to the island, he didn't turn back toward it until he was well past it, then slowed so that the motor could barely be heard as he coasted up to the shore. Skirting the side with the sharp cliffs that came down from the volcano, which looked absolutely awesome up close, he put the island between himself and the coast and now trolled along with no worries of being spotted. He studied the island's shore in earnest, his eyes popping with wonder as he did.

The first thing that fascinated Abel was that the backside of the volcano, which was several hundred feet high, was not only covered in what looked like jungle but also clouds, which clung to its sides and feathered out like frayed cotton all over the mountain and the surrounding flatlands. Abel surmised that the island, because of the volcano, had its own microclimate that gave it a rainforest-like appearance. Moist air from the ocean rose along the sides of it, cooling enough to form clouds, which in turn would cause rain to fall and which would be hard to see from the coast side.

No wonder the place looks so green, he thought. He pulled out his phone and snapped a couple of pictures.

While eyeing the volcano, he hadn't noticed that he'd been steadily drifting into a small bay. On the mountain side of this bay, jungle came right up to the shore, but toward the island, the forest thinned to just a few trees here and there, and a large meadow of very tall grass covered the land all the way to a sandy spit, which acted as a breakwater for the bay. There was also a beach area directly ahead of Abel's boat, where sand prevented grass from growing so close to the shore.

Abel did not allow his boat to cruise much farther before he throttled the engine down to an idle. He would take no chances on running the boat aground. Instead, he shut the engine off, dropped the boat's anchor, opened up a box on one side of the deck, and hauled out an inflatable dinghy. Taking it to the stern, he opened the bulwark that gave access to the boat's rear launch-and-recovery platform, inflated the boat, and grabbed his backpack. Removing his gun and putting it in his waistband, he slung the pack over his shoulder and boarded the sturdy rubber boat. Dipping the propeller of its small outboard motor into the water, he motored slowly through a hundred or so yards of calm waters and pushed the boat up onto the beach. He'd done this kind of thing with his SEAL team so often. How ironic that he was now doing the same thing just for the fun of it.

The first things that greeted his eyes as he looked up were the giant, overarching trees that formed a canopy over the jungle, which was probably another hundred yards or so inland through a plain of grass that was as tall as he was.

"Where's a machete when you need one?" he grumbled to himself, making a mental note to pick one up at the general store when he got back. He snapped a couple of pictures of the awe-inspiring view, then, using his hands and arms, did his best to clear a path for himself through the dense grass. After several minutes, he emerged onto the dirt-covered floor of the forest, which extended a few yards out from where it actually began.

Craning his neck, he gazed up at the majestic trees and their branches. They reminded him of some of the old European churches he'd seen while on leave from various deployments in Europe. Fresh breezes rustled the leaves of the trees, and, as he actually entered the rainforest, he heard an unceasing cacophony of sounds: the cries and chirps of any number of brightly colored birds that flitted and sailed about; the howls of howler monkeys, an animal familiar to many areas of Costa Rica; and the incessant sound of things falling around him from the upper layers—from waterdrops coming off leaves to tree-living animals dropping down from branch to branch. It was like a symphony of life. He set his phone to video mode and recorded the sights and sounds as he slowly walked along before catching himself and getting back to paying attention to where he was stepping.

Abel knew that what was under him could cause him far more

trouble than what was over him, as any number of poisonous tree frogs or plants could be in the shrub, and snakes and nasty insects like fire ants could be lurking on the forest floor. Proceeding with more caution, his eyes mostly down, Abel progressed farther into the forest, careful to break off shrub branches and scuff up the ground as he went so he'd be able to find his way back later.

Presently, though, when he stopped to admire the majesty of the canopy of trees once again he was greeted by a sight that almost made him burst out laughing. About fifty yards in front of him, gathered on a very thick branch of one of the understory trees, was a group of three howler monkeys. They were just sitting on the limb like preteen boys who'd climbed a tree to see what was going on in an adjacent baseball park—except they were all staring at him! Abel chuckled.

"Hola, muchachos," he called. *"¿Habla inglés?"*

The three just continued to sit there. Abel had just snapped a picture when three more monkeys showed up, this time capuchins (Abel could tell by their smaller size and pinched little faces), and they hung out in another tree as if they were checking him out.

"Guess you guys don't see humans around here too much, huh?" said Abel as he shot the capuchins with his camera. "Allow me to introduce my race to you. I'm a man, as in male of the species. Strong, handsome, amazing, if I do say so myself." He doffed his hat, bowed, made muscle poses, did turns, and struck modeling poses. The confused looks on the monkeys' faces almost made him laugh out loud.

Suddenly though, he saw that, in another tree, he was being observed by a very different audience member: a pitch-black jaguar lolling on a branch nearly within striking distance of him. He took a couple of steps back, eyeing the big cat as it eyed him back curiously.

"Sorry, sir," said Abel. "Didn't see you show up. Nice to make your acquaintance. Now, if I can just get this shot . . ."

He quickly snapped a couple of pics, then backed away a bit more, but the jaguar didn't seem inclined to move. Abel noticed that the birdsong that had permeated the woods before was now silent, and then came a chorus of strange, musical birdlike sounds from all around him. It was as if some bird (or birds) had learned how to sing like a human. Abel looked higher into the trees but couldn't see any bird in particular that seemed to be doing the singing. What he did see was a large nest, like a giant eagle's nest. And yet, there were no giant birds around either.

Suddenly, the strange birdsong stopped. Abel lowered his gaze to see that all the monkeys and the jaguar were now gone, vanished. He looked around to see if any of them were swinging or sauntering away, but there was nothing. Feeling slightly spooked, Abel decided that it was probably time for him to get back to his boat. The instant he turned his back to leave, all the sounds of the forest returned as if someone had turned them back on with a switch. Abel followed as best he could the signs that he'd left for himself, but once he could see the meadow grass, he veered a bit away.

It was then that he kicked something that made him nearly trip. He paused to check out what he'd almost fallen over and became more curious when he saw something round and quite white partially buried in the ground. At first, he thought it was just a smooth rock, but as he used his SEAL knife to dig around the thing, he could see that it was no rock. Once he'd scraped around it enough to actually lift the object out of the ground, he saw that it was, as he'd suspected, the crown and face portion of a human skull.

Abel stared at it in shock for a moment, then carefully stowed it in his backpack, hustled back to his rubber boat, returned to his ship, and pulled away from the island.

As he did, the two eyes—human eyes—that had watched him since his boat had come near the island now watched again to make sure that he and his boat left entirely and didn't turn around and come back.

12

When Abel finally got back to the pier at Playa de Palma, the sky was at peak sunset. Surfers and swimmers were being replaced by slow-strolling lovers and tripod-wielding photographers on the beach, and Monti Ruiz was just closing down his outdoor "throne room," as Abel was now calling it, and heading back up toward his house. Abel, backpack slung over his shoulder, jogged up to him.

"How was your boat ride today, mi amigo?" said Monti. "Did you catch any fish, find anything out of the ordinary?"

"I found plenty out of the ordinary," replied Abel.

"Ah, bueno, bueno!" replied Monti. "And when will the DEA be here to pick up their confiscated weapons and contraband?"

"Probably in the next couple days, but that's not what I'm needing to talk about." Monti stopped and turned to see Abel's stern face. "I went to the island," he said simply.

"You should not have done that," replied Monti. "I'm surprised you're alive."

"And why would that be?" asked Abel more forcefully. "Maybe

because of this?" He tugged his backpack open at the top and let Monti look inside. "I need to talk to you about that place."

Monti sighed. "Why is it that you *need* to talk with me so urgently about this?"

"Maybe because I'm curious," replied Abel. "Maybe because I wonder why everyone in this town is afraid of that place and calls it Isla del Diablo because of the evil thing or whatever that's out there. Maybe because I think the DEA might be highly interested to know what really goes on, on a 'forbidden' island that's just a mile and a half away from where one of their informants says he only runs a small, local operation."

It was the last part that really got Monti's attention. He sighed. "We shall meet in the morning for breakfast at the restaurant across the river from where you're staying. Good night." He turned away, but Abel didn't budge.

"No! We talk tonight at that restaurant as soon as I've finished an errand at the general store," he commanded. Abel was in full Navy SEAL mode now, and Monti could tell that he wasn't to be trifled with. And he'd also just thought of an idea that would make all this potential trouble go away.

"Fine," he said wearily. "We will stop at the general store so you can do your business, then we will walk to my home and enjoy Maria's taco salad. I have a room that is private where we can talk."

"I prefer a public place," replied Abel. "I'm not going to be looking like this dumb bastard come tomorrow morning." He indicated his backpack.

"And I prefer tomorrow morning at breakfast," retorted Monti, "but I don't want to endure the wrath of my wife and the scolding of my granddaughter because I didn't show up for supper!" His face was firm and unyielding. "So, we compromise. We talk tonight, but at my home, and I promise on the lives of those I love in that home that you will not end the evening like that poor bastard in your backpack!"

Abel finally nodded. "Okay, fine. I'll be less than five minutes in the store, and that taco salad better be good—and not too much hot sauce."

"Ah, La Catedral Verde," mused Monti as he munched on taco salad while he perused the prints Abel had gotten of his pictures. He was sitting at a neatly arranged desk in an impressive office that occupied the spare bedroom in his three-bedroom house. Abel sat across from him in a cushy chair, fanning his mouth and guzzling water like he'd just spent a week in the Sahara.

"Shit! Holy shit, that's hot stuff!" he exclaimed. "Thank God she just gave it to me on the side. What the hell is that anyway?"

"Oh, it is her special habanero chili sauce with jalapeños mixed in. She says it makes a man breathe fire from both ends," replied Monti. "I must say, Señor Forrest, for a man raised in California, you have a very sensitive palate."

"My parents were from the Midwest," Abel replied. "All Mom ever made for dinner were good old casseroles and meat-and-potato kinds of things. The only thing spicy she made was homemade chili that barely tasted like chili. I think the only kind of Mexican food I ever liked was Taco Bell."

Monti nearly spewed taco salad all over his desk with laughter, then started coughing and had to gulp water as well. "Taco Bell is an abomination!" He chuckled. "Lucia wouldn't even feed it to her dog!"

Abel chuckled, too, then asked, "So what's La Catedral Verde?"

"La Catedral Verde means 'the Green Cathedral,'" replied Monti. "It was what the few people who lived in Playa de Palma when I brought my family here from Mexico twenty years ago used to call the island because of views like this of the rainforest there." He pointed to Abel's pictures. "I remember I went there once back then and walked through the rainforest and felt like I was in a grand cathedral, like some of them in Mexico City, except there were animals and birds and trees all around instead of stone walls and people. People would occasionally go to the island, but very few had boats, so nothing really ever happened out there.

"Then, years later, after our operation here was going well and tourism was increasing, I thought of creating a nature park on the island where tourists could go, enjoy the rainforest, perhaps hike to the top of the volcano. Maybe we'd even put in zip lines and a little zoo or something for people to enjoy the animals safely, no? A real family adventure place." He now stood and paced as he continued.

"I went out with the first group of workers to survey where we should begin, what we should put where, you know, and once everybody knew what they were doing, they got to work, and I came back home.

"A few days later, though, I got a distress call from my foreman there. He was screaming for us to come get them, that a 'devil woman' was running wild through the camp along with pumas and monkeys, destroying everything and attacking the workers. Some were dead already. My son and I went with guns to try to help, but by the time we got there, it was too late. Everyone was dead, even my foreman."

He sat back down and sighed. "I sent another group, heavily armed, to the island to get rid of whatever it was out there, but they didn't return. Ever since then, no one has dared go there, and people stopped calling it La Catedral Verde and called it Isla del Diablo instead."

They were both silent for a moment, then Abel spoke. "Why didn't you go back there with the men you sent? Maybe you knew something they didn't?"

Monti gave Abel an icy look at his insinuation. "I didn't go with that group because Lucia, my granddaughter who is enjoying her taco salad out in the dining room, was just a baby then, and I knew that she'd need her grandfather around to help her grow up, that's why."

"Didn't she have a dad?" Abel asked.

"No," replied Monti. "He was the foreman supervising the workers when they were all wiped out by whatever is out there. For her sake,

I couldn't take a chance on leaving her with no father of any kind in her life. Paco, who had gone with me to rescue his brother, was only a teenager at the time."

"Sorry," said Abel. "That's a real shame."

"All of which brings me to a potential opportunity for you, should you be interested," said Monti.

Abel crossed his legs and finished his last bite of taco salad. "I'm listening."

"I have noted that you are, from all I can tell, a good man who is strong and honest and dedicated to his work with the DEA. However, it seems that this has gained you very little of the comforts of life that many like you seem to have. For example, I noted the other day that you'd brought very little to this place, yet you demanded to be put up at the finest motel in town in their finest beach house. There is some disconnect here, no?"

"Maybe I just like nice places to live while I'm in-country," replied Abel.

"Maybe you like nice places, period, but can't afford them," pressed Monti.

"Let's just say that I've had a few setbacks lately, but things are looking up," said Abel warily. He wasn't sure what Monti was getting at.

"I think things definitely are looking up for you, Señor Forrest." Monti smiled. He got up and started pacing again as if he needed to settle his dinner while he talked. "My son and I still have the dream of making our island into something more that tourists can do when they come here, and just recently, we found an investor who would like to see this happen as well. He has already committed money to the project and is hoping we can get started soon so that, by next high season, everything will be ready."

"Does he know about your little problem with the island?" asked Abel coyly.

"Actually, we failed to mention that to him. After all, we don't want to sound like superstitious fools who believe in ghosts or some evil presence that might be angered by what we hope to do."

"Certainly not," echoed Abel.

"However, we do, as you now know, have this problem, and the time has come where it must be dealt with as soon as possible. We must start whatever construction and land clearing we may need to do now before the green season arrives and dry days become scarce."

"I'm catching your drift, but I'll ask anyway. What's this got to do with me?" asked Abel.

"I have studied your background during the time you've been here, Agent Forrest," said Monti, "and I'm aware that you spent many years as one of the most elite fighting men in the world, a Navy SEAL. Certainly, such a man would be a match for any such evil presence that might be lurking out on our island. Would you be interested in a little extermination work on the side while you're here taking care of things for the DEA?"

"I might be," replied Abel. "Not sure my DEA boss will take too kindly to it, though."

"Don't worry about the DEA," said Monti dismissively. "I'm prepared to tell them of the vast amount of investigative work you're doing on our behalf to help us fend off the big cartels in Colombia from destroying our little world here at Playa de Palma. That should buy you the time you'd need."

"What's your offer?" said Abel.

"One million US dollars," said Monti, "including all the supplies, armaments, explosives, and such that you would need. Just give us a list, and it will all be here within a few days. Much we probably have on hand here already."

"I guess somebody has made an investment already," interjected Abel.

"It is as I told you. So, what say you, Señor Caleb Forrest, DEA agent and former Navy SEAL fighter?"

Abel pretended to be deep in thought, but, in fact, any niggling voice of warning that may have tried to intervene had already been politely dismissed from his conscience. This job would be like being a SEAL again, only with a vast upgrade in pay. Who needed to think about that? The future was already looking brighter. This one was a no-brainer. He raised his head. "You've got yourself an exterminator, Señor Montezuma Ruiz, king of all Playa de Palma," he said with a wry smile.

"I see that you've done some studying as well," quipped Monti.

"I'll have your Isla del Diablo turned back into La Catedral Verde inside of two weeks. I'll have that list for you in the morning. I assume I can still use that boat?" asked Abel.

"Of course," said Monti. Abel rose, and they both shook hands. "To our mutual benefit, then," said Monti.

"Hear, hear," said Abel.

ISLA DEL DIABLO

13

—

Abel was so amped up after his talk with Monti Ruiz that going to sleep was impossible, so he took the pushpins he'd bought along with his prints and did some interior decorating around the guest-house. Nothing was framed, of course, but that would change in due time. After all, he'd just made the deal of a lifetime. At least he hoped he had.

One million dollars!

Abel figured that amount could just about set him up for life. Stick most of it into his secret bank account—or at least the new one he'd have to make for Caleb Forrest—and then keep the rest of it for travel, a nice house, a nice car or two. Abel's mind conjured up all sorts of sunny scenarios as he finished putting up pictures and plopped onto his bed. As he thought more about it, his sunny thoughts began to set into the not-so-sunny, darker side of what he'd just done, and he became much soberer.

First of all, he didn't actually know that Monti had the money. He'd made a deal sight unseen as far as the actual goods were concerned. Monti was undoubtedly capable of accessing large sums of money. His "cartel" was small-time but still capable of having such funds on hand, especially if he had outside investors involved. But that was another thing. Who were these outside investors? Were they legitimate businessmen, or perhaps other shady types like Monti, sort of "good" bad guys who hoped to do good things with the money they received through not-so-good means?

And just exactly what was expected of him? It sounded like Monti wanted him to kill an actual person, someone who lived on the island and had killed others who were out there trying to do peaceful work, at least initially. That didn't sound all that bad, but he did have to ask himself what he would do if he were set up on a small island living his life and suddenly a bunch of people came and started messing with it without his permission. Wouldn't he defend it—violently if necessary—if they refused to leave?

Damn straight I would, he thought uncomfortably. *I'd kill every damn one of them.*

Then there was the fact that inside of a month, he'd again made a deal with the devil. Maybe a more benevolent kingpin than Don Vicente Galvan, but still someone who made their way in the world through criminal enterprise. What caused him, someone who had fought for his country with honor and purpose for so long, to become a mercenary who was basically for sale to the highest bidder? Abel contemplated for a minute.

Then again, it was a million dollars—*one freaking million dollars.* That could set him up for a very long time without having to do any other jobs at all. He might even be able to quit the DEA—or be forced to quit if he kept doing the things he was doing. Would they really frown on this if they knew that he, Abel, aka Caleb Forrest, was trying to assist one of their assets to build the legitimate side of his business?

Was that really what Monti wanted to do with the island, or was it just an excuse for him to get Abel to clean things up so he could engage in further not-so-legitimate business?

Abel's mind spun all these conflicting thoughts around like a clothes dryer, tumbling them over and over in his mind with their various pros and cons until he was not only exhausted but had a headache as well. He finally popped some Tylenol and flopped back down on his bed. It had been a very long day, and he was relieved that soon the gentle sound of the surf lapping onto the beach not a hundred feet from his front doorstep would be lulling him into a deep and hopefully dreamless sleep.

Up with the sunrise (which was always around six o'clock, as the sunset was also around six p.m. because of Costa Rica's proximity to the equator), Abel hustled on down to the free breakfast that the motel served. Today, he skipped the Wheaties and went for a more high-carb meal of self-made Belgian waffles slathered with butter and syrup, a half dozen sausage links on the side, and a plate of scrambled eggs for more protein. After wolfing that down, he grabbed a couple of Wheaties single-serving boxes, several slices of bread, some butter pats along with peanut butter and jelly, a giant banana, an orange, and some paper plates and plastic silverware. He hustled back to his beach house to make sandwiches and pack up a lunch to put in his backpack. Though he didn't know how many of the armaments he'd written on his list for Monti would be on hand for him this morning, he still anticipated a long day on the island, reconnoitering and mapping as much of it as he could. With his backpack loaded with food, water, gear (including one of his full-camouflage uniforms with service socks and boots), and his Glock, he slung it all over his shoulder and headed out to walk down the road to the pier by way of the general store, where he'd buy himself a couple of machetes and supplies for sharpening them.

Making a pass through the Best Western's lobby, he was glad to see that Faviola was there behind the front desk and that there was a lull in the usual morning rush of people checking out.

"Your breakfast was delicious this morning," he said. "I didn't choke on anything, and so far, I haven't died of food poisoning." He gave her a crooked smile.

"I'm glad," she said curtly as she clattered away on the front desk computer, "only, if you were to get food poisoning around here, you wouldn't die, you'd just be throwing up and shitting your pants uncontrollably starting sometime in the afternoon, so you're not out of the woods yet."

"Good thing I've got plenty of your oh-so-elegant toilet paper stashed in my backpack then." Abel smiled.

"So where are you off to today?" asked Faviola. She still hadn't made eye contact with Abel yet. "You look like you're hiking all the way to Panama."

"Actually, I'm headed out to the island," said Abel, careful not to take his eyes off Faviola when he said it. Though she tried hard not to react in any particular way, Abel noticed a definite hiccup in her clattering on the keyboard of the front desk computer.

"I hear that is not such a good place to go," she said, head still in her work.

"I've heard the same, but Monti made me an offer I couldn't refuse, doing a little side job for him out there so he and some investors can turn the place into a tourist attraction."

"And why are you telling this to me?" asked Faviola, still not looking up from her work.

"Because you asked." Abel grinned. "And because I want to know how you feel about Monti. You think he can be trusted?"

Faviola finally stopped working and looked up at Abel. For the first time, he saw that Faviola's business-suit coat and shell underneath seemed to be straining to keep her large breasts, enhanced by a push-up bra no doubt, from exploding out of them. Faviola gave him a little wink, then said, "After you have made this incredible deal with him, now you want to know if he can be trusted?"

Abel shrugged.

"It sounds like you're thinking with your bank account instead of your brain, Mr. Norteamericano."

"So?" said Abel dryly. "I still want to know."

Faviola sighed loudly. "Monti can be trusted as long as he needs your trust."

Abel gave her a doubtful look.

"It's like this motel here. Monti needs my trust because my motel gives his town legitimacy as a tourist destination. If it fails to do that, or, say, another, bigger motel moves in, he may not need my trust as much, or maybe not at all."

"So what happens then?"

"Then you don't trust him any farther than you could throw his fat ass," said Faviola. "And if I ever hear that you've repeated that, I'll slap you and call you a liar."

She went back to work. Abel still hung around, trying to process what she'd just said in light of his own situation. Finally, Faviola looked up again at him.

"There is something that you always must keep in mind about Monti. The clue is in his name. It's actually not his real name. He gave it to himself when he came here from Mexico. It is short for Montezuma, the last great Aztec ruler—"

"Yeah, I know," interrupted Abel. "I've read his DEA profile. He wants to be a king and—"

"I don't care what you've read, because obviously whoever wrote it does not understand him, and neither do you," hissed Faviola.

Abel gave her a hard look, which she answered with an even firmer glare. She now talked in a deep, conspiratorial whisper.

"He does not want to be king," she said. "He *is* king, here in this place, and his greatest goal is to be, like Montezuma, not just a king, but a fabulously rich king. All that he does, whether good or not so good in this town, is motivated by that one, single purpose. If he has made this offer you can't refuse, it's because he thinks that whatever he wants you to do at that island will make him rich somehow, and

I'm not at all sure that it has anything to do with turning it into a tourist attraction. And after you have finished whatever it is he wants you to do—"

A guest came down the elevator with her bags and moved toward the desk.

"Ah, how can I help you, Mrs. Gibson? Are you and your husband ready to check out?" said Faviola. She gave Abel a quick "be wary" glance, then went to work with the tall blond woman who had approached.

Abel made his stop at the general store, picking up two machetes, a regular-sized one with its long, eighteen-inch blade and another more compact one with a thirteen-inch blade for close-in hacking. The shorter one he tucked into his backpack, the other he bought a belt and scabbard for and hung it around his waist like a Roman *gladius*.

Ah, the weapon that conquered the world, he thought, *the Roman short sword*. One key difference: the *gladius*, though roughly the same length, had a razor-sharp point and was made for thrusting, either over a barbarian's shield into the poor bastard's face or, more gruesomely, underneath the mighty swing of the barbarian's huge but unwieldy sword or club and into the poor bastard's gut or groin. Abel's machete was sharp but had a curved point and was simply for hacking— hopefully at jungle undergrowth and not people or their animals.

He passed Monti, who was by now just setting up his throne room at the head of the pier.

"You'll find a few surprises in your boat," he called as Abel passed by. "There will be much more in the next couple of days. Have fun fishing!"

Abel waved, then headed out to his boat—or at least he might as well call it his boat. Monti was letting him use it, and the DEA wouldn't confiscate it until Monti said that Abel was finished with it, so, therefore, he considered it his boat. He smiled as he boarded the small, trawler-like vessel.

A Navy man is always happiest on his ship, even after he's retired, he thought.

He checked briefly in the cabin belowdecks to see what was there now. As he expected, the Mk 16 assault rifle was there with plenty of ammo and even a sniper-scope attachment, as were a couple of boxes of hand grenades and two boxes of MREs. There were also a couple of military-service spades for digging. His Navy SEAL M107 sniper rifle, of course, wasn't there, but as Monti had said, it was on the way. The DEA might even send one down since Monti had told them this mission was related to his undercover work. Once that arrived, he could really get down to business.

He pulled the boat out from the pier, and using the same circuitous route out to the island so as not to arouse the town's residents, he came once again to Isla del Diablo.

14

——

Abel sat on a large promontory that jutted from the steepest part of the volcano that graced the northern side of Isla del Diablo. It was a perfect spot for him to map out the island, which he carefully did now using his monocular to spot landmarks and estimate distances, then sketching them out with a pencil and the yellow notepad he'd bought at the general store. It was easy and fun, at least now that his nerves had stopped jangling and his heart had stopped racing from the craziness that had led him to the place.

Abel had changed into his camo fatigues once he'd dropped anchor in the small bay that he'd found the day before, and then proceeded onto the beach in the trawler's rubber boat as before with his full pack and gear. He'd first hacked out a trail through the tall grass to the magnificent Green Cathedral area he'd visited the day before. Once again, several animals had seemed to take a keen interest in him, but also kept their distance. These included a couple of giant iguanas that sunned themselves on a rock just on the edge of the rainforest, monkeys, and a couple of toucans that sat above him in the trees. Aside from taking a couple of pictures, he ignored them.

"You guys mind your own business, I'll mind mine, and we'll all get along just fine," Abel had told them.

He'd proceeded a little farther into the jungle and was surprised to find a substantial freshwater stream. It flowed from the direction of the volcano through the forest toward the south side of the island. He'd decided that he'd follow the stream toward the volcano to see where it originated, and hopefully find a spot to map out the island.

Retrieving his backpack and strapping on the machete, he'd hacked away at the shrubs and gradually made a trail for himself along the side of the stream. As he got higher, there was less need for the machete as the shrubbery became less dense, the steep rock not able to hold soil quite so well. The stream, of course, moved more swiftly, and at times made little cascades and waterfalls as it plunged over the volcanic landscape. There were even a few places where the water came directly off rock ledges and seemed suitable for drinking. Abel had taken note. He had enough water for today along with him, but there could come a time when that ran out, and this could be a lifesaver along with his water purification tabs.

He had finally come to a flat, very lush area where more hacking was necessary, eventually revealing the source of the stream, a spring fed from an underground source that covered an area perhaps twenty or thirty feet across with standing water, which then fell over a ledge and formed the stream. A small grove of trees provided shade for the area and gave it a fresh feeling. Abel had figured that the spring was probably an old volcanic fissure that had filled with water when the volcano was not active.

He suddenly stopped pacing the area, aware that he wasn't the only one enjoying this watering hole. Out from the trees sauntered two big cats that looked like small versions of leopards. Ocelots, Abel recalled, frequented jungles in this part of the world. They approached closer and closer, one from one side of the spring, the other from the side Abel was on. Both emitted low growls as they'd approached and gazed at him with looks that seemed to say, "Who the hell are you, and what in the hell are you doing here?" Abel backed away slowly, being careful that his escape route wasn't cut off, and slowly began to work his Glock loose from his rear waistband under his backpack.

Suddenly, as the two cats loomed ever closer, his foot had stepped on something that felt like a smooth rock and then crunched on something else that felt like stepping on fallen tree branches. He'd looked down but couldn't see anything through the thick grass that covered the ground. With eyes still on the ocelots, he'd used his hand to pull and push aside the grass that covered whatever he'd stepped in. When he'd felt something solid instead of grass, he'd ventured a glance down.

"Holy shit!" he yelled instinctively and fell onto his butt. He'd stepped on the remains of a human body: a skull, various bones, and even some shreds of decayed clothing! Both cats had then let out loud, fierce growls, as if to say, "And you're next, you dumb trespassing bastard!" Abel scrambled away, first on hands and knees, and then, regaining his feet, he ran out of the clearing and back onto the volcanic dirt that formed the floor of the forest on the steepest parts of the volcano. Checking briefly to see if he'd been followed by the ocelots, he scrambled up to a promontory.

He threw off his pack and, for the next fifteen minutes just sat there next to a rock, allowing his heart to stop racing, his lungs to resume their regular, natural rhythm, and his brain to recover from flight mode and digest what had happened. Yes, he'd invaded a watering area that the ocelots, at least for the time being, considered their territory. So their suspicions of him were natural, and he was probably lucky they hadn't attacked him.

And some other poor dumb bastard had not been so lucky, for whatever reason, a long time ago, judging from how cleanly stripped the bones he'd found were. Abel wondered if this person was one of the people Monti had sent to the island years ago who had never returned. He'd have to go back to the remains sometime—definitely not immediately—and examine them more closely.

But for now, he would finish his crude map, and then explore the rest of the rim of the volcano before descending and returning to his boat. As he peered through his monocular, Abel painstakingly noted everything of significance that he could see on his map, and as much to scale as possible. First of all, he noted that, aside from the cliffs behind him, Isla del Diablo was surrounded entirely with sandy beaches. However, in most areas, the rainforest grew very close to the shore, so the beaches were less than fifty feet wide before you entered the jungle. The exceptions were the sandbar area that formed the little bay he anchored his boat in, which was entirely beach and spread into a considerably larger beach at the point where the breakwater joined the rest of the island. And on the opposite side of the island, the eastern side that faced the mainland, there was also a sizable beach one could land on, though it had no protection from the surf.

The river meandered through the rainforest from its source on the volcano—the island's extreme north side—to its mouth on the south side. Here was another broader area of sand, and Abel noted some curious shapes under the water near the jungle's edge. Zooming in on those shapes, Abel saw that they were giant American crocodiles, some clearly over ten feet long. As he watched, he saw one lift itself up and spring with blinding speed inland to the jungle's edge. Before Abel could see what the fuss was, the damage was already done. An oblivious coati had apparently spotted a nest in the sand at the edge of the jungle and was helping itself to a delectable delicacy: crocodile eggs. More eager to eat than pay attention to its surroundings, it was now the delicious delicacy of the fast-moving croc, who Abel surmised was the female who had laid those eggs. She dragged the squealing, raccoon-like mammal into the river and plunged him under the water. Abel didn't see either again.

"Son of a bitch," Abel said to himself as he watched.

There was an unusual land feature just near the river's mouth in the heart of the rainforest, an area of flattened grass on the other side of the large meadow that he had hacked through in the morning. Then, on the other side of the river, there was a vast area of dozens and dozens of downed trees, as if something had plowed them over, with a small clearing at the end. On the other side of the clearing, there was more mature rainforest. It was almost as if, some years ago, some giant ball or something had first bounced on the meadow grass, smashing it, then came down in the middle of the rainforest, but this time skidded or rolled for a couple hundred yards until it stopped.

This phenomenon made Abel very curious, but the clearing at the end of the "skid" was just too small to make out anything through the canopy of trees that covered it like an umbrella. Checking this all out would have to wait for tomorrow as well.

Abel now began his inspection of the volcano itself. As he trudged around the summit area, which was covered mostly by volcanic rock and cinders, he noted that he had to be careful, especially near edges, because the cinders sometimes hid slick, black obsidian patches that could cause him to slip, and a slip in the wrong spot could send him over a cliff, especially on the north shore side, where they were hundreds of feet high with nothing but rocky coast and crashing waves at the bottom. Raptors like vultures and eagles had nests along the cliffs and scavenged through debris that washed up on the rocks below. On the western side of the volcano, the side that faced the afternoon sun, jungle growth returned to its sides, but not as high as Abel was at, where it was still fairly open. He noted several caves and entered a few. In the first one, he almost shat himself when he turned his tactical light on and saw that the cave was filled with bats! He turned it off immediately and dashed out. He *hated* creepy flying things like bats, locusts, hissing cockroaches, jumping spiders, and such. He caught his breath, then felt stupid for being such a wuss, but didn't return to it.

He ventured into a shallower cave and shined his light around, this time spying an even more gruesome sight, though he was getting used to it so there was no jumping or exclamation: several more skeletal remains of people. For most, their bones were scattered as if something had been feeding on the dead bodies, but a couple were relatively undisturbed. One was still coated in its nylon jacket and polyester quick-dry pants. The flesh had been devoured more discreetly—or disgustingly—by rodents, insects, and microorganisms.

Without disturbing the bones, Abel checked out what else was in the cave. He found the usual gear one would have for hiking and surviving a few days in the jungle, some backpacks, old flashlights, fancy rainproof ponchos, cooking gear, shoes, and more. There were also weapons, several vintage handguns and assault rifles, various survival knives, and some old ammunition. And there were food and water containers, most of which had not been destroyed but were all empty.

Sitting on his haunches for a moment, Abel once again checked out the human remains. It was as he suspected—no sign that anyone had died from a gunshot wound, and only a couple of broken bones, which could have come from some scavenging animal. These people hadn't been killed in some kind of violent struggle. They had been starved to death.

Stepping out quickly, he looked around once again at the island below. There were no signs of human encampments at all or any other sign of a human presence below. He got out his monocular and studied the terrain more carefully, looking for signs of old encampments, cut-down trees that might have been used as a fortification for someone trying to trap others on the volcano, but once again came up with nothing.

He did see again something he'd seen the day before: curious nests high in the rainforest understory that looked like those that might be made by large raptor birds, but there was no sign that birds had lived in them. They were also a bit larger and better constructed than what you would expect from a bird.

Suddenly, he thought he saw something—maybe even a person—zip through his field of vision so fast he couldn't make out exactly what it was. Abel quickly zoomed out his monocular to see where this figment went, but lost track of it. What could fly that fast through the treetops? He thought about a bird, but that was crazy. No bird could fly that fast, and certainly not in a straight line. Birds rarely flew in straight lines. And monkeys? Even the fastest swingers could not go so fast as to be simply a blur through the lens of a monocular.

He once again checked the nest structures. There! In one directly below him. Some creature suddenly disappeared as if it had been yanked away by a giant rubber band. Abel didn't even know which way to follow it.

He checked another nest, but just as something zapped into it, Abel's monocular went utterly dark because of a whitish-gray substance that suddenly covered everything. He saw that the afternoon clouds that had clung to the volcano the day before were returning! He needed to get down before the entire mountain became enshrouded and he wouldn't be able to see his way back to the stream and the trail he'd cut along it.

Quickly finding his pack near the cave with the multiple bodies, he hoisted it up and hustled back toward where he thought the watering hole was. It wasn't there, though, and for a few tense moments, Abel looked around, listened, and looked some more as more clouds poured in, and it became chilly and drizzly. Finally finding his own tracks in the volcanic dirt, he traced them back to the watering hole. Hoping he wouldn't surprise any other predators near the source of the stream again, he began to descend. Soon, the clouds gave way to clearer air underneath them, and the path he'd hacked out dropped farther and farther below the cloud line. Ten minutes later, he found himself where he'd started, where his main trail in from the beach met the stream.

He heard a *zing*, and then something rustled above him. He looked up, and there was something or someone in the nest he'd seen high in the Green Cathedral the day before. He fumbled with his backpack, found the pocket that held his monocular, and whipped it out, but before he could get a good look at the nest, there was another *zing* that faded into the rainforest, and whatever it was fled. Frustrated, Abel stuffed the monocular back into the side pocket of his backpack.

He walked out along his meadow trail under bright, sunny skies and looked up at the now-cloud-shrouded volcano. Once back on the beach, he climbed into his rubber boat, turned over its little outboard motor, and puttered back to his trawler. Abel thought about the last two days and realized there were many more questions about this island than he had answers to. The animals that seemed to take an interest in him wherever he went yet didn't attack him were puzzling. The idea that a group of well-armed people had starved to death in some cave high on the volcano was a total mystery, the biggest question being why they hadn't just come down from their cave and found food in the rainforest, if nothing else. And what on earth could be swishing through the trees at such a speed that he could barely glimpse it before it was gone? These questions and more excited him, and as he climbed back onto his boat, lifted its anchor, and started its engine, he couldn't wait to get back the next day and perhaps find some answers, or maybe even more questions.

He was also a little concerned. He was being paid to clean up this island and get rid of whatever the evil presence was that made everybody so terrified of it. Yet he had neither seen, heard, nor felt any evil—so far—on this island.

He had found evidence of such a thing, though, and also discovered why none of Monti's people had returned from the island. They had all apparently died. While that fact didn't exactly send a chill up his spine, it did incite his curiosity. At some point, he'd figure out how and why these people had become corpses, and he wondered if then, at that time, he'd also come face-to-face with the perpetrator.

After getting back to the mainland, he tied up his boat and once again passed by Monti's throne room. "How was fishing today?" Monti called.

"A few bites, but no catches," replied Abel cryptically without stopping.

"Ah, too bad," Monti called back. "Keep casting your line. I'm sure you'll get the big one sometime soon!"

Abel smiled and waved, then continued on, stopped by the general store, and bought some late-night snack stuff, then tromped into the All-American Diner and had himself the best steak-and-potatoes dinner since he'd lived with his folks back in Iowa. The place was slow on a midweek night—Abel was the only one there—so, Ron, the proprietor, sat down and shot the breeze with him for a while. Eventually, they got to what Abel really wanted to ask Ron about.

"So how's business here with a guy like Monti? It seems like he kind of runs the whole show."

Ron exchanged a furtive glance with Elaine, his wife, who was back in the kitchen, then said, "You could say that, I guess."

"You could say that for sure!" Elaine yelled.

"What's that supposed to mean?" Abel called back.

Elaine came out and leaned against the kitchen door. She was petite, with blond hair, blue eyes, and a feisty expression that gave her a "Don't mess with me or else" look. "It means that he rules this place like a king. A benevolent one mostly, but still, he's the only vote that really counts when it comes to town business."

Ron nodded in agreement. "I'm afraid there's no democracy here in Playa de Palma."

"So how's that work?" asked Abel.

"Well, you know, we pay taxes and such here, and all the local taxes go to him and the city council, but since the city council is his wife, his son, and him, it all really just goes to him. To be honest, he's pretty good about letting us know how it's spent, and usually it's put to good use, but we all know that he's skimming some for his own operation here," explained Ron.

"Which is . . . ?" Abel asked.

Elaine nodded to Ron, who continued.

"He runs a small-time drug cartel with his family. His territory's up and down the coast for about fifty miles or so. His main thing is keeping North American tourists happy, if you know what I mean. That's why so many of us here have such a good rapport with him. He knows

American tourists will flock to a town that has a high-quality American food place in it, for example, so he leaves us alone, and we leave him alone. In fact, we even get bonuses and reduced taxes and stuff once in a while because our *soda* brings in who he needs to make his dough."

"*Soda?*" questioned Abel.

"That's what the locals call little food places like this," Ron explained.

"Huh," said Abel. "Interesting. Anyway, it sounds like he must be pretty out in the open about what he does if you guys know so much about it."

"He can afford to be," replied Elaine. "He's got a deal with the DEA. As long as he gives them intel about his drug buddy contacts in Costa Rica, and with the big dons in Colombia, they let him slide. They even conduct fake raids every once in a while to make it look like he's legit and not an informant. Can you believe that?"

Abel just shook his head. *You'd be surprised what I'd believe,* he thought.

"It's not like we've got billboards up advertising 'Cocaine, three kilometers on the right' up on the highway or anything, but we don't pretend we don't know either," said Ron. "It's just the way it is around here. We keep him happy by helping bring in tourists, and then he keeps us happy by sharing the wealth and making this a really nice, livable community."

"He even pays some of us to be on the community patrol. It's kind of like a community-based security force," said Elaine. "Ron's one of the commanders." Ron smiled and embraced his wife.

"What would happen if someone got on his bad side somehow?" asked Abel.

The couple looked at each other with confused, worried looks.

"To be honest," said Ron, "we've never seen anything like that happen personally. Not that it hasn't, but—"

"I doubt if we'd hear much about it even if it did happen," added Elaine. "But I bet it wouldn't be pretty. Whoever it was would probably get made an 'offer they couldn't refuse' or something, you know,

like in *The Godfather*, and if we knew, we might all have a new opinion of King Monti. No one talks about Monti like that around here,
though. I don't think anyone wants to know."

"I can understand," said Abel, and everyone was silent for a minute.
Finally, he rose. "Well, thanks for the meal. It was stellar. I haven't forgotten about breakfast either." He tipped his hat, handed them a fistful
of bills, told them to keep the change, then left.

As the sun set over the Pacific and Abel strolled back down the
road to the Rio Palma bridge and his beach house, all he could hear
in his head was Elaine's comparison of life if you were on Monti's bad
side, similar to the words Faviola had used to describe his million-
dollar extermination deal with Monti that morning. He wondered if
that offer, at some point, might turn into a *Godfather* sort of offer
instead of the ticket to instant riches he thought he'd been given.

15

—

The next day started with an extreme disappointment for Abel.

He couldn't find his monocular.

He'd unpacked his backpack to repack it with fresh food and put his rain poncho in a more accessible location when he noticed it wasn't in the mesh pocket near the bottom of the left side where he'd stowed it the day before. Further searching showed that it wasn't in any pocket, and neither was it anywhere else among the things he'd taken with him the day before. Calming himself, he surmised it was probably on the island, and he remembered he'd last used it at the end of the path he'd hacked through the meadow grass. Since the island was basically deserted, it should be where he'd left it, or dropped it, and it wouldn't take long to find.

Once again, he walked through town with his backpack, dressed in a different camo outfit along with his hat and combat boots. His versatile Mk 16 assault rifle was collapsed and stuffed in the pack to avoid causing a stir while walking along the road. On the way, he stopped in at Ron and Elaine's diner just to say hi, and they wondered at his outfit.

"Just doing a little work for Monti. He's got this really remote area he wants to be explored and cleared out so it can be used as a new site for something or other. Not sure what. I use one of his boats to get there and spend my day hacking." He indicated his long machete. "Joyful work, huh?"

"Better you than me," called Ron as he served up Belgian waffles to a family of tourists.

As he passed by Monti's throne room, the king greeted him cheerfully. "Happy fishing!" he called.

"We'll see if we can catch a big one today," Abel said dryly. He wanted to be on his way because that's precisely what he hoped he could accomplish that day. There was something strange about the odd areas of the rainforest that he'd seen from the volcano the day before, the ones where the rainforest had been smashed or plowed over by something. His objective for the day was to check them all out, starting with the smashed area of meadow grass, then continuing to the river, which he'd either swing across using a grappling hook attached to a hundred-foot cable or simply wade across or swim if Monti hadn't filled his boat with more "surprises" this morning. Then he'd hack his way through the shrubbery to the area where he'd seen new-growth trees surrounded by logs and see what was at the end of it. He was sure there would be, at the very least, more clues as to what happened on the island in its past, and hopefully a lot more.

Once on the boat, Abel checked and was ecstatic. Surprises indeed! There was the portable grappling hook and cable arrangement.

No sloshing around in wet clothes for half the day, he thought.

Along with it was a sniper kit for his Mk 16. These parts gave the compact assault weapon a telescoping shoulder stock that would give it a more stable, rifle-like feel for aiming, a barrel extension to provide a bullet more spin and an accurate range of over six hundred meters, and a range-finding telescopic gunsight to enable pinpoint accuracy. If Monti couldn't get an actual sniper rifle for him, this was the next best thing. Perhaps now he'd solve the mystery of the zinging sounds in the trees and the purpose of the nests he'd seen.

Once on the island, he first followed his previously hacked meadow trail to where he thought he'd lost his monocular the day before. Alas, the monocular wasn't there. What was there Abel found to be highly intriguing. A stump of wood was propped up on the dirt at the edge of the rainforest. On it was a device that looked something like his monocular, but it had only the tiniest opening for a lens, and no place to put his eye. The stubby machine looked sturdy, as well as shiny and new.

Abel picked it up and examined it curiously. He noted a switch on one side. He flipped it, and suddenly a somewhat magnified holographic image of the ground around him appeared above the machine right at eye level. Confused, Abel soon discovered that the holographic image was of a spot of ground that the device's lens was pointed at. *What is this thing?* he thought. It did not seem possible that this was his monocular, but he couldn't think of another explanation. He changed the angle of the lens, pointing it at the trees, and the holograph became a three-dimensional view of the forest in front of him. Abel toyed some more with the device, finding that its small shaft could be turned, like turning the focus barrel of a camera lens, and that turning it one way gradually magnified the image before him, and turning it the other gave a more macro look. He turned the lens up at the nest structure above his head and not only saw a holograph of it up close and in extreme detail, but he also heard that *zinging* again. He moved the lens over the treetops that led away from the nest but saw no one.

He did see a curious reflection, though: the sun glinting off something in a place where there was apparently nothing but empty space. It was gone in an instant, though, and try as he might, Abel couldn't see whatever it was a second time. Completely confused about the object—and the apparent disappearance of his own monocular—yet needing to start his plan for the day, he flipped the switch on the holographic device, pocketed it, then hustled back to the beach. He pulled out the map he'd made the day before and began once again hacking through meadow grass, this time in what he hoped was the direction of the flattened grass area on his map. Ten minutes of chopping later, he smiled with satisfaction as he suddenly came to the blighted place. His Navy SEAL-ingrained sense of direction was as sharp as ever.

Examining the area, he quickly discovered why it was so visible from high up and far away. The first thing he noted was that it was not actually blighted, but it was depressed, and dramatically so. The ground here had apparently been punched or slammed, as though some giant fist or object had hit it in the same fashion as a person punching a feather pillow. A broad and deep indentation was left in the soft ground, perhaps thirty feet across and as much as seven feet deep. New grass had obviously been growing in the hole for years but was nowhere near as tall as the surrounding grass, or at least not in appearance, since it was growing in such a sunken bowl. He also noted that the edges of the indentation were clearly delineated. It was like someone had drawn a rough circle and pushed the ground down, making pronounced edges all along the indented zone.

Abel hacked his way to the bottom, which was well over his five-foot-nine-inch stature. He gazed at the edges. He couldn't imagine what could have done this, save some heavy machinery of some kind, and Monti had told him that the men he'd sent to this place were only heavily armed, not equipped with earthmoving tractors. He also ruled out an explosion. While a bomb or artillery shell could have made a hole this deep, the perfection of the rim made that unlikely. Also, there was no significant debris field in the grass around the depression. In fact, the only things that came to Abel's mind that could have made such an isolated, perfectly shaped hole were things not of earth: a small meteorite, perhaps, or a falling satellite or other space junk. And even that would have had to strike from straight above and been of a perfectly round shape.

Venturing out of the hole and once again hacking away at the tall meadow grass, Abel set out toward the rainforest in the direction where his map said he'd find the long slash through the jungle and the small clearing at its far end. Interestingly enough, he hadn't proceeded far at all when he ran into considerable unevenness in the ground.

Well, there is some debris, he thought. Clumps of earth that were two and three feet high were strewn here and there as he moved along. He guessed that, if everything wasn't covered with grass, there could be dozens of such clumps, especially in this direction from the depression. Whatever had made the perfectly round indentation would have entered at an angle from the western side of the island.

Continuing on once he made it to the edge of the rainforest, the going became faster. The shrub layer was not so thick as it was around the volcano, probably because the clouds around the volcano were the rainforest's source of, well, rain, and this was a good half mile from that. With such a microclimate, this would be a significant difference.

It wasn't long before Abel came to the stream, which flowed slowly here and was about eight meters wide. He hacked out a spacious spot bordered by the river so some snake or crocodile couldn't leap up and surprise him. He searched for a sturdy branch to hang his grappling hook on. He was amazed again at how high the forest canopy was, and how the trees arched over the stream. Whoever had named the island La Catedral Verde before it got its more infamous name was undoubtedly inspired.

Unfortunately, on the most likely branch of the understory trees to toss his grappling hook over, there was an audience of several capuchin monkeys, watching him intently. When he threw his hook toward the branch, they squealed and chattered, then ran out to the part of the branch he was aiming for. Apparently, they thought he was trying to throw the grappling hook to them! On his third attempt to get the hook onto the branch, one of the monkeys swooped down and caught it. The monkey held it above his head as the others screeched and grabbed for it. Abel was beside himself.

Stupid imps! Why can't they just go and do their monkey business somewhere else?

Another one of the creatures finally got the hook and started to run away with it. Grimacing, Abel pulled hard, hoping to knock the monkey off the tree and make him drop the hook. No such luck. The monkey did fall off, but he caught himself with his tail, then tossed the hook to one of his buddies. Abel yanked again and pulled that monkey off, but the third monkey grabbed the second, and they both pulled back so hard that Abel almost lost the cable.

Fed up, Abel held the cable with his left hand while reaching for his Glock with his right. Suddenly, the very distinct birdcall he'd heard two days before burst forth from somewhere. The three monkeys stopped, then the two with the hook took it out to a part of the limb that was directly over the river, looped the cable a couple of times around the limb as the hook took hold, and then they all left the area, swinging from tree to tree as they went.

Abel looked around to see where the birdcall had come from but saw nothing other than the usual colorful array of birds coursing through the understory, which, he thought was stunning.

He prepared for his swing across the river, took a running start, and leaped. He swung across, finding that the monkeys had placed the hook in a near-perfect spot. He secured the cable to a low-hanging branch on a tree near where he'd landed, then proceeded on.

Though the jungle was thicker on this side of the stream, it was only perhaps another hour before his hacking brought him to the area where it appeared as if many trees, even high canopy trees, had been flattened by some great force. There were, to be sure, more trees growing, and some were quite tall, but as he had seen from above, the forest was littered with dozens and dozens of incredibly long and also very dead logs in various states of decay. They all had fallen in the same direction, the direction he was moving in, and the blighted area went on for at least several hundred yards. Abel found himself doing a lot of walking on logs, then hopping from one to another to make headway through this most bizarre plain of destruction. Not wanting to divert back into the jungle and miss any clues along the debris field that might help explain this carnage, he continued to log-hop, but the logs seemed to go on and on, and Abel, weighted down by his backpack, had to slow his pace.

Finally, after nearly an hour spent going less than a half mile, and no wiser as to why this destruction had happened, he came to the end, and the little clearing shaded by the canopy he'd seen from afar the day before.

What he saw there made his jaw drop.

There, in the middle of the clearing, not even fifty yards away, was a giant mound of earth, perhaps thirty feet high. It was covered with shrubbery, which hid the back half of what had made Abel's jaw drop: a giant, circular-shaped sphere of shiny metal and translucent material that sat firmly in the center of the clearing.

Abel hopped off the log he was on and just stood, gazing at the object. Seeing it now made everything he'd seen so far make perfect sense, yet the thing itself made no sense at all. Abel couldn't even fathom what it might be. The first thing that came to mind was some fallen satellite, but he'd never seen a metal that looked so shiny, especially after penetrating the atmosphere. And a fallen satellite would look like a wreck and have left debris. This was a perfect, sparkling sphere, and at no point, while climbing all those logs, had Abel seen anything even sort of resembling satellite debris.

Any other ideas that came to mind after that were so unthinkable that Abel dismissed them instantly. He was curious beyond words and approached the shining ball half-buried in the mud of the rainforest floor.

Suddenly, menacingly, three black pumas like he'd seen his first day on the island hopped up onto the ball from the other side and stood silently guarding. Abel stopped, then tried to approach, but low growls emanated from all three. Abel started to reach for his Glock, but one of the pumas let out a loud roar and advanced as if to leap. Abel stopped on a dime. If this was the way things were going to be, he'd need a plan, and today, there was no time to come up with one. He backed toward the jungle. The pumas jumped down from the ball, spread out protectively in front of it, and advanced.

Abel turned and began to follow the side of the log field, hacking away at shrub when necessary. He stopped a couple of times to look back, and the three pumas were always there, spread out so he had no way to go except back the way he came.

Abel went back to the stream and swung across on his cable, back to the edge of the meadow. The pumas easily swam across the stream in slow pursuit. There, he diverted back to his original trail through the grass rather than to the depression. The pumas allowed this, keeping their distance, but escorting him out of the rainforest nonetheless.

When Abel finally came to his original meadow trail at the edge of the rainforest, he remembered the strange device he'd found there and put in his pocket. Rather than give it back, he took a pen and put it on the stump where he'd found the strange holographic device earlier. The pumas watched him but didn't seem to care. Then he turned, followed his meadow trail, motored back out to his trawler, and left, just as the rains began again on the sides of the volcano.

Leaving his boat at the pier in Playa de Palma, Abel hiked back toward the road, his mind still on that baffling round object sunken into the rainforest floor. He wasn't what you'd call a fanciful guy. There wasn't much room in his mind for imagination. Yet, the only explanations he could come up with seemed like science fiction: a shiny ball of pure silver or magnesium, or something, that had been ejected by the volcano years ago in some eruption—or the result of some failed attempt to build and launch a bizarre new kind of spacecraft that had resulted in the thing crashing. And, of course, there was the obvious but also most imaginative thought: an extraterrestrial craft that had crashed on the island. Abel's head spun.

"Ah, you've made it back again! So how was fishing today?"

Abel turned his head and nearly tripped over a board in the pier. It was Monti, of course.

"Oh, uh, pretty good actually," he said.

"And what does that mean?" asked Monti more seriously.

Abel scrambled in his mind to find words to end this conversation quickly.

"I've been doing a lot of exploring, and things are starting to make sense now. Give me a few more days, and I can probably finish the job."

Monti smiled widely. "Ah, good. I can do that for you, but I must say, by the end of next week, things will have to be taken care of. My investors would like to come here personally, and I told them all would be ready. I hope you will be finished. My associates don't like delays— or being lied to."

"You won't have to worry. It'll be wrapped up before then," said Abel. "Oh, and the sniper rifle—the .50 caliber one—it's coming, right?"

Monti laughed. "Just keep looking for surprises!" he said, then turned to collect more money from some lollipop-hawking children.

Abel walked away, but not too far. He put his pack down on one of the park benches that faced the sea and casually looked around. Everything appeared normal, and Abel himself seemed to be just a weary hiker setting his stuff down so he could rest along the beach before heading to his hotel.

But the former Navy SEAL was in intense mental turmoil. Amid the most outlandishly puzzling situation he'd ever encountered, now his well-honed, ever-wary intuition had picked up another most disturbing signal.

Monti did not want to use Isla del Diablo as a tourist attraction.

In fact, quite the opposite—he most likely wanted to use it for something nefarious, probably related to his family business. There was something about Monti's words just now, and the way he'd said them. Why such urgency? Why the timeline? It was already past the height of the high season. Tourists wouldn't be back until December— plenty of time to construct a tour of some kind, build a pier for cruise ships to dock their small boats, cut trails, build a footbridge or two, hire guides. But if Monti wanted to expand his drug operation and his investors were cartel dons, there was never enough time. Abel recalled Monti's information for the DEA that Colombian cartels were trying to move product up the coast and were looking for waystations for their ships and planes. Could giving out this information be Monti's way of hiding in plain sight, sending the DEA off looking for whichever of his competitors was plotting with the Colombian clans while he, under DEA protection, was the one actually doing the collaborating? Far-fetched, he thought, but also totally within the realm of possibility for an ambitious conniver like Monti.

Abel thought about calling Lopez to let him know of his suspicions, but that could be tricky. First of all, Abel assumed that his beach house was bugged. It would be virtually standard procedure for a drug lord with a known DEA operative in town. So he'd have to use his secure phone outside somewhere, but there could also be people watching him, another thing that seemed like protocol for a known DEA asset. And Abel also remembered that Monti was going to contact Lopez about the job that Abel was currently doing out on Isla del Diablo, but he didn't know how much Monti might have told Lopez. Did Lopez know that Monti had promised to make Abel a millionaire? It was a highly extravagant sum now that Abel thought about it. Would Lopez let him keep it if he knew?

Abel covertly assessed everything around him as his mind ran in circles. He noticed that Monti had a larger number of lollipops than usual at the end of the day.

Probably because I'm back earlier, Abel surmised.

The female lifeguard, resplendent in her form-fitting one-piece, was chatting with a young man in a blue cotton shirt and brown board shorts. She was smiling and laughing, as was the handsome man.

Flirting, no doubt. Does she know that he's one of Monti's men? Abel wondered, noting the odd bulge in the back pocket of the young man's board shorts, which almost certainly meant he was packing a compact weapon.

His suspicions were confirmed when Abel saw Paco, Monti's son, approach the young man. They both waved goodbye to the lifeguard, then ambled down the beach toward the other lifeguard tower, away from Abel, seemingly in deep conversation.

Around him and behind him, Abel saw only nondescript tourists passing by, either headed for the beach or back to the road to patronize the shops and sodas along it. *If there's any good time to do this*, thought Abel, *this is it*. He moved his backpack a couple more park benches down the beach, away from the pier and Monti, and pulled out his phone and hit a number.

"Lopez here. Good to hear from you. How goes it?"

"Good . . . I think," said Abel.

"Ruiz said he'd given you a job. Something about the island there. What's he got you doing?"

"Clearing out predators, stuff like that. He says he's got investors coming next week. They want to make it a tourist attraction."

"Your assessment?" asked Lopez.

"I . . . I don't know," Abel stuttered. For some reason, he found it impossible to say what he wanted to say.

"What's he paying you?" asked Lopez.

"Too much," managed Abel.

"Understood," replied Lopez curtly. "Carry on." He hung up.

Abel stared at the phone for a second, then put it away and casually surveyed the area again. Monti was still on the throne. He didn't see Paco and the other man, but he was confident they had been far enough away not to notice him for the short time he'd been on the phone.

He sighed and shouldered his backpack again, heading for the road. For some reason, it felt lighter. Even his boots felt lighter. Despite Lopez's cryptic remarks, he felt proud that, this time at least, he'd done the right thing, even though he had no idea how to talk about the things he'd seen or what he suspected about Monti. He needed to find out more tomorrow. That big whatever-it-was could end up being a giant-sized X factor in whatever was going on here, but for now, he just wanted to enjoy the lightness he felt for a while.

Crossing the bridge to the motel, Abel looked at the sunset that stared back at him and thought what a beautiful picture it would make to shoot the motel with the sunset in the background. He could frame it with the river on the opposite side, and it could look quite stunning. He'd love to get himself into the picture somehow, perhaps standing next to the river off to the side. He rushed into the motel lobby and was glad to see that Faviola was still at the front desk, her breasts once again shoved up by her push-up bra, this time into a space so expansive over her low-cut dress that they threatened to burst over it like a flash flood overtopping a dam.

"Hey," he called to her. "How about helping me out with a picture outside?"

"Why should I do that?" she snorted.

"Because I'm a guest and you want guests to be happy and to put up amazing shots of your place on Facebook and talk about what a great manager you are on Tripadvisor." Abel chuckled.

"You're the scalawag that took my best room for yourself," she countered.

"Yeah, but that was Monti's thing, not mine," he lied and hoped that she didn't know the truth.

"You are a bad liar, Caleb Forrest, but I do like what you say, so I will do it as long as you promise to write good things on Tripadvisor and put the picture up on our Facebook page." She came around the desk.

"You got yourself a deal," said Abel. "Now I was thinking—"

"You go down there," she interrupted, pointing to a spot down near the sandy bank of the river, "and I'll stand near the bridge abutment. That way, you'll be on one side of the picture, the motel on the other, and the sunset in between. We take one where you are turned around and looking at the sunset, so everyone doesn't have to see your ugly face, then we do one more with you looking at the camera for you."

"Did you just call me ugly?" joked Abel.

"I said your face is ugly. Too bad, because the rest of you is pretty hot. Now let's do this," commanded Faviola. She placed Abel at a particular spot on the beach near the Rio Palma, looking away at the sun, then snapped a couple of pictures with the camera on Abel's smartphone. Then she repositioned Abel quickly, closer to the river, and told him to look back at her and smile.

As Abel grinned, he suddenly heard the water being disturbed behind him. Instinctively, he turned, then did a double take. There was a crocodile! A fucking brownish-green crocodile, and it was coming right for him.

"Shit!" he screamed. "What the fuck!" He dashed across the sand back toward the motel, remembering the poor dumb coati that had become crocodile feed the other day. But the sand was soft, and he stumbled, then stumbled again, finally ending up on all fours as he scrambled all the way back to the little road that led to the motel parking lot. It was there that he turned around and saw Faviola collapsed in laughter and the crocodile ambling back to the river's edge. Abel got up and marched over to her.

"What the hell? What the fuck was that all about? I could have gotten killed, and you're standing there laughing your ass off?"

Faviola could hardly stand she was laughing so hard. "As big as that croc is, I have no idea how it could kill you." She laughed. "Look at it!" She pointed to the croc, and he looked. At first glance, he couldn't see anything other than a big ugly beast, but then he noticed its mouth and jaws.

"It's got no teeth," he said. "It's got no fucking teeth!"

Faviola laughed some more. "And look at how far it chased you!" she said.

Abel noticed that the croc, now crashed out on the beach, had barely made it ten feet out of the water before it had stopped. "What the hell?" he said. "You knew all this! You set me up, you goddamn—"

Faviola was trying to stop laughing but having a hard time. "That croc's been around here since Grandfather Juan bought this land a hundred years ago. Probably even before the dinosaurs, I think." She chuckled. "I've only seen six teeth in his mouth, and if he even makes it this far out of the water, it's a miracle. He'll probably just lie around for another hour before he's back in the river!"

Abel finally cracked a wry smile. "Well, I assume you got a good picture," he quipped.

"No," said Faviola, laughing again. "I made a video of the whole thing with my phone! You should see yourself. You look like you're a clown act in a circus! I hope all your friends will like it when I post it on Facebook!"

"Not sure that will help your business. 'At the Rio Palma Inn, we feed our guests to the crocodiles,'" said Abel. He held out his hand. Faviola slapped the phone into it.

"I lied," she said. "I took it with your phone. You can do whatever you want with it. I just couldn't resist. It serves you right, you know." She turned and walked away. "I'll be looking for that nice review on Tripadvisor!" she called back as she left.

Abel went back to the beach house and checked out the pics on his laptop computer. The one with him turned around, enjoying the sunset, really did look good. He made it his desktop wallpaper, and also shared it on the Rio Palma Inn Facebook page and captioned it, "Sunset at the Rio Palma, your home when visiting paradise, Playa de Palma, Costa Rica."

The place had turned into something like a paradise for him. The town was small, the people were friendly, the weather was perfect, and the things that had bothered him so much before, restlessness, lack of direction and security, being personally and morally unmoored, all seemed to be dissipating. The area and his job provided all the intrigue and excitement he could ever want. He was making friends here that he'd actually miss when he'd have to go back to Jacó. After talking with

Lopez, he thought that his job was secure despite the extra job he'd taken—and the enormous sum he was being paid to do it. Maybe Lopez would even let him keep it. It was no wonder he'd actually seen something beautiful tonight and stopped everything to take a picture of it—for the first time in so, so long. Perhaps life was about to take a turn.

With those thoughts in mind, he plopped down on his king-sized bed and let the gentle roll of the ocean waves lull him to sleep as the purple sky out his window gradually became black, utterly unaware that the next day his life would indeed take a turn, but in a direction so unfathomable that if he'd been told ahead of time, he'd have laughed out loud and told the teller they had gone out of their mind.

16

—

bel wolfed down another plate of Belgian waffles, grabbed some fresh fruit, and was on his way out of the Rio Palma Inn just a half hour after sunrise. He was wearing his khaki cargo pants and a roughly matching button-down shirt with his DEA utility vest over it stuffed with ammo cartridges, sunscreen, energy bars, water purification tabs, a jackknife, and the small, holographic vision machine that had been left for him the day before. He wondered what, if anything, might be left for him in place of the pen he'd left there. He also wore a fully loaded utility belt on which hung his long machete, a water bottle, a tactical flashlight, and his Glock 19, which was in a holster for the first time. In the pack he shouldered, there was the Mk 16 assault rifle, several hand grenades, more ammo, plus raingear and a new camo fatigue outfit in case he actually ended up staying on the island that night. He had no idea what to expect when he began inspecting that shiny metal thing he'd seen the day before.

As usual, he'd also stopped by the front desk to share a barb or two with Faviola before he took off, and she had obliged appropriately. "You look like everything on you is stuffed," she'd said.

Abel had come right back at her. "You look stuffed, too," he'd replied, noting her bulging chest. "You look like you could pop out of that button-down blouse any second."

"I bet you'd like that, wouldn't you," she'd come back seductively.

"Oh, yeah," Abel had agreed, "except I'd have to watch out for flying buttons. They'd pop off like bullets—a guy could get hurt that way."

"A secret weapon to keep scalawags like you from getting too close." She smiled. "Where are you going anyway, camping for a week? If you are, you'd better let me know so I don't rent out that beach house by mistake while you're gone."

"No such luck, I'm afraid," Abel had replied. "I've got to come back and get my pictures."

He'd headed out over the bridge, chuckling at the toothless crocodile, which was still lying near the river's edge. Perhaps he'd moved a yard or two since the day before.

Now, noting that Monti the King hadn't set up his throne yet (just as he'd planned), Abel hustled down the pier in hopes of getting out to sea before he came around. Just as he reached the boat, however, he heard Monti's familiar jolly call.

"Hey, fisherman!" he yelled. Abel turned and pasted on a smile. "You got your favorite fishing rod today! Make sure you use it and bring home a big one!"

Abel gave Monti a little wave, dumped his stuff on deck, and revved the boat up. He noted that it was a bit down on fuel, but there was certainly enough for the day, and he didn't want to hang around any longer. He slowly left the pier, then pulled the boat out in a more direct line toward the island, not as concerned about arousing the curiosity of tourists at such an early hour. Taking a second to check the cabin, Abel smiled with satisfaction at what he saw. There it was, the M107 .50 caliber anti-personnel/antimatériel semiautomatic sniper rifle, complete with a soft carrying case. Effective range, several hundred meters over a mile. It was the kind he'd used in his early days as a SEAL.

Seeing it now made him feel like a little bit of home had come to him. The day was definitely off to a good start.

As soon as Abel dropped anchor and motored ashore, he left most of his gear in the rubber life raft he used as a ferry, grabbed the M107 in its carrying case, hustled at a slow trot along the trail he'd cut to the volcano, and began to climb. Finally, he reached the promontory upon which he'd sat a couple of days before and made his map of the island. He assembled the M107, filled up its magazine with ten .50 caliber rounds, flipped out its attached bipod, got himself in a prone position, and, using the rifle's range-finding sniper scope, began panning around the island. He wanted to do a little experimenting.

At the mouth of the river were the crocodiles, sitting just under the water, waiting for dinner to come their way. Maybe even another unsuspecting coati. Abel peered through the scope, ran some calculations through his head since he didn't have a spotter to do it for him, calmed his excitement with some deep breathing, and then gently squeezed the trigger. The report of the rifle scattered some vultures high up on the mountain. At the same instant that the birds flew away, Abel saw a fountain of sand and water leap up on the other side of the farthest crocodile. He turned toward the east, the coastal side of the island, and exploded more sand and water on the large beach that was the farthest eastern point of the island. He sighted on his boat floating at anchor out in the little bay and splashed water just behind it. He blasted sand on the farthest point of the sandbar that formed the bay his boat was in. He fired a round into one of the farthest logs he'd scrambled over the day before—as close to the shiny metal whatever-it-was as he could get before it became obscured by trees—and watched part of the log explode into splinters.

And finally, just on a whim, he turned his rifle straight eastward, where the beaches of Playa de Palma could be seen with little ant-sized people running around on them and, behind them, tiny

Monopoly-sized houses and hotels. He brought this all into focus through his sniper scope, where now he could see actual people: the female lifeguard relaxing in her chair on the tower, a group of paddle-boarders cruising along parallel to the beach about a hundred meters out, surfers riding waves or waiting to catch one, kids running around selling lollipops to tourists in beach chairs, and Monti holding court as usual in his canopied throne room at the foot of the pier, Paco sitting next to him.

Abel's gaze lingered on them, longer and longer. He felt his heart quicken. He took some deep breaths. Then he swung a little farther to the left and spotted the old toothless crocodile at the mouth of the Rio Palma. The old guy had actually made it back into the water. He saw several groups of maids going about their work in the main complex, and someone swimming laps, however small they were, in the pool. Faviola was out inspecting, and Abel watched with a smile as she bent over to pick up some trash and burst out laughing as her breasts actually popped one of the buttons off her blouse. She casually picked it up and went about her work, now looking all the sexier.

Ah, to be in a world of Latin women, Abel chuckled.

Finally, he sighted on his beach house, the closest one to the beach and farthest from the motel's main building. Abel thought it looked very inviting and was glad he was staying in it. He did some more calculations in his head, adjusted the crosshairs in his scope accordingly, took deep breaths, and then pulled the trigger. Two and a half seconds later, another sand explosion, this time just in front of the stairs that went down from his porch to the beach.

Abel stood and surveyed everything around him—the island, its beaches, the river, the bay, his boat—then all the way around to the community on the mainland. His hunch had proven even better than expected. From this point high on the volcano's island side, he could rain projectiles down on anyone or anything on the entire island with pinpoint accuracy, something he had expected but needed to test. What he hadn't expected but thought might be possible—being able to hit targets on the mainland of Playa de Palma itself—was a shocking and sobering surprise. All this he silently contemplated as he disassembled his weapon, re-stowed it and its other ninety-four rounds in its carrying case, and searched out another small cave to cache it in. He found a space for it under some rocks where he also found the bones of another poor soul who'd given his or her life in the service of Monti, and then slowly began to descend, wishing that he had someone wiser than he to talk with about the staggering implications of this new-found power he possessed.

Once back to the beach, he grabbed his backpack and, for the first time, pulled out his Mk 16 assault rifle and assembled it for close-in use. Having seen the strange behavior of the big cats on the island already, along with the monkeys, he wanted to be ready for anything as he journeyed to the big shiny object he'd seen the day before. In just a matter of seconds, he had the weapon assembled, had snapped in a high-capacity magazine, and hung it over his neck and shoulder at "ready" height. He then slung the vastly lightened backpack onto his shoulders and hiked along his main meadow trail to the welcoming arches of the Green Cathedral.

There he stared at the ground, looking to see if the pen he'd left the night before had been replaced with anything. Incredibly, it had! Lying on the stump was a small, pen-sized cylinder, though it didn't seem to have a way to eject something with which to write. Abel stared at it curiously, picked it up, looked it over, shrugged, and moved to put it into his pants pocket when he suddenly heard the zing sound again, and an instant later, seemingly from nowhere, a human figure appeared, standing not thirty feet from him.

Instinctively, he raised the Mk 16 and aimed it at the person, his finger on the trigger. Only then did he have a chance to actually look the person over. She was a woman, probably younger than he, but definitely not a child. She was considerably shorter, but also graced with a magnificently proportioned and robust physique. Her skin was a warm brown that reminded Abel of hot, rich Colombian coffee mixed with cream and sugar. Her hair, cut straight and short above the shoulders, was a dark shade of auburn. It framed her high cheekbones and bright green eyes that were much bigger in proportion to her nose and thin-lipped mouth, giving her an otherworldly appearance. The trunk of her body was covered by a comfortably fit garment that was the color of the surrounding tree trunks (a rough-looking brown) and spotted with a green that matched their leaves. Abel had no idea what kind of fabric it was made of, but he could see the protrusion of small nipples through it across her chest, so he surmised that it wasn't thick or weighty. Her arms and legs rippled with sinewy muscle and her feet were covered in leathery shoes made from some sort of hide that was the same color as her clothes and held at ankle height by numerous laces. Except for what looked to be a small, sheathed knife strapped to her side with a thin belt around her waist, the woman appeared unarmed.

The two stared silently, their eyes taking each other in. Abel saw a human being unlike any he'd ever seen in his life. There was a side of him that figured that if Peter Pan were a woman, this is what she'd look like, the face different and captivating, like something out of a science-fiction movie. Those beautiful green eyes, so large yet not disproportionate, were mesmerizing. Though he continued to point his assault rifle at her, he couldn't imagine using it.

Suddenly, he heard the strange birdsong he'd heard several times before, including the day before when the black pumas had followed him away from the shiny metal object. This time, in his head, he heard a firm but enchanting woman's voice.

I am Rimi of La Catedral Verde. I have watched you for three days. Now, I must know who you are and why you are here.

Abel kept his eyes on her and his weapon trained. "I'm Abel—er—Caleb, Caleb Forrest."

"I'm Abel—er—Caleb, Caleb Forrest," said Rimi, this time directly to him, imitating him perfectly, even down to the stutters and his natural cocky tone.

Abel was confused by this but continued. "I've been sent here to explore the Green Cathedral. I don't want to hurt anyone."

Once again, Rimi spoke back to him the same words he said to her, in precisely the same fashion. Then she added, "I sense you are lying. You have weapons just like the others and say the same things they did before they tried to hurt us. Why do you bring weapons if you don't want to hurt us?"

"To protect me," replied Abel, still with his weapon aimed. "I don't know who you are, or who 'us' is, or where you came from, or how the hell you can talk to me in my head in perfect English."

Rimi stepped gently closer to Abel with her hands down as if to calm him.

"I can answer all your questions soon enough, but you must lower your weapon. The others would point them at us and shoot bullets into us. They killed some of us, so we killed them, as you know. Please, lower your weapon, and you and I will talk."

Abel quickly assessed his situation. He was face-to-face with an alien-looking woman who seemed harmless enough, and wanting to talk, but once you've been lulled into complacency by a Taliban woman begging for help only to watch her pull out an AK-47 as soon as you let your guard down and riddle your team members with bullets, you have second and third and fourth thoughts about lowering your weapon in any kind of standoff with an unknown. He had a sinking feeling who "us" might be, but nothing else living appeared to be around at the moment. Finally, he made his decision.

He unhitched the strap that held his Mk 16 up. "Okay, I'm lowering my weapon," he said.

She advanced a little more toward him. "This is good. All will be all right."

Abel started to put the weapon down but also backed away, not comfortable with Rimi coming closer.

"Stay where you are, and I'll put down the weapon," he said, continuing to lower it and back away.

Rimi stopped, but suddenly the three black pumas from the day before appeared. One dropped from a nearby tree, and the two others sauntered out of the shrubs behind Rimi.

Startled, Abel backed away some more and began to raise his weapon again. "What the hell? You want me to drop my weapon with those things prowling around?"

Rimi took another step forward, her hands open and calming.

"They are my friends, my guards. They go wherever I go. They will not hurt you."

Abel continued to back up. "Oh, yeah? You told them that, huh? Forgive me if I don't—"

Suddenly, Abel's foot hit a tree root behind him, and he pitched backward. He flailed his arms to catch himself, but his right hand squeezed the trigger of the Mk 16 as he was going down. Shots rang out! Abel fell to the ground on his back, his head bouncing off another hard tree root. The last thing he saw before he blacked out was three angry black pumas descending on him like avenging demons.

LA CATEDRAL VERDE

17

—

The first thing Abel noticed when he awoke was that he couldn't move. He tried and tried, but nothing budged, and with each attempt, zings of pain raced through him.

"Don't move or I'll shoot!" he heard a rather nerdy-sounding male voice command from somewhere. It had a distinct metallic sort of after-ring to it.

"Bibi, stop!" said another voice, a woman's voice, which Abel vaguely thought he'd heard before. "This is not the time to use those words. They are threatening words. Abel-er-Caleb Forrest is badly injured. He cannot hurt us."

"But he has to stop moving," the whatever-it-was that was called Bibi replied. "He'll ruin the healing process if he doesn't."

"This is true," replied the woman, "but you must use gentler words. Like this." After a brief pause, Abel saw the woman's face looking down at him. She spoke with the same calming voice that he was gradually remembering.

"Calm yourself, Abel-er-Caleb Forrest. You must continue to lie still for several more hours, or your injuries will not heal properly."

The other voice replied, "Ah, so more like, 'Relax, take it easy. Everything's gonna be fine.'"

Abel wasn't listening to the chatter. He was staring into those green eyes.

"You can just call me Abel," he said.

He then glanced around at his surroundings, noting lots of futuristic-looking electronic gadgetry on the ceiling, and the same around him inside what seemed to be a rather cramped, spherical room. He then looked down as best he could from lying prostrate on his back and barely being able to move anything. His body was naked, that was for sure, and there were many angry-looking cuts and claw marks all over it, or at least the parts he could see. The entirety of his body, save for his head, was wrapped in a transparent film made up of spiderweb-style threads wound over and over again. Thus mummified, his body was placed in a metal cocoon where a soft white light interacted with the filaments of his wrapping. He could feel things going on all over his skin but had no idea what. He looked back into the woman's mysterious green eyes.

"Where am I, and what's being done to me?"

"You are inside my escape pod. He is called Bibi, the other voice you heard. You are now wrapped in a healing cocoon, which is used by the healing cylinder to repair whatever it detects is not function-ing properly on you. The cylinder finds what is wrong, then activates the proper nanobots in the cocoon to go to work repairing whatever damage has been done. It will be several more hours before your entire body will be scanned and repaired, but it will take days more for the repairs to heal."

Abel squirmed, or at least tried to.

"Days! I can't be here for days. I've got to—"

Suddenly, Abel was interrupted by a painful shock that zapped his entire body. He instantly stopped squirming.

"Fight the healing cylinder and the healing cocoon will only cause you to have more body damage, and therefore more time that you'll have to stay in it to be repaired. And then it will take more time for the repairs to heal," said Rimi gently.

"Yeah, well, that's just great," said Abel, "but I've got stuff to do, and if I don't get back later on today, someone's going to get suspicious, so I'll just be—" He tried with all his might to break out of the mummy wrap he was in, but once again he felt painful zaps.

Rimi held him with a startlingly firm grip. "You must stop struggling, Abel. You'll only make things worse. You've already been here more than a day, and nothing bad has happened."

"What!" exclaimed Abel. He struggled more, ignoring the pain shooting through him. "Shit, Faviola's probably already given away my beach house and thrown out my pictures. Help me get out of this!" He cried out as the healing cylinder zapped him again.

"Stop struggling," Rimi ordered in a voice packed with authority.

"Not likely, sister," said Abel. "You'll have to knock me out first."

Rimi saw that Abel was actually stretching the mummifying strands to the breaking point. She'd never seen such strength in an Earth human, or such stubbornness. But she wasn't about to see Bibi's healing systems be damaged, by him or any other.

"Fine!" she said. "It shall be as you wish."

Abel, sensing he was making headway with his wrappings, grinned crazily at Rimi and was about to say something else when he noticed, Rimi's eyes change to a fiery red color, and something coming out of his peripheral vision. Then something that felt like a baseball bat hit him flush on the cheek, and he was out cold again.

Rimi dropped her fist down as she saw Abel once again was unconscious. She straightened his body gently and positioned it properly again in the healing cylinder. She found more of the mummifying material and placed it on Abel's face where her blow had connected with it, then pushed him a bit farther into the cylinder.

"See that he stays asleep until all procedures are accomplished, Bibi. I have been angered as I haven't been since the last Earth humans came here and killed some of us. I must run for a while and calm myself."

With that, she simply walked through a part of Bibi's wall that was not covered with machinery and the next second, stepped out into the clearing where the shiny ball lay half-buried, one part of it quickly closing behind her as if it were made of liquid. She began to jog, then suddenly swooshed out of the clearing so fast it was as if she'd simply disappeared.

When Abel awoke again, he was no longer in the healing cylinder, and flashy metal tentacles were peeling away the healing cocoon that was still partially around him. Remembering what had happened to him before, Abel didn't struggle this time or try to get up. Not seeing anyone immediately in his limited field of vision, he called out, "Anybody home out there?"

"Of course, I'm home," replied Bibi. "I have never not been home. It's so good to be home."

"Yeah, right . . . " replied Abel, mostly to himself. "So, are you some kind of AI robot or something?"

"I am a special kind of ground operational device called a ground operational living device. GOLDs have many purposes. Mine is to act as an emergency escape system and semi-permanent dwelling for my human owners. I am fully equipped with all options standard. What you see is what you get! I can handle anything that Mother Nature throws at my human occupants. I'm one tough GOLD!"

"Jesus, you sound like a bad car commercial," quipped Abel.

"You bet yer ass I do," said Bibi in an Old West drawl. "Where ya think I learned all that fancy lingo, any-hoo?"

"You gotta be shitting me."

Suddenly, Rimi walked through a wall in the sphere and was among them. Abel, who'd just raised himself enough to see what was being done to him, nearly dropped his teeth. Rimi went over to his side and began examining his body.

"It appears that the repairs have all been made successfully." She felt his jaw where she'd smacked him. Abel moved it back and forth, up and down. It seemed to work fine, and it felt like all his teeth were in place, but it was very sore and stiff.

"I'm especially glad that this seems to be fixed," said Rimi. "Please forgive my anger. I must learn to control it better."

"I think I asked for it," replied Abel. "How'd you do that anyway?"

"What, hit you? Well—" began Rimi, but Abel interrupted.

"No, walk through that wall," he said. "How'd you just walk through that wall?"

Before Rimi could answer, Bibi spoke up. "Another miracle of modern engineering!" he exclaimed. "My body is made of a liquid metal alloy from my home planet that can assume almost any shape and is virtually indestructible. It can be so dense that even laser beams cannot penetrate it, or so porous that someone like Rimi can walk right through it. Imagine the possibilities! Get yours now for just nineteen ninety-nine, and your shipping is free. But wait! Order now and we'll double your order. Just be one of the first ten callers and—"

"That's enough, Bibi. I will talk now," said Rimi with a sigh. "I can understand the language of most any animal innately, which of course includes Earth humans, but Bibi needs to listen to speech patterns to learn new languages. So when we came here, he used his radio wave sensors to watch and listen to television shows that were broadcast in the area. That is also how I learned much of what I know about this world."

"So you're . . . not from . . ." began Abel, not sure quite how to broach the subject of talking to an alien.

"No, I am not from this world," answered Rimi. "My parents came to this world many of its years ago as explorers. They found a civilization near this area that was very open to them, and my parents and their crew taught these people many things. They were eventually called home, but promised those people they would come back to them one day. When my parents came back, this time with me, over a hundred of your years ago, something happened. I don't know what, but there was a malfunction of some kind that dropped our ship out of orbit, and our descent was uncontrollable. My mother put me into Bibi and ejected me from the vehicle, and I have no idea what happened to it. All I know is that I am alone. There is no one else like me anywhere that I know of, and I miss my mother and father very much."

"That sucks," said Abel. He noticed that there was a tear rolling down Rimi's cheek.

Suddenly, the tentacles that had been operating on Abel dispersed and disappeared into the sphere overhead.

"Ah, you are finished. I will get your clothes and help you put them on," said Rimi. Abel sat up, looked at his naked body, and for the first time made the connection that he was lying naked in front of a complete stranger who was also a beautiful woman.

"Holy shit!" he yelled. "You've been staring at me naked this whole time."

"Of course I have. Where else was I supposed to look? I wanted to make sure that everything had turned out all right, and you are also very pleasing to look upon," she said matter-of-factly as she crossed the sphere to where he saw his things stacked.

Abel's face cracked one of his crooked smiles. "You really think so, huh?"

"Of course," said Rimi, "and what do you think of me?"

In one blinding movement, Rimi tore open a seam that stretched the entire length of her garment and let it fall to the floor. Abel gaped like some junior high kid staring at his first *Playboy* centerfold. He didn't think he'd ever seen such an example of a perfect female body.

Rimi smiled at his expression, then redressed herself almost as fast as she'd undressed.

She smiled. "I'm glad you approve. Now let's see if we can get your things back on you."

About a half hour later, Abel was dressed once again. The process had been far more arduous than he could have imagined. Apparently, all three pumas had descended upon him at the instant his gun had gone off, and before Rimi could call them off, they had used their claws to rip long gashes all over his body. Fortunately, nothing was fatal, but several large arteries had been slashed, and were it not for Rimi's ability to move from one place to another quickly, Abel could have bled to death. He had been given promptly to Bibi's healing machine, and those major wounds had been repaired, but Abel had been so weak from blood loss that Bibi had caused him to sleep through the night before the more superficial repairs were made. The machine had fused the torn muscle tissues and skin tissues together, and each would eventually become just as good if not better than they had been originally, but at this early point, the grafts were fresh, delicate, and stiff, making it difficult for Abel to walk or move his arms.

Rimi had gently helped him with his clothes, although Abel was not always the most cooperative patient. He insisted on doing as much as he could himself, which was not much. Rimi simply sat while he struggled until he finally had to ask for help. She found his bravado both amusing and admirable. She thought it silly that a man should be so stubborn and refuse the aid of another when he obviously could not do something on his own, but she also understood that, though silly, this man's refusal to allow others to help was something that made him stronger and more able to take care of himself. She also admired his ability to endure pain. Her life had been filled with pain, physical and otherwise, and she knew how much strength of mind and will it took to continue to push oneself forward in spite of it. This man, Abel, was certainly her equal when it came to that.

Once dressed, Rimi gave Abel a stick to lean on that she had used once for the same purpose, and then she showed him how to exit Bibi. There were several sections of the sphere wall that were not covered up by machines and gear, and all you had to do was think "open" when you approached the wall, and its atoms would rearrange to let you through. Abel, like most humans she'd met or seen on TV, did not seem able to understand this concept. They instead used premade openings called doors, which required a physical manipulation of a covering to enter or exit. Rimi demonstrated over and over how she simply passed through the wall, but Abel always just ran into it. He kept trying doggedly, but with no success. Rimi at one time asked Bibi if he was playing tricks on Abel, but he said no, that Abel's brain waves were not yet recognized by the nanobots that held Bibi together, probably because they contained shades of doubt if Bibi's atoms would actually move for him. Thus they remained in protection mode and would not open. Rimi finally asked Bibi to ask the wall to form a door, which it did, and Abel went through by physically opening it to the clearing. Rimi decided she'd continue to work with him until he could master this, sensing that he really wanted to and felt weak and embarrassed that he couldn't accomplish "walking through walls," as he put it, as she could.

They found one of the many downed logs near the clearing, and Rimi sat while she watched Abel struggle to walk toward her. It took him an agonizingly long time, but Rimi knew he would not want her help. She tried to encourage him and make a little joke, something that she sensed he might like from his earlier behavior.

"Do you know that there's an animal on this island called a three-toed sloth?" she said.

"I've heard of them," replied Abel.

"I think when we go back to Bibi, I'll bring it here and you two can have a race to see who will get there first."

Abel smirked. "Very funny."

"Really? Do you think so?" she said happily. "I'll give you a prize if you win."

She wasn't quite sure what this entailed, but it was something she'd heard often from Bibi about Earth humans, that they were very competitive, and winners of races or games would always get prizes.

Abel finally got to the log she was sitting on. It was high enough off the ground that he could sit comfortably on it without having to lower his rear very much. He was surprised at how tired he was from doing what seemed such little work. He'd only walked perhaps twenty feet. He felt as though he'd just run many times that far.

"I didn't know walking from there to here could wipe me out so much," he said as he caught his breath.

"Bibi says that is because of how much blood you lost," Rimi informed him. "He says that it will take your body several days to build up its normal supply again. I offered to give you some of mine, but Bibi said that it wouldn't be necessary, and besides, my blood might not be the right type for your body."

"Smart guy," replied Abel. Besides being exhausted, Abel's mind was swimming. It seemed like every time this woman opened her mouth, there was some new question he wanted to ask her. How did the stuff with walking through walls actually work? Why couldn't he walk through it like she did even though he focused all his thoughts on it? How did a door magically appear for him to go through? Was she really going to get a three-toed sloth for him to race? If so, where would she get one? How would she know where to look? Why on earth would she volunteer to give her blood to him? Where did she come from? How was it that a spherical space capsule could talk and repair human bodies? It all exhausted him even more.

He finally settled on asking one question, which he hoped was a simple one.

"So where are you going to get a three-toed sloth for me to race?" he asked.

"I'll call him, listen for his answer, then use the wires to get to him and back. Or I could just jump to him and jump back with him, but it's a little hard because you don't know if there's going to be a good place to land or not."

Seeing the confused look on Abel's face, she stopped.

You're talking too much again, she chastised herself. *These Earth people don't even believe that alien humans exist. How would he be able to understand my capabilities?*

She had done the same years before, and she'd frightened the woman whom she'd spoken to. The next day, men had come back with guns like Abel; only when they'd pointed them at her, they'd shot projectiles. She'd tried to dodge them, but one had actually struck her, and she'd had to be repaired by Bibi's healing machine.

"What's the wires?" Abel asked. It didn't look like any conversation with Rimi would be a simple one for a while, but if he could keep things narrowed down to one thing, maybe he could enjoy a little time with her before he got fatigued. He found learning about her fascinating, which made her even more attractive to him than she already was, but he'd have to go slow while his body healed, he could tell. It was something he detested but would have to gut out regardless.

"Oh, let me show you!" said Rimi, immensely relieved he still seemed to be interested. Perhaps this man would actually give her a chance to be his friend, but she still felt an intense need to be careful and not show or tell him too much too soon.

Rimi pulled out a couple of gloves and slipped them on her long, thin hands. Abel noticed that something in them glinted in the sunlight, but otherwise they appeared to just be made of some kind of sturdy material, perhaps the hide of something.

"These are my special gloves," she said. "Bibi made them for me. He made the wires, too." She gave a little leap and alighted perfectly on the log he still sat on. Abel was stunned by her graceful yet powerful agility. "Okay, here I go!" she cried, and leaped off the log high into the canopy above and then seemed to hover in the air.

"What the hell?" exclaimed Abel. "What are you hanging on to?"

"The wires." Rimi laughed. "You said you wanted to know what they were. I've strung them all around the island high in the trees. I can go almost anywhere I want on them. Watch!"

Rimi grabbed the invisible wire with both hands, swung back and forth parallel to it, then suddenly, on a forward swing, dropped one hand off the wire, and her body launched itself, with her other hand acting like a very well-greased hook sliding with the same zing sound Abel had heard before. Suddenly, she was hanging from the wire in another tree that must have been over a hundred feet away. She got there so fast it was almost as if she'd disappeared and reappeared just a second later in the farther tree.

"Holy shit!" admired Abel.

Just as quickly, Rimi was back above him, and a second later, she was standing, perfectly balanced, on the log where she'd been sitting not more than a minute before. One more second and she was sitting beside him, removing her gloves.

"Let me see those," Abel said, fascinated. *Definitely some kind of hide, but what's the shiny stuff woven into it?* "What are they made of?"

"Bibi made them from some pieces of him that fell off when we landed on this island. Then he combined it with the hide of a dead crocodile. The wires he made from the branches of those trees we knocked down when we landed." She pointed to the vast field of logs Abel had traversed when he'd first discovered what she called Bibi.

"What?" asked Abel incredulously.

"The trees contain carbon," said Rimi. "Bibi changed it from its wood form into the wires."

Abel looked at her like she'd just spoken to him in an animal language.

"I don't know how he does it," said Rimi, "but Bibi can turn just about anything into just about anything."

Abel gave her another of his crooked smiles, though this time, while his face drooped from weariness, his eyes danced with excitement.

"I'm sure there's a reasonable explanation for all this, and everything else you can do, but how about you head out and bring that sloth back here so we can have our little race. I probably need to get back inside and lie down for a while."

"I'll be back in a minute," said Rimi. She once again leaped into the trees and disappeared in another direction.

"I'm sure you will." Abel chuckled to himself.

While he waited for Rimi to return, Abel, for the first time, took a moment to look around the clearing where he was resting. It was a gorgeous setting: the giant shiny ball that was Bibi in the midst of a clearing in the rainforest, with the giant canopy of trees and the smaller ones of the understory framing the whole picture with their magnificence. Within all this, everything seemed to brim with life. Birds of endless exotic colors and varieties flew back and forth. Parrots, parakeets, and toucans thrived with more common birds like hummingbirds and robins. Beautiful, delicate butterflies also fluttered about and filled the air with even more color. For the first time, Abel noticed how abundant smaller forest creatures like red-eyed tree frogs were. They hopped around on tree limbs, and even on the log he sat on. Looking up, he saw dozens of monkeys dancing through the understory as well as a couple of big cats, probably jaguars, lurking on the sturdier limbs. Abel was stunned by all he saw and wondered why he'd never seen such beauty before. This was the fifth day he'd been on the island, yet he'd never seen anything like this. Abel guessed that, until that moment, he hadn't taken the time to notice.

Rimi came back with a big bundle of fur draped around her like a living mink stole. As she plopped back down next to Abel, she peeled the creature off her and set it down on the log. The furry animal's arms and legs seemed much longer than its body, and each of them ended in three long, curved claws.

"Don't worry," Rimi said as Abel backed slightly away. "His claws are only for hanging in trees. All he eats are leaves." Rimi cooed gently to the sloth, then set it on the ground. It immediately began its slow crawl toward Bibi.

"I guess I'd better get moving," said Abel slyly. "Wouldn't want to miss out on my prize." He stood and, with the help of his walking stick, began his slow, painful walk back to the shiny space pod. Much to his chagrin, he was gaining on the creature, but not very fast. The head start he'd given it could make a pretty tight race. Abel pushed himself a bit more, feeling pain zap through his legs and arms, but he was determined. Finally, with about five feet to go, he passed the sloth and touched Bibi's odd, shiny surface with his hand then raised his arms in victory, but quickly pulled them down because of a new zap of pain zinging through his arms.

Damn, he thought. *I can barely do anything without hurting.*

At the same time, a wave of sleepiness swept over him, almost like he could lie down right there on the ground and fall asleep instantly. He couldn't remember ever being so exhausted, even when he'd had both his knee and elbow replaced. He felt himself falling. He leaned on the walking stick, but it didn't stop him.

Rimi, in the midst of cheering for Abel, saw what was happening and was by his side instantly. She let him collapse into her arms, then carried him over her shoulder to a hammock strung between a protrusion from Bibi's side and the sturdy limb of a tall understory tree. She carefully laid him on the hammock, then disappeared through Bibi's wall and reappeared with a pillow and a blanket that she placed over him. She did this with ease and skill, the weight of the nearly two-hundred-pound man not causing her to either fall or struggle.

When she had finished, she looked down upon his face. It appeared calm and at peace, with just a hint of the crooked smile that she liked so well cutting across it. It was hard for her at that moment not to break down into desperate sobbing, so fearful was she that, as soon as he was able, he would leave the island and never come back, and once again she would be utterly alone in this world, with only her animals and the woman from the shore to keep her company. And these days, she could not even go see that person more than once or twice every few months because of how dangerous it was.

Her thoughts raced back through the last few days, how he'd come to her shore alone and unafraid, with no gun drawn or rifle ready to shoot. She remembered how he'd hacked a trail for himself through the meadow grass, and when he'd first seen La Catedral Verde, he had been awed just like she had been so many years ago. When he'd first seen her bodyguards, he had not panicked and run nor pulled out a gun to shoot. He had bravely ascended the volcano mountain, and when met by her sentries, he'd not shot at them either. He'd explored the caves where the evil people had been allowed to die and had not flinched nor desecrated their remains. She'd laughed when her monkey friends had toyed with his rope for crossing her river, and how he'd restrained himself from shooting them, then admired his toughness and tenacity as he'd climbed log over log and finally come to her clearing where he'd once again shown great respect. She'd been enraged the next day when he'd come with a long rifle, ascended the volcano again, and begun shooting, but was surprised and impressed when he'd deliberately avoided hurting any animals. If there was ever someone more suited to living life with her on her island, she had not seen them—not in over a hundred years—and who knew if she'd even be alive for another hundred years, or even a hundred days to find another.

Rimi took some deep breaths, closed her eyes, and calmed her mind, as the woman on shore had once told her to do when she was afraid. She was a strong and resourceful woman, she told herself, and she could survive anything. She could never convince anyone to stay on her island and be her companion by desperately clinging to them and begging them not to go. A person must be free and allowed to make their own choices. She was not of this world, and anyone who would be her companion would have to be able to deal with many things that no one else had to deal with. It must be that person's decision to stay. It must be because they wanted to, not because they felt sorry for her in her loneliness.

She stood a little taller and smiled down at the sleeping man next to her.

"I shall win you to me, Abel," she whispered out loud. "I shall gently guide you in understanding me, and I shall listen carefully to understand you and how to help you. If you will have me, and if I decide you're worthy, I'll give you my love, and will never leave you for as long as I live, in this world or in mine. This I promise you with all my heart and mind." And then she kissed him softly on his lips. "How's that for a prize?"

Several hours later, as the sun set behind the Green Cathedral, Rimi checked on Abel once more. He was still fast asleep, as she figured he would be. She was glad, for she was bursting to be on her way. She left some instructions with Bibi, then leaped into the trees, grabbed one of her wires, and less than a minute later stood on the expansive beach that was directly across from Playa de Palma. She checked the sun. It was at just the right spot, where no one, even if they had the sharpest eyes of any human on earth and were looking straight at her, would be able to see her because of the glare. Then, with a slight but mighty leap, she rose high into the air and out across the water like a lithe human missile. A few seconds later, she plunged like an Olympic diver into the ocean less than a half mile from the beaches of the Rio Palma Inn and, a minute later, emerged from the water just north of the beach houses. As darkness closed in, she slipped lightly into the little spit of jungle behind them and found a cache of clothing wrapped in plastic buried next to a particular palm tree. A minute later, a young woman dressed in stylish summer attire emerged and walked spryly up the little road to the main building and disappeared into the lobby entrance.

18

—

I t was the sun that woke Abel the next morning as he found himself lying in the hammock where Rimi had laid him. He sat up, rubbed his eyes, and looked around to get his bearings. He could see that his bed was slung between the silvery escape pod and a substantial tree. Feeling very refreshed and pleasantly warm, he turned to get out of the hammock but ended up on his face in the dirt instead. His delicate state of physical health had reminded him, through sharp pains in both his arms and legs, that all was not well with him, regardless of how refreshed he felt, and that his body, in general, wasn't up to its usual strength.

"Shit," he grumbled to himself. He clawed at the hammock and managed to drag himself up onto his feet, but nearly fell again when the hammock swung back as he leaned against it. "Damn!" This time he steadied himself on his legs, then used the hammock as a crude railing to help him walk to the side of the escape pod where the walking stick he'd used the other day was still standing. Now, able to firmly secure his legs, he walked forward—and fell into the wall of the pod after tripping over himself—but he didn't even know because he suddenly appeared inside the pod where he righted himself and saw that there were a small table and chair set up for him in the midst of the sphere where the healing cylinder had been the day before.

"Hello, Abel," came the metallic voice of Bibi. "It's a beautiful day here on La Catedral Verde. We've got sunny skies, calm seas, and light winds from the east at just three miles per hour. Things should remain that way for pretty much all day, with highs in the mid-seventies, and, of course, the usual afternoon rains on the mountain."

"Jesus, you sound like the morning weather report on TV back when I was a kid," said Abel. And then he suddenly stopped just as he was about to sit down. "Wait a minute. I was just out there getting out of a hammock"—he pointed to the wall—"and now I'm in here—and I didn't open the door!"

He smiled the most crooked of smiles at what looked like it might be Bibi's control panel and slammed a hand down on the table.

"Ha-ha! I did it, Bibs! I walked in just like she does!"

"Technically, you fell in," replied Bibi.

"Who gives a shit? I did it, Bibs! Ha-ha! Give me five, man!" Ignoring the pain he felt, he smacked the control panel with the flat of his hand.

"I can do better than that," said Bibi, and a tentacle with a Mickey Mouse–type hand on its end suddenly extruded from the ceiling and smacked Abel's hand so hard it sent him tumbling to the floor. He laughed in spite of the pain, and Bibi laughed a very robotic-sounding laugh.

Just at that moment, Rimi appeared through the wall and gasped at Abel on the floor.

"Are you hurt? Let me help you!" She extended her hand to Abel and yanked him up so hard he fell right into her. She braced herself, and they found themselves in each other's arms next to the break-fast table.

"Well, that was a nice surprise." Abel grinned. He allowed Rimi to let him down gently into the chair. "Nope, nothing wrong. Me and

Bibs here were just celebrating a little because this morning, I did it."
He pointed at the wall. Rimi looked at it, then back at Abel, smiling.
"That's right," said Abel. "This morning, I walked through that wall."

"Actually, he fell through," echoed Bibi.

"This is very good!" replied Rimi. "Bibi's nanobots must recognize
you now. You should be able to go in and out whenever you want from
now on. Please excuse me now. I'll ask Bibi to make our breakfast."

Abel watched as Rimi stood by Bibi's control panel, punched some
things with her fingers, and then came back to sit down with him.

"Our breakfast will be formed soon. We are having a favorite of
mine: Belgian waffles with sausage and syrup. While Bibi forms the
food, I'll go out and collect some fruit for us. I'll be back very soon."

Rimi left immediately through the wall, leaving Abel to contemplate something else that seemed incomprehensible. How could a machine "form" his favorite breakfast? And how did it just happen to be
Rimi's favorite, too? The whole thing seemed a bit too coincidental,
but then again, this entire experience was so surreal that part of Abel
was sure that at some point, he was going to wake up at his beach
house and discover that everything he was experiencing now was just
a dream. Why shouldn't some beautiful jungle woman he'd just met
have a machine that "forms" breakfast and it just so happens to be
what he likes as well? She'd probably come back with mangos and
bananas, too.

Abel had never met the likes of this woman, and he suspected he
never would again, especially if her whole alien thing was actually real.
He remembered how Rimi had shared with him how lonely she was
living on an island where her only friends were animals, and there was
no one else like her anywhere. Abel was no alien, but he sure could
relate to how she felt, especially since he'd not been able to get back
into the SEALs. He'd built his life around his team. They had been his
only real family. He had hoped to find similar comradeship when he'd
joined the DEA, but things had never really jelled for him there. He'd
thought the skill set needed for the job would be far more similar to his

SEAL skill set. Being the tip of the spear in America's war on drugs was far more drudgery and far less action than being the tip of the spear for American military operations around the world. And since—well, since losing a particular someone during his third SEAL tour, he'd felt so crushed and inept in matters of the heart that he'd never even attempted such a relationship since. Now, this woman had come into his life, someone who completely entranced him, who was actually physically stronger than he was—even when he was healthy. And who should she be but someone who said she was an alien, "not of this world," giving some pretty good indications that she wasn't kidding. And, most certainly, the very person that Monti Ruiz had offered him a million dollars to kill.

Rimi suddenly appeared through Bibi's sidewall again, carrying a large bag that she put down on the table in front of Abel, then went around to the side of Bibi's control panel. From it, she produced two plates, each filled with a large Belgian waffle covered in butter and syrup and a couple of sausage links on the side. She grabbed knives and forks from a nearby cabinet and brought them to the table.

"What would you like to drink?" she asked.

Bemused, Abel answered, "I don't know. What are you serving?"

"Bibi can make several drinks I've discovered Earth humans seem to enjoy. For the morning meal, Bibi can make coffee, orange juice, milk, or water. Which would you like?"

"Well, in that case, I'll have some coffee. Maybe I'll be able to stay awake better today," replied Abel.

Bibi piped up. "He should have orange juice and milk as well, to build up his strength."

"Jesus, Bibs, you sound like my mother," said Abel.

"I was not aware that my voice sounded female to you. Perhaps—"

Abel looked at Rimi. "Just get me the milk and OJ along with the coffee and tell Bibs his voice is fine."

As she went to retrieve the drinks, he looked in the bag she'd now put under the table. Mangos and bananas. He smiled.

"So, I guess Bibi whipped this stuff all up from . . . ?" he questioned.

Rimi gave him a guarded look.

"Right," said Abel. "I probably don't want to know the answer to that. Anything from anything, like you said. But where'd he get the pattern for this stuff? We've got machines called 3D printers that do stuff somewhat like Bibi, but they need a pattern or a sample of what they're going to duplicate. There are no waffle houses or restaurants anywhere out here."

Rimi finished chewing a bite, then said, "There are times, a few times, when I've gone to the town on the shore to see what the Earth humans are like and perhaps make a friend. I've not been very success-ful in making friends—I'm not one of them, and they can tell just by looking at me—but I have learned to enjoy a number of your foods. I've brought samples of many foods and preparations back here for Bibi to make."

"How'd you get to the mainland? I haven't seen any boats around here."

"That's because you were not meant to find them," answered Rimi. "Perhaps I will show you one day."

Sometime later, Rimi led Abel to the edge of the field of downed tree trunks near the clearing around Bibi. They both sat on a log and faced the barren area.

"Bibi destroyed all these trees when we landed. He has no landing pods or wheels like a regular cruiser would have. It was a very rough landing. I was not very old and I was very scared. All I could think was, 'Where is my mother?' and 'Where is our cruiser?' I wandered the island for many days, looking everyplace for them but could not find anything. During this time, I met some of the animals. They were sus-picious of me at first, but I learned their languages, and they learned to be my friends. They even taught their young ones to be my friends. Now, today, I've called them all here, or at least the ones that can come, so I can tell them that you are my friend, and they should treat you as their friend as well."

Abel looked up and was startled to see that the logs for almost a hundred yards before them were covered with all kinds of animals—the pumas, the ocelots, several types of monkeys, coatis, snakes, birds, and many different types of butterflies. He'd never seen anything like it.

Rimi called out using the strange song that Abel had heard his first day on the island, and all the animals stopped whatever they were doing and listened. After that, they began moving toward him.

"What's going on?" Abel nervously asked.

"They're just coming to greet you," said Rimi. "Don't be afraid. They do not respect fear."

Abel and Rimi sat on the log, and for the next hour, animals of all kinds came to Abel, flew in, landed on him, nuzzled him. Abel felt like Noah welcoming animals to the ark.

Later on, after Abel had taken another nap in the hammock, Rimi asked him to climb onto her back.

"You're kidding, right?" quipped Abel.

"No," she said with a shy smile. "I wanted to take you to meet the crocodiles who stay near the mouth of our little river. You're still too weak to walk that far, but I could take you on my back, and we could fly along the wires."

"You can't carry me," replied Abel. "You barely weigh what, a hundred and twenty pounds—maybe—and I weigh almost two hundred. You'd never even get me off the ground."

"I guess you don't remember when I caught you from falling and put you in your hammock the night before," Rimi said with a twinkle in her eye.

"No way," replied Abel. "I bet you had one of Bibs's tentacles grab me and—ow!" Rimi had kicked Abel's feet out from under him, caught him as he fell forward, and slung him over her shoulder like a sack of potatoes.

"Now, don't fall," instructed Rimi. "I'm going to help you so you can turn around, put your legs around my waist, and drape your arms over my shoulders."

She boosted Abel up until he was sure he was going to fall.

"Whoa!" he shouted, but Rimi remained calm.

"Grab my shoulders with your arms, and I'll bend over so you can get your legs around my waist," she said.

Abel grunted and cried out several times, sure he'd fall. The two looked like a couple of acrobats trying to tie each other in knots for a moment, but suddenly Rimi stood straight, piggybacking Abel. Her feet and legs had never wavered or moved.

"Jesus!" panted Abel. "How'd you get so freaking strong?"

Rimi smiled. "I have no idea. I think we're just made this way in my world. Now hold on tight."

Rimi suddenly leaped into the air, and she and Abel flew well up into the canopy of the rainforest. Rimi grabbed on to a couple of nearly invisible wires with her gloved hands and steadied both her and Abel.

"Hang on tight, and duck behind me when we go through the trees."

With that, Rimi swung her body backward, then thrust it forward, and when she did, the two were sent sailing through the trees along the wispy, barely visible cables. Abel had no idea how they didn't break. They were just a little thicker than spider webbing, but that was one reason why they flew so fast. For the first time since being a SEAL, he felt the exhilaration of flying through the air like he used to when parachuting or on HALO missions.

"Woo-hoo!" he hollered. "Geronimo!"

He ducked behind Rimi as they clattered through trees. They came to one of the nest-type constructions that Abel had seen earlier in the trees, and there they stood for just a moment while Rimi grabbed a new set of wires, and then they were off again. Abel figured they hadn't stopped for more than ten seconds. More sailing through the canopy, until, quite suddenly, he could see the trees thinning and the beach where the crocs lay.

"I'll soon be jumping to the ground," Rimi yelled back to him. "Keep your feet up, your head close to mine, and just hang on. I will do all the work."

Seconds later, Rimi launched herself from the wires, and she and Abel flew through the air like a human cannonball. They sailed through an opening in the trees and gradually descended, the beach coming up fast. And then, with a slight thud, they were down, Rimi making a perfect Olympic long-jumper-style landing in the sand, finishing on her rear, with Abel's rear coming in right behind hers.

Abel leaped up. "Whoa!" he yelled. "That's the coolest thing I've done since I jumped out of airplanes, girl!" he exclaimed to Rimi. His smile nearly cracked his face. "You have got to get me some of those gloves! When I get better, I'm gonna be doing that all day long!"

Rimi just sat and smiled. She was so glad she'd made Abel happy that she nearly cried. Her heart soared within her. She had shown him a new thing, and he'd loved it. Maybe, just maybe—she dared not think of it. Enjoy the moment, her friend had always said. And so she did. She jumped up and laughed with Abel, then allowed him to pick her up and give her a huge hug before he climbed onto her back again while she ran around like his personal mount—and dumped him into the river. When one of the crocs started to move toward him, she spoke sharply to it, and it backed away. Then she introduced the crocodiles to him before they finally wound down and sat on the beach and enjoyed the afternoon sun.

Rimi asked, "So I told you how I came to this island. How about you? So few people have come here, and so many have been bad, especially lately. Why did you come here? You are not bad. You came with guns, but all you shot was the sand, and the one you pointed at me only shot when you fell over. You came for several days in a row, every day. Why did you do this? Are you looking for something?"

Abel stared out at the lowering sun and was silent for a time. Rimi felt bad, thinking that she may have embarrassed him somehow, and she was about to apologize when he finally spoke.

"I came here looking for someone," he began slowly, "or maybe *something*. I came to the town and met with their head man. His name's Monti."

"I have seen this Monti," said Rimi. "He sits on the beach and sells things and talks to people."

"That's him," said Abel. "He told me about some evil presence or evil person or something that lives here. He said no one that's come to the island has ever come back."

"Of course they haven't. My friends and I killed them all when they started killing my friends and trying to capture me. They came with guns and pointed them at us and shot their projectiles at us. My pumas killed some in the night. Then a few weeks later, more came, and we did the same to them. Then many more came. They all had guns, and they all pointed them at us, so we attacked them. We chased them up the volcano and would kill them if they tried to come down. None of them escaped. We either killed them when they came down or left them to starve on the mountain. That was years ago, and nobody has come since. So why did you decide to come even when nobody else would?" Rimi calmed herself and hoped that she had not become too emotional or said too much. Maybe Abel would now think she was the evil one that the fat man Monti had talked about and be afraid of her also. Maybe he'd try to kill her. But he had not been afraid of her, or even of the animals. He must be different—he simply must!

Why did I even bring this up? she screamed to herself.

"I was curious," said Abel finally. "Before I came to the village on the mainland, I was a warrior, a soldier, so I wasn't afraid. I don't believe in 'evil ones' or 'evil presences' or anything like that. I was fascinated with this island from the first time I set eyes on it, and I wondered who or what was there. I wanted to explore it, so when I finished with my business in the town, that man Monti let me use a boat, and so I came out here to see what I could find."

Then Abel described to Rimi everything he'd seen and heard on his four journeys to the island. He talked about the first time he'd listened to her strange song, seen nests in the trees, and found the remains of a dead human, and how the second time he'd explored the volcano, met the ocelots, and found caves filled with bats and many more human bones. He also told her about leaving his monocular that day near the entrance to the Green Cathedral, and how the next day he'd found a curious, holographic imitation of it there.

"That was Bibi's idea," said Rimi with a laugh. "I brought it to him, and he decided to improve it rather than just duplicate it."

Abel continued, speaking of his fight with the monkeys over his river-crossing wire, and Rimi laughed.

"That was the funniest thing! Those three are so silly. They were actually just playing with you, but I finally had to tell them to stop, or you were never going to be able to cross the river."

"I could have just swum across, but I was glad that I didn't have to get wet—or kill some crocodile that might try and eat me in the middle of the river."

Rimi turned away. "I would have stopped them first if that had happened."

"I bet you would have," replied Abel. After getting to know Rimi, he was quite confident that she'd spied on virtually everything he did on the island, but given what she said about all the others who had come and disappeared, who could blame her?

Abel went on to tell of his first glimpses of Bibi after crossing the dead log field, and how odd and otherworldly it had looked to him at first sight, and finally the fourth day, when he'd found the strange instrument on the ground where he'd left his pen, how he'd taken his sniper rifle up the volcano and tested its range, and then come back to the Green Cathedral entrance, where he'd met a lovely, alien-looking woman who had both entranced and unnerved him, how he'd tripped as he'd fallen, and fired his gun.

"And so, after all that, Mr. Warrior Soldier Abel, what is it that you think you have found here on my island?" asked Rimi. "Have you found this 'evil presence' that causes whoever comes to disappear and never return?"

Abel was silent for a moment, then looked into Rimi's enchanting green eyes.

"Yeah, I think I have. The people that came here with bad intentions found a badass warrior princess and her animal allies, and so they never returned. I, on the other hand"—Abel looked down as if in thought or embarrassed, then looked back up, his voice quiet and his eyes meeting hers—"I found the most amazing, exciting, powerful, beautiful, fun person I've ever known, and I may just never return either."

Rimi looked into Abel's gentle blue eyes and saw a man who meant every word he'd said. She threw her arms around him and held him tight to her.

"You are a kind and caring man, Abel," she whispered in his ear, "and you may stay on our island for as long as you wish."

They kissed, a long, gentle kiss that seemed to last much longer than it did.

Then they both smiled at each other.

"Damn, that was amazing. I haven't done that for so long I can't believe I remember how," said Abel, even as his eyes now appeared tired and droopy.

Rimi's heart soared, but she could tell he was rapidly coming to the point of exhaustion as he had the day before.

"I think we'd better get back," he said. His words were slow and a bit slurred.

She stooped and he mounted her back again, but this time, when she stood, she felt a slight buckle in her legs.

No! she thought. *Not now!*

She carried Abel into the trees and, with considerable effort this time, leaped up to the wires in the canopy and swung them back to Bibi. When she dropped to the ground with Abel, he nearly crushed her with his weight, but she didn't allow him to fall. Carefully, and on unsteady legs, she took him to his hammock and laid him in it. He seemed to be already asleep.

At that point, she collapsed to her knees then crawled to Bibi and, with some effort, went through his wall. Abel, who was nearly asleep, watched it all with great interest before his eyes could no longer stay open and his mind could no longer remain conscious.

Inside, a tentacle with a delicate clutching instrument on its end extruded from Bibi's side, snaked into a cupboard alongside the sphere, and pulled out a small jar. Another tentacle with an even more delicate grasping instrument on its end reached into the darkened jar and pulled out a fairly large capsule.

The tentacle then floated back to Rimi, who was on her hands and knees on the floor, barely able to hold herself up. Rimi took the pill, then a glass of water another tentacle held, and gulped down the pill. She dragged herself up to a chair set against the wall of the sphere, completely spent, but now with more color and relaxation on her face.

"How many more do I have, Bibi?" she asked.

"Just three," said Bibi. "Perhaps this man Abel can help us find what we need."

"Perhaps," replied Rimi. "Perhaps he can."

And then she tipped the chair back, and it became a bed. She grabbed a blanket and pillow from a drawer underneath it and then was sound asleep.

19

—

The next morning, with both Abel and Rimi now refreshed and re-invigorated, Abel felt like flying through the trees again, except this time he wanted to try to do at least a little on his own. Bibi produced some gloves for him just like Rimi's, only larger, and the two set off down a path Rimi had made that went to one of her lookout nests she used to watch for boats coming from the mainland. As they walked, Abel asked her about what he'd seen the night before, how weak she had suddenly gotten.

Rimi was silent for a moment, not sure what to say. Could she possibly tell him the truth without him deciding to leave rather than stay forever as he'd said the night before? And yet she knew she was not a good liar at all. Indeed, a warrior like Abel would see right through whatever she might make up, or if she just ignored his question.

"Seems like you're having a little problem. Hard to talk about the idea you might be dying?" asked Abel.

Rimi responded defiantly. "I'm not dying! Look at me. I'm perfectly strong and healthy!"

She jumped high in the air, so high that she disappeared through the canopy of the jungle before descending and landing as lightly as a feather back on the path with Abel.

"Great!" replied Abel. "You're fresh from a great night's sleep, got a good breakfast in you, and probably took some medicine or had Bibs do something to you that got you going again. So how long's it going to be before you crash and burn again like you did last night, because I don't want it to be when we're out in the middle of nowhere and I'm not strong enough to get you back to Bibs, or you're carrying me around like you were yesterday, and we both end up crashing and getting really hurt."

Rimi walked along, stubbornly refusing to look at Abel. Finally, Abel stopped her.

"Look," he said. "If we're going to be a team and spend time together, we've got to be honest about these kinds of things. We can't just pretend we're fine when we're not, because we'll be depending on each other, and one of us can't hide something that might put the other person at risk."

Rimi still wouldn't look up.

"I told you that I was a soldier—a warrior. Well, I was, but not all alone. I was part of a team of other warriors. We each had our own jobs and our own roles to play, and we each had to depend on the others to do their roles and come through when we needed them. And if one of them knew they couldn't do their job, or they couldn't do it like they normally could, their job was to tell us so we could have someone else take up the slack. That's just how teams work. We've got to be honest!"

Rimi looked up. "So, we're a team, then?"

"I sure hope so!" he cried. *Damn*, he thought.

He hated conversations like this. Now he would have to spill some beans, too, just to get her to tell him what was up. "I've been looking for a team ever since I couldn't stay with my last one. The only person I ever really respected since then got himself killed, and the other one I'll probably never see again. But you're this awesome, amazing, totally out-of-this-world cool person, and a woman, which makes it about six thousand times better, and goddammit, we better be a team." He paced angrily back and forth. "There's nobody like you anywhere, and I'm the goddamn luckiest person in the whole world to know you, so tell me what the hell's wrong with you so we can figure out how to fix it!"

He stared down at her with a look that he suddenly thought must look awfully angry, but Rimi just walked up to him and put her arms around him. Sniffles in his ear told him she was crying.

"Aw, jeez, baby, it's okay. I'm not angry or anything—"

Rimi talked into his ear. "I'm dying."

Abel loosened his hold on her and stared directly into those amazing green eyes, which now looked very sad.

Rimi looked straight back at him. "You're right. There is a substance, like a vitamin, I guess you'd say, Xilinium, that my body needs and is very common on my planet, but it is nowhere to be found on this one. Because of this, my body naturally stores this vitamin, enough for years if necessary, but not enough for how long I have been here. My body ran out long ago. That's why we always carry large supplies with us on intergalactic trips—in case our natural stores run out. Bibi also had a store of this vitamin in him, and for many years, I've been slowly using that up. I've extended my supply by only using them after I'm nearly to the point of complete exhaustion, but we always knew that at some point—well, now I have only three pills left."

Abel stood, stunned. "How long will that give you?"

"Two weeks, maybe three," Rimi said simply.

Abel was so stunned at the thought of losing Rimi so soon after finally finding her that one part of his mind went numb, and another was simply angry, raging against the unfairness of it all. But it was his SEAL mindset that cancelled out all the others—having been ingrained in him for twelve wonderful, harrowing years—and suddenly, quite surprisingly, he realized that he now had a trigger, and it was time to pull it.

"So what's your plan?" he asked.

Rimi stood, confused. "Plan for what?"

"Not dying, dammit. You and Bibs knew this time would come. You must have thought of something besides just waiting for the bitter end."

Rimi now nodded but almost couldn't bring herself to say it, since it sounded so impossible to her. After all, she and Bibi had been working on it for years with no result.

"We need to find where my parents' cruiser crashed," she said. "There were enough pills on it to keep an entire crew alive for many years. If we could find where it is, maybe there would be some left. We've searched and searched around here for years and found nothing, and we have no idea where else to look or how to get there even if I knew. We've had no one who could offer us any real help."

"Well, you do now," said Abel. "We'll talk to Bibs when we get back, but right now, I want to enjoy life with my new friend instead of talking about dying. Let's do some flying instead."

Rimi smiled. She and Abel ran down the jungle path to the lookout post in the trees. She leaped up to it with him, and for the rest of the day, they flew from one end of the island to the other, stopping at various points, eating some snacks they'd brought along, and enjoying each other's friendship as neither had for longer than they could remember.

It was at their last stop, on the side of the volcano, that Rimi asked Abel about his former team. "You said that your team was a team of warriors. Who did you fight for?"

"My country. It's a lot farther north from here, the United States of America," said Abel.

Rimi nodded with recognition. "Bibi has told me of this country, and my friend also has. They say that it was once the greatest country on this planet, but now not so much. Is that why you left your team?"

"Hell, no!" Abel roared but instantly calmed himself. She had no idea what she was saying. "I mean, no. Leaving my team had nothing to do with my country or how great or not great it was. I loved the guys on my team, and I thought what we did for our country was right, at least most of the time. You don't have a choice, though. You do what the commanders say, even if they're just some idiots don't know what they're talking about. Warriors follow orders. That's how it always is."

"So were you and your team ordered to kill people?" asked Rimi.

"Sure. That's kind of what soldiers do. We killed the enemy before they came to our country and tried to kill our people."

"We killed our enemies before they could kill us," said Rimi. "It would have been nice if we could have done it before they came to the island. Who was your enemy?"

"Whoever the leaders told us they were. We went all over the world—the planet, you know. Most of the time, I had no idea who I was killing, and only sometimes why. But we didn't think about that. We just went, did our job, watched out for each other, and made sure that none of us got killed." Abel talked robotically. Every job had its downside, and for him, it was killing people—the enemy—whom he didn't know and sometimes didn't even understand. He was proud that he served his country, but it sucked that he was such a proficient long-range killer.

"So why did you leave them?" Rimi asked.

"I got shot—with bullets, you know, projectiles. They tore up my knee and my elbow," said Abel. Rimi examined his elbow and ran her finger along the scar that could still be seen from his surgery. "We have doctors that can fix our bodies if they get damaged."

"Like Bibi?" asked Rimi.

"Not nearly as good as Bibi, but they try," replied Abel. "They put my elbow and my knee back together, but they don't work the same. To be on my team, you've got to be really strong, and even though I worked and worked, I wasn't strong enough anymore. So I had to leave."

"But you are strong! This was not fair," complained Rimi.

"No, it was," said Abel. "I wouldn't have been able to do my job for the team well enough. It's like we talked about. I'd be too weak, and someone would have to pick up the slack. They can't keep doing that all the time, not for the long haul, anyway. It's better for them just to find a new team member."

"So did you go back to your country with your parents or your girlfriend?" asked Rimi. It was a nagging question that she had. Why was this fine man so far from home and not with his wife and children or his parents? Had they cast him out also? Or was he, for all he said about honesty, not being honest with her?

"No," said Abel flatly. "My parents got killed in a car crash while I was away with my team, and the only real girlfriend I ever had dumped me while I was gone—that means she left me, broke things off, whatever—so there was no family or anything to go back to. I got a job with this police force called the DEA. They look for criminals—bad guys, you know—in other countries so they won't hurt people in our country. That's what brought me here: working for them. But there's no team, and I get bored, and it doesn't pay as much. It's just not the same as being with my team."

Rimi cuddled close to Abel. "You'll never be too weak to be on my team. I'm glad you're not on that team anymore."

Abel held Rimi close and looked out over the beautiful island with its grand Green Cathedral rainforest. He never thought he'd say it, but all things considered, he was glad that he wasn't on a SEAL team anymore too.

Then he remembered something.

"Hey, Rimi, get up. Come with me. I want to show you something."

She did as he asked, and he led her to the small cave where he'd cached his M107 sniper rifle. He took it out of hiding and showed it to her.

"This is a weapon like I used to use on my team," he told her. Rimi was amazed at its size, and at how big its projectiles were. "And here's the really cool thing," he said. He set the rifle down outside the cave, and he asked Rimi to lie down with him on her stomach. She did.

Then he showed her how to look through the sniper scope. She was amazed at all she could see.

"It's just like the thing you left here when you first came, only it makes things seem even closer," she exclaimed. "I can even see Fat Monti in his chair!"

She smiled over at Abel, but he had a more serious look on his face.

"And you could shoot him from here, too," he said. Rimi looked at him, startled. "Or anyone else over there, or anywhere in between."

"Why would I want to do that?" she asked, confused.

"You wouldn't if it were just him and the people on the beach," replied Abel. "But if an enemy came from over there, someone that wanted to hurt us here, we could, if we had to, kill them before they came here."

"Just like your team would do for your country," she said, again amazed. "Do you think we'll ever have to use it?"

"I hope not, but I don't know. If we have to, we damn sure will."

They got up, and Abel took the M107 and returned it to its hiding place.

"I'm starting to get tired again," he said. "Let's go home. Tomorrow we'll ask Bibi about helping us find where your parents' cruiser crashed."

Later, after enjoying a wonderful steak dinner that Bibi produced from something in his secret storage of ooze, Abel and Rimi went out to the hammock to say their good-nights. Rimi wanted to sleep with him there, and Abel wanted her to as well but knew he was still not strong enough to enjoy that kind of activity, at least not for another day or two. Rimi promised him a night he'd never forget once he was back up to snuff, and then, after a very long, deep kiss goodnight, she retired to her own sleeping chair inside of Bibi.

Tired as Abel was, though, he found his mind not cooperating with the idea of going to sleep. Too many things were swimming around in it. Some were like peaceful schools of fish lazily drifting about when he thought of Rimi and his newfound relationship with her. Others were much more ominous, like sharks or barracuda lurking around, ready to devour the peaceful fish with much blacker thoughts. He was keenly aware, despite the blissful times he was having with Rimi, that it had been at least five days now since he had sailed his boat back to Monti's dock and reported on his progress in eliminating the "evil presence" on the island. And that, along with the three days he'd come to the island before meeting Rimi, was putting him dangerously close to the time Monti had said the job must be accomplished because his investors would be arriving. After hearing Rimi talk of how heavily armed and violent Monti's previous visitors to the island had been, he was becoming increasingly convinced that his hunch that he'd hinted at when he'd called Lopez—that Monti was preparing to use the island for nefarious purposes, like providing a refueling stop for Colombian cartel smugglers and not turning it into a tourist attraction—was in fact true. If that were so, he and Rimi could be defending the Green Cathedral against any number of vicious Colombians as well as Monti and Paco in a mere matter of days! Couple that with Rimi's impending health crisis, and there was plenty enough to keep Abel's head spinning.

One thing he'd learned in the SEALs, though, was that when in a tight situation where things seem to be spinning out of control, you look for an opportunity to take control. Never let the circumstances determine your actions. Never act in a reactionary way. Seize the initiative, take charge, and control your own destiny. And that's what they'd do at first light the next morning. Bibi would search his data files all night for anything that could help them find where Rimi's parents had crashed. It couldn't be that far away—probably within a few hours by boat or car—judging from how close the ship was to the surface when Rimi, inside Bibi, had been ejected. Once that was determined, and a plan made, Abel would take the boat back to Monti's dock, give him some explanation for his long absence, and assess how dangerous the situation might have become. He also thought that he needed to pay Faviola a visit. He had to do something with his things, and more importantly, the snarky innkeeper was probably the only one in town who would give him a straight answer if anything untoward had gone on in his absence.

With his mind now satisfied that he had a plan, and that it was a good one, Abel finally relaxed, and he was asleep an instant after that.

20

—

Fat Monti got up from his chair about the same time Abel and Rimi started for their home in Bibi's clearing, but instead of walking up to his house as was his usual practice, he turned the other way, walked along the beach, crossed the Rio Palma on the bridge, and headed to the front office of the Rio Palma Inn.

When he stepped in, Faviola was there, as he expected, checking in a new guest and his family. Faviola gave him the evil eye as she continued her work, and Monti smiled and waved, then sat in one of the plush upholstered chairs in the lobby. By the look of these guests, their clothes and luggage, they were tourists, probably from America, and of considerable means.

Ah, Favi, he thought. *Where would I be without your American Automobile Association three-diamond Best Western motel with rooms and beach houses just steps from the Pacific Ocean and an easy walk to every shop and soda in Playa de Palma? Let us hope you will continue to be a cooperative influence even as changes come to the community. It will serve you well if you do—and could be fatal if you don't, but you've always been a reasonable person, regardless of your petulant attitude from time to time.*

The guests finished registration, and a porter arrived to take them and their things to one of the beach houses.

"Welcome to Playa de Palma!" Monti said to them as they left. "Enjoy your stay." The man, tall and brawny, and his slim, very fit wife smiled graciously as their two children, probably teenagers, gave Monti a look that usually meant "What a perv" in the current index of the "If Looks Could Kill" guide to the facial expressions of high-school-age American youth.

Monti paid them no mind. He approached Faviola's front desk as if he were an old friend stopping by for a drink.

"What brings you to this end of your domain at this time of the evening? You should be at home eating tacos with Maria and Lucia."

"I wonder if we could speak in private somewhere?" asked Monti.

Faviola looked up from her work and all around the empty lobby. "Certainly. What is on your mind?"

Monti sighed, annoyed by her obstinance. "Perhaps somewhere where there is no elevator that could open at any moment, or someone might wander in asking where the nearest ice machine is?"

"I'm here by myself tonight. I can't leave the desk. What is this all about?"

Monti harrumphed. It was not unusual for Faviola to be teasingly difficult, but this had the feel of insolence, like she couldn't be bothered to accommodate his request. She knew how that would make him feel, and she was clearly enjoying it. Monti was not used to being treated with rudeness in his town, and he would not let this slight go undealt with for long. He stepped to the end of the front desk and walked around it, blocking Faviola in.

"Perhaps in your office behind the desk, then?" he said more forcefully.

Faviola gave him another evil eye, shoved some papers into a file drawer, and beckoned Monti to come. As he passed the check-in station, Monti saw the call bell that was typically used only late at night to summon the desk person from doing laundry or restocking the breakfast room and put it on top of the registration desk.

"There," he said condescendingly. "Now you won't miss anyone."

They both went into the little back office. It was cramped, with Faviola's desk and file cabinets taking up most of the space. A small coffee maker sat on top of one of the cabinets, and a water cooler and a couple of other chairs were crammed into corners. Faviola sat behind her desk and Monti in one of the chairs.

"So what is this all about?" snapped Faviola directly. "Please be quick. I have much to do."

"So snippy tonight, mi amor," cooed Monti.

"It's been a long day, and one of my clerks is sick, so it's going to be a long night as well. I apologize. What can I do for you?"

"Muchas gracias, señora," replied Monti. "I'll come right to the point. I have not seen our beach house guest in over three days now. I'm becoming quite concerned. Has he come back to his beach house over the past few days?"

"I cannot tell you that, one way or another, and you know that, mi amigo," she replied. "My guests deserve their privacy. All I can tell you is that he is still a guest of the motel."

"A guest is not a guest if he never uses his room," countered Monti.

Faviola bristled. "I do not know if he uses his house on the beach or not, and it is none of my business one way or another. He has not checked out of the motel. Therefore, he is still a guest, and that is all I know."

"Forgive me, Favi, but I was only concerned for his safety. As you know, he was a guest of some importance, and it would be bad for all of us if something . . . untoward were to happen to him."

Faviola's eyes blazed. Despite all his money had done for the community, Monti was still a snake at heart and full of shit to boot.

"If he is so important, and you wouldn't want anything 'untoward' to happen to him, why in the name of the Madre did you send him to the Isla del Diablo? No one you've ever sent to that accursed place has ever returned. Why should he be any different?"

"Where did you hear this from, that I sent him to del Diablo?" snapped Monti.

"Do you think I am blind and stupid? I didn't hear it from anywhere! He told me that you had sent him up the coast, which is probably what you told him to say, but I would watch his boat go up the coast, then, much later, go toward the *isla* from far out in the ocean. For three days he did that, and then on the fourth, he did the same thing, but whether he has come back or not, I do not know." She shook her head at Monti in disbelief. "How many people have you sent to that island with how many guns? And now you send this man and wonder where he is? Why he has not returned?"

"I would like to inspect his room," commanded Monti as he rose from his chair.

"Sit your ass back down in that chair!" Faviola ordered. "You go near that beach house, and I'll call the national police in Jacó after I shoot out your kneecaps." She drew a small semiautomatic pistol from her drawer.

Monti held up his hands to calm her. "There, there, now, mi amor. No need for violence. I am just concerned is all."

"Be concerned at your own house," Faviola said. "Get out. Go home where you belong."

"There is one other thing," Monti said, holding his ground. Faviola sighed and rolled her eyes. "I have another guest coming in the day after tomorrow, a very, very important guest, for all of us here. He is an investor, someone who would like to help us develop another tourist attraction . . . on the island. He will need your very best room. This could potentially mean millions of dollars for our community. We must all put our best foot forward. I assume that I am making myself clear?" Monti gave Faviola a hard look.

She looked down and sighed again. "Fine. What is the name of this very, very important guest so I can make his reservation?"

"His name is Vicente Galvan. He is a businessman from Cartagena, in Colombia." He narrowed his eyes at Faviola as he saw shock and disbelief wash away her former defiance. "Good evening, mi amor," he said, excusing himself, and he left.

Faviola leaped up from her desk and charged out after him.

"You're going to trash everything we have here for the sake of those snakes and your bank account?" she yelled as he crossed the lobby to the door. He opened it and left without a word. "You fucking *Mexicano!*" she yelled after him.

21

—

Abel lay awake in his hammock, staring at the glorious ceiling of the grand Green Cathedral that sprawled everywhere his eyes could see. For the first time, he homed in on various places in the canopy and the understory, noting colorful parrots and toucans that fluttered about, a group of capuchin monkeys cleaning each other on the limb of a giant tree, and a jaguar that was barely visible due to its camouflaging lounging on another limb directly above the camp. Abel wondered if it was just visiting or if it was actually on guard, one of Rimi's specially trained bodyguards. The air was crisp, and the light filtering through the trees flashed in dramatic rays, piercing the canopy that made it look like a band of angelic beings approaching from somewhere. The peacefulness and beauty of it all made him not want to move from the hammock, which swayed oh so gently in the morning breeze.

Suddenly, it all disappeared, and before he knew it, Abel was lying flat on his face on the ground listening to quiet giggles behind him. He flopped back over to see the only thing more beautiful to him than the rainforest, Rimi, chuckling nearby.

"I decided it was time for you to awaken." She laughed. "You looked far too comfortable just lying there staring at the canopy."

"And why's that?" asked Abel as he dragged himself up from the ground, the sleeping clothes that Bibi had made him a bit disheveled.

"Because I cannot join you." She laughed.

"Guess Bibi maybe needs to make us a bigger hammock," said Abel. He reached out to give Rimi a hug when she suddenly disappeared and was now standing on the other side of the hammock from him.

"Playing hard to get, huh?" He smiled and leaped at her over the hammock, but again, she somehow moved to where she was now directly behind him.

"How the hell do you do that?" Abel asked as Rimi now invisibly moved two or three more times so fast it seemed as if she'd teleported.

"I don't know." Rimi laughed as she finally came to Abel and gave him a warm hug and a passionate kiss. "It is just something we can do. Everyone from my world can do it to some extent. It just depends on how much talent you have and how much you work at it." She kissed him again, and he responded back. "Come inside and eat," she said. "Then you can talk to Bibi about the crash of my parents' cruiser."

A half hour later, Abel and Rimi stood before a large video screen that Bibi had unveiled over a part of the sphere's wall. "I have found what you asked for," said Bibi in his mellowed metallic voice. "It is what one of my external auto cameras shot as we descended to this island."

Everyone watched as the giant cruiser, out of control and descending like a missile at an unbelievable speed, zipped into the range of the camera, which then tracked it over its final few seconds. It clipped some tall trees and the volcanic summit of a rocky island not far from the mainland shore, then plunged straight into the sea just a few hundred yards away, breaking up and sinking instantly after sending a sizable tsunami toward the coast, where the water lifted up and rushed inland for a considerable distance. Fortunately, it was only palm trees and shrubbery that suffered. There was no beach settlement anywhere in the view. Everyone was silent for a moment, and Abel held Rimi close. He stroked her hair gently.

"I don't suppose anyone would have survived that," she said quietly. Abel gave her another squeeze.

"Run that again, and stop it when the ship crosses the island," Abel told Bibi. Bibi did. Abel studied the picture carefully. "I think I know this island," he said at last. Rimi looked hopefully up at him. "It's called Isla Heredia, and it's not far from Jacó, just a little farther up the coast. I went there with a couple DEA agents from the Jacó post one day while I was staying there. It used to be used by drug smugglers, and they go out there to check it out every so often to make sure no one's opened it up for business again. It looked just like that picture, and I remember the high point looked like there had been a landslide at one time, and some of the trees along this high ridge here looked smaller than the rest. There's a nice hotel near the beach there now, and surfing and scuba supply outfits. We could just drive up, rent some gear and a boat, and go check it out. It's not any farther from shore than this island is from Playa de Palma."

"So we shall go then," said Rimi excitedly. "Get whatever things you need, and then we shall fly to the entrance to our Cathedral and go in your boat."

"Actually, I'm not sure that would be best. If I don't take the boat back to Playa de Palma and report to Fat Monti, he'll probably send people out here looking for me, and we won't want that at all, especially if they get here when we're not here," warned Abel. Rimi looked disappointed. "I told you why I was sent here."

"To get rid of the evil presence here," finished Rimi bitterly.

"I don't know, but I've got a hunch that he wants to do something with this island, and it's not good. He said he wants to make it into a place for tourists to come, which might not be too bad, but just something about how he said it . . . I think he might be wanting to set up a place where bad men—really bad men—can stop in and rest. They'd come mostly on boats from the south."

"I don't understand," said Rimi. "Why here? It seems like they could rest much better in the town. There's even a pier there."

"They'd be criminals, Rimi," answered Abel. "If they ever set foot on shore, they'd have both the Costa Rican police and the DEA after them. If they use the island, they can sneak their boats in at night, rest, relax, refuel, and then leave without anyone from the town seeing them."

"So Fat Monti wants to bring criminals here? I don't understand. They could ruin his town."

"That's what I've got to find out before we go up to Isla Heredia. I don't know anything for a fact. But I can check it out today when I go back, then tomorrow we could go up there," explained Abel.

Rimi got a pouty look. "So now that you're well, the first thing you do is go back to the mainland?"

"I'm sorry," said Abel. "I don't have a choice. I've got to find out what's going on, and like I said, if I don't go back, Monti will send more bad men here looking for me."

"Will you spend the night there?" asked Rimi.

"I'll have to," replied Abel. "If I came back, it would make Monti suspicious. He might even take his boat back."

"Where will you stay?" asked Rimi.

"It's one of the beach houses at that big motel where the Rio Palma meets the ocean—the closest one to the beach and the farthest one away from the main motel. I can see the island from there plain as day, all the way until sunset, so don't do anything funny. I'll be checking up on you." Abel smiled, hoping she understood it was a joke.

"No funny stuff now. I don't want to have to shoot anyone!" chimed in Bibi. Both Abel and Rimi rolled their eyes and smiled.

"Well, Mr. No Funny Stuff," said Rimi, "it just so happens that I can see that beach house all the way from the east beach on this island, so no funny stuff yourself."

Abel grabbed his backpack, threw his weapons and other things into it, slung it over his shoulder, and found his hat, and then he and Rimi stepped through Bibi's wall. They donned their special gloves.

Abel climbed on Rimi's back, and she leaped with him up into the nest above. They both found wires to fly on and *zinged* out of sight.

Moments later, they stood on the beach together where Abel's rubber boat lay just as it had for days now.

"I'll tell Fat Monti that I still have to clean a few things up out here tomorrow, and when I come, we'll hide you down below in the boat and bring you back. Then we'll take my Jeep up and check out that island." He gave her a huge hug and another kiss. "Stay alive until I get back," he told her. "Remember, we're a team now." One more kiss and he was off to the rubber raft, and moments later, his small trawler's motor fired up, and Rimi waved as he sailed away, feeling an unfamiliar ache as if someone were pulling on her heart inside her chest.

ISLA HEREDIA

22

—

Abel was still well offshore when he knew that Monti Ruiz had seen him. That was because Fat Monti did what he usually only did at the end of the day just before sunset—he got out of his chair—and started to walk down the pier. He stood at its end, and when Abel finally pulled the old trawler up alongside it, Monti grabbed ropes from its side along with Abel and moored it securely. Once that was done, he gave Abel a big bear hug and clapped him on the back.

"I knew it, by the Madre!" he cried. "Our hero has returned to us, as no one has for years and years!"

"Better be careful," said Abel under his breath. "Someone might think I was out on the island rather than down the coast."

"Ah, you are right. Of course, my friend," he confessed, "but you can't imagine how concerned I was. After all, it is tomorrow night that my investors arrive, and the next day, they will tour the 'facility.' I am assuming that it is now safe and that no one going over there will be disappearing into thin air?"

The two began walking toward Monti's throne room. "I'm afraid no one ever disappeared into thin air over there," said Abel. "Their bones are all over the place, plus old weapons, ammo, food containers, shreds of clothes, you name it. That's what I've got to do tomorrow—make sure everything's cleaned up, burned, whatever." The two sat down under Monti's big umbrella in a couple of comfy beach chairs. "I can sure see why they used to call that place the Green Cathedral. The jungle's breathtaking. The clouds that form on the volcano keep things cool. The stream's amazing as long as you don't mess with the crocs. It's an awesome place to set up some kind of eco-tourist stuff. I wouldn't mess too much with it, though. Just wouldn't want to see someone fuck up the beauty."

Monti gave Abel a strange look as he went on about the island. "There must truly be something spooky about the place," he said finally. "You look different, like you're glowing or something. And I've never heard you call anything beautiful or amazing or awesome before. It's almost like you're in love or something."

Abel silently kicked himself in the ass as he continued. "Well, I am, I guess—with the island. It's just like paradise. I've never seen a place like it. You really are going to make it into a nature attraction, right, not Disneyland or whatever? To see that place destroyed like that would just about break my heart. I mean, it's one thing to look at it, but a whole other thing to actually be there. That's why I didn't come back here overnight. It's a whole other world at night. When the moon's full, it shines out there like a big light bulb in the sky, and—"

"Yes, yes." Monti sighed. "I will see what I can do, but it will be almost all up to my investors. Now, I must know," and here he lowered his voice considerably, "what was the evil presence on the island that caused people to be terrified and killed all my men so many years ago?"

Abel gazed away for a moment, took a deep breath, and then said, "It was a girl."

"Madre de Dios, you are in love!" moaned Monti.

"Hell if I am!" answered Abel. "She was some wild child, as feral as a lone wolf. Could talk to the animals and all that shit, moved like a cat, hissed, and talked funny. Must have been some kid that got washed up there after some shipwreck somewhere and didn't have any way to get to the mainland. Her fingernails and toenails were all like claws, and she may have even had bigger canines than normal people in her jaw."

"How old would you say?" asked Monti. He was fascinated.

"Don't know," said Abel. "Could be teens, twenties, maybe even thirty. Hell if I know. She was like chasing a ghost to track down, but I finally did. I had to kill her, and when I did, a bunch of big cats attacked me, jaguars, ocelots, even a couple of black pumas. They got the drop on me, but I finally got them all. That's another reason I had to stay out there so long—I couldn't walk for a couple days." He showed Monti his scarred legs.

Monti was amazed. "What about other animals? Is the place safe now?"

"Pretty much," said Abel. "The tamer ones like sloths and coatis and the monkeys and all the birds are still there. And there may be a big cat or two. I'll check again tomorrow when I go out there. Oh, and thanks a ton for getting me that sniper rifle. I bet I killed off every croc in the whole place, and all from such a long range that I never got anywhere near them. Reminded me of target practice when I was with the SEALs."

"This all sounds very exciting, and you cannot imagine how relieved I am that you are back and have given such a full report. Tomorrow night, I shall welcome my investor, and the next day, we will visit the island for his evaluation. You may come if you wish or stay here in town. I will not transfer your fee until after I have been to the island with the investor. If I like what I see, and we all feel safe, I will send you your one million dollars regardless of what the investor says."

"No good," said Abel dryly. Monti did a double take, as if no one had ever disagreed with him on a deal before (which they hadn't). "I've just spent I don't know how many days out there groveling around in the jungle, hacking my way through grass taller than I am, tracking down some monkey child that knew every inch of that island like the back of her hand, been attacked by multiple big cats, *and* made it back safely, and I get nothing at all unless you like it? I want half now, and I'll take the other half when you've been out there."

Monti laughed out loud. "Who do you think I am, some fool like the people that run the sodas here? With that kind of money, you'd skip town and say to hell with the rest, even if I was killed by a crocodile as soon as I stepped onshore. I can give you twenty-five thousand now, that is all."

Now Abel laughed. "That's not enough to even put a down payment on a house. What if I missed a croc, and you do die out there? I get nothing."

"Because you didn't make it safe," retorted Monti.

"And maybe that croc wasn't even there the day before!" boomed Abel. "I get where you're coming from, but I've got to have at least two hundred thousand upfront today. That's twenty percent. I'd say that's pretty generous of me."

"One hundred fifty thousand, and I give it to you in cash tomorrow morning," said Monti. "That's the best I can do."

Abel sighed. "It's a deal. I'll meet you here—when there are plenty of people around."

Monti frowned. "I don't flash cash around like that in front of others."

"You won't have to," said Abel. "Bring it in a duffel bag. I'll check out what's inside, and we'll all go home happy."

They rose and shook hands. Monti said, "And if I like what I see two days from now, I'll transfer the rest to whatever account you wish, but if I don't—"

"Let's not be negative," said Abel. "Two days from now, we'll both be very happy men." He picked up his backpack and slung it over his shoulder. "And now I'm off for a nice double cheeseburger and milkshake at Ron and Elaine's, and then I'll head over to the inn and make sure Faviola hasn't given away my beach house."

Monti laughed. "I can make no guarantee of that!"

23

—

After stuffing himself with cheeseburgers and a giant milkshake at Ron and Elaine's All-American Diner and shooting the shit with them for an hour or so, Abel walked into the midmorning sunshine and headed for what he hoped was still his motel. No offense to Bibs, but the cheeseburgers he made from whatever he made them from were nothing compared to the real thing at Ron and Elaine's. And the milkshake? Well, Bibs had never really gotten the knack for making those.

Abel felt quite good about how things had gone so far in his visit back to Playa de Palma. His main goal with Monti had been achieved with comparative ease. When he picked up that duffel bag in the evening, he and Rimi should have enough cash to suit whatever they might need moneywise for quite some time, and who knows, maybe Bibs could figure out how to duplicate tens, twenties, and hundreds by the time they ran out. The rest of the money he honestly didn't care about, which shocked him somewhat when he realized it as he strode down the road to the bridge over the Rio Palma. Being with Rimi and living in the Green Cathedral must really have been changing him if he didn't care about whether he closed on a million-dollar job or not. The only use for it, as he could see now, would be to possibly buy the island from the town (if that's who it belonged to) and just tell Monti to keep his money. It would be nice if things could be so simple.

After talking with Monti, Abel was much less calmed by his references to his investor and what he envisioned for the island. He didn't seem particularly interested in the island itself and what was there, just that it was safe and that whoever or whatever had killed his men years ago was now eliminated. As before, Abel had a very wary feeling about what Monti was up to, and he hoped that when he talked with Faviola, she might be able to tell him more.

When he came to the bridge over the Rio Palma, he checked around the mouth of the stream, and sure enough, there was the toothless crocodile lurking lazily beneath the surface where the stream water and the saltwater met, his snout and his eyes making little protrusions in the otherwise smooth surface. Abel smiled, crossed the parking area, and went into the lobby. A young man, the same one who had met him when he'd first come to the inn, was standing at the front desk, straightening displays of brochures and dusting the counter. Because it was midmorning, there was no one in the lobby.

"Hi," said Abel. "My name's Caleb Forrest. I'm renting the guesthouse closest to the beach, but I've been out of town for a few days unexpectedly. I'm hoping that it's still in my name."

"Yes, Mr. Forrest. I remember you. I can help you with that, sir," said the young man in perfect English. "Can I ask you, did you check out before you left?"

"No. That's what I mean," said Abel. "My absence was unexpected, so I didn't get a chance to check out."

"Well, then, we should still find it in your name. Let's just see now . . ." The young man fiddled with the front desk computer. "Ah, here it is! Yes, Señor Forrest, the first beach house is still assigned to you. Do you have your key card?"

"Actually, probably not. Can you make a new one for me?"

"Of course," said the young man.

As he went about his work, Abel asked, "So where's Faviola today, taking the day off?"

The young man laughed as he handed Abel his new key card. "Ha! That is funny, señor! Señora Faviola misses about as many days of work as there are rainy days during high season! She is out making her morning rounds. She's usually picking up trash on the beach by now. If you're going to your beach house, you'll probably see her."

"Well, I'll just do that then . . ." Abel squinted at the young man's smart-looking name badge, "Javier. That's right. I remember now. I'll mention how sharp you are behind the desk, too."

"Gracias, Señor Forrest. Enjoy your beach house, and if anything has been disturbed, please let me know."

Abel shoved open the door and headed down the little road through the palms to his beach house, impressed even more by Faviola and the tight ship she ran at her inn.

Sharp woman, he thought. *And sly as a snake, too.*

When Abel got to his beach house, he was amazed to find that nothing had been disturbed. The bed had been made up just as always during the days he'd been there. The bathroom had been cleaned, and the towels changed. Most importantly, every one of Abel's pictures was still push-pinned to the wall, exactly where he'd left them. Looking them over, he was disappointed that, for all the time he'd spent with Rimi and Bibi, he had no pictures of either of them, or of the myriad activities they'd done, things they'd seen, or anything.

Just as he was about to chastise himself for this appalling oversight, his more practical side reminded him of some crucial things. Though he felt safe, especially now, at the inn with Faviola in charge, he was not necessarily among friends in Playa de Palma. Ron and Elaine had as much as told him that when they'd spilled the beans about how they and most everybody else knew of Monti's "business" and understood their roles in it. And Monti, for all his obsequious behavior toward him because of his DEA connections, was no more his friend than the serpent had been to Adam and Eve. Anything Abel might have that showed who the wild child really was and that she was very much alive, as well as Bibi and all the rest of what the Green Cathedral was about, could not only be used against him but could put Rimi and her entire way of life at risk. Perhaps some subconscious instinct he'd developed after so many years living a clandestine life had kept him unwittingly in check. He heaved a sigh of relief after realizing what such perfectly normal carelessness could have cost him and Rimi.

Suddenly, he felt a presence in the room, and, a voice interrupted his thoughts.

"So, the prodigal scalawag returns at last!"

Faviola stood, smiling a sly grin, on his front doorstep. She had a ridiculously floppy sun hat on and wore flip-flops rather than her spiky high heels, which made her hip-hugging business-suit skirt and camisole-like shell look utterly incongruous.

Abel gave her one of his crooked grins. "I'm guessing the suit is a corporate thing, right? The manager of the property always has to be professionally dressed, even when she's doing garbage-picking duty on the property's beach?"

"You never know when the big bosses might show up," Faviola replied.

Abel tossed a few things out of his backpack—sans the weapons— and began to put them away in drawers and the bathroom.

"Well, if they showed up now, you wouldn't have to worry about the front desk. Your man Javier's one consummate professional. Got any future plans for him?"

"He's going to university right now. He'll return as soon as high season is over. He has two more years, and then he'll be my full-time assistant manager. That's good because I'm not getting any younger. One day, he hopes to buy out the franchise from the bosses in San José," explained Faviola.

"He sure seems sharp enough," said Abel as he continued to rummage around.

"That he is, mi amigo, and he'll learn even more in the university, but, of course, I'll also have to educate him a lot as well." Her smile disappeared as she and Abel exchanged knowing glances. "Perhaps we can take a walk on the beach." Abel nodded, and they left out the front door.

"I'm glad we're out here," said Abel. "I think Monti may have—"

"Of course he has," interrupted Faviola as the two walked along the line where sand and surf met. Both were barefoot. "He has bugged the rooms of just about any important guest that's ever come here. He still has to come to me and inform me who he's listening to and why, but there's not much else I can do about it. He pays my bosses well." Faviola paused for a moment, then continued. "I need to let you know of two things," she continued. "The first is that I know you've been on the island this whole time."

Abel gave her a puzzled look.

"I have a friend—more than a friend—who lives in La Catedral Verde," said Faviola. "About twenty-five years ago, when I had just taken over the motel, I started seeing her walking around the town as if she were lost. I watched her many times. She would go in and out of the shops and the sodas. Sometimes, she would eat something, sometimes buy something. And then she'd be gone for a long time, then suddenly show up again. No one really talked to her, and she never approached anyone to do anything more than get directions or find out how much something cost. She was always dressed like she'd just come from the jungle, and her green eyes seemed so big. I always knew when she was back because others would talk that the 'green-eyed girl' was in town once again.

"Once when I was going through town during high season, I saw her being teased by some high school bullies who were home from school. They were especially making fun of the blood that was dried all over her thighs. She didn't understand, but I could see that she was becoming outraged, and I was afraid of what might happen, so I scolded those kids and took her back here to the inn. The inn was much smaller then. I had inherited it from my father when he and Mama died." She stepped delicately around a hermit crab that skittered along the sand as she continued.

"When we came to the inn, I helped her with the blood. Of course, it was her time of the month, and apparently, she knew nothing about how to take care of herself. I showed her what to do and gave her some products. We had dinner together at my home, which used to be on the same property as the inn, and then she said that she had to go home. I asked her where that was, and she didn't say, only that she stayed with someone named Bibi, who would be worried that she hadn't come back."

"Son of a bitch," said Abel with surprise. "You're Rimi's friend that she comes to see in town. She talks about you a lot but never says what your name is or where exactly you are. I sort of thought she was making the whole thing up."

Faviola turned, and for the first time, Abel saw her for who she really was instead of her brash facade. Her smile glowed, her eyes danced despite their wetness, and she looked as though she would burst with both pride and affection.

"From that day on, Rimi has come to see me many times and on many occasions. We've bought clothes so that when she comes, she will blend in rather than stick out, and we have learned so many things together. At first, she hid from me who she really was, but over time, as she trusted me more, she told me who Bibi was and where she lived and so many other amazing things. She is not from this world, you know. And she and her kind age very slowly here. Her first memory is of seeing a little Costa Rican boy and his white-skinned father on her island shortly after she landed there. I think she saw my grandfather Juan when he was just a little boy. She says that the boy she saw was with a lighter-skinned man. My great-grandfather was a white American who had worked on the railroads to Puerto Limón long ago."

"How long ago?" asked Abel, intrigued.

"Around the turn of the century, the twentieth century," replied Faviola.

Abel was incredulous. "What the—so how old is she?" he exclaimed.

"Realistically, not any more or less than you, I suppose, but as to years on Earth, she is well over one hundred."

Abel just shook his head. "The more I find out about that woman—"

"She is a most unique treasure," said Faviola.

She paused for a moment, then resumed her narrative. "I was horrified when Fat Monti started to talk about making her home a tourist attraction, but then he'd send people there, and they'd never return, and later he sent men with guns, but they never returned either. When she finally revisited me after all those incidents, she asked me if I wanted to know what happened to them. I told her no. I didn't want to think of my Rimi as being—you know . . ."

"She definitely knows how to take care of herself," said Abel.

"She is so much more to me than my friend, mi amigo," continued Faviola. "She is *mija*, like the daughter I never had before my poor Alfonso died. I've invited her many times to come live with me, but she always politely refuses, even though she talks so much about how lonely she is. She says that her friends the animals are better companions than most of the people she's met. How can I disagree?

"But then," said Faviola, this time with her more familiar snarky tone, "one day early this week she came to me and told me of this amazing man who had come to her island, and how he was not like the other men who had come. On and on she went. She couldn't stop talking, and her face glowed like moonlight. Imagine what I thought when she told me that the man's name was Abel-er-Caleb Forrest?"

"That I truly can't imagine," said Abel through his crooked smile.

Faviola smiled like the cat who'd caught the canary. "I just told her to take good care of you—she said that you were injured—that I knew you from the inn, and that I thought that, even though you are a scalawag, you just might be the perfect companion for her."

"Aw, shit, Favi, you got to be kidding. You got me weeping over here."

"Actually, I'm not," replied Faviola, a twinkle in her eye, "but if you ever hurt her, I'll kneecap you with my *pistola* just like I almost did to Fat Monti the other night."

"What was he up to?" asked Abel.

"That's the other news I have for you, and it is much more serious. The investor that is coming tomorrow night to look over the island is a Colombian. I am sure that he is no ordinary investor. I felt like shooting that fat idiot right there in my office. If he makes a deal with the Colombians, you know what will happen with this place! You are with the DEA! They will never let him continue to operate. They will take him out and the Colombians as well, and the whole town will be caught in the cross fire, not to mention what it would mean for you and Rimi. What will you do? They will be coming to your island the day after tomorrow!"

Abel stood with the warm Pacific lapping at his bare feet, frozen both in mind and body. This was terrible news, though not totally unexpected. He had never actually thought Monti's investors were legitimate, but the fact that they were Colombians made it potentially much worse for him personally.

"Did he give you a name or anything?" he asked.

"Sí," said Faviola, "a man from Cartagena, Vicente Galvan. He'll probably be staying in the beach house right next to yours."

"Shit!" Abel cried, then instantly calmed himself, his SEAL training once again coming to his aid. "This is all really nasty stuff, Favi, but we've got a bigger fish to fry first. Rimi's dying . . ."

"What?"

"Some nutrient that her body needs that we don't have on this— well, this planet. She's running out of it. She's only got a couple weeks left. She knows that the ship her parents were in has a lot more of it, and we think we know where the wreck is."

"Where is that?"

"Off an island I've been to just north of Jacó. We're going there to-morrow morning in the Jeep. Once we get there and hopefully get the stuff, we'll get back here and figure out something about the next day. Do you know anyone with a dock up the coast?" asked Abel.

"Yes. A friend of mine runs a scuba school just a few miles from here. They have a boat and a small pier."

"God, you're a lifesaver. Maybe we can borrow some gear from him, too. We'll have to do some diving," replied Abel. He gave Faviola a big, heartfelt hug.

"I'll call him tonight and make sure all is ready," she said. "Abel—that is your name, correct? What if you don't find anything there?"

Abel looked into her worried eyes and smiled. "We're not crossing that bridge yet, and neither should you. We're going to go there, get what we need, and then probably end up kicking some Colombian asses somehow."

"So you know this Galvan?"

"To put it mildly, yeah," replied Abel. "Let's just say he's the reason you've got to call me Caleb Forrest when we're around literally anyone else, even though my name's really Abel."

"I'm confused," said Faviola.

"It's a long story."

"Perhaps later we can talk more."

Minutes later, as Faviola hurried back to the main building, Abel plopped down on his bed and lay back on a pile of pillows, staring at the ocean. He couldn't imagine anything worse than Don Vicente Galvan climbing back like some unkillable cockroach into his life at this very moment. The gods did not seem to be smiling, and depending on how things went, they could all be weeping very soon as well. But hard times bring out the best in men—and women. That's what the SEAL attitude was. A mountain is there to either be climbed over, bored through, detoured around, tunneled under, or blown up, and it was the SEAL's job to figure out which ones to try, and then execute that plan.

Abel's gaze strayed to where the island and its volcano stood off the coast like a sentinel. That was home to him now, and the one person he now lived for called it her home as well. They were now his trigger, and tomorrow he'd pull it as they dived for the wreck, and the next day, he'd pull it again and again and again, as many times as needed. He would not die during these days, and neither would Rimi, for he simply would not allow either event to happen.

As the sun set behind the volcano, Rimi, with her small knife sheathed by her side, stood on the eastern beach of the Green Cathedral. She pulled the weapon out. It was unimpressively small, but its pulsating blue glow gave it an exotic and dangerous look.

"I sense that I may be needing you soon," she whispered to it. "I know you won't let me down."

Replacing it in its sheath, she stared across at the mainland, its beach, its shops and pier, the river mouth, and the inn. She had told Bibi she'd be gone for a day or two, that she and Abel were going to find the wrecked spaceship and the pills she needed to stay alive. Bibi had questioned her. Hadn't Abel said he'd return to get her the next day, and then they'd go? Yes, she had replied, but she had a surprise for Abel, so she would have to leave tonight.

She smiled now, then looked to the sky and leaped high out over the water into the sunset just as she'd done so many times before when she went to see her dear friend. But this time, she was going to see a more special friend, the man she was going to spend the rest of her life with, whether that was many years or only a couple of weeks.

Abel was dozing in his bed after having dinner with Faviola at the inn's restaurant. There, for two hours, he'd poured out the whole story of the dizzying and much misguided last few weeks of his life. As he'd talked of his many foolish actions as well as all the second chances he'd been given by people like Victor Garza and Colonel Ochoa, he was appalled anew at his foolishness and arrogance. But then, amid repeating the same sins, he'd been hired to rid the evil presence from Isla del Diablo, and that had led him to Rimi and, finally, the complete change that occurred. He now not only appreciated the beauty around him both in Rimi and her island home but also felt an acute sense of both gratitude and shame—gratitude that he'd been spared time and again from the deadly clutches of Don Vicente Galvan and finally found things to live for so much more valuable than money, and shame that he had neglected to thank any of those who had helped him along the way, not his commander Victor Garza, the Panamanian Colonel Ochoa, or even the Uber driver who had gotten him out of Cartagena. He was determined to do right by them all finally, to help Rimi find what she needed to live, and then do whatever was necessary to protect Playa de Palma from whatever Don Vicente Galvan and Fat Monti were cooking up, and free himself and Rimi from the specter of this man forever.

All these things Faviola listened to without question or comment. Then, she spoke.

"When I first heard of you, I thought you must be some arrogant ass like so many of Monti's guests, and that is why I brought the family down that you were displacing, so you would have to face them. You did not seem so arrogant after that, and you even had a sense of humor. But then you did something that I found very extraordinary. You asked for my opinion about what Monti had offered you. Why is this so extraordinary, you ask? Simply this: Regardless of how much progress Costa Rica has made in comparison to other Latin countries, there is one thing that is true of any of them. That is that no man cares what a woman thinks, except maybe if his shirt and pants match or silly things like that. I know you are not Latino, but to this woman, who has spent almost her whole life in this little town, it is still quite shocking to be asked such a thing from a man. And not only did you ask, but you listened to what I had to say. It was at that time that I knew you were different. And that was confirmed a few days later when you didn't come back to the motel. Instead, mija came as I told you, glowing like a full moon and carrying on and on about you, even though you were injured. You can learn a great deal about an arrogant ass when they are injured. One is if they stay an arrogant ass, or if they allow themselves to be changed by their experience. From all I could tell, you were the second type, and I was glad, because mija was truly happy, and I had come to enjoy you as well." Faviola sat back and looked Abel in the eye.

"So here is what you'll get from me in this present situation. It will take great courage from all of us to put a stop to this evil man who seeks vengeance against you and our fat friend who wants to invite him here. But before that is dealt with, you must find what Rimi needs to continue to live. I will call my friend with the pier and the scuba gear as I said, and I will drive my Jeep from here to there so that you and Rimi can stay on your boat once you leave her home and not have to come back. Rimi can drive the Jeep if you need, but you'll feel like you're going to die the whole time she does. It will also help me cover for you here. Your Jeep will be here where it should be if you're out on the island as they think.

"And I leave the rest to you, mi amigo, you and mija. There are no two people anywhere in the world more capable than you two of ridding this town of the cancer that has infected it ever since that fat man showed up here from Mexico.

"Now go—shoo! You have a long day coming up, and you'll need your rest. And I have to close down the front desk." The two stood and embraced. "I'm glad that mija has found a man of honor and courage," said Faviola, and then she left after asking the maître d' to put the meal on her tab.

All this gave Abel great comfort and encouragement as he went back to his beach house, threw off his clothes, and plopped onto the bed, his mind in a place of peace and clarity that he'd seldom been in save when staying with Rimi on La Catedral Verde.

And so, as he was dozing off in the darkness, it wasn't with alarm that he heard a splash or two interrupt the steady rhythm of the waves that ebbed and flowed from the beach for a moment, and then saw a figure coming toward his beach house out of the sunset, a woman who moved with grace and complete silence. She seemed to float up the stairs to his deck, and then through his open door. It was only then that Abel could discern that the woman was Rimi. She slipped her finger down her front, loosening her garment, and it fell to the floor.

"I've come to give you a gift, my dear friend," she said softly, then glided onto his bed like a soothing, seductive spirit.

Abel felt an electric-like spark of excitement tempered by an overwhelming feeling of peace and gratitude. As Rimi touched him, and he touched her, time seemed to disappear, and the two wrapped themselves around each other and enjoyed the pure ecstasy that comes when two lovers finally become one.

24

—

When Abel and Rimi woke up with the sun the next morning in the same bed for the first time, having an early breakfast wasn't the first thing on their minds. But after considerable time, and with considerable effort, they finally managed to pull themselves apart and got ready to meet the day. Abel dressed in his camo and boots, as if ready to head back to the island for a long day of work, while Rimi found her cache of "Earth clothes" near the tree behind Abel's beach house and dressed in a cute shorts-and-top combo with flip-flops, as if preparing for a day at the beach. Then Abel packed his backpack with work gear and made sure his weapons and ammo were all there. He saw Rimi slip a small knife that seemed to glow faintly into one of her pockets.

"Hey, what's that—er—thing?" asked Abel, catching himself before he said words like "knife" and "island." *Damn,* he thought. *This place is bugged, remember?* He regained his composure quickly. "Just something you like to carry around, huh?"

Rimi gave him a knowing look as she folded her jungle outfit and put it into one of Abel's drawers. "Only if I may have need of it," she said quietly.

Abel gave Rimi a curious look. "Seems pretty harmless," he said as he finished packing.

Rimi shot him a glance like he'd never seen from her before as if sending him a warning. "I assure you, it is anything but harmless."

Abel stood silent for a moment, then shrugged. "Okay. Just curious. Let's get going."

Rimi smiled widely and gave him a little kiss. Then they left and stopped by the front desk and surprised Faviola, who was working in the back while Javier handled guests who were checking out.

"You both look so perfect together, though the choice of clothes is odd," she said. "Go over to the breakfast room and have some waffles or a bowl of gallo pinto, and I'll be right there."

"Actually, we're headed to Ron and Elaine's for breakfast. I told them that sometime I'd stop in for breakfast, and I figured that since I had a date to go with me, we'd go together," said Abel. He and Rimi smiled at each other, but Faviola frowned.

"And just how are you going to explain this to locals who have seen this woman come and go for many years?" she asked sternly.

"I'll just say that she came into town last night and we hit it off, so we decided to make a day of it today. It's not like anyone really knows her except that they see her with you a lot when she's here, so it all makes sense. And I'm just a tall, dark, handsome single guy that anyone would swoon over, so—"

"Ack!" spat Faviola. "You both act like *pollos con las cabezas cortadas*!" she grumbled. "Go! Have your fresh eggs and sausage with hash browns or whatever they call it."

"I'm having pancakes." Rimi smiled.

"Well, at least you don't have to worry about getting fat. But please, mijo y mija, you must be careful. This will draw attention to you that you don't need on a day like today. Don't let anyone take your picture. Don't talk to Monti any longer than is necessary," implored Faviola.

"Don't worry, it's breakfast, then to the boat, then we do everything as planned," said Abel.

The two strolled into the All-American Diner, and Abel was quickly hit with a taste of the reality Faviola had tried to get them to understand. The place was packed, and everybody they passed as they squeezed around tables on their way to a booth off in a corner did a double take when they saw Rimi, then another to check out the man she was with.

Maybe this wasn't such a good idea after all, he thought as they sat down.

His fears evaporated as he watched Rimi's face when she first tried some pancakes slathered with butter and maple syrup. Her green eyes became even bigger. She groaned with gastric delight and cried out, "This is soooo good!"

She worked her fork like a very efficient robot whose sole purpose was devouring pancakes. Abel, enjoying his diced ham and scrambled eggs with hash browns, thought she might stuff herself so much she'd puke. She finished when he was barely half done and immediately asked for more.

"Not a chance, girl," he said. "Let's see if you can hold that without it all coming up, or going out the other way, then maybe some other day we'll do more."

Rimi pouted playfully, but finally just smiled and laughed and tried to master how to use her fork to scoop up every bit of leftover crumbs and syrup she could.

"Well, look who's in town," came the voice of Ron over Abel's shoulder. "I see you've met Faviola's daughter, eh, Caleb?"

Rimi instantly gave Abel an astonished look, which he quickly shook his head no to.

"Yeah, she just came in last night for a while—and we hit it off right away, so we decided to make a day of it," Abel said, sounding perfectly natural and smiling.

"Well, isn't that nice." Ron grinned. "How're the pancakes?"

"Oh, so, so good! Your wife is a magnificent cook!" gushed Rimi.

"Well, I'll just be sure to let her know." Ron smiled again and moved along to talk to the folks at the table behind them.

Abel gave Rimi an astonished, admiring look.

"I can be such a perfect Earth human when I wish." She grinned mischievously.

Later on, as they strolled down the road toward the pier, they could each feel more looks coming their way. It made Abel feel troubled, but Rimi played it up so much and so well, both in English and Spanish, that pretty soon no one was paying attention anymore.

Faviola's done wonders with this woman, Abel thought. *She acts just like any sassy Latin American lady who's scored with the new guy in town.*

He bet anything that Faviola had been the same way years ago.

Arriving at the pier, Abel told Rimi to take his backpack and head down to the boat while he spoke with Monti, who was already holding court under his pavilion.

"Ah, my friend! It is good to see you again today. And I see that you're ready to go back down the coast and finish your job," he gushed.

"That I am. Just here to pick up my little down payment like we talked about," Abel replied.

"Ah, you'll find it in a bag behind my chair. Perhaps you'd like to inspect it once you get out to where you're going."

"Sounds like a plan," replied Abel. He found the small duffel bag, took a peek inside, saw bundles of money, and quickly zipped it back up. He would most definitely count it once he was on the island.

"Who is the *chiquita* you're taking with you?" Monti asked with a snarky grin.

"Oh, Faviola's daughter. She came into town last night, and we hit it off right away, so we decided to make a day of it. She'll lie on the beach while I do the grunt work in the jungle."

"And I bet you take an extended break for lunch and a siesta." Monti laughed. "Just make sure that all is ready for tomorrow. My investor has confirmed that he will be arriving sometime later today."

"Don't worry. I don't want to miss my payday!" Abel replied.

After the trawler was well on its way, Rimi asked, "Why is it that the man in the diner called you Caleb rather than Abel? I remember one time after Bibi fixed your wounds you said your name was Abel-er-Caleb Forrest, and then later you told me just to call you Abel. I don't understand this mystery."

Abel sighed and tried his best to explain, in an abbreviated form, all that he'd recounted to Faviola the night before. It was difficult without getting into too many details, and several times he begged Rimi to try to understand until some later time when they could talk about it more. He told her that what was most important to know for now was that, because of things that had happened weeks ago in Cartagena, a very kind colonel in Panama had made it seem that he, Abel, had been killed there while trying to escape, and that now, for everyone else besides her and Faviola, his name was Caleb Forrest and not Abel, and they must remember that when talking to others.

"There's something else, too," said Abel as the boat rounded the volcano and headed for the little bay formed by the sandbar. "That man, the one from Cartagena who wanted me dead, he's coming to Playa de Palma sometime this evening. Fat Monti's making a deal with him to bring lots of evil people to the Green Cathedral and use it to help them do bad things. Nothing will be the same. That's why I came out here in the first place. Monti wanted me to find you—the evil presence on the island—and kill you, and your animals, as well, at least the ones that could kill a person. That bag over there"—he pointed to the duffel bag he'd gotten from Monti—"it's full of money, part of what Monti's paying me to get rid of you. I get the rest when he comes here tomorrow and finds you're not here anymore."

Rimi looked confused. "But when you came here, you were kind to the animals. You had your gun, but you didn't use it. You could have shot me a hundred different times, and you never did. And I am not leaving the island by tomorrow—we are coming back tonight, and staying for the rest of our lives, aren't we?"

The boat was nearing the shore now, and Abel cut the motor and tossed out the anchor. Then he sat down by Rimi. She looked into his eyes with her green ones that seemed even bigger now, pleading for him to reassure her somehow.

"That's exactly what we're going to do," said Abel as he looked straight into those eyes. "We're going to find your parents' cruiser, get you what you need to survive, and then we're coming back here to live forever. The only reason I took that money from Monti this morning is that we might need it from time to time. I don't give a hoot about the rest of it. You're worth so much more than that to me. I guess what I'm saying is that now, things are more complicated. We'll have to fight for this place like you've never had to before—"

"But you are here now, a great soldier, and my friends and I are still here as well, and—"

"There's one other thing," interrupted Abel. "If the man that's coming to see Fat Monti, the one that wanted me dead, should see me somehow, recognize me, and figure out that I'm not dead like he thinks—"

"He'll have you killed immediately," said Rimi soberly. After a moment of silence, she looked up at Abel and smiled. "So, we will make sure that that does not happen. We are a team, remember? We will work together. We will find the pills I need to survive, and then, together, we will stop these bad men." She stood. "Come, my amazing companion. Tell me what I should do here to help you, and then we shall be off to do what we must do today."

Abel rose as well. "Okay. You take that bag with the money in it back to Bibi and leave it there. I'll be burying some bones that aren't far from the shore here. The rest I don't care about—they're not going to put up anything here anyway. Then we'll go."

They both boarded the little rubber boat and motored onto the beach. Rimi grabbed the duffel and dashed for the meadow path and the entrance to the Green Cathedral. Suddenly, Abel called out, "Oh, and ask Bibi to check out the money inside and see if he can figure out how to make more of it!"

Rimi smiled a sly grin. "*Mi madre* has told me that you're a—how she says—scalawag!"

Abel shrugged and grinned back. She disappeared, and he shouldered a spade and headed into the meadow grass to dig up and bury the skeleton he had fallen over on his first-ever visit to the Isla del Diablo just a couple of weeks ago, a period that now seemed like a lifetime ago to him. *Actually, it was a lifetime ago*, he decided with a smile.

Rimi came to the grand entrance to the Green Cathedral at the end of the meadow path. She leaped into the nest directly above it, the place from where she'd seen this man Abel the first time as he had gazed at the beauty around him, and she, wary as always of Earth humans, had called her friends to come and watch with her. She remembered how different he'd seemed. His only weapons had been the two machetes he'd used to cut a path through the grass from the beach to the rainforest, and yet he'd been unafraid, even when one of her pumas had shown up and stared down at him from the trees. He was definitely attractive, much more than anyone she had seen on the mainland during her occasional visits to her adoptive mother. How far they had each come in such a short time. From perfect strangers suspicious of each other to the closest of friends, and now lovers as well. It was a miracle, just what her mother had told her about when she and her father had met. Now, today, she might possibly see her mother and father again. Yes, they would not be alive, but regardless, she could share, in some fashion with them, that she had found her miracle, too.

Grabbing her gloves from where she'd left them, she took one more look at Abel, now fully caught up in digging at the edge of the tall grass near her, and *zinged* along her cables to Bibi's small clearing. She walked through with the duffel of money and tossed it down.

"Live from Studio One-A in Rockefeller Plaza, this is *Today*, with Bibi and Rimi," greeted Bibi.

"Bibi, hello. I have some instructions for you, and then I must go again. First, this bag is full of money. Abel would like you to identify all of its types and find a way to make more of it. When we return, you can tell us what you've come up with. The next thing is that I will soon be leaving with Abel again to try and find the Xilinium supplies that were on my mother and father's space cruiser. We're going to where Abel thinks their crash site is, which is not far from here. We hope that we'll be successful.

"Also, I need the bracelets we talked about last night. Are they ready yet?"

"They are here, exactly as you ordered," said Bibi. Even as he was speaking, two silvery-looking bracelets appeared from the shiny metal of the side of the sphere where Rimi and Abel usually entered. Each was inlaid with several sparkling crystals of different colors, and one clear crystal in the center.

Rimi allowed each to fall into her open hand as they slowly extruded. Finally, she was holding both of them. She gazed at them with wonder and a smile.

"Oh, Bibi, you've done it! They're just like Father's and Mother's!"

"So all is well with the Earth human, Abel?"

"All is very, very well, but things are about to become very dangerous, Bibi. You must be ready to defend yourself if necessary in the next day or two. You must not melt away, however, because we may need your healing webs and cocoon."

"Is there a chance that something could be fatal to you or Abel?" said Bibi in his usual flat tone.

"Yes, I'm afraid that this is a possibility," said Rimi, much more soberly.

"I shall prepare accordingly," chimed Bibi.

"Thank you, my friend. I must go with Abel now to find my mother and father. We shall return as soon as we can. In the meantime, expect visitors, and if it seems like they are going to be harmful, don't hesitate. Exterminate them, as we did with the other hostile Earth people before."

Rimi walked through Bibi's wall, the mysterious bracelets now in the pockets of her shorts, leaped to the nest in the trees, and sailed off back toward the meadow.

25

—

It was a couple of hours later when Abel and Rimi sat in Faviola's Jeep on a deserted beach just north of Jacó and gazed out at the rocky island they'd seen in Bibi's external surveillance footage from the day of his crash over a century ago. Abel could see more now why the owner of the scuba rental facility at the nearby motel about a mile up the beach had warned them about diving there.

"We've been asking the government to close down that area for years," he'd said. "There was a seismic landslide that came off that island years ago, and it threw up all sorts of debris and boulders all over the beach and under the water, too. It's totally unstable. We get injuries every year from people messing around down there on the rocks and slipping and falling when they shift, and divers who get cut on the underwater rocks or get attacked by jellyfish. And shark attacks happen a lot out there, too, mostly bull sharks that use the boulders as cover and lurk around looking for schools of fish to go after."

Abel had signed an equipment rental agreement that said, among other things, that he had been informed of the dangers of diving, and that if he died, he waived the right for anyone who was related to him in any way, family or legally, to sue the company for damages. Abel had mentioned that he was an experienced diver, but had not divulged he'd been in the SEALs for twelve years.

Along with individual gear for him and Rimi, he'd rented a harpoon gun, two headlamps, a couple of foldable digging tools, and a crowbar. He'd also bought some underwater flares and a small, motorized, underwater sled they could put supplies into and also help them get where they were going with less effort. And Rimi, for some reason, bought some water shoes.

Now, as they geared up, they formulated their plan. "We should stay near the surface for as long as we can," explained Abel. "That will keep us from having underwater troubles with those boulders. The video looked like the cruiser clipped that mountainside on the island and then just plunged straight down, so I'm thinking we'll probably find it submerged just off the shore of the island. That's over a mile of swimming. You think you're up to it?"

Rimi, who had put on the wetsuit and weight belt she'd been given but had put on the water shoes rather than the fins Abel was donning, replied, "'Up to it' is a good description. But before we go, I have a surprise for you."

Abel gave her an incredulous look, remembering her surprise for him the night before. "Not to say I wouldn't like it, but this isn't the time or the place—"

Rimi laughed. "Not that kind of surprise," she said. "I have something for you. Here, hold out your hand." She grabbed his right hand. Abel noticed a jeweled bracelet around her right wrist, one of the ones Bibi had made for her. She now stretched over his wrist the other one with the clear crystal on top. The ends of the bracelet, as if by magic, wrapped around Abel's wrist and fused themselves perfectly.

"This is a special bracelet that humans from my world use to show their lifelong commitment to one another. It is also precious and very practical. The crystals are specially attuned to my energy, and as long as I am alive, the clear crystal will shine, and its point will direct you to where I am. See?" She took a few steps back and forth, and the directional crystal, its tip darkened, turned with whatever way she walked.

"If I am above you, the crystal will point straight ahead, and the blue one next to it will flash, and if I am below you, the red one on the other side of it will flash. And if I am no longer alive, the clear crystal will no longer shine," she said.

"Does yours do the same thing for me?" asked Abel.

"Of course." Rimi smiled, and she showed him.

"What's the range?"

"I'm not sure here, but in my world, my mother's and father's worked even when they were thousands of your miles apart. So, you see, now neither of us will ever be lost again."

"That's quite the way of putting it," said Abel, and he wrapped Rimi in a warm embrace. "I guess we'd better get going on this. You better finish getting ready." He grabbed the harpoon gun, strapped on his rebreather and face mask, and powered up the underwater sled.

Rimi slipped her small bluish knife between her weight belt and her wetsuit. "Okay, I'm ready."

Abel gave her a curious look. "Aren't you missing a few things—like something to breathe with, for starters?"

"I'll be just fine." She grinned. "Here, give me some of those flares." Abel handed several to her, which she also stuck underneath her weight belt. "I'll meet you there!" And with that, she leaped high into the air and out over the water, and before Abel could even get into the water himself, he saw her plunge into the ocean just a few hundred yards from the island.

Abel shook his head and smiled his crooked smile. "Glad she's on my side," he said, and then eased himself into the water, flipped on the underwater sled, and let it drag him out to where Rimi already was, helped along by the powerful push from his flippers.

Meanwhile, Rimi, headlamp turned on, allowed her weights to slowly pull her down while she observed what was below her. True to what they'd been told, there were many boulders, some very massive, littering the ocean bottom, which was probably only thirty or forty feet deep at this point. But then she noticed there was an area of relatively clean sand and mud between the beginning of the boulder field and the shore of the island. It was as if some giant had shoved a massive pile of rocks out into the sea to make a space for him to sit that would be free of stone. Finding this both curious and encouraging, Rimi allowed herself to settle onto the ocean floor just on the other side of the boulder field and then began to walk slowly through the mud and sand. Rimi stared around her and felt with her feet for some huge object that might be her family's cruiser buried in the mud, smiling to herself at what Abel's expression would be when he saw that she could breathe underwater just as easily as she could breathe above it. It was a gift that Earth humans considered miraculous, but for her, it was nothing special at all. Everybody where she came from was able to do the same. It was apparently an adaptation that her particular species of humans had developed that the Earth human species never had.

Looking around, she saw a true underwater wonderland. The sun above looked a bit like the moon did at night, with most of its light dissipating just a few yards above her. It was like being just under the clouds, able to see the clear sky while being shrouded in the darkness just a little farther down. She saw small schools of fish swimming in the curious, singular behavior that reminded her of how flocks of birds acted in the sky. There was an occasional larger fish that wandered among them. One, which Rimi sensed was a predator, was directly above her. She sent out a telepathic warning in its direction, and it instantly skittered away.

Checking her wrist crystal, she saw that Abel was still above and behind her, but the quickening blinking of the crystal indicated that he was coming rather fast. At the same time, she suddenly felt as if she were walking gently upward, even though she was still walking in mud and sand.

I'm just ahead of you, and I think I've found something, she thought to him.

What the hell? Is that you, Rimi? she heard back from him.

She chuckled. *Of course it is. Who else do you know that can get into your head so easily?*

Nice! On my other team, we all had to wear radio headsets.

Bibi would say that you've made it to the majors, like in baseball.

Nah, we're in a league of our own. Abel chuckled. *This crystal thing says you're right below me.*

Rimi looked up. She could see his shadow hovering over the veiled sun. *I'm walking on the ocean bottom and have started to go gradually upward. And as I go, the mud I'm in feels firmer.*

It could just be that you're getting closer to the island, observed Abel. He was clearly adjusting well to communicating through his mind, because his telepathic messages were getting very clear. *It's only about two hundred meters to shore from here. I'll come down with some of the tools and see if there's anything under you. Light up one of those flares so I can see where you're at. I'll be down in a second.*

Rimi popped the top off one of her flares as Faviola had shown her once when her Jeep had run out of gas just short of getting home and she'd called Fat Monti to bring her enough to get back to Playa de Palma. When he'd called out to them, and she could see headlights far in the distance, she'd done the same thing to let him know where she was in the pitch black of the rural Costa Rican night. Rimi now tossed the burning flare, impervious to water, out a ways in front of her, and she continued up the gentle slope, dragging her water shoes through the mud to see if they contacted anything hard or metal.

Suddenly, as if by magic, Abel was before her. She gave a little start of surprise.

Ha! I made you jump! came his thoughts as he stood there, smiling.

It's because you look so scary dressed like that! thought Rimi to him. *Like a sea monster from some of the movies mi madre's shown to me!*

And you standing there with no gear on makes you look like a mermaid or a sea nymph, either of which would have made me the envy of my old team if I ever saw one. Come on now, let me take this crowbar and do a little poking around with it.

Abel lifted off the ocean floor and drifted just above where Rimi was walking, poking with the straight-claw end of the crowbar. She walked along with him as he swam. Finally, after going together for perhaps fifty feet, the crowbar hit something hard. Rimi's heart beat faster as Abel banged several more times, then used the other end of the bar to push aside mud and sand. Suddenly, the light from his headlamp was reflected back to them by an impossibly bright, shiny surface. Rimi gasped. It was the hull of her parents' space cruiser.

Faviola was just finishing a late lunch over at the motel café when her cell phone beeped, and she answered.

"Señora Faviola, there are some men here at the front desk who wish to see you. One is Señor Monti, and the rest I've never seen before." It was Javier, and he sounded on edge.

"Fine. Tell them I'll be there shortly," she said. She quickly paid her bill, left a tip for the waiter, a nice young man from Jacó whom she'd hired for the high season, and left, her high heels clicking on the asphalt that led from the restaurant across the road to the parking lot of the main building.

"Just like Fat Monti," she groaned to herself in disgust. Why couldn't he be on *mañana* time like everyone else in Costa Rica? No one ever actually showed up on time in Playa de Palma. It was against the *pura vida*, the Costa Rican expression for their laid-back lifestyle, to hurry around. Monti even came from Mexico, where being on time was considered rare. But he was always on time, and sometimes even early! She cursed him as she so often did. "No siesta for me," she huffed. "I'll make sure he doesn't get one either."

Walking into the lobby, she observed a group of men (and one woman) who looked like stone statues sitting in the comfortable chairs. Everyone was stiff as a palm tree. One in particular was so large Faviola knew he could break her in half over his knee if he chose to. The woman was the only one who wasn't motionless. She feverishly tapped keys on her cell phone as if she were having a silent debate with someone.

Standing at the counter was Fat Monti, who looked extra fat standing next to his companion, who was barely over five feet, five inches tall and was stylishly dressed in a light-colored business suit, his facial hair coiffed into a striking, pointed goatee.

"Ah, Señora Faviola!" Monti said lavishly as she entered and strode behind the front desk. "I want you to meet our new potential investor, Señor Vicente Galvan of—"

"Don Vicente Galvan," corrected the man in a very staccato voice.

"Ah, yes," cowered Monti. "Don Vicente Galvan of Cartagena is here as I told you he would be. He would like accommodations for him and his wife, as well as his men, as we talked about."

"We talked about him, not his wife or his band of . . . gentlemen. I will see what I can do." She quickly punched up Vicente Galvan's beach house. "Señor Galvan, we have for you—"

"*Don* . . . Don Vicente Galvan," corrected Galvan.

Faviola's temper simmered, ready to explode, yet she held it in check. "Señor Vicente Galvan, I don't know what you're used to in Cartagena, but here in Costa Rica, we do not have knights or lords who own castles like the Spanish who conquered this land hundreds of years ago and ruled over everybody. We have *señor y señora y señorita*, and that is all. If you must be called 'Don,' perhaps you'd prefer to stay at Señor Ruiz's house up the road." She saw Monti cringing behind Galvan.

Vicente Galvan looked as if his temper was simmering, ready to explode as well, but he also held it in check. "Señora Faviola," he said as smoothly as a Latino crooner, "forgive me for not understanding how crude things are here in this tiny town in Costa Rica."

He signaled to the giant sitting in the lobby, and the man stood to his full height, which was over a foot taller than Faviola—and Vicente Galvan for that matter—and walked stiffly over and stood next to

Galvan. Galvan made the slightest nod at the bell sitting on the front desk, and the giant grabbed it in one of his massive hands and squeezed. Faviola watched in terrified awe as Galvan continued.

"Thank you for informing me so I will not unintentionally offend someone else, and I do hope things will go well with us here at your inn, so I don't have to show you how we deal with difficulties in big, beautiful cities like Cartagena. Now, you were saying?"

Faviola was still mesmerized by what the big man had done to her bell. It was now merely a mass of twisted metal on her front desk.

Finally, she shook herself visibly and said, "Señor Galvan, you and your wife will be staying in one of our best accommodations, a beach house right near the mouth of the river and the ocean. Here is a list of its amenities."

At this point, Monti intervened. "Señora Faviola, a word with you for a moment." He scuttled behind the front desk and dragged Faviola into the back office with him, smiling goofily at Vicente Galvan as he did. Galvan rolled his eyes.

In the back office, Monti's face turned red with the strain of keeping his voice down. "Señora Faviola, Don Vicente Galvan was to have your finest accommodation, not your *next* finest accommodation. I thought I made myself clear—"

Faviola interrupted. "And I thought I'd made it clear that Señor Forrest is still the occupant of that beach house—at your request—and since he has not checked out today, it is still his beach house and will remain in his name! What is your problem with this Vicente Galvan, your *investor*? House number two just sits back a little from the beach. That is all. Otherwise, it is exactly the same as the other."

"Exactly," hissed Monti. "Because it sits back, its view is inferior, and you know it. Now, you will send your boy to clear all of Señor Forrest's things out of Guesthouse Number One and put them into Guesthouse Number Two. Your maids will put fresh sheets on the beds and linens in the bathroom, and I will hear no more about it."

He moved to walk back out, but Faviola stepped into his way. They glared at each other eye to eye.

"Who do you think you are, Fat Monti? Has this man convinced you that you are a don now, too, that everyone will bow and scrape to you like serfs just because you say so? I don't know what you and your investor have planned for this place, but if it involves bowing down to you and serving people like those out there, the population will not have it. They will run you out on a rail. I will contact Best Western and tell them that this is no longer a safe place for tourists, and your money will stop flowing as if someone turned off the water. This will be a haven for no one except surfing bums and nature lovers. See if you can get rich on that!"

Monti didn't bat an eye. "Once Don Vicente Galvan and I are finished with that island, there will be no need any longer for tourists, or this motel for that matter. The money that our operation there will bring in will make me far richer than you can possibly imagine—and others as well if they choose to cooperate. How about you, Señora, will you cooperate, or that DEA agent, Forrest?"

"Estúpido!" spat back Faviola, straining to control the volume of her voice. "You will ruin everything we have here, everything! And for what? So you can get rich, you and this Don Galvan? You think the DEA is going to allow you to continue to operate as they have in the past? They'll shut you and your friend's operation down before it even gets started. How could you be so blind?"

"Because Don Vicente has already taken care of the DEA. Not only will they not shut us down, but they will also share in the profits, and we will hand over to them all of our competitors."

Monti stopped and looked into Faviola's face, now a mask of shock and horror.

"Please, mi amor, see if you can find a way to cooperate. No one wants to see you crushed like that bell out there."

"Javier!" she called out.

Javier appeared immediately in the back office door. "Yes, Señora?"

"Take one of the crews of maids that are still here and go down to Guesthouse Number One. While the maids clean it up and change the towels and linens, you are to gather all of Señor Forrest's personal effects and take them over to Guesthouse Number Two. Everything, please. Go now—do it quickly."

"Sí, señora," said Javier, and immediately exited. Monti gave Faviola a commiserating look, but she did not look to him at all.

A half hour later, Javier returned to the front office. Monti and the other men were gone, as was Señor Galvan and his wife, who had arrived in Guesthouse Number One just as Javier and the maids were finishing up. Javier had collected everything of Señor Forrest's and taken it all to Guesthouse Number Two, all his clothes, his duffel bag (which seemed unusually heavy), and food from the kitchen. Lastly, he took down all of Señor Forrest's pictures, some of which looked very beautiful, and zipped out of the house just as Señor Galvan walked up the front stairs. As he hastened away, Señor Galvan called out to him.

"Hey, muchacho! You dropped one of your pictures!"

Javier returned to Galvan, and Señor Galvan was just about to hand it to Javier when he stopped and looked at the picture more carefully.

"So, muchacho, who is this man in this picture?"

It was a picture of Señor Forrest standing outside the All-American Diner, the soda run by the two Americans, Señor Ron and Señora Elaine.

"That is Señor Forrest, the man who was using this beach house until now."

Javier was startled to see that Señor Galvan was visibly angry and having a hard time controlling his temper. "Thank you for this information," replied Galvan, almost grinding his teeth as he answered. "Now be gone."

Javier was frightened for Señor Forrest because of the look on Galvan's face, and so now, as he sat with Faviola in the office behind the front desk, he told her everything. He was afraid even more when he saw fear and anger welling up in Señora Faviola's eyes as well.

"Have I done something wrong?" pleaded Javier. "I'm so sorry. I was sure that I had all the pictures. Why would this man become so angry about a picture?"

Faviola looked at him with pity, and she tried to sound gentle. "Nothing is your fault, Javier. Nothing. Now, please handle the front desk for me while I make some phone calls."

26

—

For the next half hour, Abel and Rimi feverishly worked. They continued up what they knew now was most likely the roof of the space cruiser and did not have to go far to find where it was no longer buried in mud but exposed completely. There, Rimi determined within minutes that the space cruiser was definitely dead.

If it were still living, she thought to Abel, *it would act as Bibi does, and I at least could enter it from anywhere by walking through the hull.*

So Rimi led Abel to various places where she remembered hatches or doors in the event of an emergency. The ship's hull was remarkably undeteriorated due to an anticorrosive alloy Rimi said all space-traveling vehicles from her world were coated with to give them durability in a variety of planetary environments, but it was also smashed and misshapen in many places, the result of the monumental force that their collision with the planet had generated. The aft part of the ship was only about twenty-five feet down, and the sunlight above caused a dazzling reflection off all its surfaces, showing how truly vast it was. Abel likened it to finding something the size of an airliner buried in mud and rock.

They finally found a hatch that would open near the rear of the main section of the craft, which seemed to be shaped roughly like a classic airplane, except the two wing sections actually had long, covered walkways along them that led to pods of sleeping quarters on each end. Entering the ship, completely filled with water and dark except where sunlight penetrated a cracked area or a window, was an eerie experience for Rimi. Though it had been over a century ago, seeing the ship now made it seem that it was just yesterday she and her parents and the rest of the crew were sailing through space, heading for Earth so that her father could fulfill his promise to the people he and his former crew had helped so much and come back to see how they were doing.

Now, Rimi used her headlamp to guide her through the main compartment, recalling as she went things like where observation decks were, the areas that she and several other children used to play, the areas where data analyzers had come out of the walls, the crew relaxation areas, and on and on. More importantly, though, she did not remember the exact location of the healing centers, where the vital, life-giving boxes of Xilinium, enough for the entire crew to exist for a year on an alien world, would be stored.

Grotesquely, wherever they went, there were bodies, or at least parts of bodies. Thankfully, most were unrecognizable, their flesh having been eaten away by microscopic sea bacteria and other organisms. Others had obviously been food for sharks and other predators. What was amazing to Rimi and Abel was how many crew members, or what was left of them, were still tethered with emergency tentacles. It was like looking at a macabre wax-museum reconstruction of the ship at the exact moment of impact.

As they worked their way into the darker parts of the ship, Abel led with his harpoon gun in one hand and the crowbar in another, clearing rubble and making sure it was safe, as it was much harder to see what sort of sea life might be around the next corner.

They came to a partially open door, and Abel used the crowbar to shove it open.

Watch out! he thought to Rimi as a large bull shark lazily drifted through the doorway. Rimi telepathically ordered it to leave, and it swished away. Then she went inside with Abel.

Looks like we finally hit the jackpot, he said. Surrounding them were several healing cylinders and compartments filled with strange devices and many boxes of what looked like medicines. As in the other areas, most personnel were tethered by emergency tentacles. Another body was actually strapped into a healing cylinder, like it had been being given some kind of first aid when the ship crashed. It appeared that the sharks had been particularly active here, as more bodies looked like they'd been fed on by some kind of carnivore.

Probably was more blood in here right after the crash, speculated Abel. *Come on, let's start checking out these cupboards. What are we looking for?*

They would probably be encased in large, waterproof chests or containers, and if some had spilled, they would be in watertight bottles with a large "X" on them.

It wasn't long before they found what they were looking for, a closet full of five plastic-like chests with the letter "X" on them.

These are it, said Rimi, *but there's probably more somewhere else. This is not near enough for the entire crew.*

The two bulldogged the containers onto the motorized water cart Abel had brought. They quickly opened the first container once they got it up to the surface to check its contents. Rimi smiled when she saw the boxes lining it, and inside each box, several bottles labeled Xilinium.

"You are a genius, Abel!" said Rimi triumphantly. "I shall not be dying in the next few weeks."

She smiled at him, gave him a kiss, and then they got seriously to business. Abel retrieved the other cases and several other boxes from the water-filled healing area, then Rimi used her "go fast" ability and her incredible strength to get the crates quickly to the beach and stack them up, along with the loose boxes and bottles.

After their first haul was out, Rimi thought to Abel, *I think this may be too many to carry in Faviola's Jeep.*

Yeah, I thought of that. Come on back here for a minute, replied Abel.

She did, and they talked as they held on to the side of Abel's sled.

"Where's the rest likely to be? Are there any cargo holds or something like that that maybe are below the living decks?"

"Yes, I believe so. They would be under the floor of the ship."

The two went to work again, this time with much more light because they were near the ship's more exposed stern section. After about ten minutes of banging on floorboards in the large aft storage area, they found a metal covering that rattled more than most. Yanking it off, they discovered a storage area belowdecks that encompassed the lower level of the entire ship. And lining the ship's right side from the aft area as far as their eyes could see were more "X"-marked crates.

Yup, I'd say a few too many to carry in the Jeep, Abel thought to Rimi.

We can't take them now, but as long as we keep this place a secret, they will always be here for us. That will give us time also to figure out a way to store them on the island once we get them there. Come! We should go now. The sun is well past noontime.

Rimi, thought Abel to her, *there's one more thing.* She gave him a curious look through her face mask. *What about your parents? Do you want to go farther forward and see if you can find them on the bridge?*

Rimi had been so busy that she'd put this same thought to the side ever since they'd entered the wreck. It was definitely easier not to think about it. But Abel was right. She had had very little time to say goodbye to her mother, and none at all with her father. Perhaps it was time to, say one final goodbye after being so suddenly and totally separated.

But then she thought of the grotesque, ghostly look that even the bodies inside that hadn't been ravaged by predators or microorganisms had, and also the fond memories that she had of her parents when they were alive.

No, she thought.

She wanted to hang on to those good memories, and not have

them tainted by whatever a century in the ocean had done to her parents. She realized that she'd said her goodbyes a long time ago, and there was no need to tarnish those images now.

There is no need for that, but thanks for asking.

And with that, the two swam away with their haul. What they failed to notice, though, was a faint, flickering light that momentarily penetrated the thin sand covering the cruiser's midship area as Rimi passed over it.

When they got to the beach, they packed up all five chests of Xilinium, as well as the loose boxes and bottles, and headed back to the highway and the motel, careful to stop and erase as much of their tire tracks and other markings they'd made in the sand as possible. That end of the beach would remain a dangerous place nobody had gone to in years, just like before.

But even as they did these things, back with the underwater wreck, a faint, pulsing light began to emanate from the bridge area of the spaceship, the one part of the decimated cruiser they'd decided not to explore.

Meanwhile, back in Playa de Palma, Fat Monti was getting a swift education in what it was like attached at the hip to a Colombian drug lord. As soon as Don Vicente Galvan discovered that DEA Agent Caleb Forrest, whom Monti Ruiz had been dealing with, was actually the supposedly dead DEA Agent Abel Nowinski, he moved into action, and things began happening so fast that Monti couldn't keep track.

First, several "technicals," military terminology for a civilian vehicle like a pickup truck or other SUV with a mounted armament in the back bed or on the roof, suddenly appeared out of the jungle and drove straight through Playa de Palma in front of all the town's shops, sodas, and small hotels. Each carried a mounted automatic weapon of some type (Monti thought perhaps a smaller-caliber machine gun) and four or five men. Patrons of the shops stared in alarm, and people along the beaches stopped what they were doing to watch. And then everyone, eventually, turned their heads to Monti Ruiz's pavilion, with those close by running to it to find out from Monti what was going on.

Monti himself was apoplectic, screaming into his phone at Vicente Galvan, who was still at Faviola's inn.

"What the *fuck* are you doing to my town? We keep our guns to ourselves here! Why are you parading these vehicles around like the cartel bosses in Mexico? You're scaring the tourists!"

"I'm sorry for the inconvenience, Señor Monti," replied Galvan over the phone. "This is my personal protection detachment. They go wherever I go in case I require them, and I'm afraid that a situation has developed where I do."

"What 'situation' are you talking about? There is no situation that requires vehicles mounting machine guns and militias barrelling through my town! Get them out of here—now!"

"Your town?" replied Galvan, his voice calm and smooth. "I was under the impression that our deal makes it *our* town and *our* island, and therefore, I shall do as I please. I would have discussed it with you, but the situation is immediate."

"What situation?" shouted Monti so loud that those around him in the pavilion backed away.

"Obviously you did not know, or you would have told me, I'm sure. Your man Caleb Forrest, the DEA agent who has been working with you, is actually not Caleb Forrest."

"What?" shouted Monti.

Galvan's silky voice continued through Monti's phone. "He is a corrupt DEA agent that was supposed to see to the protection of my shipments to Miami from Cartagena. His real name is Abel Nowinski. I paid him a large sum of money, which he took, and then, that very night, my shipment was seized by the DEA before it even left the international waters around Cartagena. He caused me to lose over one hundred million dollars in product."

Monti was so shocked that all he could do was sit with his mouth open as Galvan continued.

"I have called in my guard so that we can plan a way to deal with him as quickly as possible. The man obviously is very resourceful, and we do not want him interfering with our little project on the island. Oh, and speaking of that, I have ordered my construction crew into your harbor as well. They should be arriving by boat soon. Once the current situation is dealt with, they will head out to the island, and our plans will begin immediately. I cannot afford delays—I have shipments coming, and our new allies in Jacó will be expecting a payout soon, as will you."

Monti continued to be gobsmacked.

"Perhaps you can find places where these men might eat and refresh themselves while they are ashore. There will be around thirty of them. Gracias, my friend. We will soon be rich men." Don Vicente Galvan clicked off Monti's phone.

Perhaps thirty people in and around the pavilion stood silently, waiting for Monti to speak. He looked at each of them. Some narrowed their eyes as if saying, "What have you done, you stupid fat man?" Most just looked at him with wonder, almost like children waiting for their father to tell them what to do.

"Obviously, there are going to be some changes around here, but it has happened much sooner than I anticipated. These men who look like militias will soon be gone, and hopefully will never return. I apologize to you all for their intrusion. There is a . . . situation that I was not aware of which has brought these men here. It will be resolved soon." The people still stood around, needing to hear more, and Monti, of course, had more to tell.

"The other things are more permanent changes—to our island off the coast. Men will be arriving in a short time who will build things there that will lead to much more money that can be invested in our community. They will only be here for as long as it takes them to build the facilities, and then they will leave, but for now, we must hasten to make accommodations for them. There will be thirty or more men and perhaps women, too. Any of you who run sodas or motels, please prepare yourselves for a much larger dinner crowd than usual."

Ron, from the All-American Diner, asked, "What sort of facilities will they be building on the island? Is this the tourist attraction you've been talking about?"

"I am not at liberty to say," replied Monti softly, "but for now at least, no, it will not be a new tourist attraction."

A collective groan went through those assembled.

"Perhaps that will come in the future," added Monti through the din.

Then someone else called out, "I thought the island was haunted. We sent many men there with guns to clear out whatever was there, and none of them returned. Many here do not remember that because it was long ago, but I do. I lost two of my sons to that island! What has happened to make it safe to build these facilities?"

Monti sighed. At first, he wasn't sure what to say, but then, as if the Madre had spoken to him Herself, he had an epiphany.

"I will tell you the truth, my friends. For the past two weeks, I have hired the DEA agent who came to our town several weeks ago to do just that—to clean out the evil presence that has haunted our island and caused so many of our people to disappear and never come back. He has been fearless. For several days, he went there and came back, assuring me that all was going well. Then, on the fourth day, he did not return, and I was horrified. Had he disappeared as well? But, no! Nearly a week later, he returned! Some of you may have seen him. He told me that the evil presence, an insane woman who had been there for many years, had been eliminated after he had battled her and been seriously wounded. And so, thanks to this fine man, our island is liberated. If you should see him around over the next few days, be sure to show your gratitude to him. He is a hero who nearly gave his own life so that our families can be at peace, and our island is useful again."

Monti smiled around at them all, and inside he thought, *And so now, my friend Caleb Forrest, or Abel Nowinski, or whatever your name is, perhaps at some time when you most need it, if you survive Don Vicente Galvan, you'll find an unexpected friend here ready to help you. You know, I really did like you, at least before today.*

"Look, I see a boat approaching!" called someone.

Monti saw what looked like a large trawler with men crowded on the deck.

"Come, my friends. We must be ready for them when they get here."

EL DIA DE LA MUERTE

(The Day of Death)

27

—

Just as they left the outskirts of Jacó on the way back to where they'd left their boat, Rimi and Abel got a call on Rimi's cell phone that Faviola had given her to use while visiting the village. It was also paired with the Jeep's sound system so that both Abel and Rimi could hear the call. It was Faviola.

"I'm afraid I have bad news," came her voice over the speakers. "The man Galvan has already come to town, and by chance, he saw a picture of you, Abel, one that you took outside Ron and Elaine's diner. He recognized you immediately and is crazy with anger and revenge."

Rimi and Abel exchanged wary glances as they listened.

Faviola, beaten and bloodied with swollen eyes, a broken nose, and her clothes in tatters, continued from the back office as Javier, also showing scars and bruises, ministered to her wounds. "He has a personal entourage of bodyguards that he has gone north with to intercept you. Thank God I couldn't tell them where you were, because I didn't know, but I had to tell them something, or they would have killed us both, Javier and me. I did not tell them that you would have to turn off the highway to go get your boat, though, so maybe you can get there before they catch you on the highway."

"Are you hurt, mi madre?" asked Rimi.

"I have not hurt this much in a long time, mija, but Javier and I are both alive, and now you must take steps to make sure you stay alive as well," replied Faviola. "If you can get to your boat and can get to the island by tonight, you can prepare for them perhaps."

"How many bodyguards are we talking about, Faviola?" asked Abel as he drove. His ex-military mind was already strategizing.

"It looked like around fifteen, in three vehicles. Each one had some kind of machine gun on it. Galvan went in his car with his giant personal bodyguard."

"Okay, thanks," replied Abel. "One more thing. Is there any way you and Javier could get some of my gear to me? What I need is the real hefty duffel bag. If you guys could get it, it would really help us once we get back to the island. You can drive my Jeep over to where the boat is and just throw the bag over the side if you have to."

"I know which one it is," said Javier to Faviola as they listened on Faviola's speakerphone, "and right where I put it."

"And Galvan is gone, but what about the woman?" asked Faviola.

"I don't know. I didn't see her," replied Javier.

Faviola spoke into the phone. "Yes, I think we can. We will try. Be safe, both of you." She clicked off her phone.

Rimi and Abel looked at each other with expectant expressions.

"Well, babe, sounds like things could get a bit exciting," said Abel.

He stopped Faviola's Jeep on the side of the road, got out, and took out his ever-present backpack.

"Never know when you might need this stuff," he quipped as he assembled his Mk 16 assault rifle, strapped on a bulletproof vest, and filled its pockets with extra magazines. "We'll keep this up front with you." He handed her the gun, then got in and started the Jeep back up. "Seriously, honey. This is going to get really hairy—that means crazy—and there's a good chance we could get hurt. Not a pleasant thought, but I'm just saying—"

"I'm not worried," replied Rimi. "We are a team now, and you've never had a teammate like me before."

Don Vicente Galvan seethed as he rode behind his driver in his bulletproof car. How could he have been so stupid, to be duped by some colonel of Panama's PNP force and then believe the words of bounty hunters and his own men in Panama that the crispy corpse they'd found in the plane they'd shot down was actually DEA Agent Nowinski, the one who had made a fool of him by taking his money, then allowing Galvan's shipment to be taken just minutes after it left Cartagena? The old saying "If you want something done right, you do it yourself" definitely applied to running a burgeoning drug cartel. It was only by chance that he had seen the picture of Nowinski, and this time, he personally would make sure that nothing went wrong. He had started by overseeing the interrogation of the feisty motel owner and her desk clerk after discovering that Nowinski had been seen around town early in the morning with the motel owner's daughter, allowing Jumo, his bodyguard, to pound the shit out of both of them until they talked, but yet not so much as to render them unconscious or dead. They had dutifully confessed, as he knew they would. They were not hardened criminals and were easy to break.

Now, he carefully planned a multilayered ambush for Agent Nowinski along the highway from Jacó that even he, with all his ex-Navy SEAL experience, would find impossible to elude. "Jumo," he called to the huge man in the shotgun seat, "get on your radio. Tell all drivers to stop."

Jumo did as he was told, and Galvan's car, along with all three vehicles behind it, came to a halt.

"Tell Alejandro to pull off the road under cover of these trees here and have his men take cover on both sides of the road. They are to disable the traitor's vehicle and kill the girl but capture the man alive. He is for me. If for some reason they fail, they should continue pursuing the vehicle."

Jumo again did as he was told. The vehicle closest behind them pulled off into the deep shade of the trees on the right side of the road. The men filed out of the truck, and Alejandro, a small man in a broad-brimmed hat, ordered three of the men to find hiding places along the road. Each was armed with an assault rifle. One manned the machine gun mounted on the roof of the SUV cab by standing up through a moonroof in the back part of the vehicle. Then Alejandro returned to the driver's seat.

"*Excelente,*" commented Galvan. "Tell the rest to turn around. We shall go back down the road where another vehicle will wait in ambush."

Again, Jumo repeated his boss's words to the others in Spanish. All the vehicles turned around as best they could on the narrow, pitted highway and proceeded back toward the Playa de Palma turnoff. About a half mile down the road, Galvan ordered another vehicle to set up their ambush, and then, another half mile away, he and the third vehicle both waited in ambush. Vicente Galvan couldn't imagine even a Navy SEAL getting past two traps where the men were well hidden and experienced enough not to give themselves away too soon, but if he somehow did, he would never get past him and his ambush. He savored the thought of executing the man who had cost him so much both in money and prestige in Cartagena. Then he would get to work building the narco sub and ship docks on the backside of that Fat Monti's island so he and any other don with half a brain in his head could use them to smuggle drugs into Mexico and California, leaving the Caribbean altogether and making Vicente Galvan of Cartagena the most powerful among them.

Abel and Rimi proceeded slowly along the Costa Rican Pacific Coast Highway, partly because it was so filled with potholes, but more because they were wary of the possibility of ambush. And yet, they needed to get to the turnoff to where their boat was docked as quickly as possible.

"Damn potholes," cursed Abel. "I'd be cautious, but I'd sure be moving faster than this if it weren't for fear of blowing a tire or bottoming out the transmission."

"Mi madre always says the same thing," said Rimi. "This ambush you talk about. What is this thing?"

"Same thing you and your friends did to some of those guys with guns that showed up on your island," replied Abel. "You hide somewhere out of sight and then pounce on your enemy before they know you're there. Classic surprise attack. See these trees on the sides of the road?" He pointed out several. "Their shadows are really vivid and dark. There could be a whole car or truck parked in an area like that, and you wouldn't know it until it was too late."

"Don't worry about your speed," said Rimi. "I will help you see."

Abel looked over at her with a confused expression, then he pulled off the road and simply stared at her. "What the hell did you just do?"

"Nothing really," replied Rimi. "It is just something that anyone from my world can do, but I guess Earth humans cannot do." What Rimi had done was pull back the skin from around her already large eyes, making them look twice as large.

"When I do this, my eyes can see clearly for much farther than they normally do, and I also can see much more to either side."

"Jesus, you're like a freaking owl," marveled Abel.

"What is an owl? I've not heard of this thing."

"A big bird. It doesn't live in this part of the world, but it's got eyes like that seeing machine I left on our island. They can magnify things that are far away, can see things in the dark, stuff like that," answered Abel.

"My eyes can do those things as well. I will watch the road far ahead of us. You just continue driving," said Rimi.

"Fine with me." Abel shrugged. He pulled the Jeep back onto the highway and continued, driving a good deal faster. Rimi stared ahead with her super-eyes. Abel glanced down at the jeweled bracelet on his wrist. As advertised, the center clear crystal emitted an intense but small, rapidly flickering light, and its sharp end was turned toward Rimi beside him. He wondered what other marvels his new companion had in store for him.

"I heard that," Rimi said with a smile. "You shall see plenty!"

Back at the Rio Palma Inn, Faviola and Javier had patched themselves up enough that they could at least walk. Javier, who was the more mobile of the two, went and got a maid's cart for them to put the duffel bag on, and they both set out for Guesthouse Number Two, Javier walking ahead while Faviola hobbled along behind, carrying her pistola that she'd threatened Monti with.

"This is good." She grimaced. "I can watch to make sure there's no funny stuff going on with that man's woman while you're inside."

Javier approached the beach house as if he were just coming to change the towels and linens. He tried to walk naturally, but both kneecaps were horribly bruised by Galvan's giant's police wand, so it was hard. Javier winced, thankful that he had the maid's cart to lean on. He pushed it up to the back door of the beach house, the one by the outdoor shower that opened into an entryway and then the kitchen straight ahead, and the master bedroom down a small hallway to the side. Because this beach house was set somewhat back from Guesthouse Number One, its backside was not in ready view of the porch or open windows of Guesthouse Number One.

He left the cart outside, grabbed a handful of towels, and kept the charade of delivering linens as he went in and diverted toward the master bedroom. Opening the door, he instantly saw the black duffel bag that had been so heavy for him to move earlier in the day. He dumped the towels on the king-sized bed, then went for the duffel bag and hauled it up off the floor. It seemed every muscle in his body ached, especially his back and arms, which had also taken their whacks from the giant. He heaved the duffel bag's shoulder strap around his neck and shoulder so that his hands would be free, then staggered along the wall to the door he'd just come through. Then suddenly he heard shots and bullets ripped through the walls of the hallway he had nearly stepped into.

"Stop!" yelled Rimi.

Abel swerved the Jeep sharply off the highway and under some trees.

"There are five men ahead who have guns," cried Rimi. "Three are hiding in the trees on this side of the road, the other two are in a big car like mi madre's Jeep, only bigger. There is a big gun on the top, and a man standing in a hole in the roof ready to shoot it. There is also a driver."

Abel said, "Here, give me the gun." Rimi passed over to Abel his Mk 16, and Abel stepped out of the truck, drew up the weapon's shoulder stock, aimed it down the road, and peered through its sniper scope. "Son of a bitch," he mumbled. "You're right, and so was I." He sat back down in the Jeep. "We've got to make a plan. If you've got any more surprises for me, now's the time to let me know. My gun can't hit them from this distance, and if we moved into its range, there's a chance they'd see us, and that machine gun they've got could take us out."

"I can hit them from here," said Rimi. She pulled out her little knife that glowed a soft blue color. Abel nearly laughed out loud—the look was like that of a child pulling out their little toy gun and saying they were ready to go blast the enemy—but he was glad he didn't. Rimi was dead serious.

"My knife will fly to whatever I am looking at. It is made of a very dense material not found on Earth. When my parents came here first, they showed the people how to use blades made from this mineral to cut huge stones to exact specifications for building impressive structures. When I throw it, it will fly at nearly the speed of one of your bullets. I guide it with my eyes, and it will go through whatever I want it to destroy. Then it will return to me, or usually, I am there to get it. It does not get sticky or dirty or dull because its outer covering sheds debris, and it is so much harder than any material on Earth. I am your plan! I will destroy these men and their guns who lurk like crocodiles beside the road waiting to hurt you."

Abel looked at Rimi and the little knife and could say nothing. They both seemed so small and so unthreatening. Probably like what David of the Bible, armed with his sling and stones, must have looked like to the Philistine giant Goliath. So small, so vulnerable. Yet the boy David had felled Goliath with one precisely hurled missile to the giant's head. Could Rimi be such a warrior as well? Seriously?

Rimi, reading his thoughts, groaned. "Why do people of this world always think that someone small is also weak? I shall go. You watch through your eyeglass. These crocodiles shall be dead before they know what has killed them."

With that, Rimi stepped out of the truck and motioned Abel to do the same. Somewhat startled, he grabbed his Mk 16 and stepped out of his car again, training it on the three men on their side of the road, who, though standing or lying down with their assault rifles at the ready, were talking and chatting rather than vigilantly watching the road. Suddenly, the head of one man literally exploded, only silently, and before the others could even react, another's head blew up, and the other looked down at the enormous hole in his gut before falling to his knees, and then onto his face.

A second later, Rimi was there and caught her dagger, then threw it like a missile at the truck. Its windshield immediately exploded into tiny pieces, and a great red splat filled the front seat. In the next second, the other man collapsed through the moonroof, apparently eviscerated, and a second later, the knife, flew into Rimi's hand on the other side of the road. She caught it as if she had simply been playing catch.

Faviola stood behind the tree where Rimi usually kept her clothes buried in a particular hole that she'd dug. Faviola could feel the hard cover of the hole underneath her high heels as she stood there.

Estúpido, she railed at herself. *You can barely walk, and you've still got these ridiculous shoes on! How foolish!*

She hadn't thought of anything else except helping Javier get the things Abel needed since they'd talked with him on the phone, and now, it was too late to be thinking about shoes. She was about to kick them off when she saw her—Galvan's little woman—creeping out from Guesthouse Number One like some disgusting spider. She even carried a weapon, a *pistola* with a suppressor on its end.

Faviola felt like spitting but didn't want to give herself away.

Faviola and the spiders that lived around her inn actually had an unwritten rule that they all followed. As long as the spiders behaved themselves and didn't come out to scare the guests, they could continue to spin their webs and rid her inn of *cucarachas* and beetles and mosquitos and flies and whatever vermin they caught in their webs. But if a spider violated the rules by coming out in plain sight somewhere, well, then it was fair game and it had to go. She or her staff would punish it for its ill behavior, which always resulted in a smashed spider. Faviola had killed many rule-breaking spiders, and she knew that you couldn't kill a spider if you were not careful as you approached it. You must be silent, patient, and then, when all is ready, pounce like lightning.

And so Faviola watched as the woman—the spider—crept to the side of Guesthouse Number Two, then skittered along the wall toward the open door and the linen cart. Her eyes were looking at nothing but her prey.

Faviola stepped from behind the tree, planted her feet so she could partially lean against it to steady herself, aimed her gun with both hands, and fired, one shot after another after another.

The first three shots missed high. The woman whirled in shock and tried to shoot back but was caught by the next two bullets, which hit her squarely on both sides of her chest. She fell back against the wall and dropped her gun, then took two more shots to the gut. She finally fell to the ground. Faviola could tell that this spider was still alive, but not for long.

"You may come out now, Javier!" she called.

Faviola limped toward the back door of the beach house. She needed to grind her shoe into this spider to kill it. Javier appeared, threw the duffel onto the linen cart, then turned, took one look at the gasping, flailing, bleeding woman next to the wall, and vomited into the linen cart's garbage bag.

"I'm sorry you had to see this, mi amigo," said Faviola. "This spider was a messy one to smash, but I got it. Go, take these things to the beach house parking area. Find Señor Forrest's Jeep and take them to Pablo's just down the highway, you know, the one who runs the scuba school. That's where Señor Forrest's boat is. He says the keys are in the Jeep."

Javier, looking pale, nodded, then looked back at the woman. "But she's not dead yet," he said.

The woman seemed to be mounting a pathetic attempt to regain her gun, which was lying on the ground a couple of feet away from her.

"She will be," said Faviola, "once you are gone. Quick. Go now. Señor Forrest could be at his boat any minute."

Javier shoved the cart back up the pathway, and Faviola looked down at her victim, who was bleeding out all over the back-door area of Guesthouse Number Two.

"You're going to be a mess to clean up, you know that?" As she pointed her gun at the woman's head, the woman made one last, desperate lunge for her weapon. Faviola re-aimed and fired, but she also felt her left leg go suddenly weak and then collapse. Faviola's bullet had hit its target. The spider was as dead as dust. But Faviola's ankle had been shattered by the spider's last attempt to bite, and Faviola knew that there would be no walking back to the front office for her. She propped herself against the other side of the doorway from the dead woman, tore off a strip of cloth from her skirt, and wrapped it tightly around her leg just below her knee, hoping she wouldn't bleed out before someone found her.

Don Vicente Galvan and Jumo had just heard a frantic cry from Alejandro, something about exploding heads and a woman, when there was a loud crash, and the radio suddenly went dead. This was cause for concern. The brief transmission sounded like Alejandro's post was being attacked from afar by heavy-caliber weapons, the kind a SEAL sniper might use.

This ex-Navy SEAL seems to have brought some of his favorite toys, Galvan thought.

"Jumo," he said. "Give me the radio." Once he had it in hand, he raised his other ambush team. "Pedro, it's Vicente. Our adversary is very clever. Move your team down the highway until you pass my position, then keep going until I tell you to set up a roadblock."

"Set up a roadblock on the main highway? Is this wise, Vicente? There could be many tourist cars coming by."

"Fuck the tourists," Galvan answered. "Do as I say."

Abel and Rimi continued down the highway. She had come back, seconds after her attack, and they'd gotten back into the truck.

"I've never seen anything like that," Abel said. "You're the most lethal person I've ever seen, and I worked with very lethal people."

"You're a very lethal person yourself, my friend," Rimi replied.

"You're right there," Abel said.

Now, they passed the carnage that had once been Alejandro's ambush team, and Abel didn't slow a bit, just another pile of dead bodies and a shattered vehicle. Nothing new there. Where were the next targets? His SEAL sensibilities were returning right on time.

Rimi was peering ahead again and reported something curious.

"There is another group of men ahead, but they are getting into a pickup truck with a big machine gun in it and going down the road the same way we're going. It's like they're running away from us."

"The guys you killed must have had the chance to use a radio before you got them—a few seconds at least. They're going to plan B."

To Rimi's confused look, Abel said, "It means they're changing to a new plan. That's good. You got them riled up, but I don't think they're scared actually."

"They should be," said Rimi.

"No argument there," replied Abel through one of his crooked grins. Rimi managed a tiny smile in return. "They may try a roadblock somewhere down there and then see if they can box us in. They'd have someone hidden around here that will pop out from behind us somewhere once we get close to the roadblock."

"But what about the other cars that passed us, and the two that are behind us right now?" asked Rimi. "They're just tourists. Can they block the road for them, and what happens if shooting starts?"

Abel shook his head. "Sad to say, Rimi, but guys like these are so violent and crazy they'll shoot someone even if they look at them wrong."

"Then I shall not feel bad about killing such evil people," she replied.

"That's good," said Abel. "They sure wouldn't feel bad about killing you."

They continued driving, other cars passing them from time to time. Rimi kept her eyes on the machine-gun truck (which tourist cars gave a wide berth to) as it traveled for another mile or so, and then, Rimi reported, they stopped in the middle of the road. Five men got out, she said, and went to either side of the road, and one stayed in the truck next to the big machine gun.

"That's it, just like I thought," said Abel.

Unbeknownst to Abel and Rimi, though, they were just a quarter mile from where Don Vicente Galvan's bulletproof car was parked in the shade just out of sight on an upcoming side road off to the left, as was the other technical with its crew of five men and a driver. Rimi was fixated on the pickup ahead and hadn't noticed, and Abel was concentrating on the right side of the road. He knew that the little drive down to Pablo's scuba school was in the area somewhere near, and he was straining to see its little handmade sign along the highway.

"Rimi," he said, "check along your side of the road just a couple hundred meters off to the right. Can you make out a sign that's next to a little road entrance?"

Rimi replied excitedly, "Yes! You're right, my friend! It's the scuba school sign!"

Abel sped up a little, and within thirty seconds he was making a sharp turn onto a little road through the jungle that would eventually spread out into a dirt parking lot in front of a small adobe building out of which Pablo, Faviola's friend, ran his scuba school. Moored to Pablo's pier would be their boat, which meant they would soon be back on their island.

"Sorry, Señor Don Vicente Galvan, sir, but we're skipping the little party you had planned for us." Abel chuckled. He smiled over at Rimi, reveling in the action and happy to be on someone's team again while he did it.

"They have *what?*" screamed Don Vicente into his radio.

"They turned off the highway. I think just before getting to the road where you're hidden," came Pedro's voice.

"Which way?" snapped Galvan. The woman Jumo had beaten behind the front desk of the motel had said nothing of this.

Lying bitch, he thought. *I'll blow her head off with a machine gun when I see her again.*

"They made a right-hand turn, toward the ocean," came Pedro's voice.

"I will find the road and chase them into the sea and drown them if I have to!" yelled Don Vicente into his radio. "You return this way and watch for where we turn, then block the road so no one can go in or out."

He clicked off the communicator, then whapped his driver on the head with his hat. "Get going! What are you waiting for, your funeral?"

The driver gunned the gas, and Don Vicente Galvan's tank of a car leaped forward, screeched a turn to the right, and sped away, with the technical SUV right behind.

28

—

Ron stood behind his restaurant's bar and surveyed his dining room. Who would have thought that in midafternoon near the end of high season the place would be packed? Besides those stopping in for a genuine American-made chocolate milkshake or banana split while taking a break from lying out on the beach or surfing or shopping, there were now twelve big, hearty men from the boatload of construction workers that had recently docked at the pier. Most spoke English, and they were looking to fill their bellies before their boat left again.

And, goodness, they had such bellies to fill! Not that they were all fat, but each was a huge man compared to Ron, and they ordered two and three dishes consecutively. They'd vacuum down the double cheeseburger and plate of fries, inhale a milkshake, then order a California burger, and as soon as that was delivered, the same thing would happen, and then they'd order again! Ron had called in his other two cooks and all his waiters and waitresses, promising them double wages for as many hours as they were needed. He threw in that the customers were especially big tippers. He didn't actually know that for sure, but they had the look of men who would happily pay well for the chance to eat good, greasy American food.

It turned out that Ron's hunch had been right. These men played with money like it grew on trees. It was not unusual for his waitresses to get hundred-dollar bills for tips. One man put ten one-hundred-dollar bills into the payment folder to pay for him and the three other men with him, and then told the waiter to keep the change! The men were boisterous, but not overly loud or fearsome. It was like something out of Ron and Elaine's expat dream when they first opened their soda: a room full of happy customers, happy workers, and great American food—and lots of money in the cash register.

Suddenly, Ron noticed that one in the group of workers was José, a tree cutter from farther down the coast who was clearing land just north of Quepos where a new beachfront motel was to be built. He came up the highway to Playa de Palma a couple of times each week to have American Night with his family. Ron squeezed himself through all the customers eating at his tables to greet him.

"Ah, José," he called over the din. "So glad to see you here. So your guys are part of this project for our island?"

José wiped a milkshake moustache from his face and smiled up at Ron. "Sí, my friend," he said. "We are all part of a new crew that this businessman has put together. We're to clear some land on your island here."

"So I was told. Kind of a rush job, huh?"

"Ah, sí!" said José. "We all thought we'd come tomorrow, but we got a call earlier that a boat would pick us up and we'd go in today, and each of us got ten thousand US dollars in cash as a bonus! Pretty great, eh?"

"So, do you know what's eventually going to be built there?" asked Ron.

"No, señor, but I don't care. I just know we're clearing land. Some of the other crews are building some kind of structures, but we don't know. We just do our job, right?"

"That's for sure," said Ron.

So these men don't know anything more than we've been told, thought Ron. All this secrecy made him worry about the dark speculation he and other community patrol members had heard. The community patrol, as Monti called it, was a group of men and a few women who lived year-round in Playa de Palma and regularly patrolled the roads behind the beach, the beaches themselves, and the road up to the school and the highway each night to keep the community safe. Each wore a bright orange vest with "Community Patrol" emblazoned on it in reflective paint and carried a utility belt that held a police wand, pepper spray, a tactical flashlight, and a holster with a small semiautomatic pistol. Once each week, patrol people had to check in on their own time at the firing range near a big warehouse up by the highway and spend time shooting and practicing self-defense moves with a partner. Several times when Ron had gone there over the past few weeks, he'd heard others talking, usually in Spanish, about Monti getting tired of his small business and reaching out to more big-time kingpins in the region. The talk always centered around the island and something about a waystation.

Ron wasn't sure what it all meant, and he certainly had no idea what sort of waystation the men might be referring to. Something was definitely afoot that Monti was not being up front about. Ron wondered if it had something to do with the guest Monti took to the Rio Palma Inn earlier, and the parade of armed men and trucks that had trundled through town not long after.

Suddenly, one of his waitresses, Marta, a single mother who lived near the river, came up beside him. Ron was shocked at the look on her face: one of utter fear and terror. "Marta, what is it?"

"You must come to the break room immediately."

Marta grabbed Ron's wrist and yanked him around. Ron could barely wave to his friend José before he was marched through the dining room, through the kitchen door, and into a small room in the back that served as the employees' break room. Sitting on a chair in a corner, crying, was Marta's ten-year-old son, Enrique. Marta sat Ron down in another chair that she dragged over from the break room table.

"Tell Señor Ron, mijo," said Marta to her son. "Tell him what you saw. He is a good man. He won't hurt you."

Enrique just sat with his hands over his eyes and quietly cried.

Marta saw Ron's confusion and pity for the child. "He has made friends with one of the little boys whose family is staying in one of the beach houses at the Rio Palma. He was going to their house to find his friend and play, and he saw something."

She turned again to Enrique. "Mijo, you must tell Señor Ron what you saw. Tell him now!" Her words were filled with both understanding and urgency. Enrique finally lowered his hands and peered at Ron with his reddened eyes.

"I saw two women on the ground beside the second beach house. Neither one was moving, and there was blood everywhere!"

Javier finally pulled Señor Forrest's Jeep into the small dirt parking lot in front of a small building with a crude sign that said "Pablo's Scuba" on it. The journey had been longer than usual and scary, to say the least. After leaving Playa de Palma, Javier had gotten onto the highway and turned left to go the four miles or so to the scuba school. All had been fine for three miles, but then in front of him, he'd seen the strangest and most frightening thing he'd ever seen on any highway. Driving down the middle of the road was a big pickup truck. Three ugly men were sitting in the bed of the truck. Two were carrying assault rifles, and the other stood leaning on a big machine gun that was mounted in the bed. Javier had slowed his Jeep and pulled to the side to pass the truck, and as he'd gone by it, he'd seen two other ugly men in the cab, both with assault rifles, and another man driving. Javier fought the urge to stare. Staring would get their attention, and these were the kind of people whose attention he definitely did not want. He drove along, gripping the steering wheel a lot tighter than usual, and finally came to his turnoff, but just before he got there, his peripheral vision picked up something odd just down a road that went off to the right, barely visible in the shade of the trees. He turned his head instinctively, but he'd already gone by the road junction and only saw trees. He could have sworn there was another pickup truck with a machine gun in its bed just like he'd seen driving down the road less than a mile back.

Unnerved, to say the least, he was relieved to make his left-hand turn onto a dirt road marked with a tiny sign that said "Scuba School."

Then, however, he got another unwelcome surprise. The school was not just a little way off the main road. The dirt road, barely maintained and filled with holes and dangerous dips and steep little hills, seemed to wind through the jungle for miles. It must have taken him fifteen minutes, going very slowly, to finally reach the welcoming parking lot. There were only a couple of other cars there, also SUVs, and it looked like there was one person inside the building behind the counter. He also noted the little fishing trawler moored to the small pier that extended into the ocean from a tiny beach.

Señor Forrest's boat, he thought. He was glad he'd gotten there in time.

Javier parked in front of the building and went inside.

"Hola," he said to the man, who looked to Javier like he had just awakened him. "I have a delivery from the Rio Palma for Señor Forrest, the owner of that boat out there. He is expecting it."

"So what? Go ahead. Make your delivery," mumbled the man, who obviously was not Pablo, the scuba teacher. "You get beat up or something?"

"Oh, you mean these bruises? No, just fell down the stairs at the inn. Clumsy me!" Javier laughed.

He then went back out, dragged the duffel bag out of the car, and then suddenly, all hell unexpectedly descended upon him. He heard a loud buzzing coming from the jungle, bullets struck the dirt all around him and whizzed through the trees, and then, dashing into the parking area from the jungle, was Caleb Forrest, running like a madman and shouting and waving his hands.

"Stop!" he cried. "Stop! Drop that bag. Drop the bag!"

29

—

When Abel and Rimi had turned off the highway, they had both breathed a sigh of relief. It seemed like they had most certainly ditched a trap that had been laid for them by Don Vicente Galvan and his guards, and now, they juked and jolted down the pitted dirt road to Pablo's, feeling a lot less tense than they had for quite a while.

The feeling didn't last long.

Suddenly, they heard the heavy sound of an old .50 caliber machine gun, and the mini-missile-like rounds kicked up dirt on the road, shattered tree trunks with loud pops, and made hissing sounds passing by their open windows.

"What the hell!" yelled Abel, and he glanced into his rearview mirror. There, barely a hundred yards behind them, was another technical! It must have been very near, for the one they'd seen in the road could never have gotten to where they'd turned off so quickly. Fortunately, it appeared that the treacherous road was making it almost impossible for the machine-gun operator to fire accurately.

"Shit!" yelled Abel. "I hate it when I'm right. This must be the crew that was going to close the trap on us if we'd stayed on the highway. They would have been a lot closer to the turnoff." There was more gunfire, this time from an AK-47 assault rifle (Abel had heard too many of those to ever forget their distinctive racket). Once again, bullets seemed to fly everywhere around the Jeep.

Rimi kept her head down and looked up at Abel expectantly. "So what's our plan?" she asked.

"We've got to get this Jeep to the dock and unload the stuff onto the boat, and we'll never do that if that machine gun gets a good shot at us. Those bullets will rip this thing apart like a cardboard box!" Abel yelled as he sped the Jeep up. The increased bouncing up and down and sideways that this caused helped them be a harder target to hit, even if it was bone-rattling. Abel checked the side mirror because the crates of Xilinium were stacked so high it was hard to see out the rearview. The truck pursuing them had sped up, too, but that made their shooting even more ridiculously inaccurate. The man firing the fifty caliber got off a few more rounds, one of which slammed through the Jeep's tailgate, but a second later, he nearly flew out of the truck.

"My knife will be inaccurate as well," Rimi called back. "I would have little control over it because our vehicle is bouncing so much. I could jump out and leap into the truck. I'm much quicker than them."

"But there's five of them plus a driver, and it only takes one bullet in the wrong spot and you're dead meat, and besides—" Abel stopped himself as he glanced in the rearview again. There was another vehicle, a sedan-style car, lurching down the road several hundred yards behind the machine-gun truck.

Galvan himself, Abel thought immediately. "There's a car coming behind the truck. Not sure if they'll make it. This road might beat it up too much."

He returned his attention to the road ahead, speeding up once again. He and Rimi bounced up and down in their seats.

"Okay, this is what we do. I'm going to get ahead of them a little here, and then I'm bailing out with my rifle. You move in and drive this thing down to Pablo's. When you get there, heave those things into the boat and get it ready to leave. I'll be along, don't worry. It shouldn't take long to get rid of these clowns. I'll run cross-country and get there hopefully not long after you. Then we're gone."

He turned to Rimi. She actually looked eager.

Where has this person been all my life? thought Abel.

"Okay, we're coming up to this little flat spot." Abel grabbed his Mk 16. "See you on the boat!" He threw his door open, fell out so that he was already rolling when he hit the ground, and Rimi seamlessly slipped into the driver's seat after him. She quickly worked the controls to adjust the seat, then gunned the engine and sent the car forward. She could hear more machine-gun fire, but no bullets zipped around the Jeep.

They must be shooting at Abel now, she thought. *Please stay alive, my dear friend.*

Abel slipped into the thick undergrowth that lined the road. He must have been seen by someone in the truck because a barrage of AK fire peppered the area where he'd hit the ground. Of course, he was no longer there, having run deeper into the jungle as soon as he'd gotten up.

The truck slowed noticeably, and Abel smiled. He hadn't wanted to tell Rimi the other reason why he wanted to bail out of the Jeep. He knew that Galvan was after him—him and only him—and that if he bailed, and Galvan knew, then Rimi would be home free with the Jeep's cargo and would make it safely to the boat. Not that he had a death wish, and not that Rimi couldn't handle things nearly as well as he in this situation, but he was a guy, and he wanted to keep his girl safe, and he didn't care how old-fashioned that sounded. That's the way he was.

Abel crept from tree to tree through the dense jungle, looking for the perfect spot where he could get off a few bursts of well-aimed rounds at the truck, which was now moving barely faster than he was. He could see everyone with their eyes peeled, staring into the forest, mostly in the wrong place. Abel finally found a spot with a clear view, aimed the Mk 16, and sprayed the bed of the truck with a full automatic burst. A second later, all three shooters in the bed were dead, riddled with bullets. At the same time, the truck sped up. Those inside fired into the forest, but none of them really knew where he was.

Abel now stepped out from behind a tree beside the road, aimed at the pickup's back window, and fired several more bursts. The truck spun sharply to the left and then turned over.

Great, thought Abel. *That will block the road for the car behind if it manages to get that far.*

He turned, expecting to either see the car a few hundred yards back or for it to not be visible at all, but suddenly, he got the shock of his life.

The car had somehow morphed into something like a monster truck. Its chassis was now a good three feet off the ground, with heavy-duty shocks and springs underneath, and its engine roared like an off-road Hemi. Worst of all, he saw something that looked like an M134 20mm Gatling gun mounted underneath. Abel had never felt more like a dead man. His body, if hit directly by the gun's spinning barrels, which were capable of firing thousands of rounds per minute, would simply disintegrate. He dashed back into the jungle and ran as fast as he ever had on a perpendicular course. At the same time, Abel heard the dreaded *buzz* of the weapon. The tree that he'd been near was obliterated. It actually fell down—across the road! Abel almost chuckled. That would be tough for even this highly elevated monstrosity to get over. He aimed and fired his weapon at the car's windshield, but all that he saw were sparks as his bullets bounced off.

Great, he thought. *It really is a tank—bulletproof and everything. What did these guys do, steal a presidential limo?*

Abel watched before deciding his next move. He noticed that the Gatling gun, for all its ferocity, was not on an electrical, remote-control swivel, but something that was hand-operated, perhaps by a steering wheel or a hand crank. It was turning in his direction, but not instantly as a military-grade weapon would. In a split second, Abel knew what to do. As the *buzz* of the cannon began again and more forest got shredded, getting ever closer to him, he took off running away from the gun's path, dodging trees, leaping logs, plowing through shrubs, all the way behind the car and to its other side.

There he dealt with a different threat. A man was standing with his door open and holding an AK-47. And not just a man, a giant man. His head was on a level taller than the freaking jacked-up car! Abel recognized him. It was Don Vicente Galvan's giant bodyguard who had stood watch when Abel had made that fateful, foolish deal with the devil over a month ago. Was it just that long ago? The giant was just aiming his AK, leading Abel's path. Abel stopped abruptly, brought his weapon up in a flash, and squeezed off a few more auto rounds. Then he took off again, glancing over to see if any damage had been done. The giant was no longer standing outside the car, and his AK was on the ground.

Chased inside at least, thought Abel. He continued to race around the car. He leaped the tree that had fallen and ran directly in front of the vehicle. Seeing a door open, he held out his Mk 16 and blindly fired it on auto at the car until his magazine ran out, hopefully once again driving any shooters back into the vehicle.

Having outraced the Gatling gun all the way around the tanklike car, and with no time to stop and pop a new magazine into his Mk 16, Abel ran through the jungle like a steeplechaser on steroids, dodging trees, leaping over or plowing through bushes, tall grass, fallen logs, sure that the tank, now blocked by the fallen tree, would simply turn into the jungle and four-wheel it straight through to the pier.

He glanced up as often as he could, trying to keep his bearings and not just blindly plunge through the forest. He knew that the road where he'd left it was one of the sections that paralleled the beach, so he ran perpendicular to that last point as much as possible. And then, unexpected help! He caught just a glimpse of Rimi and their Jeep. It was far off to the right, some sun rays glinting off its windshield on a section of road that paralleled Abel's path. *That's good!* Abel knew that the road would soon turn back toward his path and then make a right into the dirt clearing that served as Pablo's parking lot. If he just angled to his right as he ran, he should end up right near that junction.

Suddenly, though, Abel could hear pops and zings as bullets flew to his immediate left. He veered right a little and started to zigzag. He knew that the Gatling gun would be just like the truck's machine gun, almost impossible to aim accurately, but frankly, Galvan didn't have to be accurate with such a weapon. He could sweep it from side to side like a scythe in a wide arc in front of his tank-car.

The car's firing stopped, but the roar of its motor and the crunching of the heavy vehicle on the forest floor continued unabated. Since the sound came from behind him and to the left, Abel figured they must be having a slow go of it, despite their adaptations. He was probably running faster than they were going.

The *buzz* came again, this time its effects hitting first to his left, then coming toward him. Abel jumped behind the nearest tree and lay flat on the ground as a blizzard of bullets swept through the jungle all around him. Keeping his head down, he heard the ground explode just to his left, then suddenly the deadly buzz saw tore through branches high in the trees before him and to the right. They must have started firing level, then dropped into a hole, and then pulled up out of it; their bullets pounded the ground before sending a cascade of leaves and small tree branches falling from the trees around him.

Abel leaped up and ran again on the same track, now trying to think what he'd do once he did get to Pablo's. If this tank-car made it through, and there was no reason to believe it wouldn't, what would he and Rimi do then? Just a few seconds of direct hits from the Gatling gun would render their boat useless, if not sink it altogether. His Mk 16 was inept against an armored vehicle, and no one had any—

Wait a minute, thought Abel. Faviola and Javier were supposed to have left his big, heavy duffel there at Pablo's with the boat. There was a reason it was so heavy. It was not only filled with a variety of weapons but also a good supply of hand grenades he'd asked for from Monti. The Nammo HGO-115s were called scalable offensive grenades because several could be stacked securely to double or even triple the explosive power of a regular hand grenade. Abel had premade several two- and three-stacks that were in the duffel, knowing that, while stacking didn't take much time, there were far too many situations when any time was too much. If he could get to Pablo's, get to the boat, grab the grenades, and have them ready before the car made it to the parking lot, they'd have a chance. Abel spurred himself even faster. He must get to that parking lot. And then he thought of something else.

Rimi!

30

—

Javier's mind was utterly blown. What had happened in the last ten seconds played over in his head like a super-slow-motion sports replay. Only this sport was in real time and deadly. There was the man, Caleb Forrest, whose duffel bag he struggled under, leaping out of the jungle on the other side of the dirt parking area at the same time bullets started pelting the ground around him like a deadly hailstorm.

"Stop!" Forrest yelled. "Drop the bag! Drop the bag! Get down!"

With bullets flying all around, Javier didn't need convincing. He threw the duffel bag clumsily toward Caleb Forrest, then fell toward the ground, but bullets were kicking up dirt all around him. He was sure he was about to be killed when suddenly something swept him up, and the next moment he and Señora Faviola's daughter, Rimi, were flying high toward Señor Forrest's boat. Then, in the next second, Rimi, who was carrying him, alighted on the ship as softly as a bird landing on a branch, put Javier down on the deck, and then swished away again so fast he couldn't even see her.

Javier scrambled to the boat's rail to see what was going on. The shooting had stopped, and Caleb Forrest and Rimi were frantically pulling things that looked like stacks of big green Legos from the bag. Suddenly, the shooting started again, this time behind the building, then riddling the two SUVs parked nearby. One exploded spectacularly. And then the ocean itself was churned by the gunfire. Javier turned again to Abel and Rimi. They stood behind trees at opposite ends of the parking area. Javier heard the roar of an engine. Creeping out of the jungle into the parking area was a large car that looked like it was on giant truck stilts. It had a gun on its front that was moving around slowly, then zeroing in on the boat. Javier gasped. It was going to shoot at the boat!

Suddenly, he saw Abel dash at the car from behind and toss two Lego stacks under the vehicle and streak back to the jungle. Rimi had done the same, but so much faster that it was blinding to Javier. Four massive explosions erupted underneath the car. Its tires and wheels shot out in four different directions. The giant truck stilts were turned into debris that flew everywhere, and the vehicle itself was thrown high in the air and came crashing down onto what was left of the truck stilts, flipped over on its top.

There was silence in the parking area. Rimi and Abel both came out of the jungle. There was no movement at all from the vehicle. It sat like a giant dead beetle that had flipped over onto its back.

"I'll go get the Jeep. You stay here with Javier and make sure no one comes out of that thing," said Señor Forrest, and he took off at a quick jog up the road from the parking lot. Rimi took a little leap and was once again in the boat.

Rimi took one look at Javier, and her eyes widened. "What has happened to you? What has happened to mi madre?"

When Abel got back to the parking lot with Faviola's Jeep, he pulled it up to the pier so they could unload the Xilinium, but before he could get out of the Jeep, Rimi was by his side, her large eyes nearly red and her whole countenance twisted with rage.

"What the hell?" asked Abel. And then, for the entire time it took to unload and pack the Xilinium chests, Rimi told him what Javier had told her, about his and Faviola's interrogation by Galvan and his monster Jumo, about the shoot-out with Galvan's wife behind the beach house, and the uncertain fate of Faviola.

"I shall use your bombs to blow that up again and kill anything that's inside," she hissed.

"No, you won't. Those bombs aren't strong enough. That thing's armor-plated, and if anyone is still alive in there, they'd be waiting with a gun as soon as we tried to crack a window. Besides, we don't have time. We need to get back to the island before he and his men start to occupy it. If we don't, we'll never be able to defend it. As good as we are, we're not good enough to fight off thirty or forty men."

"Then when we leave, I shall use my knife, and when we pass by the inn, I will go and find mi madre."

"Actually, we'll all go to the inn, in secret, and not for long. We've got to get Javier back there, and while I do that, you can check on Faviola. But we can't stay long. No one can know we're there.

"And as for your knife, you can do whatever you want with it, my friend, but think before you do it. You can't see in those windows, so you can't direct it, and everything about the vehicle is bulletproof. I hope none of it will slow it down or snag it. I'd hate for you to lose it."

"I shall focus on the windshield glass, and it will come out the back—and I'll pray that it will tear that evil man's head off on its way through."

Abel started up the boat, and it pulled slowly away from the pier. Leaning on the stern rail, Rimi focused intently on the wrecked vehicle they were leaving behind, now lit by the flickering flames of the SUV that had exploded. Then, in the smoothest throwing stroke that Javier had ever seen, Rimi threw something that looked like a tiny blue missile at the overturned car. There were two shattering sounds just milliseconds apart, then the blue bullet returned to Rimi's hand as if by magic.

Javier walked back to the bridge as Rimi stood at the stern silently.

"Anything I can do for you, guy?" said Abel as he calmly steered the craft.

Javier just leaned against the bridge rail and stared at the sun, which was now getting low in the west. "No," he said. Abel patted him gently on the shoulder and gave the boat a bit more gas as they sailed toward Playa de Palma.

Back at Pablo's, a burly man and two people, a young couple dressed in swim gear, went to the overturned car and cautiously checked it out.

"Holy shit. What the fuck?" said the woman, who was wearing a sexy bikini.

"Look, the front windshield has a hole in it," said her husband. His wife got down on her hands and knees to check it out with him while the burly man, Pablo, stood beside the car, kicking at the unbroken glass on the passenger-side window.

What the hell happened here? he thought. *And who killed my desk clerk, Curly, and shot up my building?*

Suddenly, Pablo heard two little sounds, and when he looked down to where they came from, he saw both the man and the woman he'd trained that day with the backs of their skulls blown entirely off. Horrified, he tried to look away, but then he heard the same sound, felt a sharp pain in his spine, then no feeling at all. He collapsed to the ground as he watched blood gush from a hole in his neck, then all went black.

As the three bodies bled outside the wreck, a weak but defiant voice spoke in Spanish.

"Get someone here, quick. We're alive but trapped and injured. And bring the big trawler in. We'll need weapons, and more men, too."

Ron felt exhausted.

He and several of his most trusted companions in the community patrol had quietly armed themselves, excused themselves from whatever they had been doing, and all met on the bridge over the Rio Palma. There'd just been four of them, two other men and one woman, so they wouldn't attract undue attention.

"Hey, look," the woman, Lara, the owner of one of the souvenir shops, had said. "Those construction guys are all headed back to the pier. Must be going to the island."

Ron had been sorely tempted to speculate more with these three, all longtime shopkeepers along the road between the pier and the river, about the purpose of these workers' island excursion, but he'd quickly put it out of his mind. They had to stay focused. He had to stay focused.

"All right, here's what's up," he'd said. "Marta's little boy says that behind one of the beach houses at the Rio Palma, there's a couple of women's bodies and a lot of blood. Since Javier, the desk clerk, is gone, and Haley, the afternoon clerk, doesn't know where either he or Faviola is, I'm thinking, assuming the kid just didn't have a nightmare or something, that one's probably Faviola."

The others had let out little gasps, and Juan, one of the owners of the general store, had said laconically, "I guess that's what I'm doing with these Ziploc freezer bags and fifty-five-gallon drum liners."

"I didn't figure you'd have body bags in stock," Ron had said grimly.

"Could have ordered them, though," Juan had replied.

They had all gone together, acting as normal as possible, through the parking lot to the little road that led through the small spit of jungle down to the beach houses, then walked on until they could see the back ends of the beach houses through the trees.

"He said Guesthouse Number Two," Ron had said quietly, and sure enough, as they'd peered through the trees, they'd seen the ghastly scene.

Ron, fighting nausea himself, had taken charge on the fly. In the process of checking things out and cleaning them up, they'd found first and foremost that Faviola was definitely one of the victims, but was breathing, though unconscious. He'd immediately sent Lara to ask Haley if there were any doctors at the inn. Since there was no doctor in Playa de Palma, Faviola would offer doctors and their families free lodging if the doctor showed his medical ID and signed on as an on-call doctor who would handle the immediate treatment of medical situations that might arise and mitigate them until an ambulance came from Parrita. Fortunately, there'd been one, an orthopedist from Modesto, California, who came to Playa de Palma every year to get away from the baking summer heat there.

He had been called, and the dead body had been hastily bundled into a couple of Juan's oversized drum liners and taken around the side of the building so the doctor wouldn't see it. Lara had also talked Haley into letting her borrow one of the maid's carts, and she'd stocked it with soap and brushes and bleach and brought it down, and then she and Juan and the other man, Horatio, had scrubbed things as best they could. Ron had met the doctor, a quiet, tall man in his fifties, and explained that his job was only to examine and treat the woman, nothing else.

With laser focus, the doctor had immediately gone to Faviola, woken her up, checked her vital signs, assessed and treated her many bruises and scrapes, and set her ankle with an air splint after cleaning and bandaging a bullet wound that was covered with dried blood. All the while, Faviola had drifted in and out of consciousness, always mumbling something about "stop him." The doctor had told Ron that she'd been badly beaten but had no visible broken bones other than the shattered ankle and her nose. She had lost a large amount of blood, though, and should get to a hospital or clinic for more thorough treatment and a transfusion if possible. Otherwise, she'd just need to rest—she wasn't hemorrhaging anymore. Then he'd left.

The four of them had all gingerly taken Faviola in through the back door of the beach house, which seemed to be unoccupied, although there were someone's things stashed in the bedroom. They'd put Faviola on the bed and covered her. She had briefly woken up and mumbled, but that was it.

She now lay calmly, and were it not for the bruises, she looked quite serene.

The four then went out onto the porch and sat in the chairs and watched the sun slowly sink lower over the ocean, each one silent with their own thoughts and in various states of emotional and physical exhaustion. Ron asked, "Well, what do we do now?"

"Maybe we should call the clinic in Parrita," said Horatio. "It is the closest. They'd send an ambulance for sure."

"We can't do anything like that without telling Monti first," replied Lara. "He'd probably kick us out of town if we didn't."

"Fuck Monti," said Juan in a menacing voice. "He's probably part of this somehow—him or that asshole with the big car that came into town this morning and paraded those militias down the road later on."

"Good answer," came a sarcastic voice from behind them. Each was so startled that they instantly turned around, Horatio nearly falling out of his chair.

"Whew! Agent Forrest! You scared the shit out of us. What are you doing here?" stuttered Ron, his heart still in his throat.

"This is my beach house. I was staying in Number One, but they moved me over here this morning so Don Vicente Galvan, the guy that came into town today in that big car you were talking about, could have it for him and his wife. I'm guessing that's her in the drum by the side of the house."

The four nodded grimly.

"You guys got some tough decisions to make. Your man Monti's the one that's invited this guy into your town. Just so happens that he's out to kill me this time, but it won't be the last time stuff like this goes on. If they build on that island what I think they will, you're going to have clientele like Galvan and his thugs coming into town every week. Your tourist trade will vanish. You'll have stuff like what went on behind the house here go on all the time. I've seen it in Cartagena, and it'll be worse here."

"What does he want to build out there?" asked Lara.

"They're called waystations, I think," Ron said before Abel could answer. "They're safe places where drug-smuggling boats can stop and refuel. A guy in the diner I know said they were hired by 'some guy' to clear land on the island. He's mentioned waystations before. They got paid ten thousand dollars each up front."

"Fuck," spat Juan. "That's drug money for you. Fat Monti's sold us out so he can get fucking rich."

"He's been into drug money for ages," replied Ron, "and he spreads the wealth pretty well."

"A lot of that's been DEA money," said Abel, "and he won't be in control this time. He thinks he will, but Galvan's just playing him. Once he doesn't need Monti anymore, he'll be dead as a doorknob. I'd be surprised if he's alive next year, and if this town's around much longer." Abel rose. "Like I said, it's not my town, but you guys need to figure out what you're going to do. Monti talks big, but he's still dependent on you guys for now, but not for long if that thing gets going on the island. I wish you luck. Rimi and I have to get going now."

"Where are you going, Señor Forrest?" asked Horatio.

"To defend our island," said Abel.

"Your island," sneered Juan.

"Rimi's island—she's lived there for a hundred years, her and the animals, and I'm with her, so you bet your ass *our* island," Abel snarled back to him.

"So, you mean that Rimi—Rimi's the evil presence on that island, the reason they call it Isla del Diablo?" questioned Ron. "How the hell—she's just so small and plain and—"

"Trust me." Abel smirked. "She's your worst nightmare if you're not on her side. Oh, and one other thing. If you could move Faviola out of town somewhere, we'd be much obliged. Things could get really crazy around here, and she's had enough of it."

Caleb Forrest disappeared into the beach house, and just a minute later, the four community patrol people saw him and Rimi appear from behind the house and head down the beach and out of sight.

Once again, there was silence on the porch for a moment. Then Ron said, "Horatio, I think you and Lara should take Faviola to the clinic in Parrita, and Juan, I think you and I should have a little talk with Monti."

"Here, in this place, the scene of the crime, with no one else around but the rest of the patrol," Juan concurred.

31

—

Abel steered the boat toward the north side of the island. Since there was no boat and no activity on the big beach on the island's mainland-facing side, he figured Galvan's men must have rounded the island and found the same inlet he had discovered two weeks before and were probably in the process of setting up operations there. Had it just been two weeks ago? It was amazing how time seemed to have flown since he'd come to this island, first as a predatory visitor looking to kill whatever it was that haunted it so he could get a million dollars and go do—go do what? That was the question he'd never had clear answers for until he'd come to this island. Now, they were as clear as anything he'd ever envisioned. Rid the island of these men. Rid the world of Don Vicente Galvan. Put Fat Monti back in his place. All so that he and Rimi could preserve the beauty of their Green Cathedral, their new relationship, and their unique way of life without interference from others. That's what it was time to do. He and Rimi had a plan, and now, it was time to execute it.

Rimi came up from below the deck with several of the loose boxes of Xilinium stashed in a plastic bag and tied to the waist belt of her jungle outfit, which she'd retrieved while at the beach house. Tied on to the other side was a scabbard containing her glowing blue knife.

"You sure that's enough?" asked Abel.

Rimi nodded. "For several years—at least." She had that eager "let's get it on" look in her big green eyes that Abel loved so much.

"Okay, babe, this is it. Do your flying leap thing, stash that stuff in Bibi, and then you and your friends get busy. Remember, scare first. If they leave, good for them. If they fight—well, bad for them, I guess."

"Remember, you can think to me. I'll hear you."

"And I'll hear you," said Abel. He wrapped her in a tight hug, and they kissed. "I'll never let you die," whispered Abel.

She held up her bracelet. "Remember also your lifeline to me. Remember, we'll never be lost again!" And with that, she took two quick steps and leaped off the side of the trawler high into the setting sun, and a second later, Abel saw a small splash not far from the mainland-side beach.

He headed the boat around the volcano slowly, and as he neared an anchorage on its other side, he saw that his hunch was right. The construction crew, who must have numbered at least thirty, was unloading equipment at the very same little bay that he'd used so many times to anchor his boat and go ashore. There were lots of chainsaws, explosives, and machetes, but also, ominously, a good number of AK-47s and small arms as well.

A cartel construction crew for sure, thought Abel. These guys wouldn't be scared easily.

He tossed out his anchor and slipped the rubber raft into the water. He threw in his backpack carrying his Mk 16, as many hand grenades as he could fit, and extra ammo, then made for the shore. He beached the little motorboat and then hustled across some open ground into the jungle, where he quickly hooked up with his jungle trail that headed along the stream and up the volcano. After five minutes of the most vigorous hiking he'd done in years, he was well up the side of the volcano in his sniper nest. He dug the big M107 Light

Fifty out from its cave hiding place, along with the ammo box, and set himself up. He also scouted out several areas that he could move to so he couldn't be pinpointed. Who knew if the armaments of the construction crew might include RPGs or mortars? He didn't want to be in the same place for more than a minute or two.

As he returned to his main sniper nest, he reminded himself out loud, "Ninety-four rounds. That's all you've got. Ninety-four rounds, after that, you're human again. Ninety-four rounds—don't lose count."

Suddenly, he heard a loud, musical bird call that echoed off the volcano and all around the island.

Rimi, thought Abel. *She's ready.*

He took aim at a stack of AKs and other weapons piled on the beach near the path he'd cut two weeks before. Construction crewmen were using it to move equipment and manpower in toward the Cathedral entrance. He fired three rounds into this stuff and watched the guns leap up and shatter spectacularly, and a box, which must have been filled with either mortar bombs or grenades, blew up with a deafening explosion. Several men nearby went down with shrapnel wounds. Other men dove for cover.

"Oops," said Abel. "Ninety-one rounds left."

Then he heard another sound, that of a construction crew member screaming, and the loud roar (though far off) of a big cat. There was a short AK burst, and then another man screaming.

Rimi and friends in action.

He turned his sniper scope to the Green Cathedral entrance, where several men had already started in on some of the majestic trees with their chainsaws. Abel aimed carefully and fired.

"Ninety, eighty-nine, eighty-eight," he said to himself.

At the Cathedral entrance, José and his crew had just started working after José had said admiringly that this place looked like the entry into a church. Suddenly, he cried out as something ripped the chainsaw from his hand. Two of his other men had the same thing happen, and they all ducked when their refueling can exploded.

"What the hell?" shouted José. "This place was supposed to be safe. Pass out the weapons and take cover!"

Meanwhile, at the river, Rimi saw a boat full of equipment, including torches, being pushed into the water and several men began rowing it across. She called to the crocodiles at the mouth of the river with her mind. They slid into the river and headed upstream. There was also a man with an AK rifle who had found Abel's cable. He was about to swing across to provide cover for the others. Rimi called out in a screeching sound, and suddenly, the three monkeys that had descended on Abel weeks ago now leaped from the trees and landed right on the man's head. The man screamed with fear, and in his panic, he fired his machine gun wildly. Bullets flew everywhere. Rimi, who was hiding high in a nearby tree, heard bullets smack into trees all around her. She ducked behind a tree trunk, but not before a bullet clipped her throwing arm. Rimi tried to shake off the injury—it wasn't deep—but it could affect how hard she could throw her knife. She decided not to tell Abel at this time. These men were scared and might go away soon.

She turned and saw that the men in the boat had made it to the other side, and one man was onshore and had set fire to an area using an accelerant. She contacted Bibi through her mind and then watched as three crocs leaped from the water and dragged the two men who were still in the boat into the river. A fourth rose up on the riverbank and chased the man with the torch, who ran away and set more forest on fire in his panic.

Suddenly, the man saw two long, slender metal tentacles snaking through the shrub near him. He jumped back in horror as one went into the river, and the other began spraying river water all over the fires he'd just set. The water had such force that it doused the blaze in seconds, and then caught the man full in the chest and sent him careening back into the river—and the croc slithered back in after him.

Abel had most of the construction crew on the run. Using precision firing, he'd shot up virtually all the munitions the workers had brought ashore. MRE boxes had been riddled. A big one-hundred-gallon water tank had been shot through with several bullets and water was pouring out all over the construction headquarters that was being set up. A portable satellite dish had been blasted, along with communications equipment.

Abel, now with seventy bullets left, noted the chaos as some of the men were panicking. Some ran out of the jungle, screaming that it was haunted, that animals were in rebellion against them. Many were bloodied in some fashion. Rimi had let him know that these men had been attacked and that several were now actually crocodile dinners. When these panicked people saw their comrades at the edge of the Cathedral and at the beach headquarters were pinned down by sniper fire, they spread the panic to others.

Abel now turned his sniper rifle on the rubber boats that had brought the men ashore, and those still ferrying supplies in from their large ship.

"Sixty-nine, sixty-eight, sixty-seven, sixty-six," he counted as he squeezed off each shot, two in each rubber boat on the beach, two more into the two boats acting as ferries. As the frightened workers saw their comrades sinking and their boats being riddled, they panicked even more. At least a dozen left their heavy utility belts and boots and dashed into the water, hoping to swim for it.

One group, though, didn't panic. It was José's group, those who had been eating at the All-American Diner earlier in the day.

Contrary to what José had told the American expat proprietor, his men were not just journeymen construction workers who went where the money took them. They were all seasoned soldiers of the cartel in Cartagena, land clearers for sure, but experienced killers as well, brought to this area by Don Vicente Galvan some time ago to be in a position to start work immediately on this project. They would be the core of the construction force.

When they saw other panicked workers fleeing through the jungle, bleeding from animal attacks, they either stopped the men or simply killed them if they wouldn't stop. Meanwhile, José had been searching for the sniper. Knowing that the volcano would make a perfect post, he'd been scanning with his monocular for where the devil might be, and now he had found him.

The man was using several different locations around a small cave on an exposed side of the volcano, which gave him an unobstructed view of the entire island, but also gave José an unobstructed view of where he was, aside from the rocks he was hiding behind. There were several ways to deal with a sniper once you knew where they were. One was to have your own sniper take him out, another was to engage him so much that you could resume your work. José's unit had no sniper or sniper rifle. Another choice would be to target the sniper with air-strikes or barrages from nearby boats or an artillery battery, but they had neither of those as well. Those might be coming later, but this guy could have shot them all up by then. The other way, much less preferable and much more dangerous, was to go after the sniper in his nest with men on the ground. This would almost certainly involve casualties, but it was the only option, and if something weren't done soon, all would be lost—he and his men would be all that was left of the construction crew.

And so, as an occasional bullet from above crashed through more supplies or blew up another box of dynamite, he had sent several of his men out to scavenge for assault rifles, and they had returned with five, mostly picked up in the jungle or the meadow where panicked workers had abandoned them. There were still a couple of their own assault rifles that were usable, and there was some extra ammunition as well. José told them where their objective was and what their plan was.

Of course, this movement had not gone unnoticed by Abel. He watched as the group climbed the slope up the very trail that he and Rimi had used, and how several had split off, forded the creek as it narrowed farther up the hill, and swung around the mountain in a long arc just at the edge of the tree line, thinking they were undercover. This would be almost too easy. He thought to Rimi what was going on, telling her to go after the second group with whatever animals she could find. Meanwhile, he continued to fuel the panic among the others on the island, shooting at their large boat, causing the men to go wild with fear, running and swimming and flailing at the water to get to the ship before it was disabled and all hope of leaving the island was dashed. He would lull these men coming up the mountain into thinking that he had not seen them, and then, when they were closer in and exposed, he'd deal with them with his Mk 16, saving the precious .50 caliber bullets in case they were needed later.

José and his five men approached the little pool where the creek originated. They heard the explosions of the .50 caliber gun as it rained its destruction below. A couple looked down and saw how far up they'd come and cringed, but José snapped at them.

"Turn around. We have a job to do! I will see where the sniper is, and then we'll attack accordingly. We will drive the hornet from his nest, and our friends will finish him off."

With that, the four others took cover, and José crept out to get a better view. He poked his head up over a rock just the slightest bit and glanced around. The loud report of the sniper gun quickly gave away its user's position. José smiled.

Suddenly, though, he heard screams and cries from the area where his other team should be. Something was happening to his other team!

But the sniper was still here! He raised up again, and this time saw one of the men from his other group—with a wild cat on his back growling and biting at the man's neck. The animal pierced it, blood sprayed like a fountain, and the man collapsed.

Forgetting himself, José was transfixed, when suddenly, there was a burst of machine-gun fire from somewhere. He was walloped by so many bullets that he was thrown back against a rock. He bounced off it and plunged downward past where his men watched in horror. Those men screamed and ran back down the trail, where the machine gun mowed them down like someone killing rats driven out of a hole.

And then, there was the telltale whistling sound of incoming fire, and the whole area was rocked with an explosion.

Abel ducked behind the rocks as he heard the whistle of the incoming bomb. It blew up about thirty feet away, basically where José and his men had been before Abel had slaughtered them. Figuring that the bomb was meant for him, Abel changed position to another of his sniper nests, then did a quick survey of the area, trying to pinpoint the origin of the bomb. Even as he began this, another explosion forced him to duck, but it came closer to his old position, not really near where he was now.

Rimi surprised him from behind.

"There are no more killers behind you. My friends have eliminated them all." Abel turned, and she gave him a hug. "We have driven all the bad men away! They are all leaving, but where have these explosions come from?"

"I'm trying to figure that out now. It could be from the air, but I don't think—"

"I've found it—where they're coming from!" said Rimi excitedly. "Look, out to sea!"

Abel saw another boat of some kind coming toward the island from its ocean side, heading for the little harbor where the construction crew boat was just beginning to ease out. Abel trained his sniper scope onto it.

"Watch out! It has sent another bomb our way!" cried Rimi. The two took cover together near the rocks that surrounded them as another explosion pounded the other sniper's nest. Abel quickly retrained the sniper scope back on the boat. His eyes popped!

Where the hell did Monti, or even Don Vicente Galvan, get a ship like that?

What he was looking at was an old US Navy Mark III Patrol Craft Fast, better known as a swift boat, a craft whose heyday had been in the Vietnam War! Old weapons systems of many types were up for sale on the dark web all the time, but something this old that was still serviceable was remarkable. And dangerous. The old swift boats had been armed with two mounted .50 caliber machine guns and an 81mm mortar that could lob its big shells for almost three miles. That must be what was pounding them now—the mortar. Fortunately, a boat-mounted one wouldn't be that accurate, but all it would take was one direct hit, and Abel and his gun would be history. The other thing that the swift boat had was an abundance of deck space, and this one was covered with armed men who didn't look like glorified construction workers. Abel counted another thirty or so, plus the crew of the boat.

"This could get bad, Rimi. That's a heavily armed boat out there, and there are lots of men on the decks, all armed. What do you think you can do with your knife on that?"

"Not much until it gets closer. My arm was grazed by a bullet fired wildly by an evil man being attacked by my monkey friends."

"What? Let me see," said Abel.

Rimi continued as Abel examined her. "I cannot do so much to the boat if it is armored, but plenty to the men. If they stay out on the boat's floor like that, I can hit many with one throw. But it must come closer."

"You don't look too bad, babe, but be careful. Listen. Go back on down, get yourself to where you can use that knife. We've got to keep these guys off the land if we can, or we'll be overwhelmed."

"Overwhelmed or not, we will win, my dear companion. This is our Green Cathedral, and we won't let evil people take it from us!" She turned to go.

"Wait!" cried Abel. She turned just in time to meet Abel, who smothered her in a crushing embrace. They kissed passionately and then squeezed each other hard again. Abel stared into her big green eyes.

"Don't die," he said. "Life without you would be—Jesus, I don't know, really shitty." He kissed her again.

"Don't worry, dear friend," she smiled back. "No one is dying today except those invaders." She kissed him. "I love you, dear Abel!"

Rimi then turned and bounced down the mountain like a deer, Abel never taking his eyes off her.

Watching her is like watching a never-ending miracle, he thought.

Time to pull his trigger again. No way was he dying today. Not even a chance!

There was another explosion, this one more random. Abel raised his sniper rifle again, putting the mortar right in his sights. He squeezed off four more rounds, ripping to shreds the body of one of the operators and damaging the mortar. It was a good shot, but now he was below fifty shots left. He fired another two shots at the men coming to replace the mortar crew, then redirected his fire to the boat's bridge, scattering several men and putting giant holes in the bridge's armor. As the men recovered themselves after Abel's salvo, Abel scoped the bridge again, hoping to kill the captain. And that's when he saw that the apparent captain was none other than Monti Ruiz!

32

———

I t had been one hellacious day for Monti Ruiz.

At first, all seemed to be going very well. Don Vicente Galvan and his crew of heavily armed men had left, and the meeting with the shop owners had seemed to go well, especially when the construction crew arrived and the shops and sodas filled up with friendly customers who had full wallets and big appetites. All had seemed well as the construction crews drifted back to their boat and readied to head to the island, which Monti assumed was safe thanks to DEA Agent Caleb Forrest.

And speaking of Caleb Forrest, it was troubling to discover that he was actually a DEA agent from Cartagena named Abel something-or-other who had caused Don Vicente Galvan much loss, and even more disturbing that Galvan was hell-bent on getting immediate revenge by going after this Abel, who had gone with Faviola's adopted daughter to the island. Monti was glad that Galvan and his men had left and secretly hoped the DEA agent prevailed against the don. Then, perhaps, he, Monti Ruiz, could assume control of their heretofore joint project.

But then things had begun happening thick and fast, so much so that Monti couldn't even figure out which were good and which were bad. He'd gotten a desperate call from Don Vicente. He was trapped in his armored car, which apparently the DEA agent had blown up. He needed help and also wanted his big boat and his armed soldiers taken to the island. Monti had called in the boat and sent Paco and some men to Pedro's scuba school to see what they could do there, but just moments later, his entire community patrol had shown up at his pavilion, armed and in full uniform, wanting answers.

They'd told him what Vicente Galvan had done to Faviola and related Javier's story of what had really happened to the don at the hands of Abel and Faviola's daughter. They had then demanded to know everything, or they'd take him into custody that moment and put him on trial before the entire town. Fearing for his life, Monti had told them about the waystation, about how it would be set up and run by Don Vicente Galvan and Monti jointly, and how he would get a share of the profits, which he swore he'd share with the community, even though he hadn't been so sure about that just a half hour before.

It was after this conversation that the community patrol had proposed a plan. Monti would immediately see to it that Don Vicente Galvan was eliminated. He would then assume command of the cartel soldiers that Galvan had called into the area and ensure that they eliminated the two occupants of "the town's island," as they put it. Though Monti heard some groans and outcries at this, they were quickly shouted down by others. It seemed they were thirsty for revenge for lost loved ones the "evil one" on the island had killed in the past, even though that would mean killing Faviola's daughter, something that clearly did not sit well with many in the meeting. Once these things were accomplished, Monti would supervise construction of the waystation until it was done and the cartel workers were gone. Then he and the patrol would consider all options—legitimate and not-so-legitimate—of what to do with the island and together come up with something that would benefit the entire community. Every part of the plan, though carried out by Monti, would be overseen by patrol personnel.

If Monti went along with it, he'd be able to continue as he always had as the leading citizen of the town. If not, he would be put on trial, and at the very least run out of town and shot on sight if he ever showed up again. Not much of a choice, and yet, the community patrol was actually being quite generous with him, come to think of it. He'd said that he'd accept their plan, and then, in front of them all, had made a call to Paco, who was already on his way through the jungle to Pedro's, having found the road to the scuba school blocked with a downed tree and a disabled vehicle. Everyone listened over Monti's speakerphone as the first part of the plan, the elimination of Don Vicente Galvan, was then executed with cold precision.

Paco had brought one of Pedro's boats to the pier. He had picked up Monti along with Ron and Juan, the patrol's overseers. All four had donned face masks and other clothing worn by Don Vicente Galvan's guards, and then left for the island, even as they heard the near-constant sound of gunfire coming from it. It was unnerving, this sudden and shocking introduction into big cartels and their soldiers. But with his life literally depending on the day's outcome, Monti steeled all of them for their mission.

A few minutes later, their small boat met up with the Clan de Cartagena's most recent acquisition, a former US Navy swift boat that Vicente Galvan had bought from a Vietnamese government official Monti and his entourage had boarded the boat, and in what Monti considered a rather grand speech, he told Galvan's hardened soldiers who sat on the deck about the tragic death of their leader, of his appointment to the head of the Costa Rican arm of the clan, his resolve to fulfill Don Vicente's dream and to heap vengeance on those responsible for his murder. After a cheer from everyone aboard, Monti ordered the boat full speed ahead to the island.

As they drew near the island's ocean side, Monti had been shocked at what he'd seen through his binoculars. The area near the rubber boat landings was covered with panicked construction workers. They were all jumping into rubber boats and hurrying to the trawler that had brought them there. Some simply abandoned all their equipment and plunged into the water on foot, swimming for the trawler. The entire meadow area between the beach and the grand rainforest trees that gave the island its other name, La Catedral Verde, was covered with dead bodies, boxes of supplies, land-clearing munitions, and ammunition, most of which had been destroyed.

Monti was going to pass the binoculars to Ron, who stood next to him, when he heard distant gunfire, and one of the rubber boats was suddenly riddled with holes. As it went down, leaving its load of eight men to thrash around in the water and try not to drown, Monti looked toward the volcano, the direction of the shot report, with his binoculars. There, protruding from some boulders, was the barrel of the very gun he had looked so hard to find for Agent Forrest when he was supposedly clearing out the evil presence from the island, the .50 caliber sniper rifle that had an effective range of nearly a mile.

This could be very bad, he thought.

Monti handed his binoculars to Ron and stepped out the back of the bridge. Spying the boat's mortar crew, he yelled, "Raise the mortar! Set its range for the volcano, and fire at those boulders up there!" He pointed to the mortar's spotter, who looked through his binoculars, then gave his crew and Monti a thumbs-up. The gunner pulled the lanyard, and the 81mm round was on its way.

There was an explosion on the side of the volcano, but the round had missed. The rifle once again peered out, this time from a different set of rocks.

"Take cover!" yelled Monti, but he was too late. He looked back just in time to see the spotter's body blown apart after being hit in the midsection by one of the sniper's big .50 caliber rounds. The gunner's arm was severed, and the range-finding mechanism of the mortar was shattered. Monti yelled for someone else to take up the mortar, but suddenly, the bridge area was hit. One bullet went through the glass and narrowly missed Ron's head. He and Juan, next to him, ducked, but for Juan, it was tragic. A bullet came straight through the bridge's armored bulwark facing and lodged in his eye, too spent to explode his head, but not to blind him. As Ron tried immediately to get the sizzling round out of Juan's head, he looked up at Monti. Both were terrified.

Ron had never in his life seen such carnage, and Monti only briefly, while still in Mexico. Both would have chosen to leave this kind of work to real soldiers while they waited on the beaches of Playa de Palma for word of the outcome. But this was their plan, and each had their job to do. So Ron grabbed a first-aid kit off the wall, and Monti gave a command into his intercom.

"Full speed ahead! Ready the boats!" And then, looking behind him as his men scrambled for cover on the crowded deck, he commanded, "Whoever has an RPG, be ready to fire on those rocks once you're in range! And the same for you muchachos with the machine guns!"

Before he could turn around, Monti saw one of the gunners splatter all over his machine-gun emplacement, and the heads of five cartel soldiers exploded simultaneously as they crouched in a line along the boat's deck. Some blue streak swished around and took out three more soldiers on the other side of the deck. Swallowing the bile that came up into his mouth, Monti called out to his men.

"Take cover below. Take cover wherever you can find! You'll all be ashore soon!"

Then he ducked below the window level of the bridge while his helmsman did the same, steering the boat with just his eyes peering over the brink. Today, Monti decided, he'd find out just what kind of fighter he could be. If he proved good, he might live. If he didn't, he'd most surely die, if not by the hand of Agent Forrest, then by the hand of the community patrol after his trial.

33

—

When Abel saw the swift boat speed up, he knew that the end for him and Rimi could be near. Closing the distance between them and the land would almost instantly take away his advantage of being able to rain bullets down on the boat while he was out of range of their armaments. Even the ship's mounted .50 caliber machine guns would have had a hard time hitting him since he was up so much higher than the boat. He'd just picked off one of the gunners and had seen a whole line of men dissolve in bloody gook after being decapitated by Rimi's knife when the boat gunned its engines hard, and it leaped forward. He tried to hit the other gunner but couldn't be sure of the shot. The target was simply moving too fast. Every one of his dwindling supply of bullets counted.

Since the boat was now going at top speed, some of its hull below the waterline was exposed. Abel decided to see if he could put some holes in the hull. The rapidly closing range of the boat combined with the speed of his antimateriel rounds might punch through even if the hull was armored. He was about to fire away when something streaked across his sniper scope. The next thing he saw was a long slit opening down the entire length of the boat's hull that was exposed before continuing on.

Rimi! She must have used herself as a guided missile with her knife as its point, dragging it through the hull of the swift boat and eviscerating it. The boat instantly began sinking, its racing motor actually driving more water into it by the second. It suddenly stopped, bottomed out in the shallow water before the deck was submerged, and hurled panicked cartel soldiers into the sea, some in boats, some thrown all the way up into the shallows of the beach, and others simply dunked into the drink. Suddenly, there was panic near one of the boats. It was sinking, and the water around it was filled with blood as if a shark had attacked. Abel knew it wasn't a shark.

Come on, girl, get out of there, he thought, hoping that Rimi would pick up on what he was thinking.

An instant later, he saw Rimi shoot from the water as if launched by some catapult. He pulled his gun back and watched as she flew high in the air and came down somewhere in the jungle behind the meadow. He had no idea if she had been wounded or not.

What he did see was that, once again, the cartel soldiers were like sitting ducks, waiting to be taken out. He squeezed off more rounds, carefully targeting each victim all the way until he saw their bodies explode into pools of blood and gore.

Suddenly, though, he saw a fiery swish erupt from the boat's deck and head his way. RPG! He ducked just in time to let the rocks take the brunt of the explosion and not expose himself to too much shrapnel. He peered out and looked for the rocket man as droves of cartel soldiers continued making their way to shore. No dice—couldn't pick the guy out, so he took aim again at the waterlogged soldiers, but then, another swish, and another explosion. Whoever was in charge down there was no dummy. He was pounding him with explosions while his exposed men went ashore. Abel tried again to aim, but this time, .50 caliber machine-gun fire raked his position.

Time to move, he thought.

Abel grabbed his backpack and made a mad dash to one of his other sniper nests. Hurling himself down just in time to see another RPG round pulverize where he'd just been, he smiled. He loaded another clip with .50 caliber rounds, which were now down to fewer than twenty. He had to make these count. Each one must put at least one soldier out of commission, preferably more. He'd have to fire as many shots as he could in the minute or less that it would take the gunners below to locate his new position and blanket it with fire.

He creeped out on a ledge in front of his rock hideaway. The whole scene was below him, cartel soldiers paddling to shore and unloading on the beach, then dashing into the meadow grass for cover, and for the first time, he saw the gunners on the bottomed-out swift boat holding position and ready to fire up at him with their machine guns and RPG launchers. Suddenly, a streak of blue ripped through a boatload of men, sinking the boat and slicing up two or three of them.

Rimi again, thought Abel. *I'll live through this day for you, girl.*

With that in mind, he set his scope on the three gunners on the swift boat and fired pairs of rounds at each. Seconds later, their bodies were blood splatters on the deck, and their weapons unmanned. Abel now targeted the guns themselves. He took out both machine guns with one shot each, but several brave men ran in and snatched up the RPGs and their ammo boxes. Abel hit a couple and managed to disable one of the RPGs, but the others escaped into the meadow grass. One pulled out some binoculars and looked his way, and Abel made sure that that was the last thing the guy ever saw. But then his clip was out. He loaded his last ten bullets, and as he did, an RPG round exploded just yards to his right. Luckily, he was down so low that any shrapnel hits were only a nuisance.

So what would he do with his last ten shots? Abel peered through the sniper scope. He couldn't see the RPG guys in the meadow grass, all the cartel soldiers were now on land. He could pick some off, but not enough. What about a leader, though? Shooting the person in charge would probably end this whole affair! And at the same time that revelation hit him, Abel knew whom he must target—Fat Monti.

Casting about with his sniper scope, he finally found him. There he was, crouched behind a tree with another man. He had a bullhorn and was directing fire at some trees near the entrance to the Green Cathedral.

He must think he's found Rimi, Abel thought. He looked over and saw Rimi zip back and forth between trees, always seconds ahead of hailstorms of bullets. *That will end*, Abel thought.

He trained his rifle on Monti, who was hidden so completely behind the tree that he had almost no shot at all. As he did, a thousand thoughts flooded his mind. This was Monti Ruiz, the town's heretofore benevolent drug dealer, a small-time operator who had fled the cartel wars in Mexico and set up his own little operation in a peaceful Costa Rican village. With it, he'd brought prosperity and progress to it. He'd cooperated with the DEA and was respected by them for the valuable information he'd shared. He'd hired Abel to do a job for the tidy sum of a million US dollars.

It was Monti who had brought Abel to the Green Cathedral, and soon after, the most amazing woman he'd ever met. Shouldn't he feel some gratitude to the man? How would Playa de Palma go on without him? He relaxed his aim for a second . . . but only for a second as other thoughts poured through him.

Things had changed in these last two weeks. Abel had found beauty and purpose through Rimi, the woman from the stars who had miraculously come into his life on this enchanted isle. A million dollars was the furthest thing from his mind at this moment. All he cared about was protecting his faithful and beautiful friend. He checked his crystal bracelet at the thought—yes, she was still alive and well, somewhere in the forest, protecting the Green Cathedral.

Frustrated with his lack of a good shot, Abel hustled back to his former sniper's nest, lay in his prone firing position, and once again trained the sniper scope on Monti. Aha! It wasn't a great shot, but it was doable. Enough of Monti was exposed to fill his crosshairs, as was the soldier who always seemed to be near him. Abel steadied, let out a breath—

And just as he was squeezing the trigger, he heard the hiss of the RPG, and an explosion just behind him lifted him off the ground and tossed him forward.

"Aiyeee!"

Monti screamed as wood from the tree trunk behind his head exploded and sent sharp splinters of wood flying everywhere, including into his neck. Ron, who was next to him, got a face-full of slivers himself.

"Ack! My eye! I think the wood got it!"

At the same time, the RPG operator stood up in the meadow and cheered. "I got him!" he yelled. "I think I got him!" Monti looked up just in time to see the man cut in half by the blue streak he'd figured out by now came from Faviola's "daughter," Rimi, who seemed to fly between the trees at an incredible speed. They'd cornered her in a few trees near the churchlike entrance to the island's rainforest, but she still was highly lethal.

"Estúpido!" growled Monti to the now-dead RPG operator. *He better have gotten the sniper—Agent Forrest.*

At any rate, the sniper had almost single-handedly destroyed over half his force of cartel soldiers—he and his jungle companion—and Monti wasn't sure how much more they could take. And yet, the community patrol's instructions had been clear: eliminate both the DEA agent and Rimi, who, sadly, under normal circumstances most everyone in town liked. Not enough to have them stand in the way of the town's use of the island, though. Aside from the revenge factor, Ron, Juan, and the others had heard them declare that the island was *their* island, and they'd defend it from anyone encroaching on it. How presumptuous of them. Who cared if the woman had lived there for years and years? The island represented a tremendous opportunity for growth for their burgeoning community, and one person, or two, couldn't be allowed to selfishly stand in the way of that. As long as an armed force of Colombian cartel soldiers was on hand and doing the dirty work (and getting killed) anyway, it was best just to eliminate both of them now.

So much easier said than done, thought Monti.

He was tired of this slaughter. He picked wood shards out of his neck, and Ron, the American food soda owner and the community patrol's last observer, was having one removed from his eye by the cartel detachment's corpsman. Monti decided he'd had enough. His men would attack the trees with as much force as they could muster, and that would bring the sniper down from his perch. He must be nearly out of ammunition anyway. Monti had only given him one hundred rounds with the gun, and he'd been continuously shooting for hours.

"I need men, here at the arches, now!" he commanded through his bullhorn. "Bring hand grenades if you have them and stay undercover. We'll drive this woman into the open and bring her sniper friend to us."

34

—

Rimi sat in a tree, the same tree with a platform she'd sat in the very first time she'd set eyes on Abel as he'd approached the entrance to the Green Cathedral.

Abel sat in a tree as well, though one nearly a half mile away by the source of the stream. He'd been tossed into it after being vaulted from his sniper position by the RPG explosion.

Both were exhausted. Both were in love. Both desperately wanted the other to live as they engaged in a hurried telepathic conversation they feared would be their last but would not admit to the other.

How are you, dear friend? asked Rimi.

I've been better, replied Abel as he looked at all the cuts and scrapes that covered his arms and his shredded shirt and pants. Shrapnel from the RPG round and rocks that he'd tumbled over during his fall were to blame, so were the tree branches that saved his life when he landed in them. He had blood on his hand from where he'd wiped his forehead and no weapon in it. That was far above him in his sniper nest. The sniper rifle was out of ammo anyway. In his backpack, also in the sniper nest, was his Mk 16, bulletproof vest, ammunition, and hand grenades. In fact, the only weapons he still had were his Glock 19, his SOG-SEAL knife, and a few shards of obsidian he'd scraped up after one of the earlier RPG explosions had showered him with them. He never knew when some black glass might come in handy.

How about you?

Rimi gazed over her pummeled body. Her legs and arms were covered with cuts and scrapes from tree branches, as well as several more severe flesh wounds she'd gotten from random machine-gun fire from cartel soldiers as she'd darted back and forth from her destructive forays into their midst. Now both arms were wounded and weakened. Her right leg had been grazed by a bullet. This one had caught her as she'd escaped from sinking the big boat. She still had her knife but could barely use it in her depleted state. Even her eyes, which she used to guide it, were exhausted from the strain.

I've been better, too. Much better.

You're at the Cathedral entrance, by the meadow? asked Abel.

Yes, she replied. *On the platform where I first saw you.*

Gee, that almost sounds romantic, said Abel with a chuckle.

Of course it does. You know me.

I'm coming to you, on the wire from here, said Abel.

No! shouted Rimi in his head. *I am surrounded! The evil men are everywhere. They are just waiting to kill you!*

Don't worry. I've got a plan.

Do you have any weapons?

A few, replied Abel. *I could use some help from that knife for just a few seconds when I drop in. Can you do it?*

Of course. I'll be ready. Please be careful!

Monti had gathered seven men around the tall trees that formed the high arches of the Green Cathedral, including one man who had picked up the RPG launcher from the corpse who'd held it last and reloaded it. He was about to order his men to open fire full bore into all the nearby trees when he heard a zinging sound, and suddenly, out of the sky fell DEA Agent Caleb Forrest not ten feet in front of him. The agent shot two soldiers who were closest to Monti, and the blue streak took out two others who heard the shots and turned. All this gave Abel the few seconds he needed to kick Monti hard in the nuts, sending the fat man to his knees, then get behind him, between him and the tree, put him in a choke hold, and put his Glock to Monti's head.

"Drop your weapons, or I blow his head off!"

Everyone in the area froze, and other soldiers stood to see what was going on. One, who was out of Abel's sight, raised his assault rifle but was instantly splattered into pieces by Rimi's knife.

"I said, drop the weapons, or I will blow this man's head off!" yelled Abel.

There was still no movement from the cartel soldiers. It was almost as if they wondered if the death of this fat man who had assumed command of their group would be such a great loss.

Ron quickly answered their question.

"Drop them now. He's the only one alive who can access Galvan's bank accounts. He dies, no one gets paid!"

Instantly, weapons clattered to the ground all around the meadow and the Cathedral entrance.

"Rimi," called Abel. "Come on down."

There was an audible gasp from those near the trees as the small, bloodied figure with the large, glaring eyes lowered herself on a nearly invisible cable that seemed to come out of her wrist. She stood menacingly by the tree she'd descended from, brandishing the glowing blue knife. It was as if a small but infinitely powerful avenging angel had suddenly dropped into their midst from heaven itself.

"Abel, come quickly to me!" she cried. "Grab onto me, and I can lift you up, and then we'll fly away!"

Abel gasped himself when he saw her. Covered in cuts and blood, he wondered if she could actually do what she said she could.

Don't worry. I'm injured, but still strong in my heart. We will not die today! she thought to him.

Abel now quickly went through his options. In his present position, he was safe but also trapped. He needed to get to Rimi, who was some thirty to forty feet away, too far to just dump Monti and run. The cartel soldiers near the trees would be on him before he could close the distance. He could try forcing Monti to cross the gap with him, but the man weighed at least two hundred and fifty pounds, and Abel wasn't sure he could control him, even with the gun to his head, or if he might not end up shooting Monti accidentally, which would most likely lead to a fusillade of gunfire before he and Rimi could get clear.

"Things are a bit more difficult than you thought," taunted Monti. "Neither of you will make it out of here alive this way. Throw down your gun, and we will let both of you live."

Abel laughed out loud. "You're really funny, you know that, Ruiz? You should try stand-up. It'd be a lot safer than drug smuggling."

"Ah, but where's the profit?" answered Monti.

Suddenly, Abel heard Rimi in his head.

I'm coming for you now! Grab onto me, and we shall be gone!

Abel looked and saw Rimi readying to jump. He wanted to tell her no—that he'd come to her—but there was no time.

"Just a friendly bit of advice," he said to Monti, then shoved him aside just as Rimi took one of her signature leaps toward him—but there was something wrong this time! Instead of instantly zipping through the air to him, her flight seemed stunted, almost ordinary both in speed and height. Abel could see that she would get close to him, but not close enough. He dashed toward her even as she landed ten feet from him and barely kept her feet. Abel grabbed on to her lithe body. She held him with a strong but trembling arm, raised her other hand, and the thin cable that came out of her crystal wrist band began to retract.

Abel now saw cartel soldiers running at them from all around.

"Get them!" yelled Monti. "Don't let them escape!" The closest soldiers grabbed on to Abel even as he and Rimi began to rise. He fired his Glock into the face of a couple of them, but then a man clamoring onto his back knocked the gun free, and it fell to the ground. Another soldier grabbed his feet. Abel kicked him away, but the pull had loosened his grip on Rimi and her grip on him. The cable hauled them inexorably up, but they couldn't regrip. Abel found himself grasping frantically at Rimi's leg that had been previously wounded. Gunfire could be heard, and bullets now whizzed around them. He had to let go, or they'd both die.

NO! came a scream in his mind! *You can't! We can make it!*

No, he thought back. *You can make it. Leave! Get as far away as you can!*

And then he let go.

Abel landed in a mosh pit of cartel guards. He punched and kicked furiously, knocking one out with one punch and doing great bodily harm to two others, only to be assailed by several more. He did see one of his attackers, who came at him with a knife, drop dead when his head was split by a small blue knife, but the blade stayed in his head, and Abel knew that Rimi, wherever she was, had just spent her last ounce of energy in his defense.

"Don't kill him, dammit!" he heard a booming voice say from behind him, and then he felt a mighty blow on the back of his head, and everything went black.

35

—

When Abel returned to his senses, he was being tied up by a couple of burly cartel guards. Standing in front of him was Fat Monti. He smiled a jolly smile as he saw Abel's eyes blink open.

"Ah, good! You are waking. I'm glad because before we take you back to camp, I wanted to illustrate something for you."

Abel instinctively checked his crystal bracelet—the clear crystal still glowed faintly and pointed to some trees nearby.

Abel noticed that a loaded RPG launcher was lying on the ground. Monti turned, picked it up, took a few steps toward what Abel now realized was the same tree Rimi had been hiding in before he'd been knocked out, and before anyone could say anything, he shouldered the weapon, aimed it at the leafy areas underneath its tallest limbs, and fired. Two seconds later, the target exploded spectacularly, and a body dropped out of it and fell heavily to the ground like a sack of cement.

It was Rimi.

Monti unceremoniously dropped the RPG launcher, walked to Rimi's body, kicked her over onto her back, pulled out a semiautomatic pistol, and pumped three shots into her chest. Abel, so appalled that he couldn't even cry out, rechecked his bracelet. The clear crystal had gone dark.

Monti walked back toward Abel, who was now on his feet.

"You see how easy that was?" he called. "Kill the evil presence on the island. Did you see? That's how simple it would have been for you to do it." He shrugged, then motioned for the cartel soldiers to bring him along, which they did with great difficulty because Abel couldn't take his eyes off Rimi's lifeless body.

Abel was hustled down the very path he'd cleared himself through the tall meadow grass, and when he came out onto the beach, he was surprised to see that the same construction workers he and Rimi had driven off earlier in the day (at least those who hadn't been killed) were busy as bees doing all sorts of tasks. Dock builders had already driven posts deep into the ground using a portable post-pounding machine they'd assembled, and it was clear they would soon be connecting them with long, heavy planks and constructing a temporary pier out toward the bay. A scavenging crew was out on the beached swift boat removing anything of value from it, and a demolition crew was busy rigging it with explosives so, once it was totally stripped, the carcass of the ship could be pulled out into deeper water and blown up. A crew was busy scouring the beach, the meadow, and the nearby jungle for dead bodies. They were being brought to the beach and thrown into a huge hole where it looked as if they'd be burned later.

It was all just one more shock to Abel's shattered emotions, so much so that it made almost no impression at all on him. These were, after all, hardened criminals who dealt with killing people and destroying dead bodies all the time. Why should a little distraction like that keep them from their work?

Monti directed that Abel should be restrained, sitting down next to one of the big poles that would one day be the pier pilings. It was right near where the meadow trail met the beach. As he was being led there, Abel carefully slipped one of his hands into the back pocket of his ripped-up khaki pants.

Once bound up, Monti dismissed those guarding him, and he sat down beside Abel in the sandy dirt.

"You know, I didn't want to say this in front of the other men, but what I showed you out there, that really is all you had to do, and I would now be transferring to your bank account eight hundred and fifty thousand dollars, the total balance of what I owe you for the job I gave you. I am not crooked. I don't break promises or beg out of contracts. I had the money already—from Galvan!"

Abel spat in the sand beside him.

Monti ignored the gesture.

"Even your DEA boss had approved it. Think of it—you, a rich man, me, even richer, a waystation nearly set up that would bring money to the community as never before. It would have been so simple!"

Abel spat again.

Monti continued. "Instead, we are way behind schedule, there are dead and wounded people everywhere, people are angry and upset, Don Vicente Galvan is dead—"

Abel looked straight over at Monti. "Why didn't you kill me like you did Rimi?"

"Oh, be sure that I would have liked to. You have caused me so much trouble, but not killing you is actually a way for me to get a little payback for all my losses today. You see, you killed Don Vicente Galvan, and—"

"I didn't kill Galvan. We just disabled his vehicle."

"Oh, I know, señor, but everyone will think that you killed him. Paco actually killed him after he found him trapped inside his car. His arm had been severed, so he would have bled out anyway, I'm sure, but we couldn't wait. My community patrol demanded it, and they were right. He was no longer needed." Monti picked up some dirt and absently played with it.

"But his family in Cartagena doesn't know any of that. They'll just know what we tell them—that you are responsible for Don Vicente's death—and then we'll negotiate an exchange. I'm sure they'll give us something for you, especially if we tell them that we'll set you free if they don't."

"You've got it all figured out, huh?"

"Of course. I always do," replied Monti with a smile as he leaned in closer to Abel, "because I'm not a fool like you who puts passion and beauty before practicality." He stood up. "Good night, Señor Whatever-Your-Name-Is. Enjoy your pole. Tomorrow, we will take you back to Playa de Palma and find a nice jail cell for you to stay in until the Galvans come for you."

Monti walked off, and Abel watched him placidly, while behind his back, he slipped the obsidian shard he'd taken from his back pocket and began using one of its edges to slice at the duct tape that bound his hands.

A little while later, Ron came over and plopped down by him. Ron was dressed like a cartel soldier, which Abel found very odd, and now had a patch over one eye as well.

"What the hell are you doing here?" asked Abel. "Especially dressed like that."

Ron explained to Abel all that had taken place between the community patrol and Monti and the deal they'd struck with him about jointly planning, financing, and sharing in the profits of whatever they decided to do with the island. He also told him about the regrettable but necessary decision they'd made to get rid of both him and Rimi.

"You couldn't have just talked to us about it?" asked Abel.

"To be honest, that's something a number of us proposed," said Ron. "No one was all that comfortable with the idea of killing you two. Personally, I thought it would be murder. But Rimi killed a lot of people back in the day, Agent Forrest: fathers, uncles, brothers, even some sisters and aunts and mothers . . ."

"She was only defending herself!" barked Abel. "Herself and the island."

"I don't think you'd see it that way if you were one of them," interrupted Ron. He gave Abel a sharp look in the eye, and Abel stared right back. After a moment, Ron continued. "Everyone had ideas on what to do with the island to help the town, but none included you guys, and I guess between that and the revenge-mongers hollering, it kind of came down to, Why talk about it? You guys thought the island belonged to you, and even if you'd wanted to share it, the patrol didn't. They didn't want someone complicating things for whatever plans they might come up with. And, hell, the Colombians were here. They could take care of…well, you know."

Abel looked at Ron with the same disdain he'd looked at Monti with. "What did you tell me all this for?"

"Well, I just felt kind of bad, you know. I mean, you're a cool guy, and we got on good and Rimi was always a real sweetie and—"

"Fuck you, Ron—you and your whole goddamn community patrol. You're all just the same as Monti and Galvan: greedy sons of bitches looking for ways to get rich, and you don't give a shit who you stamp out to get there." Ron's face contorted in shock. "Still think I'm a cool guy that you 'get on' with?" Abel smirked.

"Sorry I bothered," mumbled Ron. "You know, they made me do this—come along with Monti. Juan wanted to, but I . . ." Abel wasn't listening. Ron got up and walked away.

Ten minutes later, Abel was able to pop the restraints on his wrists, but the timing wasn't right. The sun was just going down, and the cartel soldiers and construction workers were just beginning to eat around a roaring fire. One soldier had come around right after Ron left to check him over, but Abel faked that his hands were still tightly wrapped, and the guy, obviously eager to eat, had gone without really checking anything.

Now is the time to think and plan, thought Abel. Once these guys were either fast asleep or roaring drunk, he'd slip away, and there would be much to do before the morning.

36

—

It had been dark for well over an hour. Abel had watched the cartel soldiers and the construction workers slowly drift in from their tasks, line up at a makeshift chow line that had been set up near the fire, and take their dinners to various logs that had been brought in to serve as seats. Some food had been brought to Abel by a couple of guards, but he'd refused it. He didn't want the guards to see he'd already freed himself from his bonds. He knew he needed sustenance, but that would have to come later, after he'd escaped. As he'd expected, some of the soldiers and workers simply keeled over after eating and fell asleep, while others, the more boisterous types, began drinking heavily, singing, and playing cards.

A couple of reluctant guards had been assigned to him, and they were both bored to distraction with their job. They talked among themselves in both Spanish and English, and sometimes Abel even interjected a comment or two. As the two became more comfortable with him, he casually began a discussion he hoped would lead to the one thing he really needed to know before he set his plans in motion.

"How many bodies have they brought in?" he asked at one point.

"Who knows?" said one, a large man who looked like he'd prefer being a gentle giant rather than a head crusher. "Maybe forty, forty-five, fifty."

"And then men come in from the jungle with more," chimed in the other, a smaller, skinny guy who sounded snide and sarcastic. "Mostly killed or maimed by animals. It's crazy, like that devil woman was making them attack us."

"Why do you want to know, anyway?" asked the bigger man. "You're the one who killed most of them. You think you're going to brag about it or something? I got news for you. The Galvans—"

"Take it easy," said Abel calmly. "I had a job to do just like you. The DEA said to keep the cartel from occupying the island. What else was I supposed to do? I was the only one they sent. I found the devil woman, and she didn't want anyone here either, so we worked together. Nothing personal, just like it wasn't personal when your kind came after me. We're soldiers, right? We do what the big boys tell us."

"Big boy is right." The skinny guy laughed. "I can't believe how well that fat man moves. Maybe he played American football, eh?"

"I doubt it," replied Abel. "So what did they do with the devil woman's body, anyway, just throw it in with the others?"

"Oh, no," replied Skinny Guy. "She still lies right there where the fat guy killed her. No one dares to go near her. Everyone's afraid she'll come back to life as a witch or a zombie or something. Personally, I can't blame them. She's too spooky for me."

"Yeah, she was pretty spooky for me, too," agreed Abel. He was relieved to get this bit of information finally. Rimi's body would be his first priority of the night, and now that he knew she was still just down the meadow path at the gateway to the Cathedral, he could wait for the right moment, make his breakout, and get on with his tasks.

That moment came an agonizing hour later when Big Man finally snoozed off into a deep sleep. Abel told Skinny Guy that he needed to take a piss before he fell asleep, and as soon as Skinny Guy got him up, Abel headbutted the guy so hard that he almost knocked himself out. Skinny Guy dropped in a heap. Abel took off the guy's utility belt and put it on, then used the man's knife to slit his throat, and then he did the same to Big Man. He felt bad for both of them in some part of his being and was glad in a way that he seemed to be, at long last, developing a conscience again, but his SEAL constitution quickly compartmentalized those thoughts and gave him perfect clarity as to what he needed to do.

The utility belt, he noted earlier, had most everything he needed for his first tasks. There was a tactical flashlight attached to it, which he could use discreetly to find his way in the blackness, the knife, of course, and a Glock 19 semiautomatic with four extra clips. He started to head out but, on a whim, turned back to check around the area where the pier was being built. Hastily looking around by the light of the dying fire, he finally found something he was looking for. It was a tool, like a scythe, that was used to cut down tall grass. It had a long handle and a curved blade at the end. He grabbed it and was off.

It wasn't more than a minute or two of jogging before Abel was kneeling next to the lifeless, broken body of Rimi. Gently, he raised her up, then threw her over his shoulder and continued into the Green Cathedral. He used his light to keep himself on the path he'd cut through the shrubbery just a couple of weeks before. Here and there, his light flashed over the dead bodies of animals, monkeys, a sloth, a couple of jaguars. All had been shot to shreds by automatic weapon fire. He felt pangs of hurt, but he forged on. It took him ten minutes, with periodic thirty-second rest stops, to reach his stream crossing. Moving the flashlight over the water, he saw several dead crocodiles floating upside down, and then a reflection glinted off what he was looking for.

Just as he'd anticipated, his cable for crossing the creek was still there but was dangling uselessly over the middle of the stream. Abel carefully laid Rimi's body down, and using the long-handled tool he'd brought with him, he was, after several attempts, able to snag the cable and pull it back toward the shore. He picked Rimi up once again, grabbed the cable with both hands, took a little run, swung himself across the creek, secured the cable to the tree he'd used previously, and then continued on his trail alongside the vast wasteland of fallen trees. Finally, a half hour after leaving the beach camp, he arrived at the clearing in the woods where Bibi sat, just as he had the first time Abel had seen him. Abel hoped that the AI alien escape pod would still recognize him and let him in. Carrying Rimi, he walked to the pod's side, and voila, they were in.

Lights came on instantly. Bibi greeted them.

"Hello, Caleb Forrest. It appears that Rimi is injured. What has—"

"She's dead," Abel interrupted. "Get out the medical thing. I want you to repair her and see if you can save her."

"You mean, bring her back to life?" asked Bibi.

"Of course, I mean bring her back to life. Repair her and see if that can bring her back to life," replied Abel impatiently.

Bibi raised the medical cocoon, opened it, and Abel laid Rimi gently inside of it. Instantly, robotic tentacles appeared from the side of the pod and began to extrude the silky threads that would soon cover Rimi.

"I have never made a human come back to life before," Bibi said as he worked.

"Have you ever tried?" asked Abel.

"No," replied Bibi.

"Okay then, there's a first time for everything, right?" Abel allowed himself to slow down and be weary for just a moment. "Look, do your best, okay? She hasn't lost too much blood, so once she's repaired, there should be plenty in there to revive her if her heart gets beating."

"But what about her brain?" asked Bibi. "I can tell already that there's no activity at present, though structurally, it does seem intact. I have no knowledge of how to make it active again."

"Well, just try stuff, you know, shock her with electricity or something. That works in Frankenstein movies. I don't know. Just do what you can. I've got to go, but I'll try and stay around somewhere. We've got the crystal bracelets on that you made. If you somehow bring her back, I want to know."

"Staying close will not be necessary if you don't wish. The range of crystal transmissions is normally over ten thousand miles," instructed Bibi.

"I'll keep that in mind, but I'd still like to be around," replied Abel. "I've got to go now. The island's been attacked, and there are all kinds of strangers here on the other side."

"I've detected as much," said Bibi.

"They get really spooked by creepy stuff they don't understand, so don't hesitate to use those tentacles to scare up some inexplicable calamity if they ever get close. If they think this area's haunted somehow, they should leave you alone." Abel watched as Rimi was now completely covered in cocoon strands. "Take care of her, Bibs. I'll be back for her whenever you get done. Now, I've got to go."

"Goodbye, Caleb Forrest," Bibi answered. "I will do as you've asked. Oh, and there's food in the bay of my duplicator if you care to take any along."

Food, thought Abel. He'd totally forgotten.

"How'd you know, or is it days old from the last time I was here?"

"I sensed it immediately in your thoughts when you came through my walls," replied Bibi. "I hope you'll enjoy it—it could bring back some happy memories."

Abel stepped over to the duplicator and opened its bay, and there was a plate filled with Belgian waffles.

Five minutes later, after wolfing down his and Rimi's favorite synthetic meal, Abel reappeared in Bibi's clearing and headed back to the stream, where he once again swung across, but this time went up the river trail he had cut and up the side of the volcano, frequently using brief flashes of his tactical light to make sure he didn't miss a step and end up injuring himself any more than he was already. Once he'd passed the pool of springs that was the source of the creek, it wasn't long before he regained his sniper nests—or what was left of them—and to his great relief found his backpack. Drawing out his Mk 16 and locating the hand grenades and other supplies he always took with him, he smiled. The first part of his busy night had been all about saving Rimi. The second would now be all about setting things right.

Or is it really just revenge? Though that motivation was definitely present, what he was now planning was about so much more. It was about upholding the law and about saving both an environmental wonder and a peaceful community from those who would victimize them. It was about pride and honor, and the satisfaction of finally taking an irreversible stand to do right instead of wrong.

Satisfied now as to his cause, he edged his way down the north-facing slope of the volcano, a somewhat more gently sloping hill compared to the cliffs just a little farther toward the east, using moonlight and an occasional burst from his tactical flashlight to avoid obstacles. There was the small inlet at the bottom where he'd anchored his small trawler after sending Rimi off with the Xilinium earlier in the day.

He smiled one of his most crooked smiles when he saw the moonlight silhouetting the boat's tall bridge as it bobbed on gentle waves. He had played a hunch when leaving the ship there earlier in the day and had ended up getting lucky.

Bingo, he thought. *Score one for Rimi and me.*

When he got to the rocky beach below, he even found that the rubber boat he'd used to ferry himself to the shore was still there, so he loaded it up with the supplies in his backpack and motored back out to the boat, fired up the engine, slowly moved around the island, and anchored himself a few hundred yards from where the big trawler that had brought the construction crew to the island now stood at anchor.

Abel stuffed virtually every hand grenade he had in the pack into a watertight bag he kept on board, then slung the bag onto his shoulders, threw a pair of swim fins on his feet, and soundlessly slipped into the water off the stern platform and set out for the big trawler doing a short, steady breaststroke he'd used dozens of times on SEAL missions when having to haul munitions to a target without the benefit of a boat. Keeping his head up, he fixed his eyes on the bigger boat's running lights, and fifteen minutes later, he was beside it.

Not hearing anything from the deck of the trawler, he circumnavigated the entire boat, listening, peering up, listening some more. He finally moved to the stern and crawled up on its water-level platform. From there, he looked all over, wishing that he had night-vision goggles with him, but could neither see nor hear any signs of life. It appeared the boat was just sitting at anchor and that its crew had gone ashore. Carefully, he slipped the backpack from his shoulders, crawled over the stern rail, and then lifted the pack over. He was now aboard.

With his knife in one hand and the hand grenades and some duct tape in another, he stealthily tiptoed along the deck until he reached the ladders amidships. One led up to the bridge, the other down to the cabin, the hold, and the engine room. Silently setting down his gear, Abel brandished the knife as he crept up the ladder to the bridge. The door was open, and Abel thought he saw something bulky sitting in the captain's chair. Quietly, he crept up behind the chair. Yes, he was right. There was a man in the chair, asleep. Quickly visualizing his plan of attack, Abel in one lethal motion rose, grabbed the man's head, pulled it back, and slit his throat. Blood sprayed all over the ship's instrument panel as Abel silently snuck out. Dying without even knowing how it happened, not the way Abel wanted to go, but at least the poor bastard didn't have a chance to feel anguish or fear.

He crept back down the ladder and slithered down into the ship's cabin. Another man there was also sound asleep. Abel moved into the cabin but stubbed his foot on the entryway. The man gave a start and looked around as if he'd been awakened from a deep, dreamless sleep. By the time he saw Abel, it was too late. Abel had already sliced his throat, then dived to the side to avoid the blood shower that ensued.

Creeping back out and being careful to neither step in blood nor trip over the entryway again, Abel went down to the ship's engine room. No one around. He climbed back up the ladder, grabbed his backpack, then slid back down. Scanning with his flashlight, he quickly located the engine block and the fuel lines that led aft to the fuel tank. He lashed several hand grenades to the engine block with duct tape. Once started, the engine block would start heating up, exploding the hand grenades. He put a couple of more hand grenades where the fuel line came into the engine room. Once the other grenades exploded, these would then explode, and then in quick succession, the fuel tank would go up as well. The ship would be blown to pieces so small there wouldn't be anything big enough to use as a life preserver, and anyone on it, if they didn't die in the explosion itself, would most likely be too injured to swim and would drown.

Having finished this work, Abel found some bleach in the ship's cabin. He hauled both bodies out from where they were and tossed them overboard, then went to work on the bloodstains. He didn't want whoever came out to the boat to be tipped off that something might be dangerously wrong until it was too late. He scrubbed furiously using the ship's cleaning supplies on the bloody floors and instrument panel and tossed out the bloody bedding from the cabin. In the dim light of his flashlight, it probably wasn't the most thorough job, but for what he had planned, it didn't need to be. Finally, he shouldered his backpack again, put his swim fins on, and headed back to his own boat. Once there, he climbed on, pulled out the rest of his hand grenades, checked his Mk 16, put on his bulletproof vest, then sat in the captain's chair and waited for daylight, snoozing off and on. Three hours later, it happened.

37

—

Fat Monti woke from a peaceful slumber on the beach like all the rest of his men did—to the sound of automatic weapons fire.

Bullets zinged in horizontal rows along the beach just meters from where the fire had been and where people were sleeping. Then there was an explosion that blasted a hole in the deck of the half-sunken swift boat. Instantly, the beach became a scene of confusion and panic. Men dashed back and forth, trying to find shoes and guns, or get out of the way of bullets. Another spray of automatic weapons fire blanketed the fire pit, this time bullets striking some of the men who'd crashed out there. Monti quickly gathered his wits. It seemed that at this stage anyway, he was out of range of the bullets. That meant they were coming from the ocean. He scanned the bay, and it only took a few seconds for his eyes to fall on something very familiar—his own small trawler, the one he'd given to Agent Caleb Forrest to use to get to the island and back. It was standing less than a half mile offshore, just at the mouth of the bay. He grabbed around until he found his binoculars, then trained them on the boat.

No, it can't be!

At that moment, someone ran up to him. It was Ron from the community patrol.

"Monti, Abel's gone, and the guards are dead!"

Monti stared again through the binoculars. *Yes, it could be.*

More bullets spattered the sand about twenty-five yards away. Ron ducked and covered.

"Is it—"

"Agent Forrest? What do you think?" interrupted Monti, a look of godlike fury on his face. He saw just enough of the man on the deck of his boat to know that it was his former prisoner before the DEA agent dashed up the stairs to the bridge and gave his boat some gas, and the ship began to flee out to sea. But both Monti and Agent Forrest knew that the small trawler was not a fast ship, not near as fast as the big ship that had brought in the construction crew. Monti cast about for his bullhorn and finally found it.

"Now hear this! This is Monti Ruiz! Stop what you're doing. The danger is over, and we're about to teach our former prisoner a lesson he'll not forget. This man has killed enough of us for a hundred life-times. Now, we will have him at last. Soldiers and crew of the trawler, to the rubber boats! We'll be off to our own ship, chase this little fly down, and smash him like the nuisance he is. Bring the RPGs and your assault rifles. Our boat sails in five minutes. The rest of you, pre-pare breakfast! When we return, we'll have another celebration."

Instantly, the entire camp sprang into purposeful action. Soldiers grabbed guns. A couple went back and found the RPG launcher. The big trawler's crew were in their rubber boat inside of a minute and had set sail for their boat. One by one, the motorized rubber boats took off, filled with armed men. Monti looked at Ron.

"Come with me, my friend. You'll not want to miss this!" He hauled Ron up, and they both dashed for one of the last boats headed for the trawler. Even as they did, though, more machine-gun fire splattered the water twenty yards out into the bay.

"Curse that fucking man!" yelled Monti. "I'll chop his head off myself if we don't blow him up with his boat first!"

When Monti's boat arrived at the trawler, the deck was alive with crewmen and cartel soldiers. Some were hauling out a 20mm Gatling gun that was stored below. Others were setting up its mount on the foredeck. The captain had fired up the engine.

"Cast off!" yelled Monti to him, and the captain opened the throttle, swung the big boat around, and set his course straight toward the smaller trawler, which was chugging away from them about a half mile up the coast and a mile from the mainland.

"Get that gun ready! Be quick!" ordered Monti. He left Ron amidships and tromped up to the foredeck. As he passed soldiers, he ordered them to fire at will when they felt they were in range. As he stepped on the foredeck, he saw that the Gatling gun was mounted and a couple of soldiers were rigging its ammo belt. Monti stepped behind the weapon.

"Clear away," he told the others on the foredeck. "When you've got that all cocked and loaded, show me how to shoot it. I'm going to blast that man and his little boat into a million pieces! You hear! A million fucking pieces!"

Abel kept his trawler on a steady course away from Playa de Palma but not too far in front of Monti's ship. This would be a delicate act, and eventually, if things didn't work out right, he'd be a goner if he played things too close. Yet he had to keep the bigger boat going for a while longer so that its motor would get good and hot.

Suddenly, he heard that telltale *buzz* he'd heard the day before and saw the ocean churn like a swarm of piranhas was chasing him.

Shit, he thought. *Another freaking Gatling gun!*

The range a thing like that had was way more than an AK, and it could sink him with just one direct hit. He gave his boat all the gas he could, and the trawler tried hard to respond. He also began to steer the ship in a zigzag pattern to throw off the aim of the gunner. Another *buzz* and more water churned up, this time in a line perpendicular to his boat that would have cut it in half just seconds before. His boat was making better speed now, but so was the big trawler. Any second now, the somewhat erratic gunner on the big trawler might figure out his range, and that would be the end of everything. Another *buzz!* Another train of churned water heading on a perpendicular line toward his boat. He turned the wheel hard to the left, to avoid the sweep, and then—

Boom!

And then another boom!

Abel turned in time to see the final explosion, a gargantuan blast that shot a ball of flame into the air and sent pieces of the big trawler flying everywhere and showering down for hundreds of yards around it. What was left of the boat quickly disappeared underwater. Abel was glad he didn't have any binoculars. He'd have been tempted to go to someone's rescue, he was sure. Instead, he watched for another moment, then spun his wheel around and headed his trawler north past Playa de Palma, a place that, he realized now, he'd come to both loathe and love, and was the home of the only person he knew who would still be his friend.

EPILOGUE

———

Two Weeks Later

Abel sat inconspicuously at one of the outdoor dining tables on a patio outside the Rio Palma Grill, the restaurant and bar across the bridge from the inn. It was six a.m., and he had a standing date with his good friend there every weekday morning. It was a tradition the two had agreed upon two weeks before, right after the Day of Death, as it had become aptly known.

Carissa, the head waitress of the morning crew, fiddled with the grill's front door lock and officially opened it for business.

"Hola, Señor Forrest!" she called to him. She wore the same bright, cheery smile every morning, no matter what. It was something Abel found charming and also something that elicited fond memories of Rimi as well. Rimi had never seemed to be without a smile. "You may come in. I have your regular booth all ready for you and the señora."

"Thanks, Carissa," said Abel as he walked in. "You're a total peach."

Carissa blushed a little as she walked him to his booth and left two menus. Abel opened one up and studied it. The grill had some great breakfast dishes, typical of Costa Rica, Mexico, and the US, and

Abel always checked them out before putting the thing down and just getting one of his three regulars, diced ham and scrambled eggs with hash browns, Belgian waffles, or a full stack of pancakes with sausage on the side.

He heard Carissa call out, "Hola, señora! He's already at the booth." He looked up to see Faviola limping in with her walking cast, looking incongruous with her freshly pressed navy-blue skirt and immaculate white blouse, which was, as usual, unbuttoned very low.

"What are you looking at?" said Faviola in a joking way as she approached.

"What I'm always looking at when I'm looking at you." Abel chuckled.

"Pervert," she huffed, then smiled as she sat down. "So, my dear friend, how goes your project on the island?"

"Almost done," said Abel. "All the bodies have been found and removed. They'll work on identifying them up at Jacó. The vets and zoological types finally packed up yesterday. They figure they've found all the dead animals and will start repopulating next week. Cleanup crews are still working, though."

Carissa came to take their orders. "Gallo pinto with a fried egg over easy and fried plantains, please, and some water with ice," she said to Carissa.

"And my regular number one with coffee, and ice water, too," chimed in Abel.

"Ah, the diced ham and eggs. They will be coming right up," Carissa said and left.

"So, how are you finding your accommodations, Señor Forrest?" asked Faviola, as she did nearly every day.

"Same as always. With the high season almost over, most of the time I feel like I've got the beach all to myself," replied Abel.

"Do you know yet if they're going to let you stay?"

"No, but I'm thinking they will. What took place here, and what was going to take place here, really has got everyone shook up. They're taking a look at a lot of islands up and down the coast. Assuming they let me stay, I'll probably be patrolling a bunch of them in the area besides ours," speculated Abel. "How's business?"

"Winding down, but this morning I may have to leave at any minute. There is a tour group checking out that has to catch the seven o'clock bus to San José, and they are all on separate accounts."

They both sat silent for a moment, and then Faviola asked another question she always asked. "Have you been over to—"

"No," replied Abel. "Not yet. There's no clean up to do over there, and—"

"I know," said Faviola. "Do you really think there's a chance—"

"If there is, I'll be the first to know," said Abel, nodding to the crystal bracelet he still wore. The center clear crystal was still dark.

Suddenly, Faviola's phone dinged, a text message.

"I was afraid of this. I must go."

She arose, and Abel did as well. They gave each other a warm embrace.

"Have a good day," said Faviola. "Oh, and I almost forgot. Elaine from the All-American soda says that Ron would like to see you in the hospital in Parrita if it's okay with you. She says that she thinks he feels estúpido and wants to apologize. Check it out with her sometime. Now, I must go." She turned and walked to the door, calling out, "Carissa, have mine made to go, and send it to me at the office!"

Abel sat back down. That was good to hear about Ron. He was the sole survivor of the exploding cartel boat, though horribly injured and burned. Abel wondered what the guy might be thinking these days. He was glad he'd get a chance to find out.

Carissa came with his diced ham and scrambled eggs, along with his water and coffee. Abel reached for his napkin to lay across his lap when he stopped and dropped it instead.

He stared at his wrist, blinked, then stared again. He shook his wrist, then stared again. There was no question. It wasn't an illusion or the way the now-rising sun was coming through the windows.

The clear crystal on his bracelet was glowing, pulsing, and pointing straight out of the grill's seaside windows at the island—La Catedral Verde, the Green Cathedral!

"Carissa," he called and caught her eye. "I'm going to need this to go, too. Oh, and can you do up a nice big Belgian waffle with strawberries and syrup, too?"

Kerry McDonald Collection
(Action and Adventure)

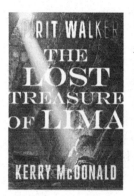

ISBN: 978-1-933769-98-1

When a wealthy playboy is paralyzed and nearly consumed by depression, he discovers his ability to astral project to his estranged twin brother. Logan and Landon Flint embark on a high-stakes adventure to restore their relationship and find the Lost Treasure of Lima.

ISBN: 978-1-64630-000-6

When a neo-Nazi group discovers that the legendary lost Nazi Gold Train also contained a biological warfare agent specifically targeting Jews, Landon and Logan Flint must find the train first to avoid a new worldwide holocaust.

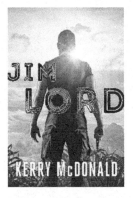

ISBN: 978-1-933769-96-7

After botching his response to a school shooting, a disgraced former cop, hiding out in Jamaica, is challenged by a local gang and decides to take down their powerful boss, seeking the redemption he so desperately wants.

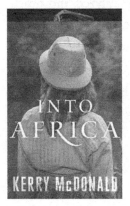

ISBN: 978-1-933769-94-3

When her famous missionary brother, David Livingston, sends word that he is dying, a scared-of-the-world, racist Scottish woman must organize a rescue mission and go on an extraordinary adventure in far-away Africa. What she finds will change her view of the world, and herself, forever.

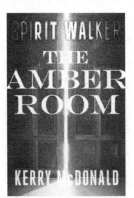

ISBN: 978-1-64630-040-2

When Landon and Logan Flint uncover evidence that the Amber Room contains holographic images from an alien civilization, they must locate the room before unknown alien technology falls into the hands of terrorists.